Archie
MEETS KISS

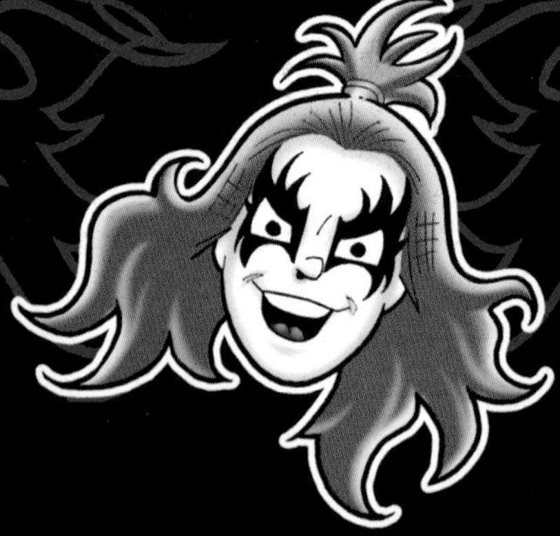

ARCHIE Meets KISS: Collector's Edition (Hardcover)
ISBN: 978-1-936975-14-3

ARCHIE Meets KISS (Trade Paperback)
ISBN: 978-1-936975-04-4

Published by Archie Comic Publications, Inc.
325 Fayette Avenue, Mamaroneck, New York 10543-2318.

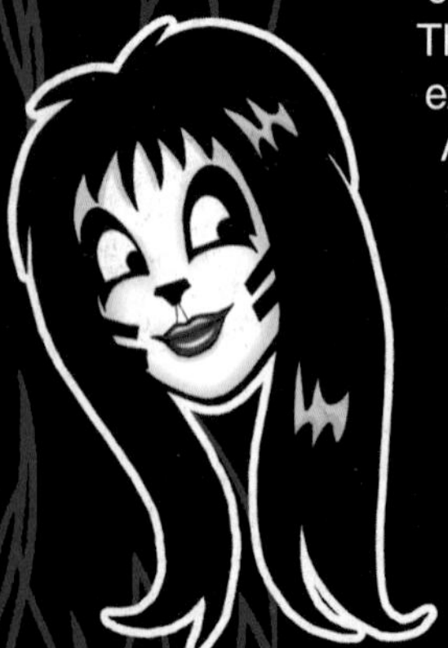

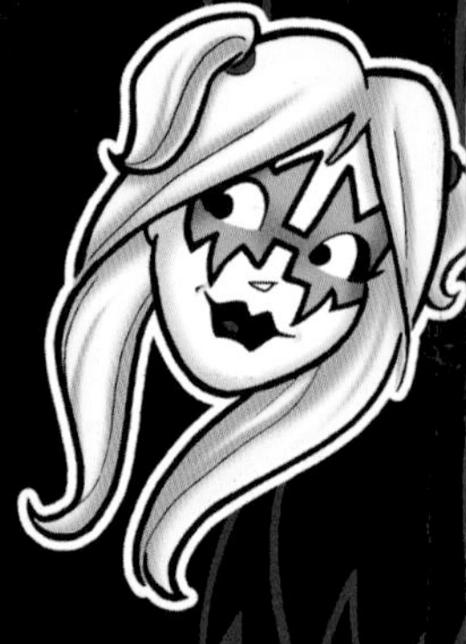

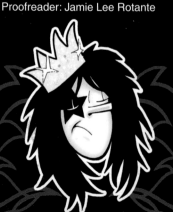

Publisher/Co-CEO: Jon Goldwater
Co-CEO: Nancy Silberkleit
President: Mike Pellerito
Co-President/Editor-In-Chief: Victor Gorelick
Director of Circulation: Bill Horan
Executive Director of Publishing/Operations: Harold Buchholz
Executive Director of Publicity & Marketing: Alex Segura
Project Coordinator & Book Design: Joe Morciglio
Production Manager: Stephen Oswald
Production: Rosario "Tito" Peña, Suzannah Rowntree, Jon Gray, Steven Scott
Proofreader: Jamie Lee Rotante

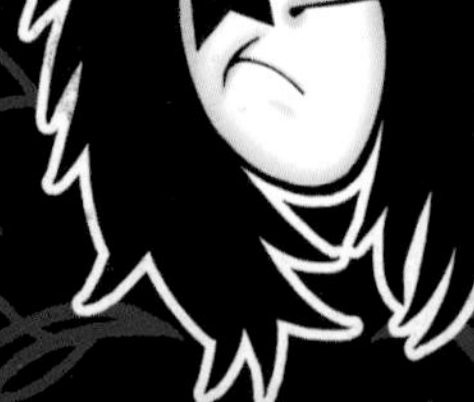

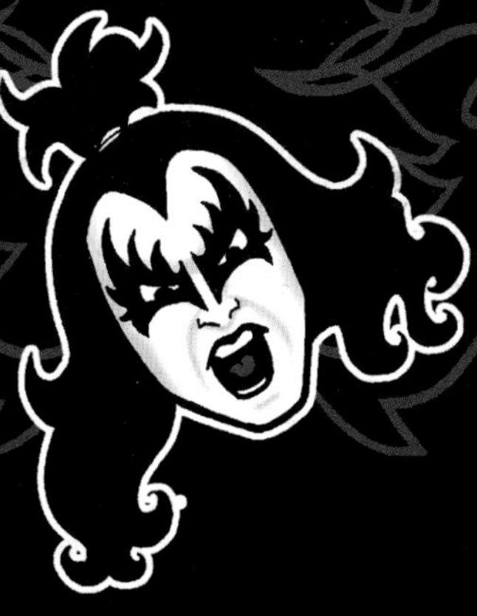

Written by ALEX SEGURA

Pencils by DAN PARENT

Inking by RICH KOSLOWSKI

Lettering by JACK MORELLI

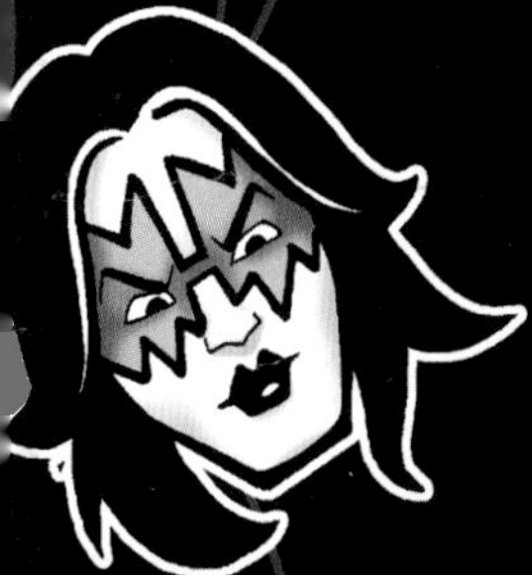

Coloring by
DIGIKORE STUDIOS

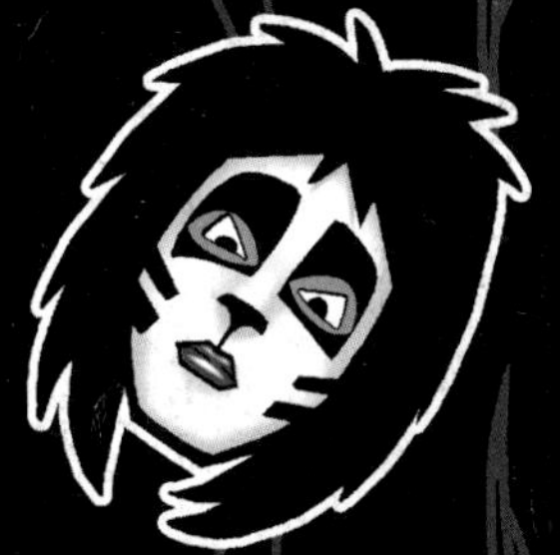

Collector's Edition
Cover Artwork:
FRANCESCO FRANCAVILLA

Trade Paperback Cover Artwork:
DAN PARENT

Special Thanks:
Gene Simmons, Paul Stanley,
William Randolph, Doc McGhee, Del Furano,
Keith Leroux, Janet Dwoskin,
and the entire KISS Army!

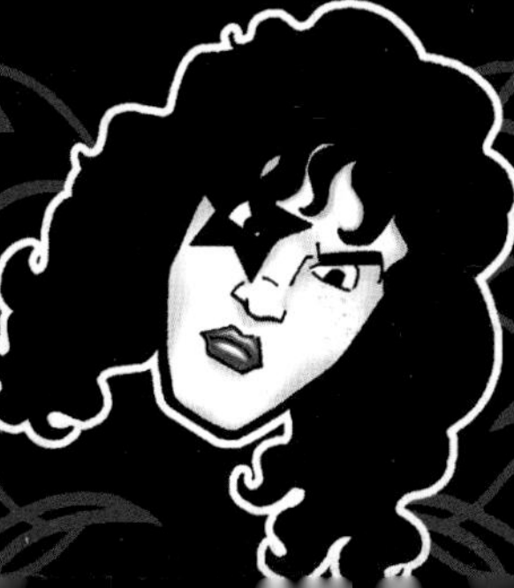

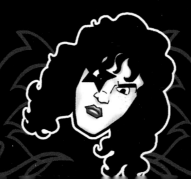

Archie MEETS KISS

FOREWORD BY GENE SIMMONS

Archie is one of America's enduring iconic characters. From one generation to the next, Betty, Veronica and Archie have attracted new fans. KISS is approaching our fourth decade. It continues to be the juggernaut of music licensing and merchandising. But at its heart, KISS was born as an idea and as an ideal, to put together the band that we never saw on stage. Since then, KISS has gone where no band has gone before, and continues to break new ground every year. KISS and Archie bravely combined their respective worlds and the results, I have to say, have been outstanding, and this is just the beginning!
Stay tuned!

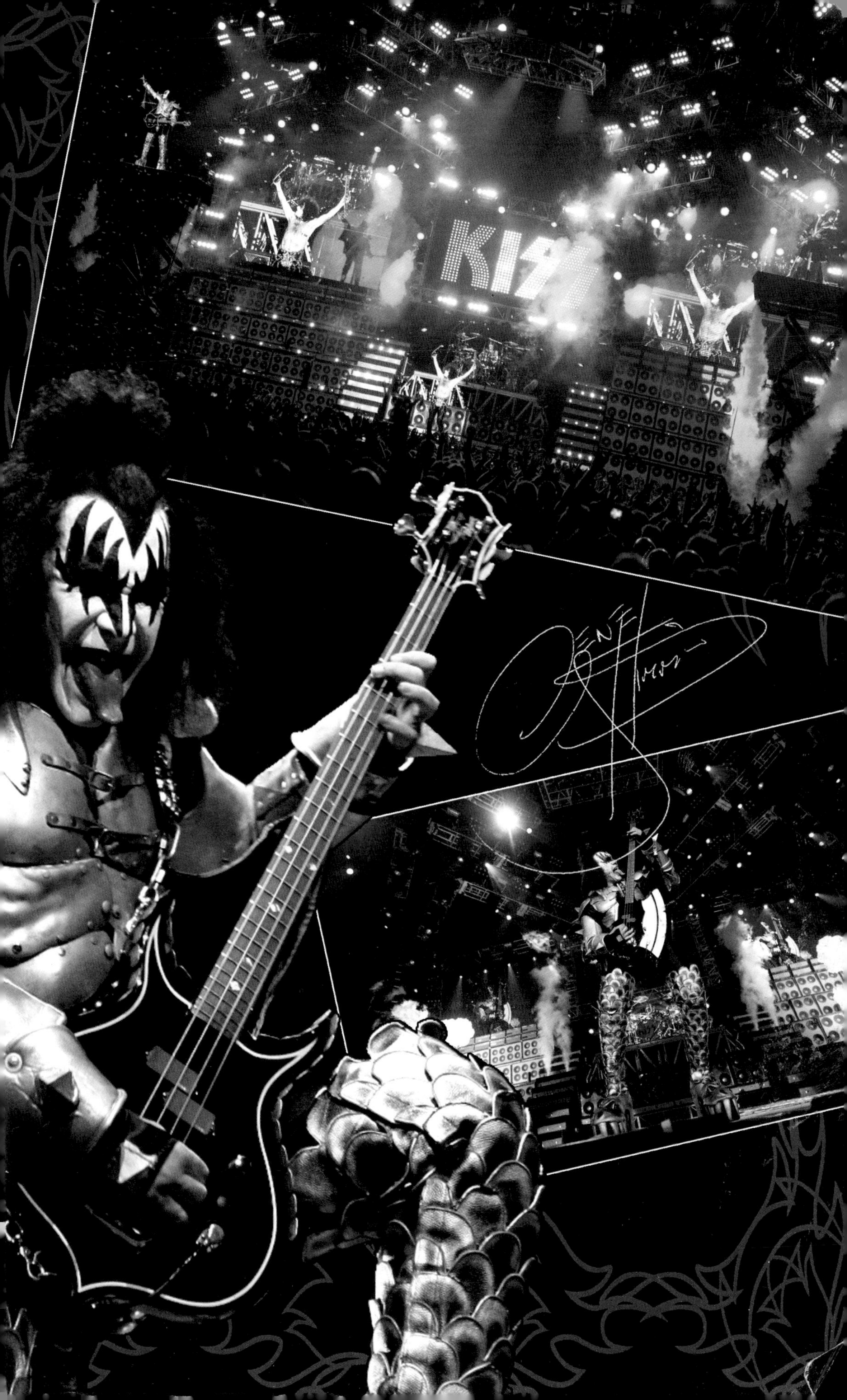
KISS

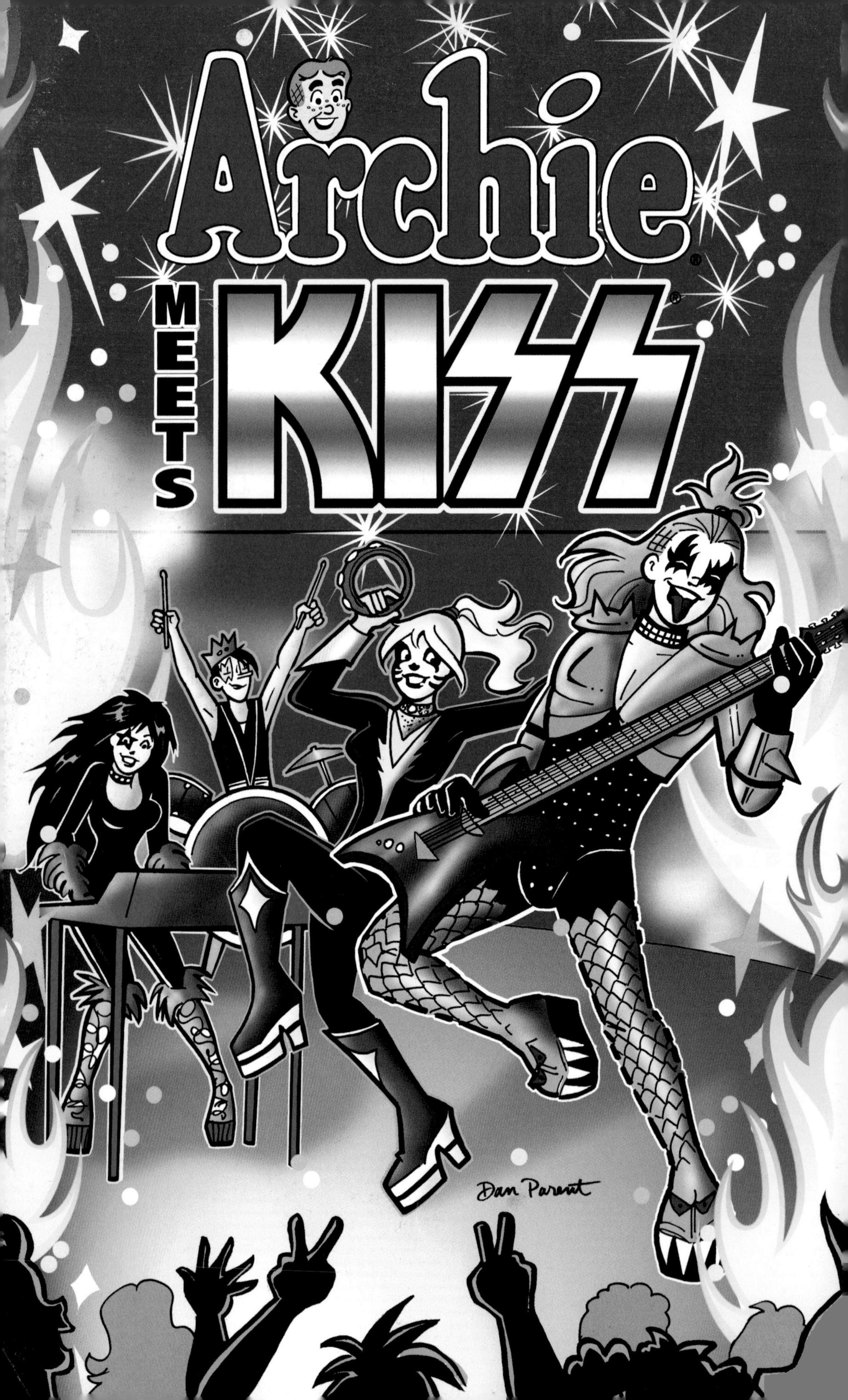
Archie
MEETS
KISS
Dan Parent

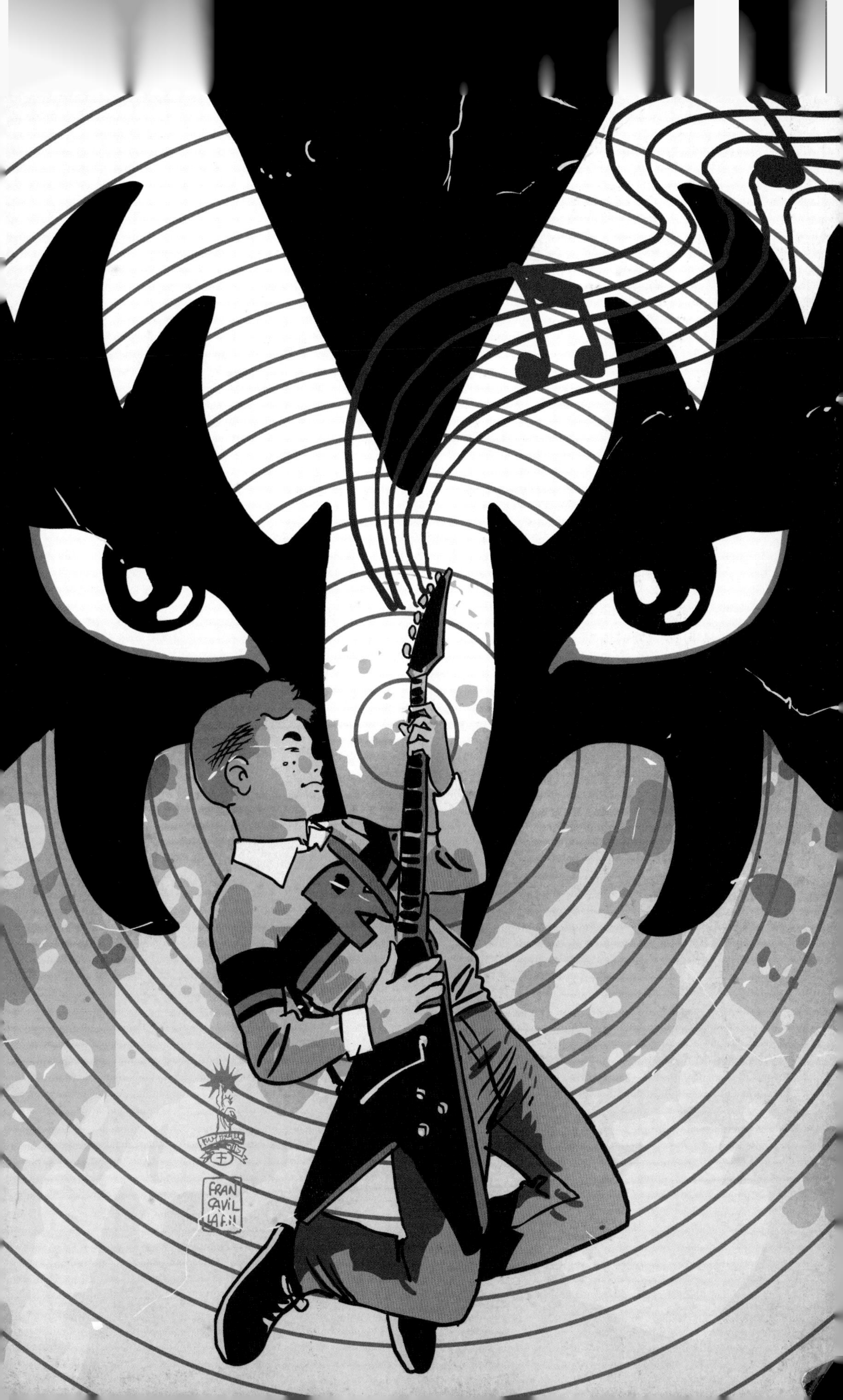

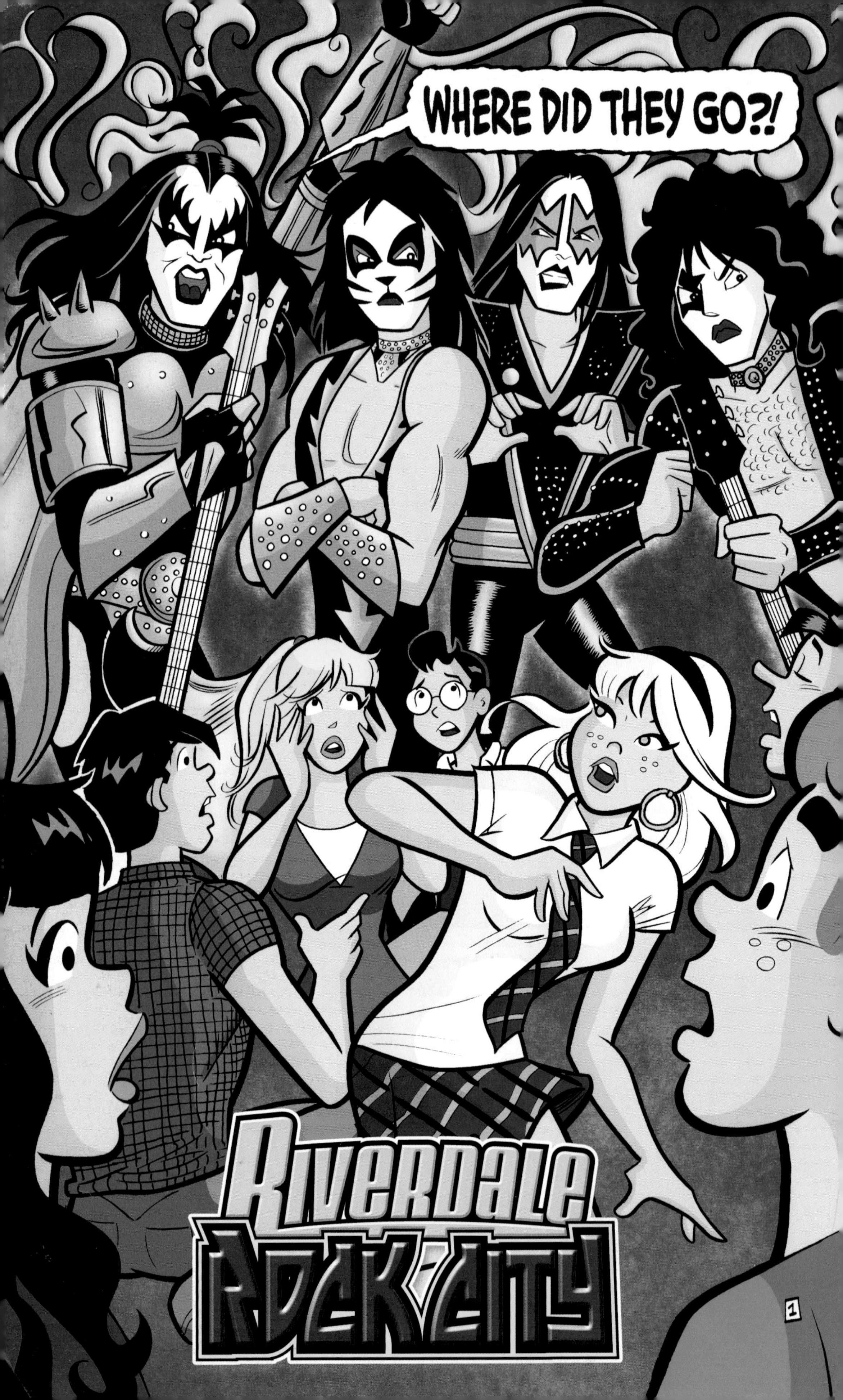
WHERE DID THEY GO?!
RIVERDALE
ROCK CITY
1

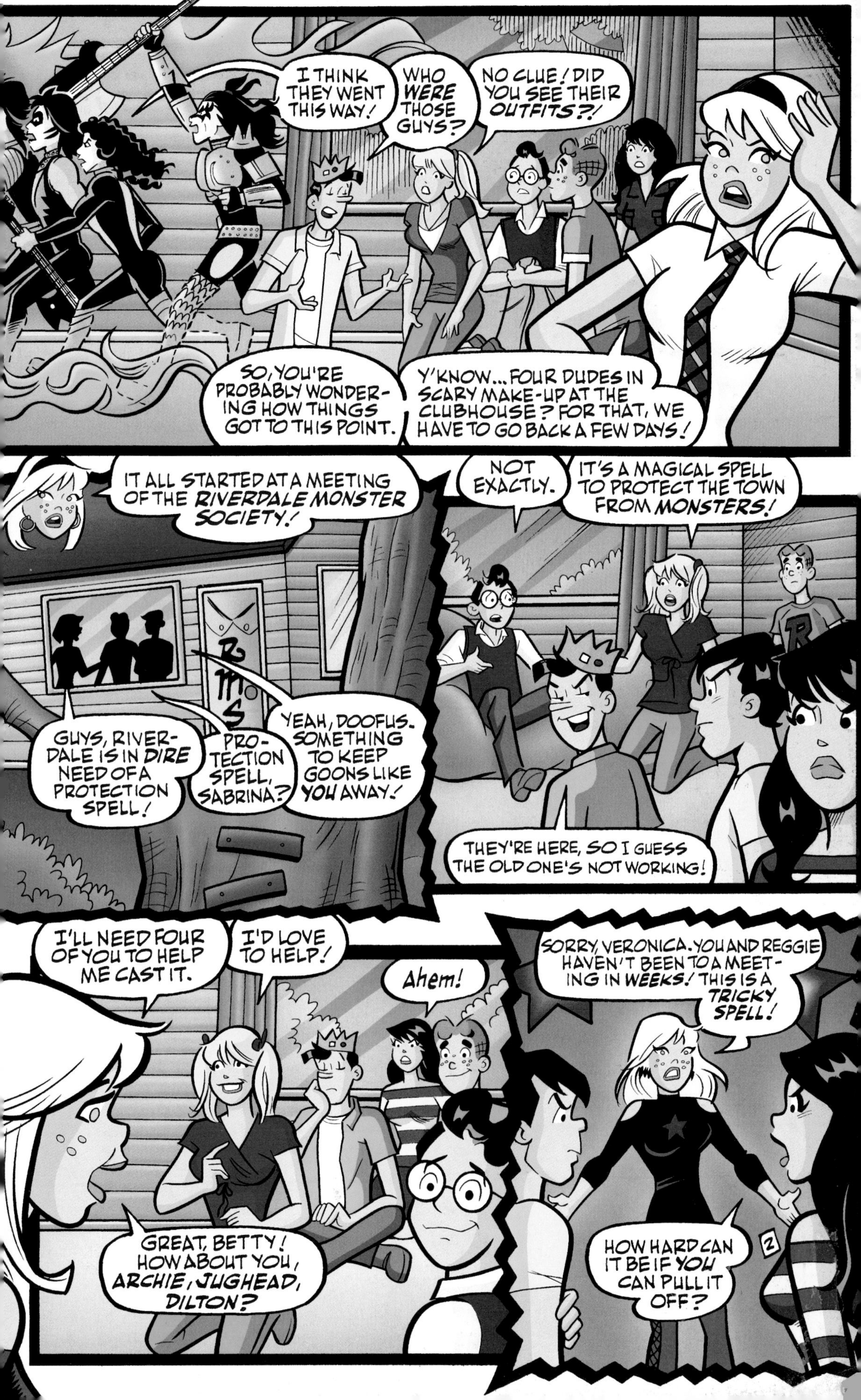
I THINK THEY WENT THIS WAY!
WHO WERE THOSE GUYS?
NO CLUE! DID YOU SEE THEIR OUTFITS?!
SO, YOU'RE PROBABLY WONDERING HOW THINGS GOT TO THIS POINT.
Y'KNOW... FOUR DUDES IN SCARY MAKE-UP AT THE CLUBHOUSE? FOR THAT, WE HAVE TO GO BACK A FEW DAYS!
IT ALL STARTED AT A MEETING OF THE RIVERDALE MONSTER SOCIETY!
GUYS, RIVERDALE IS IN DIRE NEED OF A PROTECTION SPELL!
PROTECTION SPELL, SABRINA?
YEAH, DOOFUS. SOMETHING TO KEEP GOONS LIKE YOU AWAY!
NOT EXACTLY.
IT'S A MAGICAL SPELL TO PROTECT THE TOWN FROM MONSTERS!
THEY'RE HERE, SO I GUESS THE OLD ONE'S NOT WORKING!
I'LL NEED FOUR OF YOU TO HELP ME CAST IT.
I'D LOVE TO HELP!
Ahem!
SORRY, VERONICA. YOU AND REGGIE HAVEN'T BEEN TO A MEETING IN WEEKS! THIS IS A TRICKY SPELL!
GREAT, BETTY! HOW ABOUT YOU, ARCHIE, JUGHEAD, DILTON?
HOW HARD CAN IT BE IF YOU CAN PULL IT OFF?
2

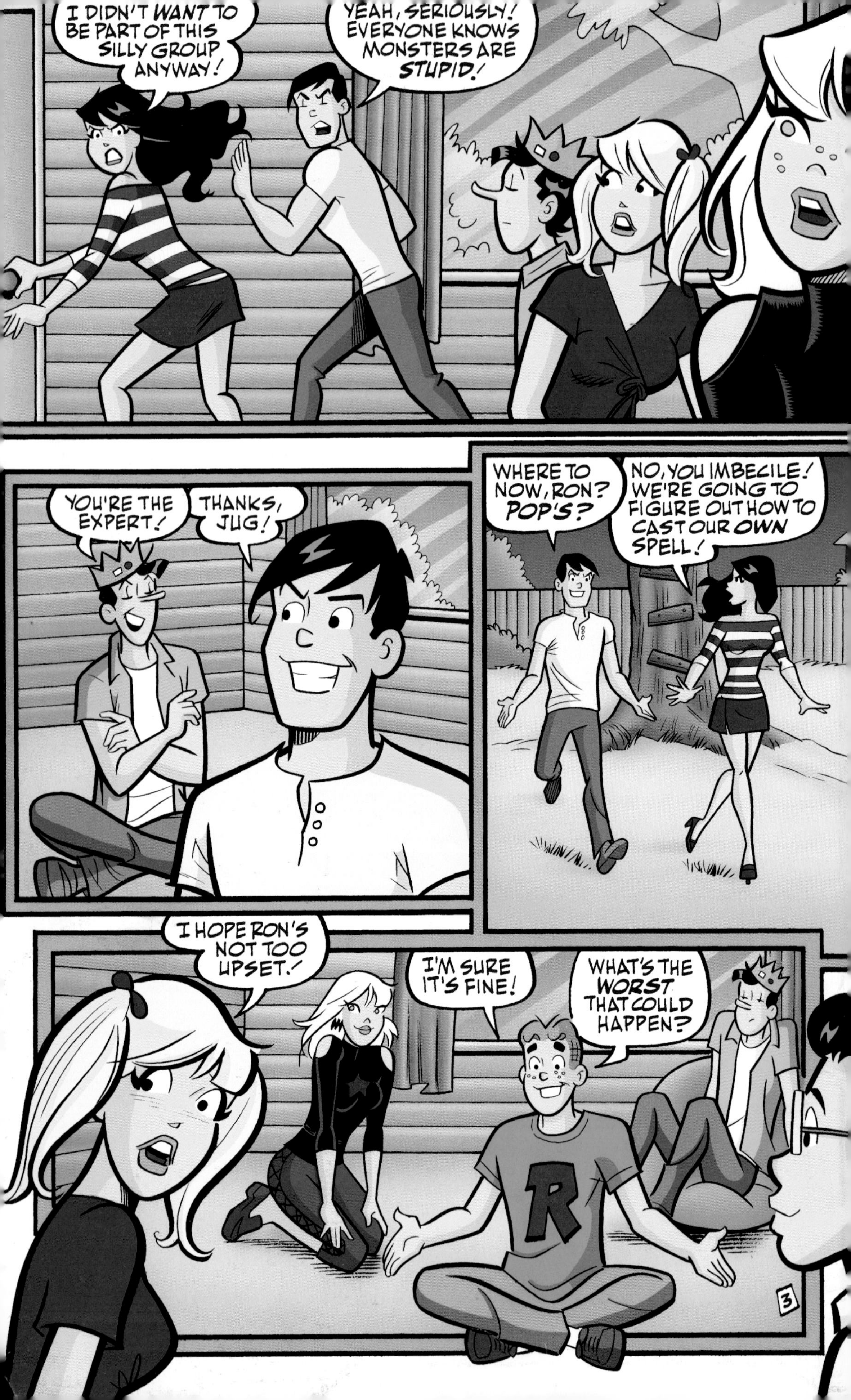
I DIDN'T WANT TO BE PART OF THIS SILLY GROUP ANYWAY!
YEAH, SERIOUSLY! EVERYONE KNOWS MONSTERS ARE STUPID!
YOU'RE THE EXPERT!
THANKS, JUG!
WHERE TO NOW, RON? POP'S?
NO, YOU IMBECILE! WE'RE GOING TO FIGURE OUT HOW TO CAST OUR OWN SPELL!
I HOPE RON'S NOT TOO UPSET.
I'M SURE IT'S FINE!
WHAT'S THE WORST THAT COULD HAPPEN?
3

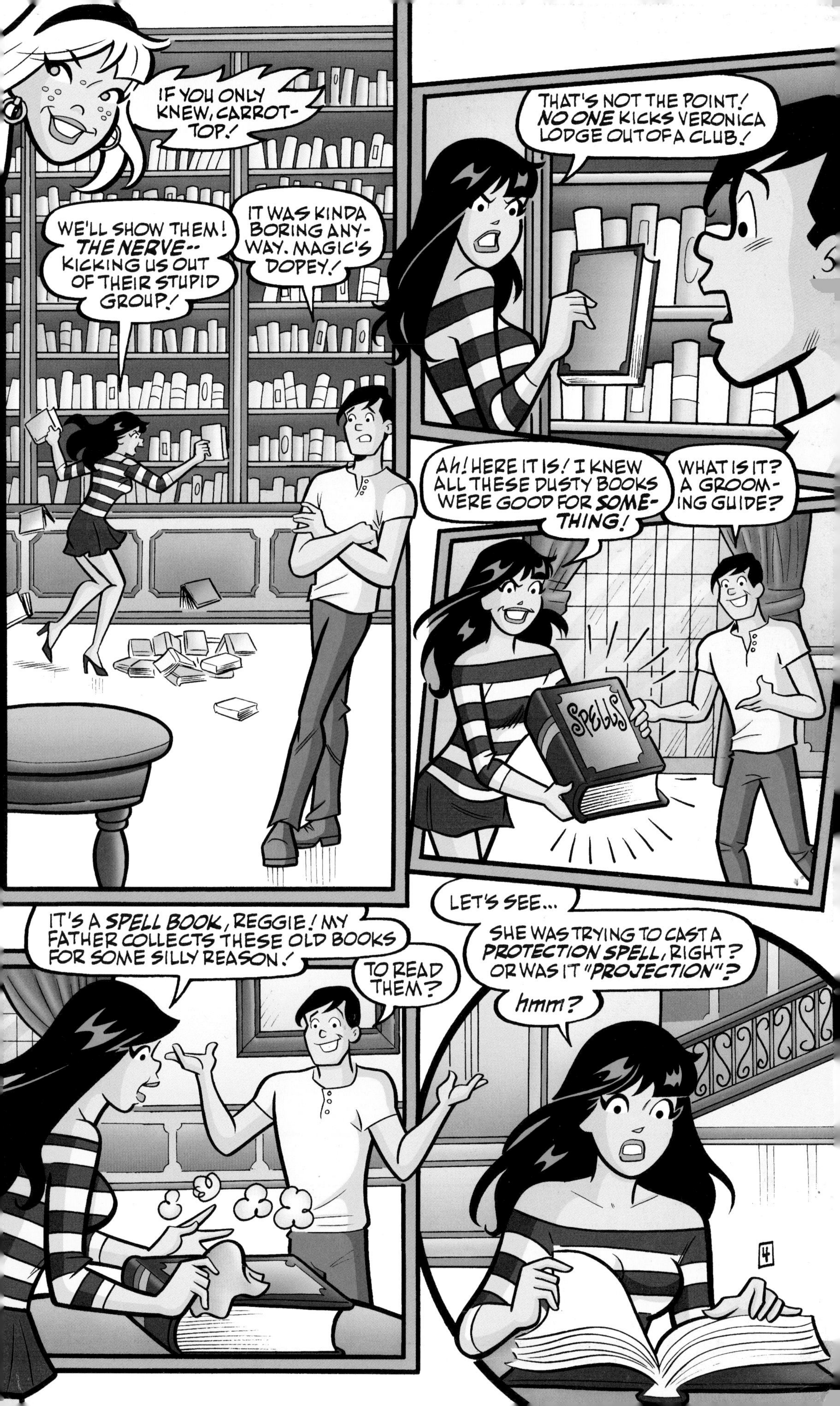

IF YOU ONLY KNEW, CARROT-TOP!
WE'LL SHOW THEM! THE NERVE-- KICKING US OUT OF THEIR STUPID GROUP!
IT WAS KINDA BORING ANY-WAY. MAGIC'S DOPEY!
THAT'S NOT THE POINT! NO ONE KICKS VERONICA LODGE OUT OF A CLUB!
AH! HERE IT IS! I KNEW ALL THESE DUSTY BOOKS WERE GOOD FOR SOME-THING!
WHAT IS IT? A GROOM-ING GUIDE?
SPELLS
IT'S A SPELL BOOK, REGGIE! MY FATHER COLLECTS THESE OLD BOOKS FOR SOME SILLY REASON!
TO READ THEM?
LET'S SEE...
SHE WAS TRYING TO CAST A PROTECTION SPELL, RIGHT? OR WAS IT "PROJECTION"?
hmm?
4

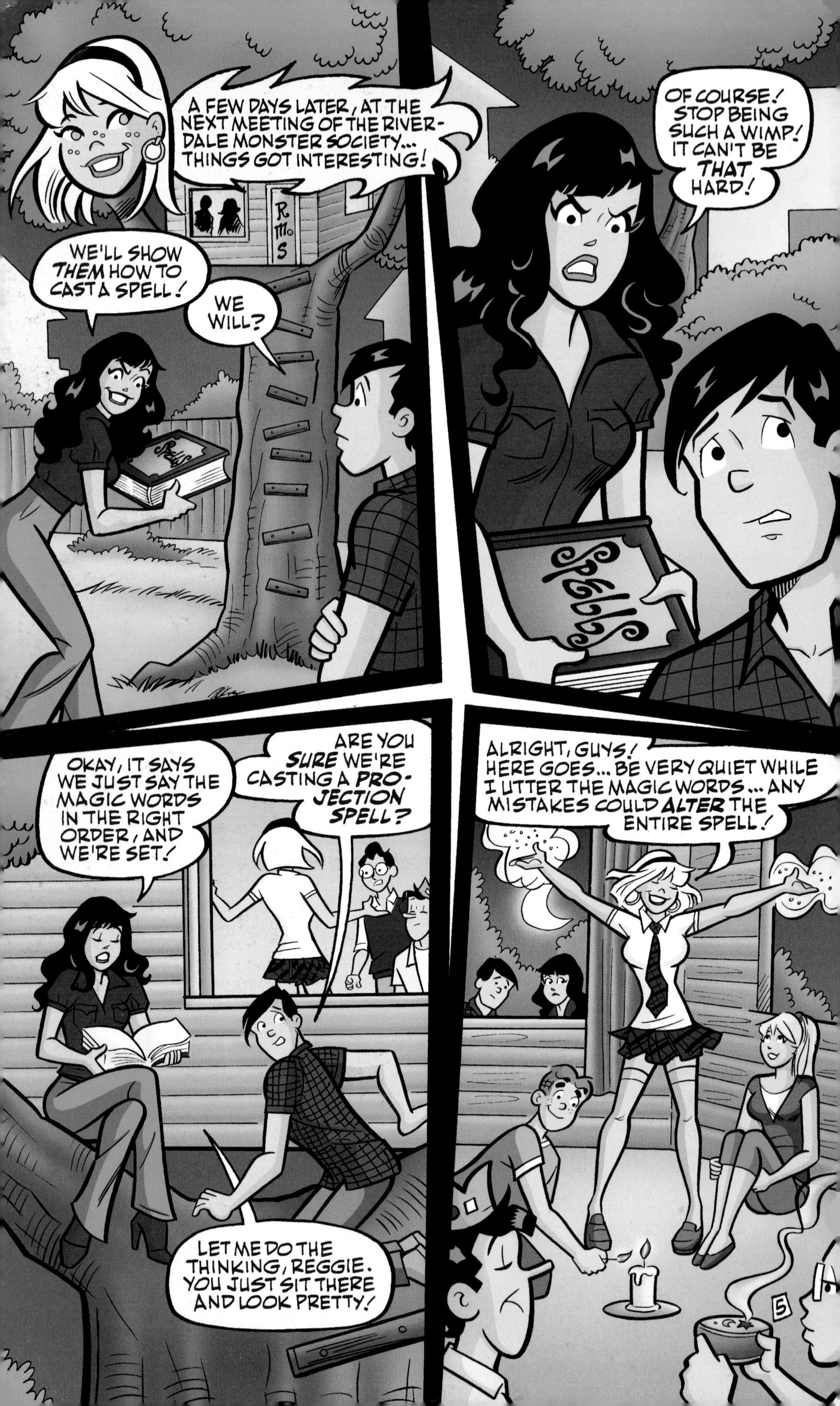
A FEW DAYS LATER, AT THE NEXT MEETING OF THE RIVER-DALE MONSTER SOCIETY... THINGS GOT INTERESTING!
R M S
WE'LL SHOW THEM HOW TO CAST A SPELL!
WE WILL?
Spells
OF COURSE! STOP BEING SUCH A WIMP! IT CAN'T BE THAT HARD!
Spells
OKAY, IT SAYS WE JUST SAY THE MAGIC WORDS IN THE RIGHT ORDER, AND WE'RE SET!
ARE YOU SURE WE'RE CASTING A PRO-JECTION SPELL?
LET ME DO THE THINKING, REGGIE. YOU JUST SIT THERE AND LOOK PRETTY!
ALRIGHT, GUYS! HERE GOES... BE VERY QUIET WHILE I UTTER THE MAGIC WORDS... ANY MISTAKES COULD ALTER THE ENTIRE SPELL!
5

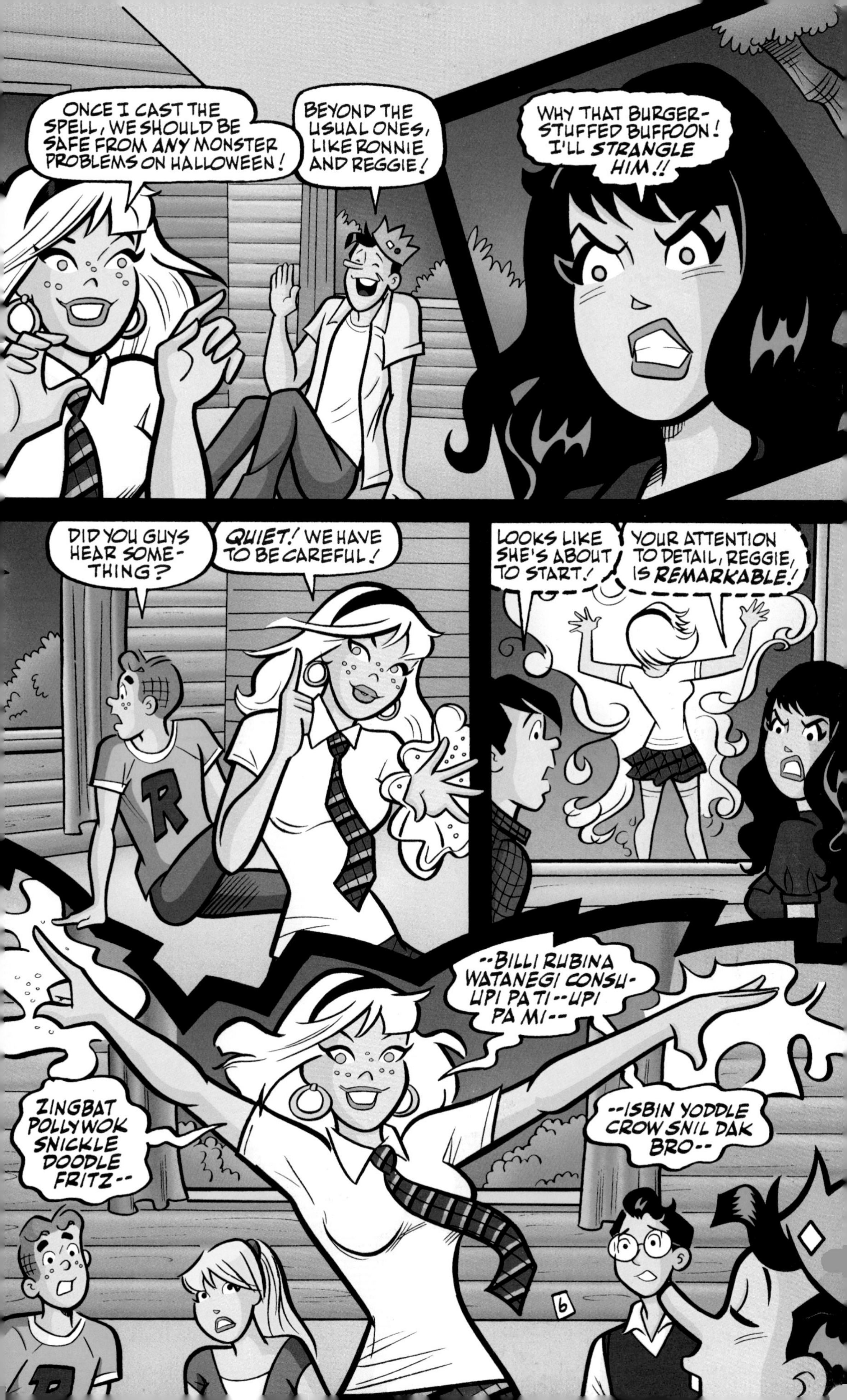
ONCE I CAST THE SPELL, WE SHOULD BE SAFE FROM ANY MONSTER PROBLEMS ON HALLOWEEN!
BEYOND THE USUAL ONES, LIKE RONNIE AND REGGIE!
WHY THAT BURGER-STUFFED BUFFOON! I'LL STRANGLE HIM!!
DID YOU GUYS HEAR SOME-THING?
QUIET! WE HAVE TO BE CAREFUL!
LOOKS LIKE SHE'S ABOUT TO START!
YOUR ATTENTION TO DETAIL, REGGIE, IS REMARKABLE!
ZINGBAT POLLYWOK SNICKLE DOODLE FRITZ--
--BILLI RUBINA WATANEGI CONSU-UPI PA TI--UPI PA MI--
--ISBIN YODDLE CROW SNIL DAK BRO--
6

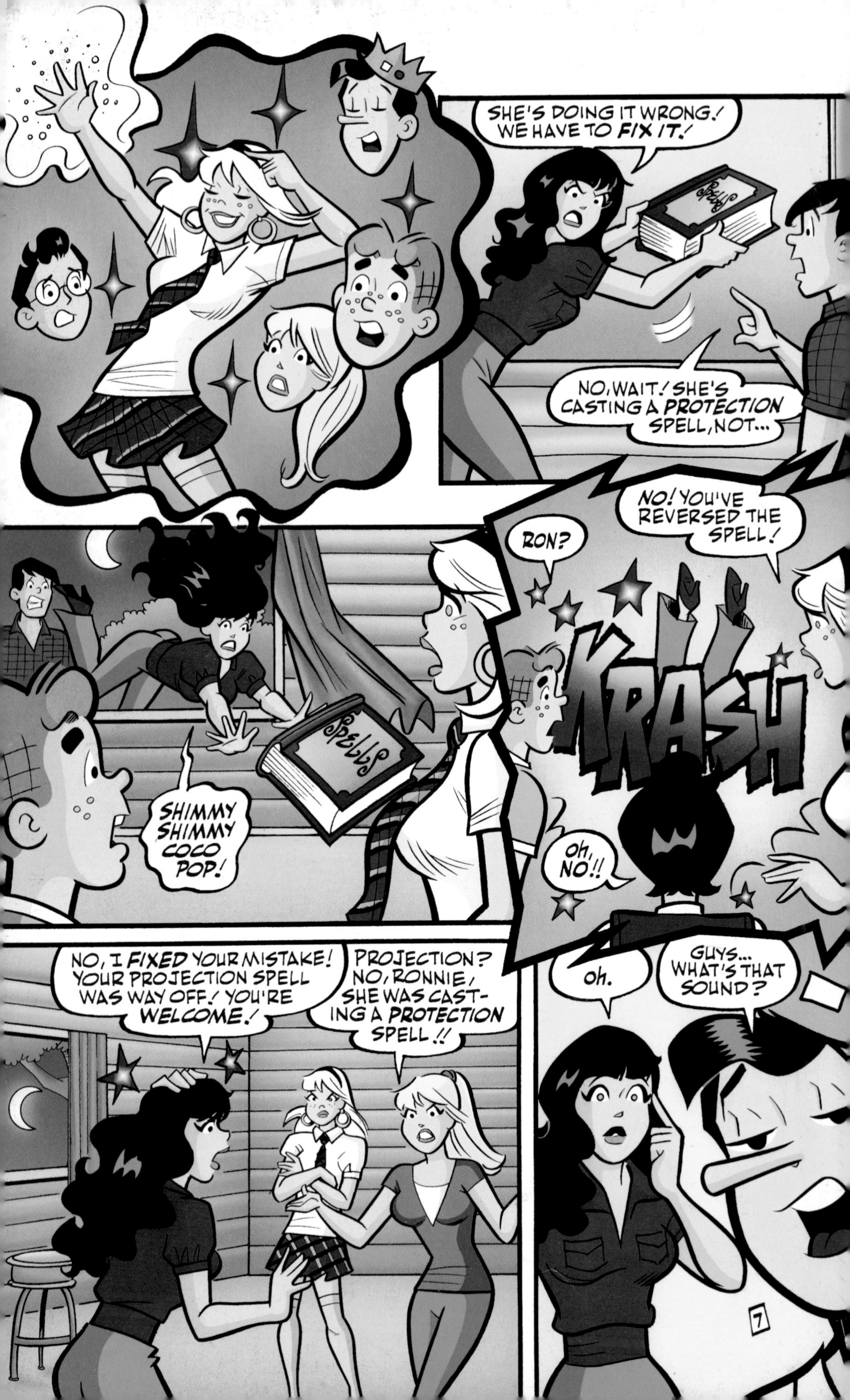
SHE'S DOING IT WRONG! WE HAVE TO FIX IT!
NO, WAIT! SHE'S CASTING A PROTECTION SPELL, NOT...
SPELLS
SHIMMY SHIMMY COCO POP!
RON?
NO! YOU'VE REVERSED THE SPELL!
KRASH
OH, NO!!
NO, I FIXED YOUR MISTAKE! YOUR PROJECTION SPELL WAS WAY OFF! YOU'RE WELCOME!
PROJECTION? NO, RONNIE, SHE WAS CASTING A PROTECTION SPELL!!
OH.
GUYS... WHAT'S THAT SOUND?
7

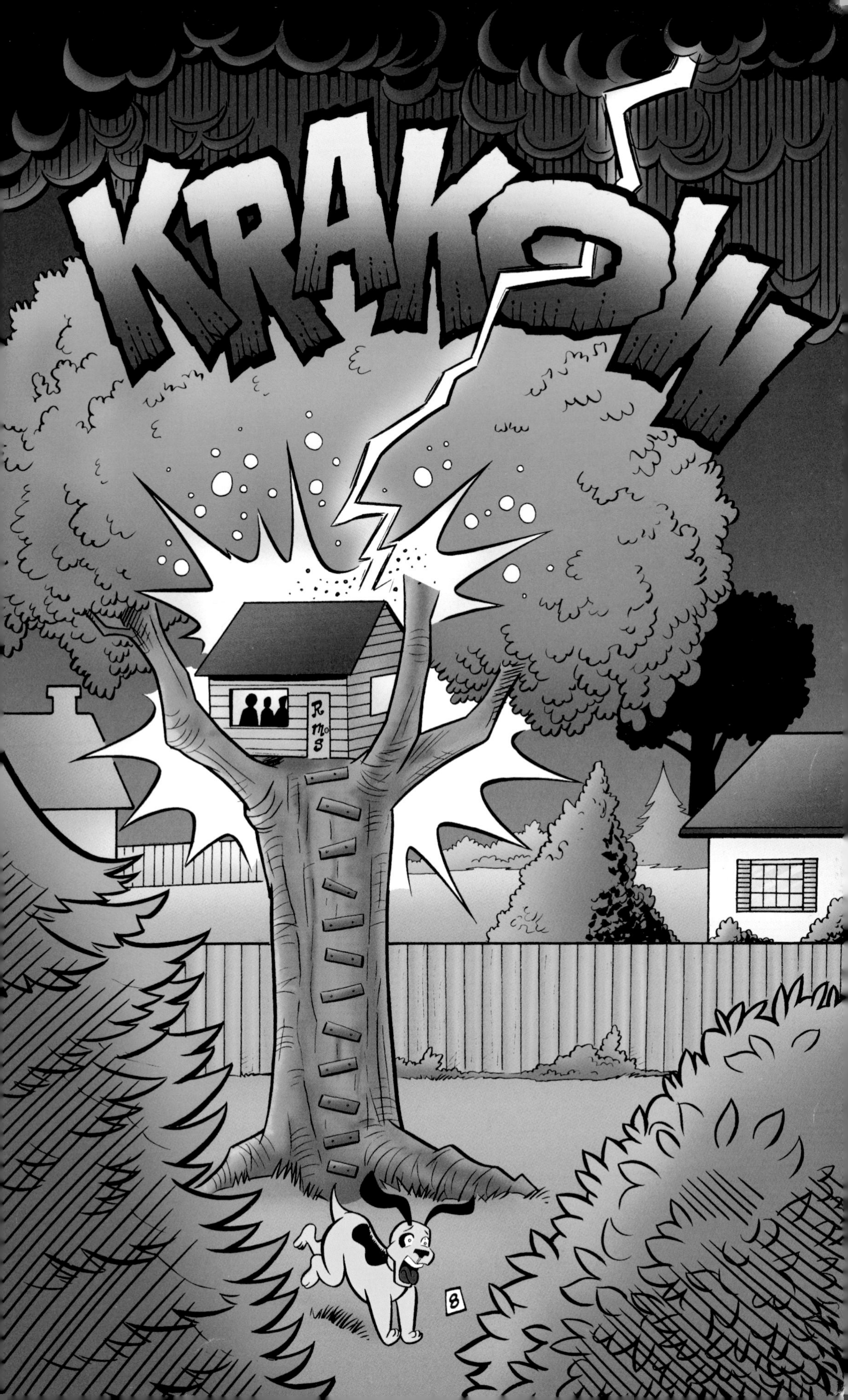
KRAKOW

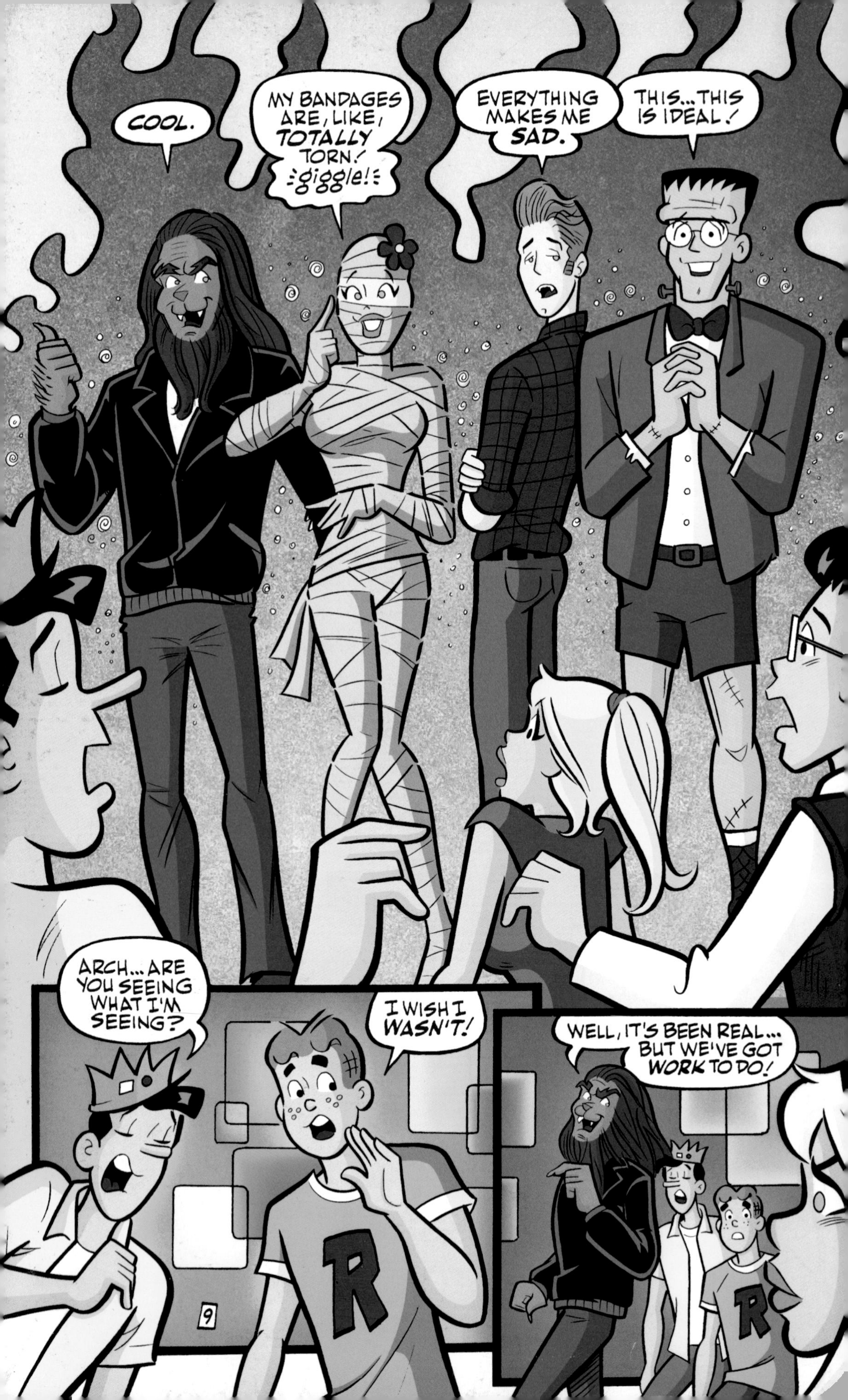
COOL.
MY BANDAGES ARE, LIKE, TOTALLY TORN! giggle!
EVERYTHING MAKES ME SAD.
THIS... THIS IS IDEAL!
ARCH... ARE YOU SEEING WHAT I'M SEEING?
I WISH I WASN'T!
WELL, IT'S BEEN REAL... BUT WE'VE GOT WORK TO DO!
9

It's going to be, um... totally cool to, uh...

Drain this place of any personality? Should be easy enough!

Are you happy now, Ron? You've unleashed MONSTERS on Riverdale!

Oh, Betty, don't be SO NAIVE! Those aren't MONSTERS, they're NERDS!

Yeah, seriously! They're probably biding time between Renaissance fairs!

This dive will be PERMANENTLY LAME and BORING!

Sabrina, WHAT WERE those things?

I'm NOT SURE, but they're NOT FROM AROUND HERE!

And, judging from the instability that portal caused upon opening, we may be in a highly temperamental geographical area, akin to a WORMHOLE!

Dilton. ENGLISH.

Um... guys? I hate to sound like a broken record, but...

10

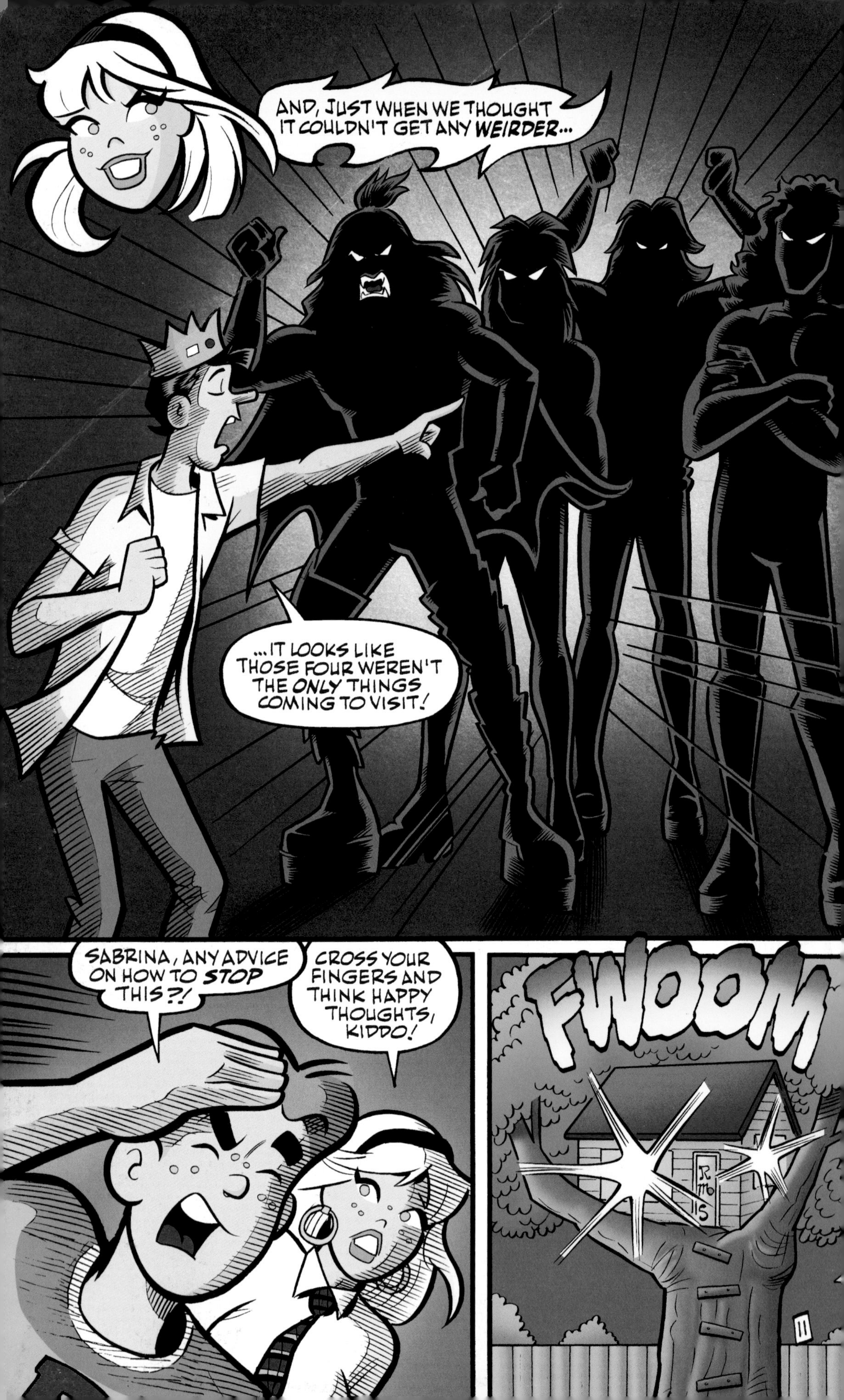
AND, JUST WHEN WE THOUGHT IT COULDN'T GET ANY WEIRDER...
...IT LOOKS LIKE THOSE FOUR WEREN'T THE ONLY THINGS COMING TO VISIT!
SABRINA, ANY ADVICE ON HOW TO STOP THIS?!
CROSS YOUR FINGERS AND THINK HAPPY THOUGHTS, KIDDO!
FWOOM

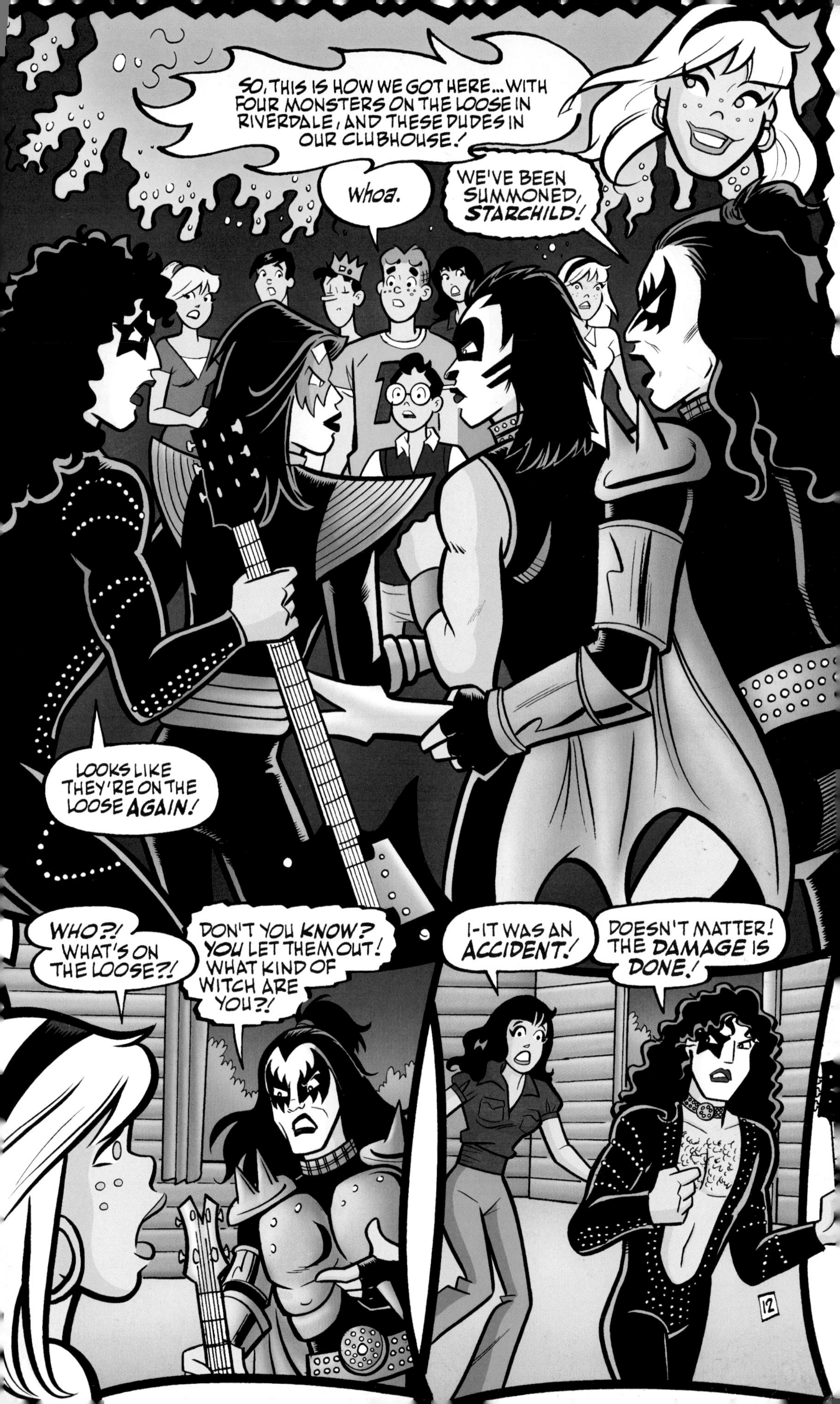
SO, THIS IS HOW WE GOT HERE... WITH FOUR MONSTERS ON THE LOOSE IN RIVERDALE, AND THESE DUDES IN OUR CLUBHOUSE!
whoa.
WE'VE BEEN SUMMONED, STARCHILD!
LOOKS LIKE THEY'RE ON THE LOOSE AGAIN!
WHO?! WHAT'S ON THE LOOSE?!
DON'T YOU KNOW? YOU LET THEM OUT! WHAT KIND OF WITCH ARE YOU?!
I-IT WAS AN ACCIDENT!
DOESN'T MATTER! THE DAMAGE IS DONE!
12

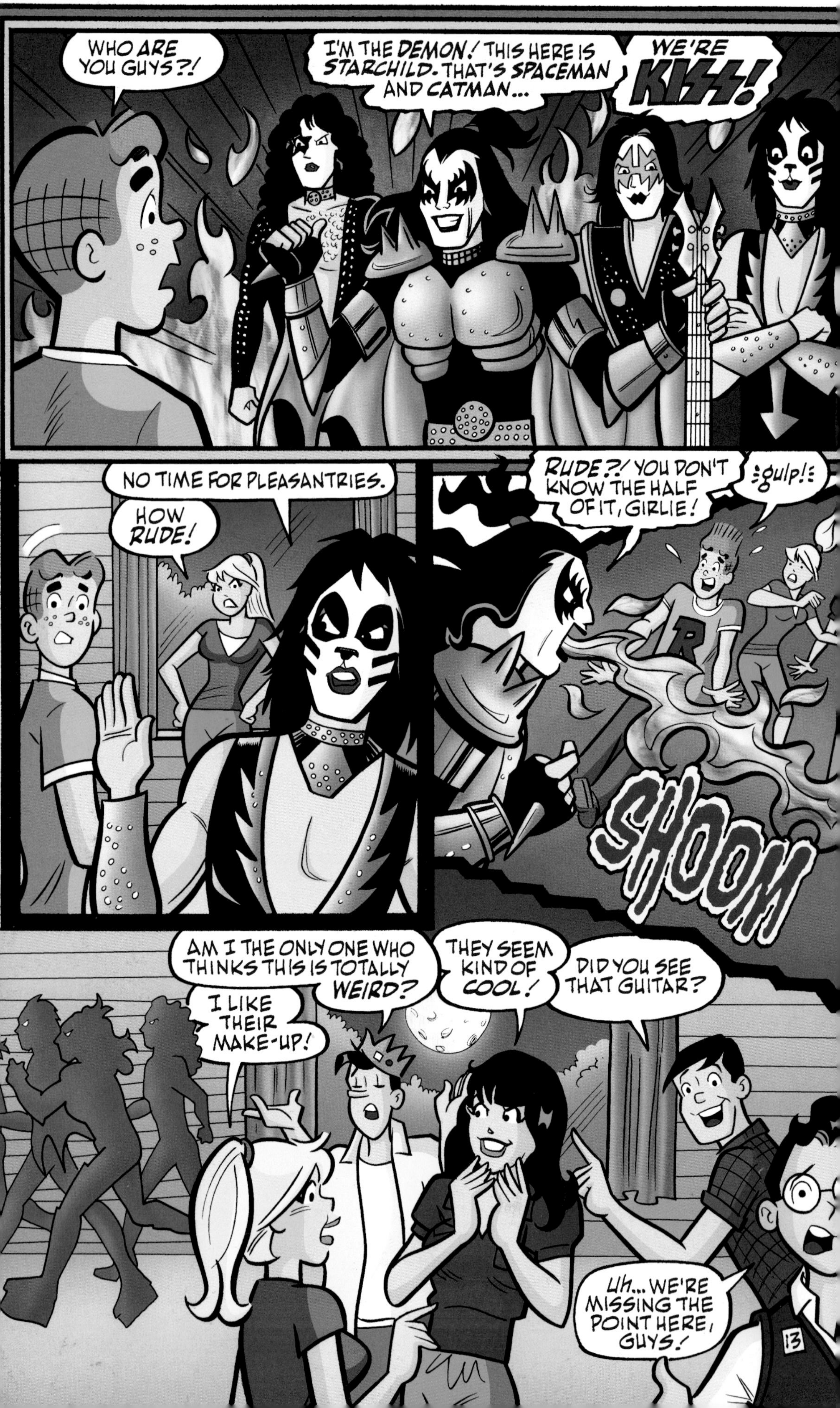

WHO ARE YOU GUYS?!
I'M THE DEMON! THIS HERE IS STARCHILD. THAT'S SPACEMAN AND CATMAN...
WE'RE KISS!
NO TIME FOR PLEASANTRIES.
HOW RUDE!
RUDE?! YOU DON'T KNOW THE HALF OF IT, GIRLIE!
gulp!
SHOOM
AM I THE ONLY ONE WHO THINKS THIS IS TOTALLY WEIRD?
I LIKE THEIR MAKE-UP!
THEY SEEM KIND OF COOL!
DID YOU SEE THAT GUITAR?
uh... WE'RE MISSING THE POINT HERE, GUYS!
13

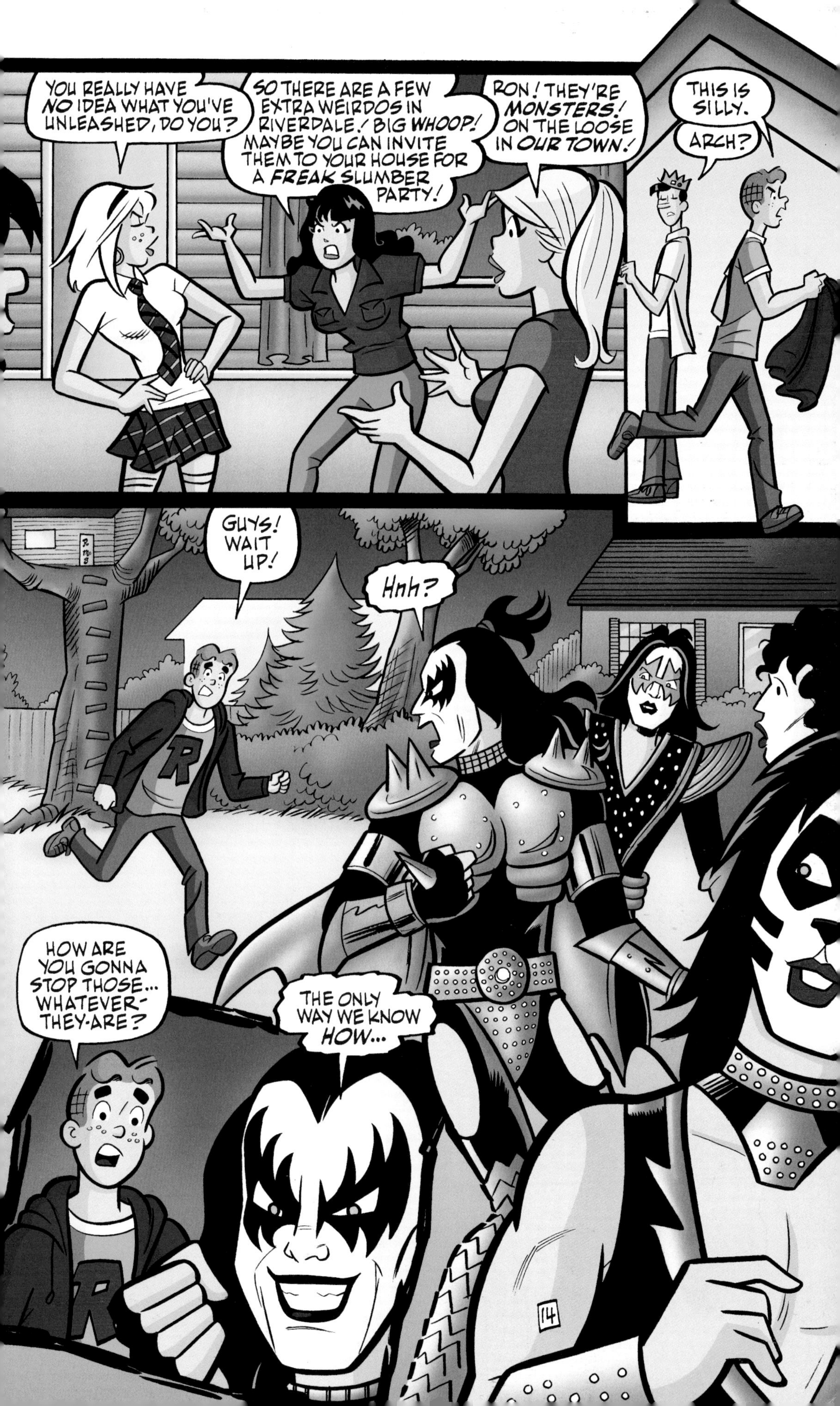
YOU REALLY HAVE NO IDEA WHAT YOU'VE UNLEASHED, DO YOU?
SO THERE ARE A FEW EXTRA WEIRDOS IN RIVERDALE! BIG WHOOP! MAYBE YOU CAN INVITE THEM TO YOUR HOUSE FOR A FREAK SLUMBER PARTY!
RON! THEY'RE MONSTERS! ON THE LOOSE IN OUR TOWN!
THIS IS SILLY.
ARCH?
GUYS! WAIT UP!
Hnh?
HOW ARE YOU GONNA STOP THOSE... WHATEVER-THEY-ARE?
THE ONLY WAY WE KNOW HOW...
14

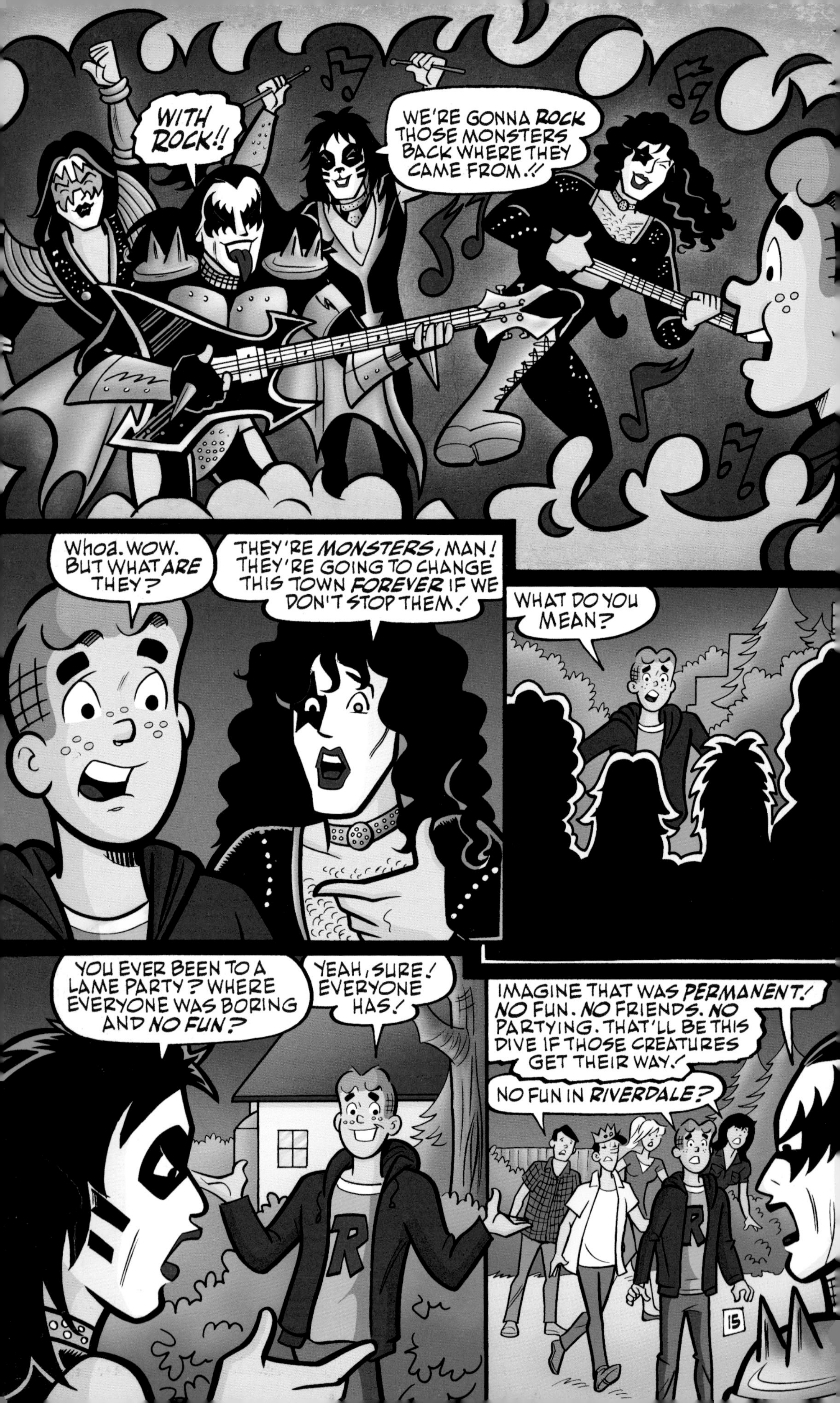
WITH ROCK!!
WE'RE GONNA ROCK THOSE MONSTERS BACK WHERE THEY CAME FROM.!!
Whoa. WOW. BUT WHAT ARE THEY?
THEY'RE MONSTERS, MAN! THEY'RE GOING TO CHANGE THIS TOWN FOREVER IF WE DON'T STOP THEM.!
WHAT DO YOU MEAN?
YOU EVER BEEN TO A LAME PARTY? WHERE EVERYONE WAS BORING AND NO FUN?
YEAH, SURE! EVERYONE HAS!
IMAGINE THAT WAS PERMANENT! NO FUN. NO FRIENDS. NO PARTYING. THAT'LL BE THIS DIVE IF THOSE CREATURES GET THEIR WAY!
NO FUN IN RIVERDALE?
15

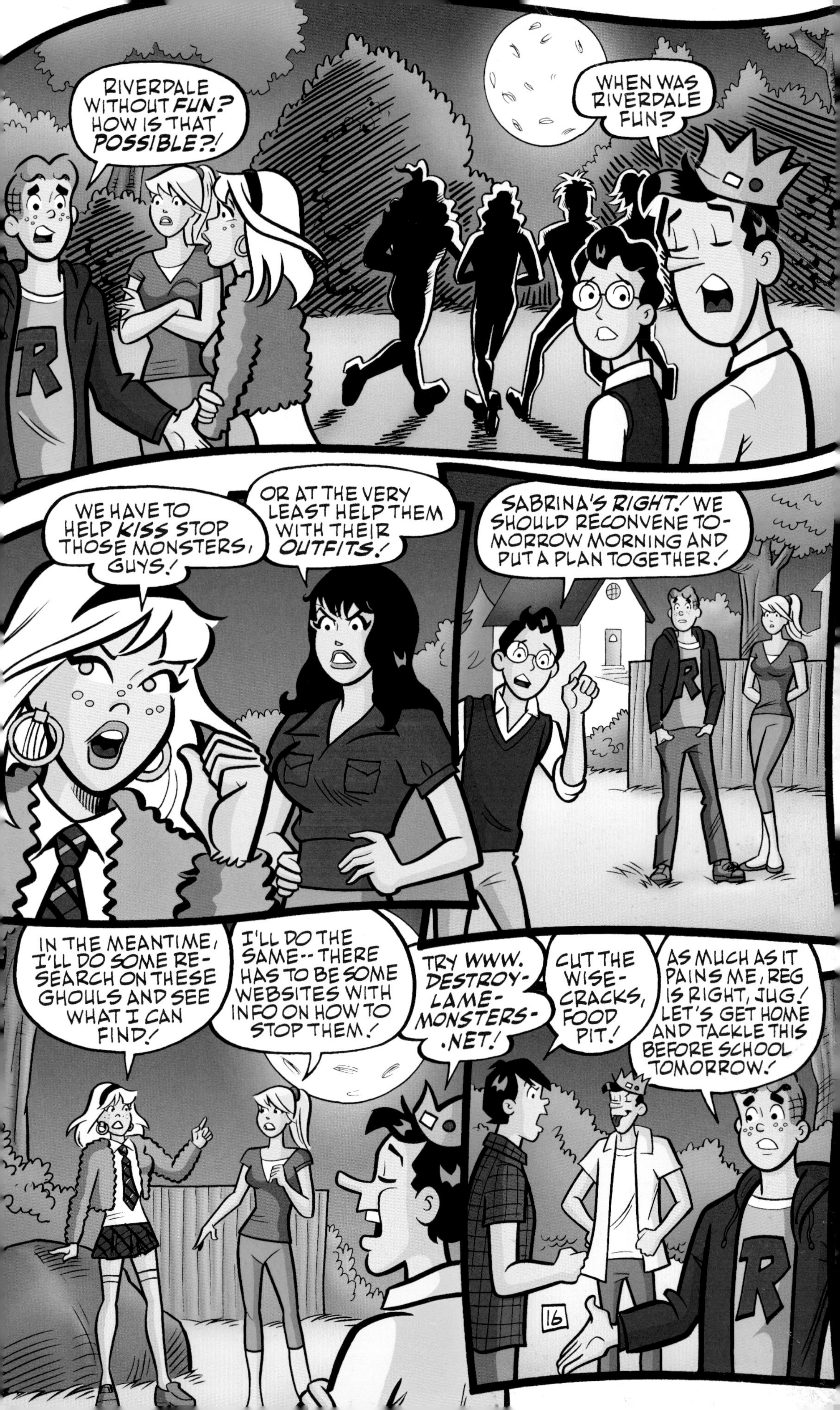

RIVERDALE WITHOUT FUN? HOW IS THAT POSSIBLE?!
WHEN WAS RIVERDALE FUN?
WE HAVE TO HELP KISS STOP THOSE MONSTERS, GUYS!
OR AT THE VERY LEAST HELP THEM WITH THEIR OUTFITS!
SABRINA'S RIGHT! WE SHOULD RECONVENE TO-MORROW MORNING AND PUT A PLAN TOGETHER!
IN THE MEANTIME, I'LL DO SOME RE-SEARCH ON THESE GHOULS AND SEE WHAT I CAN FIND!
I'LL DO THE SAME-- THERE HAS TO BE SOME WEBSITES WITH INFO ON HOW TO STOP THEM!
TRY WWW. DESTROY-LAME-MONSTERS-.NET!
CUT THE WISE-CRACKS, FOOD PIT!
AS MUCH AS IT PAINS ME, REG IS RIGHT, JUG! LET'S GET HOME AND TACKLE THIS BEFORE SCHOOL TOMORROW!
16

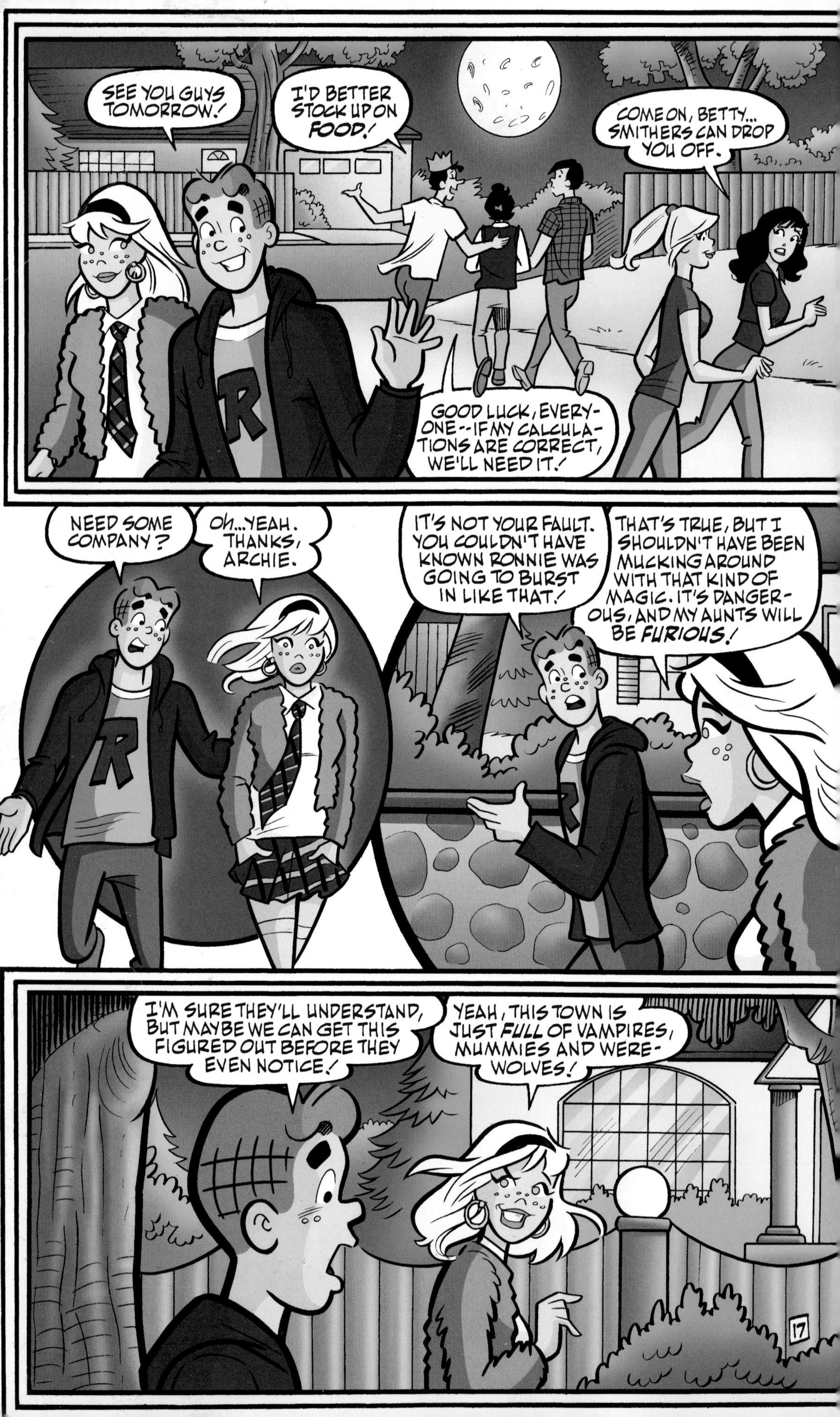

SEE YOU GUYS TOMORROW!
I'D BETTER STOCK UP ON FOOD!
COME ON, BETTY... SMITHERS CAN DROP YOU OFF.
GOOD LUCK, EVERY-ONE--IF MY CALCULA-TIONS ARE CORRECT, WE'LL NEED IT!
NEED SOME COMPANY?
Oh...YEAH. THANKS, ARCHIE.
IT'S NOT YOUR FAULT. YOU COULDN'T HAVE KNOWN RONNIE WAS GOING TO BURST IN LIKE THAT!
THAT'S TRUE, BUT I SHOULDN'T HAVE BEEN MUCKING AROUND WITH THAT KIND OF MAGIC. IT'S DANGER-OUS, AND MY AUNTS WILL BE FURIOUS!
I'M SURE THEY'LL UNDERSTAND, BUT MAYBE WE CAN GET THIS FIGURED OUT BEFORE THEY EVEN NOTICE!
YEAH, THIS TOWN IS JUST FULL OF VAMPIRES, MUMMIES AND WERE-WOLVES!

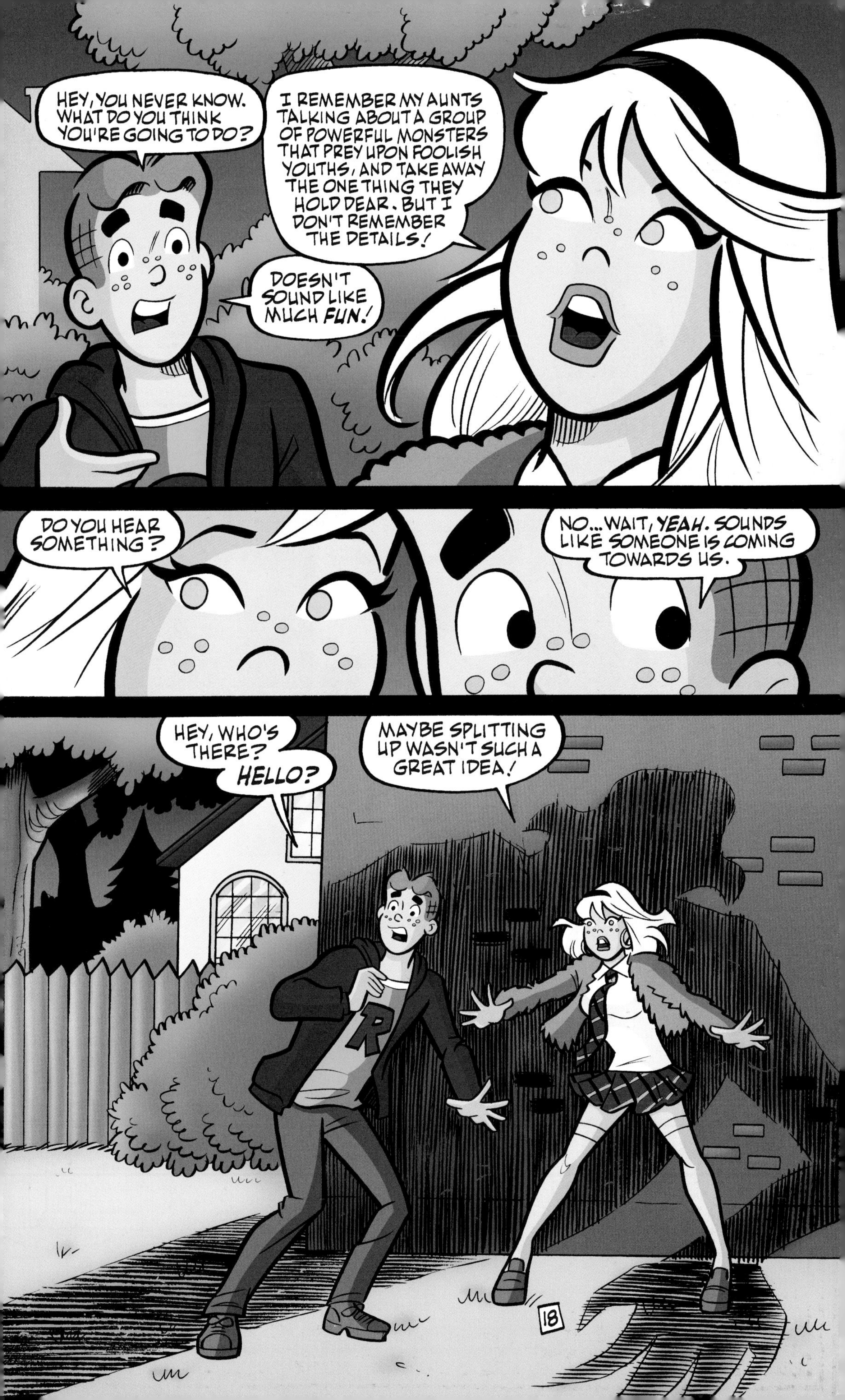
HEY, YOU NEVER KNOW. WHAT DO YOU THINK YOU'RE GOING TO DO?
I REMEMBER MY AUNTS TALKING ABOUT A GROUP OF POWERFUL MONSTERS THAT PREY UPON FOOLISH YOUTHS, AND TAKE AWAY THE ONE THING THEY HOLD DEAR. BUT I DON'T REMEMBER THE DETAILS!
DOESN'T SOUND LIKE MUCH FUN!
DO YOU HEAR SOMETHING?
NO...WAIT, YEAH. SOUNDS LIKE SOMEONE IS COMING TOWARDS US.
HEY, WHO'S THERE? HELLO?
MAYBE SPLITTING UP WASN'T SUCH A GREAT IDEA!
18

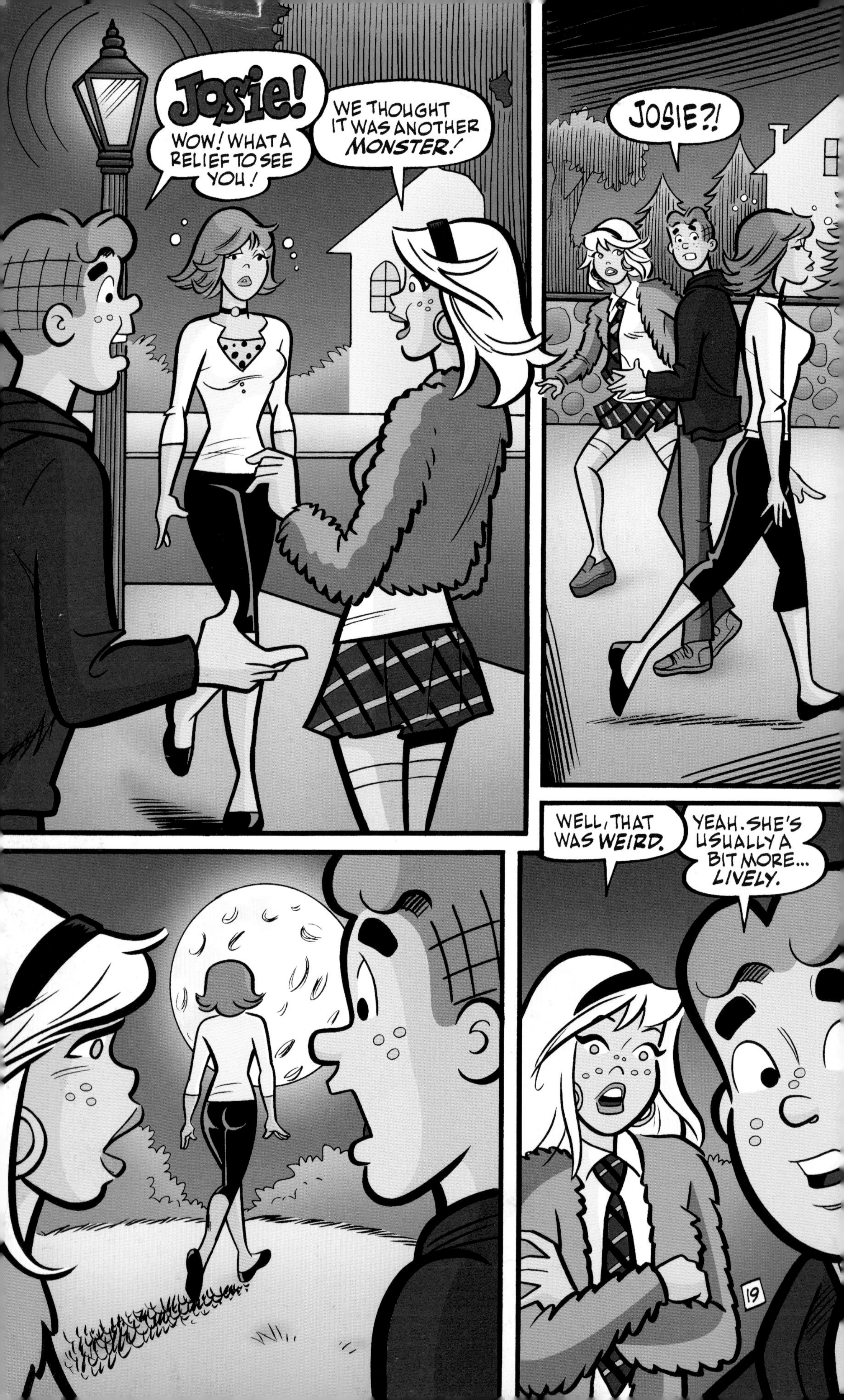

JOSIE!
WOW! WHAT A RELIEF TO SEE YOU!
WE THOUGHT IT WAS ANOTHER MONSTER!
JOSIE?!
WELL, THAT WAS WEIRD.
YEAH. SHE'S USUALLY A BIT MORE... LIVELY.
19

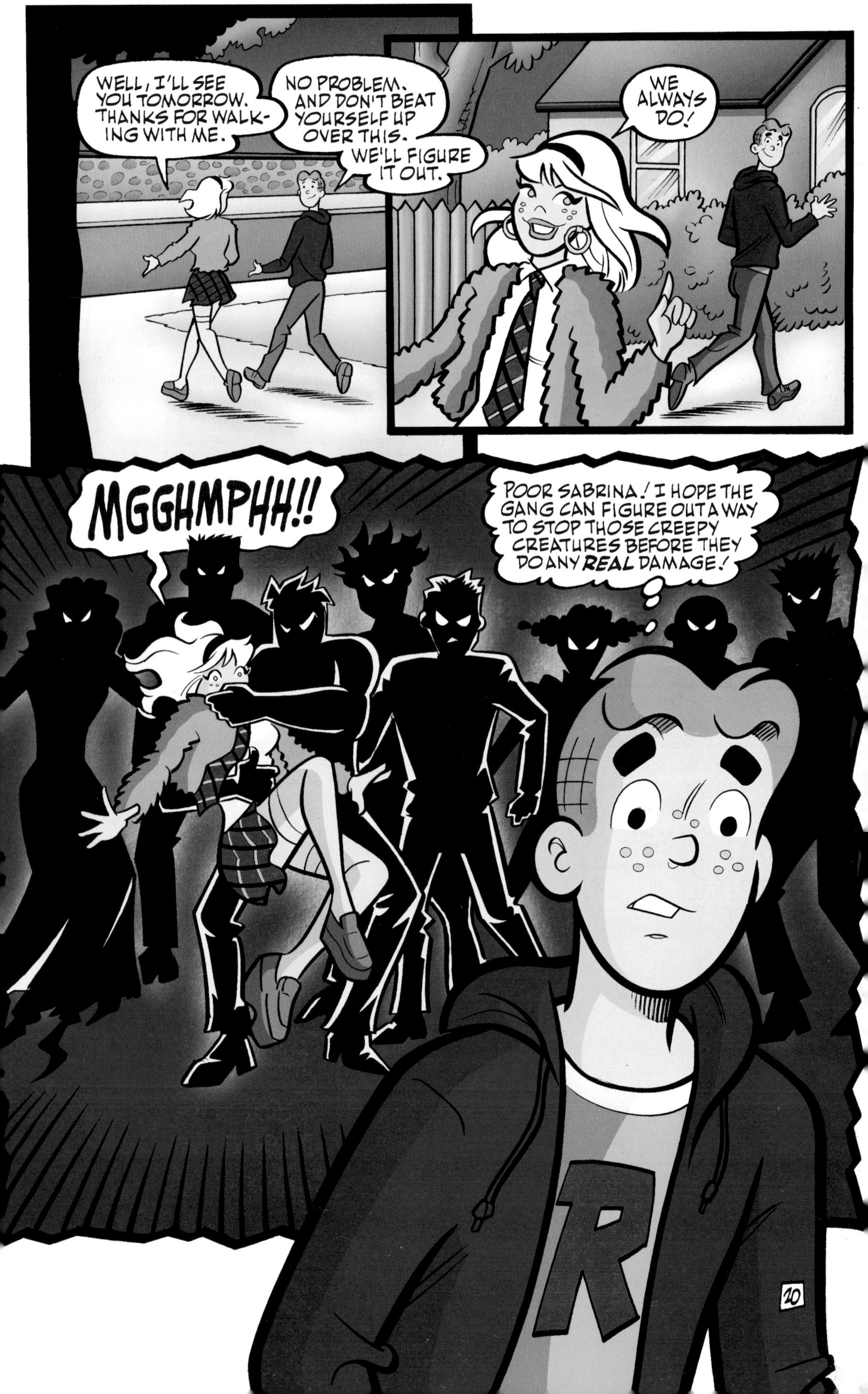
WELL, I'LL SEE YOU TOMORROW. THANKS FOR WALKING WITH ME.
NO PROBLEM. AND DON'T BEAT YOURSELF UP OVER THIS.
WE'LL FIGURE IT OUT.
WE ALWAYS DO!
MGGHMPHH!!
POOR SABRINA! I HOPE THE GANG CAN FIGURE OUT A WAY TO STOP THOSE CREEPY CREATURES BEFORE THEY DO ANY REAL DAMAGE!
20

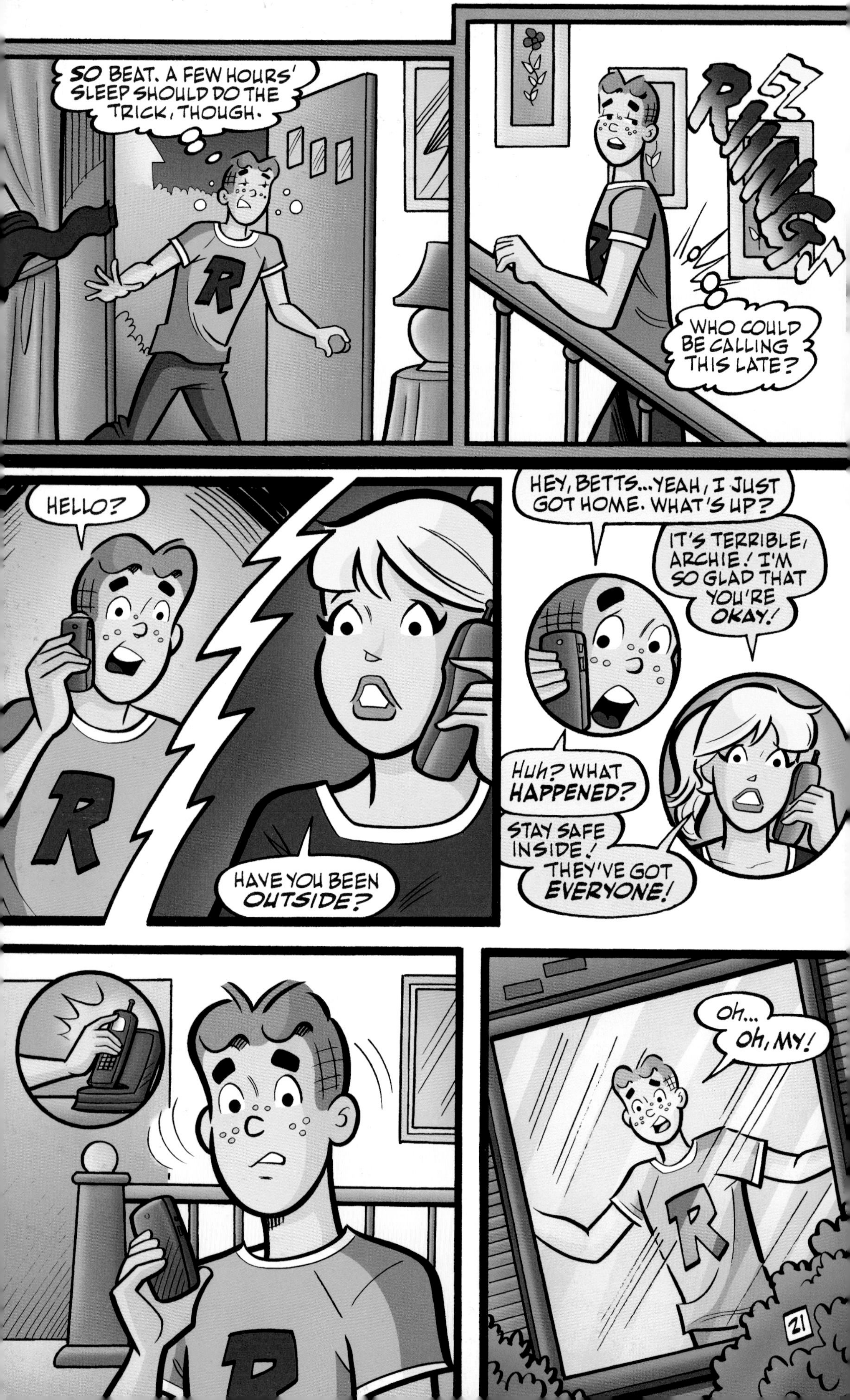

SO BEAT. A FEW HOURS' SLEEP SHOULD DO THE TRICK, THOUGH.
RIIING!
WHO COULD BE CALLING THIS LATE?
HELLO?
HAVE YOU BEEN OUTSIDE?
HEY, BETTS...YEAH, I JUST GOT HOME. WHAT'S UP?
IT'S TERRIBLE, ARCHIE! I'M SO GLAD THAT YOU'RE OKAY!
Huh? WHAT HAPPENED?
STAY SAFE INSIDE!
THEY'VE GOT EVERYONE!
Oh...
Oh, MY!
21

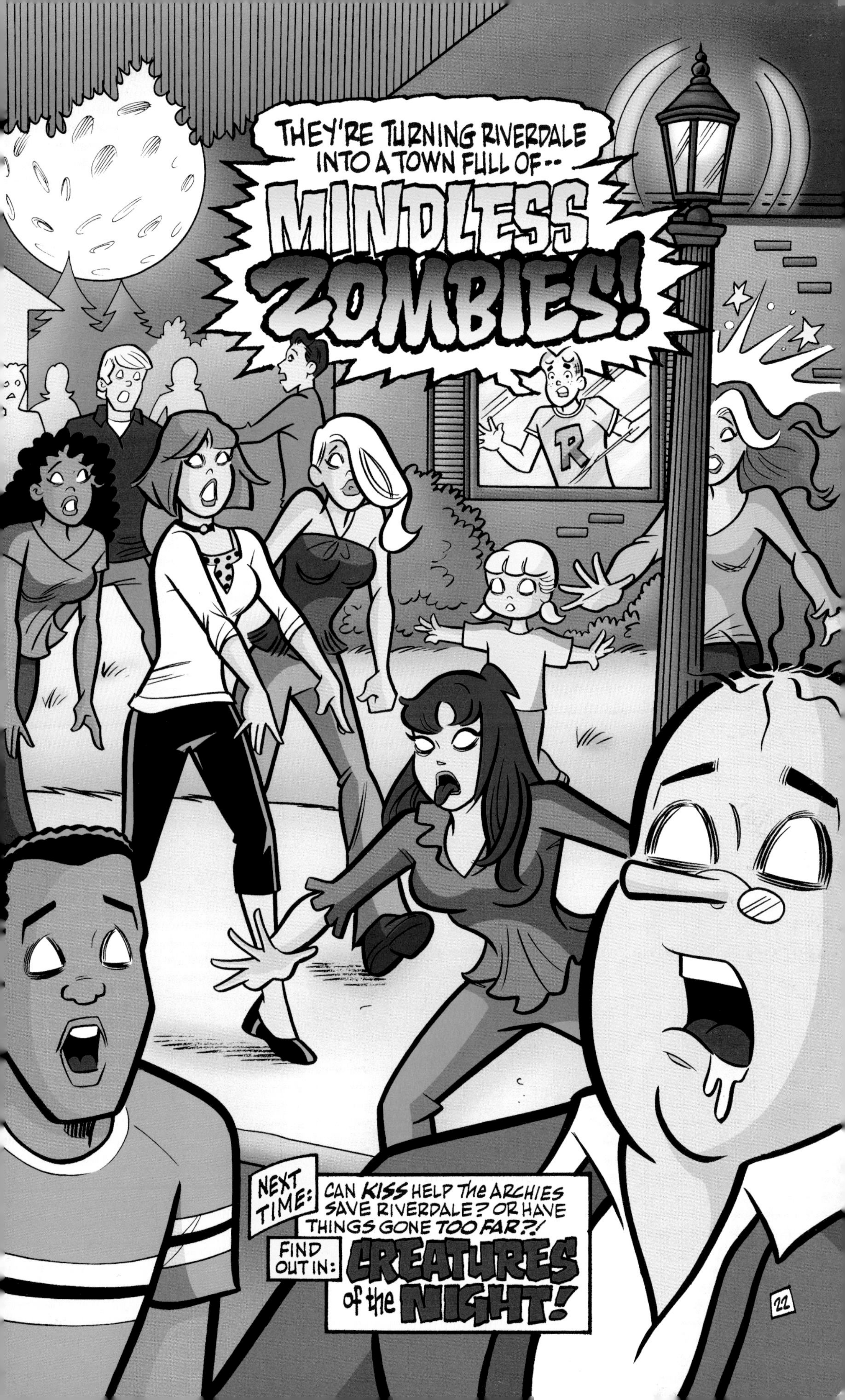

THEY'RE TURNING RIVERDALE INTO A TOWN FULL OF-- MINDLESS ZOMBIES!
NEXT TIME: CAN KISS HELP THE ARCHIES SAVE RIVERDALE? OR HAVE THINGS GONE TOO FAR?!
FIND OUT IN: CREATURES of the NIGHT!
22

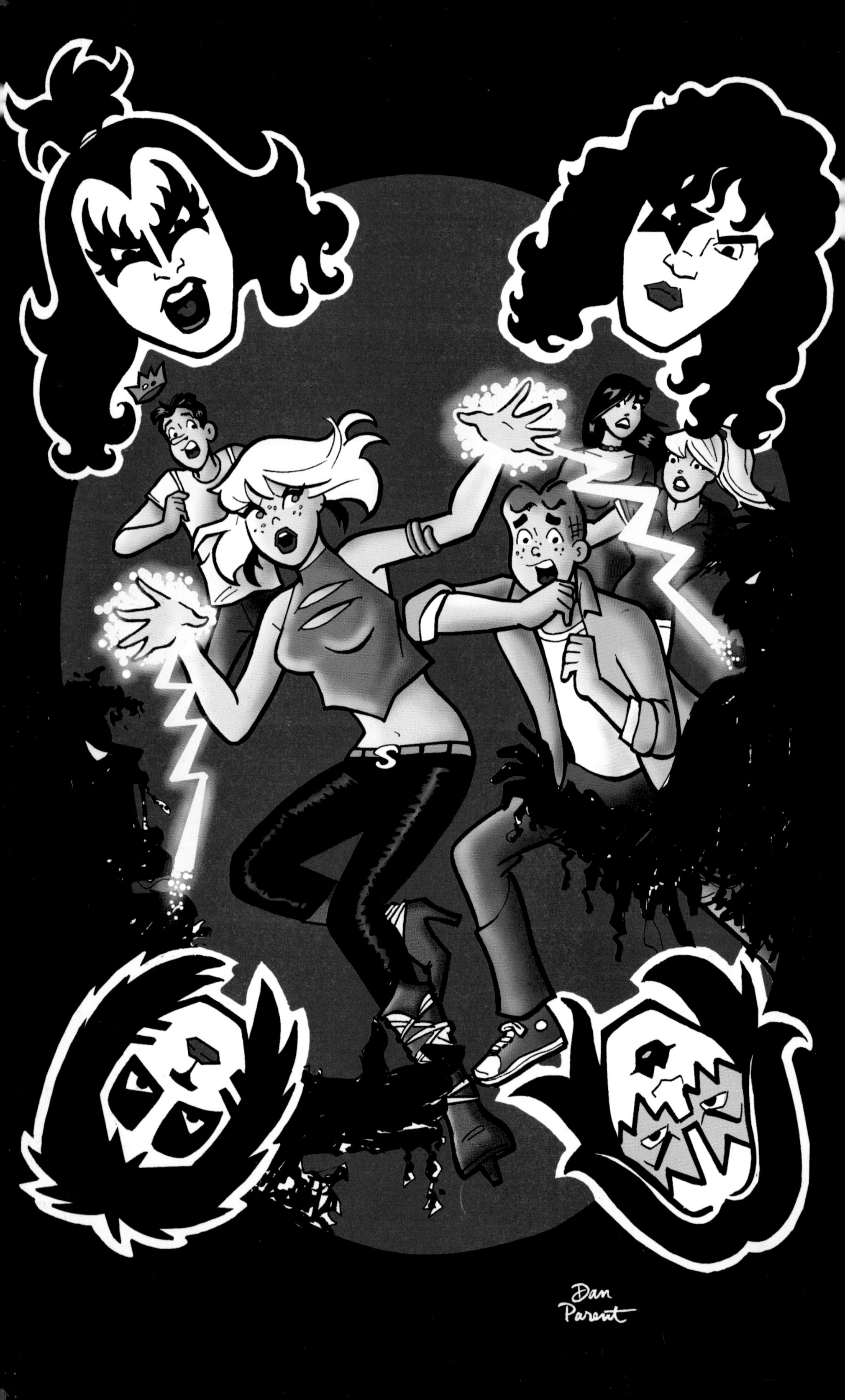
Dan Parent

Chapter Two: Creatures of the Night

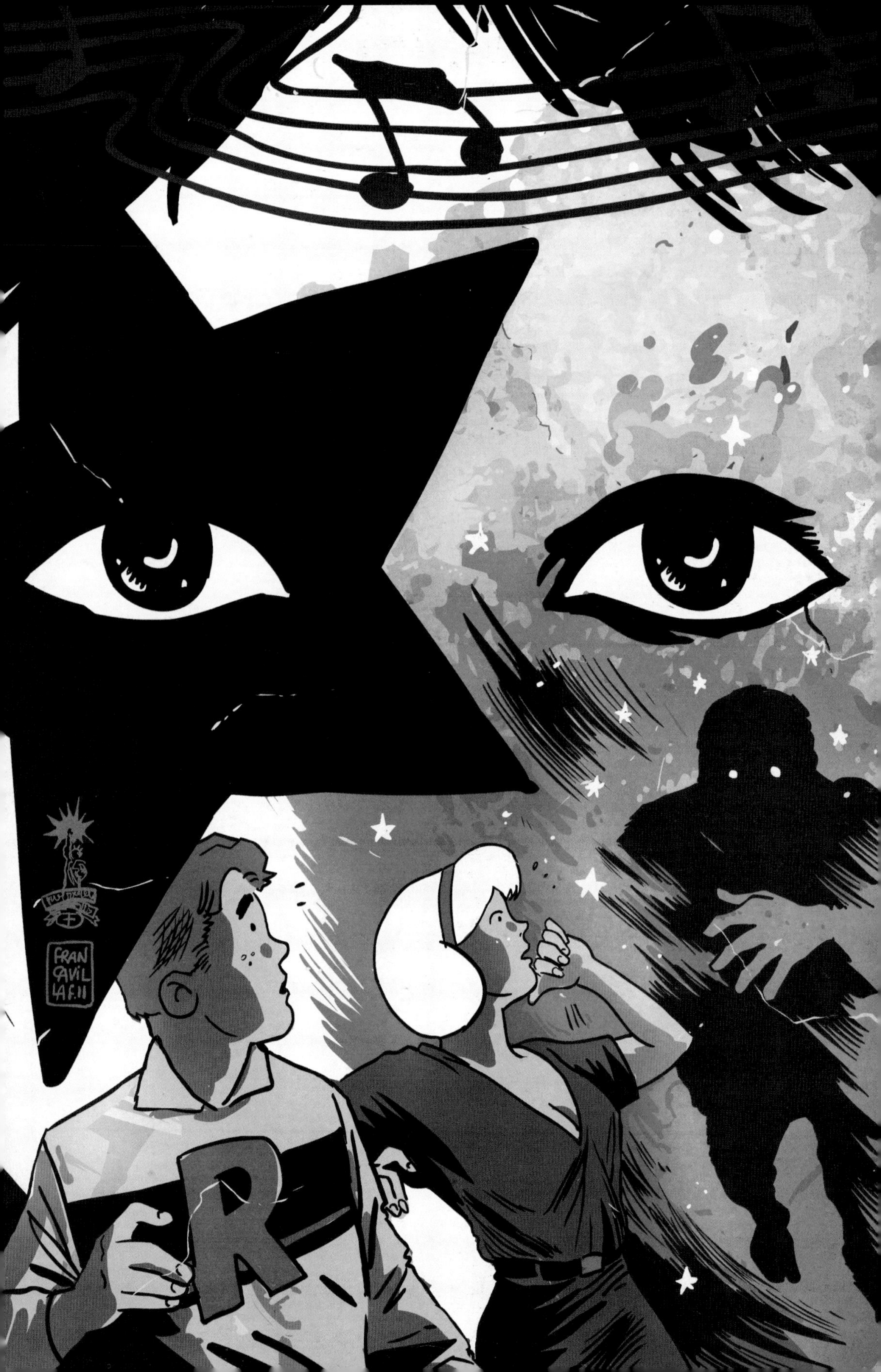

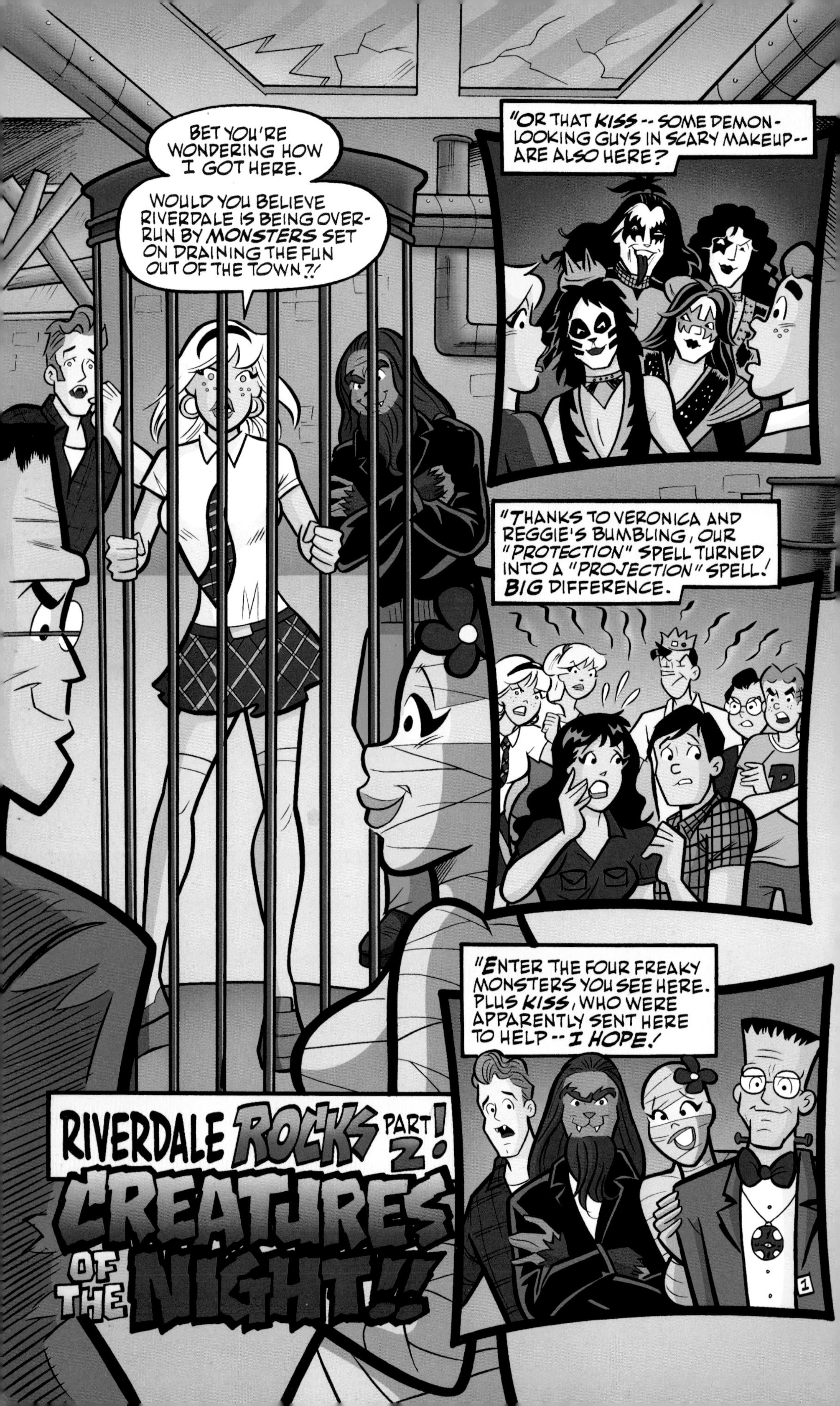
BET YOU'RE WONDERING HOW I GOT HERE.
WOULD YOU BELIEVE RIVERDALE IS BEING OVER-RUN BY MONSTERS SET ON DRAINING THE FUN OUT OF THE TOWN?!
"OR THAT KISS -- SOME DEMON-LOOKING GUYS IN SCARY MAKEUP -- ARE ALSO HERE?
"THANKS TO VERONICA AND REGGIE'S BUMBLING, OUR "PROTECTION" SPELL TURNED INTO A "PROJECTION" SPELL! BIG DIFFERENCE.
"ENTER THE FOUR FREAKY MONSTERS YOU SEE HERE. PLUS KISS, WHO WERE APPARENTLY SENT HERE TO HELP -- I HOPE!
RIVERDALE ROCKS PART 2!
CREATURES OF THE NIGHT!!
1

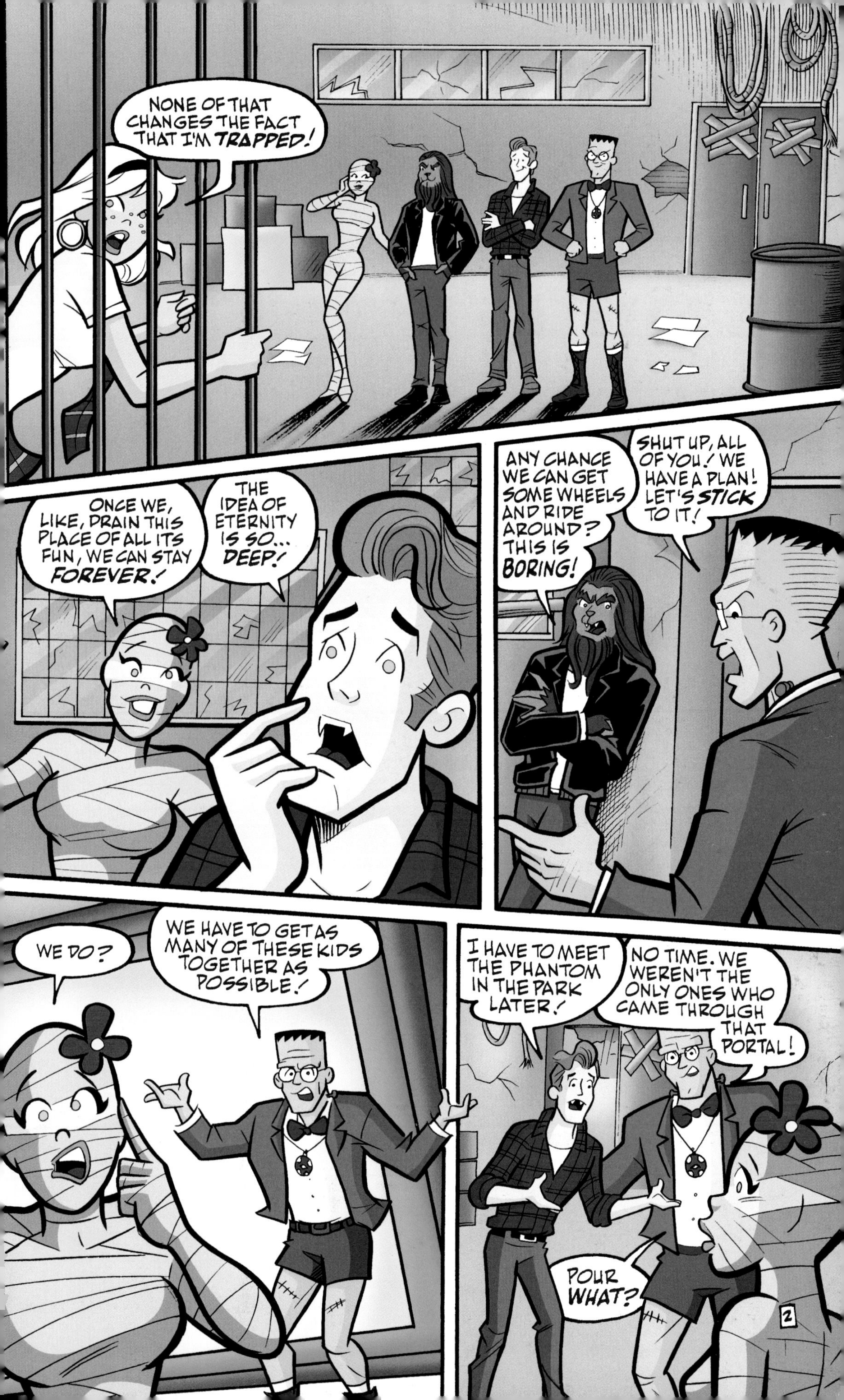
NONE OF THAT CHANGES THE FACT THAT I'M TRAPPED!
ONCE WE, LIKE, DRAIN THIS PLACE OF ALL ITS FUN, WE CAN STAY FOREVER!
THE IDEA OF ETERNITY IS SO... DEEP!
ANY CHANCE WE CAN GET SOME WHEELS AND RIDE AROUND? THIS IS BORING!
SHUT UP, ALL OF YOU! WE HAVE A PLAN! LET'S STICK TO IT!
WE DO?
WE HAVE TO GET AS MANY OF THESE KIDS TOGETHER AS POSSIBLE!
I HAVE TO MEET THE PHANTOM IN THE PARK LATER!
NO TIME. WE WEREN'T THE ONLY ONES WHO CAME THROUGH THAT PORTAL!
POUR WHAT?
2

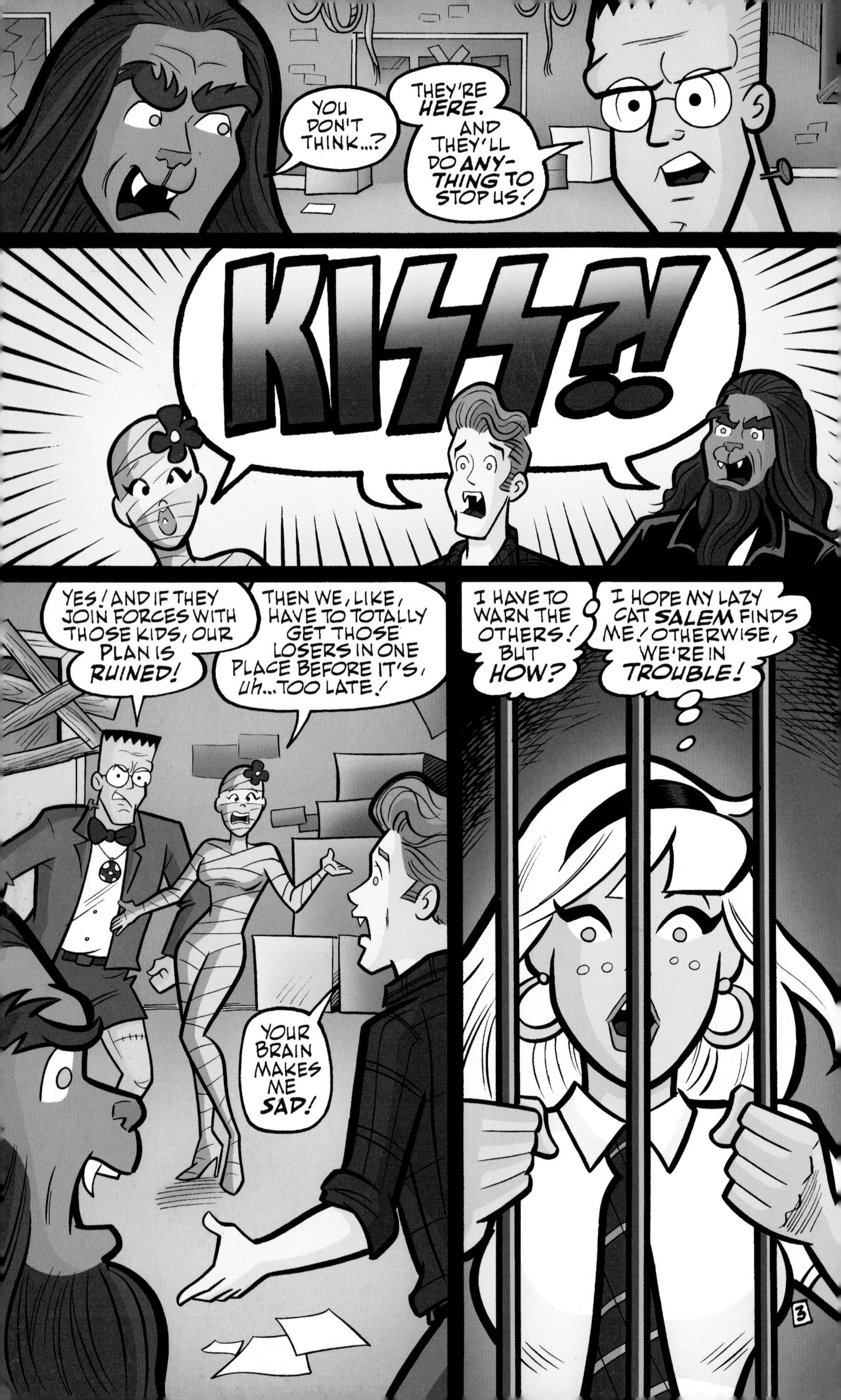
YOU DON'T THINK...?
THEY'RE HERE. AND THEY'LL DO ANY-THING TO STOP US!
KISS?!
YES! AND IF THEY JOIN FORCES WITH THOSE KIDS, OUR PLAN IS RUINED!
THEN WE, LIKE, HAVE TO TOTALLY GET THOSE LOSERS IN ONE PLACE BEFORE IT'S, uh...TOO LATE!
YOUR BRAIN MAKES ME SAD!
I HAVE TO WARN THE OTHERS! BUT HOW?
I HOPE MY LAZY CAT SALEM FINDS ME! OTHERWISE, WE'RE IN TROUBLE!
3

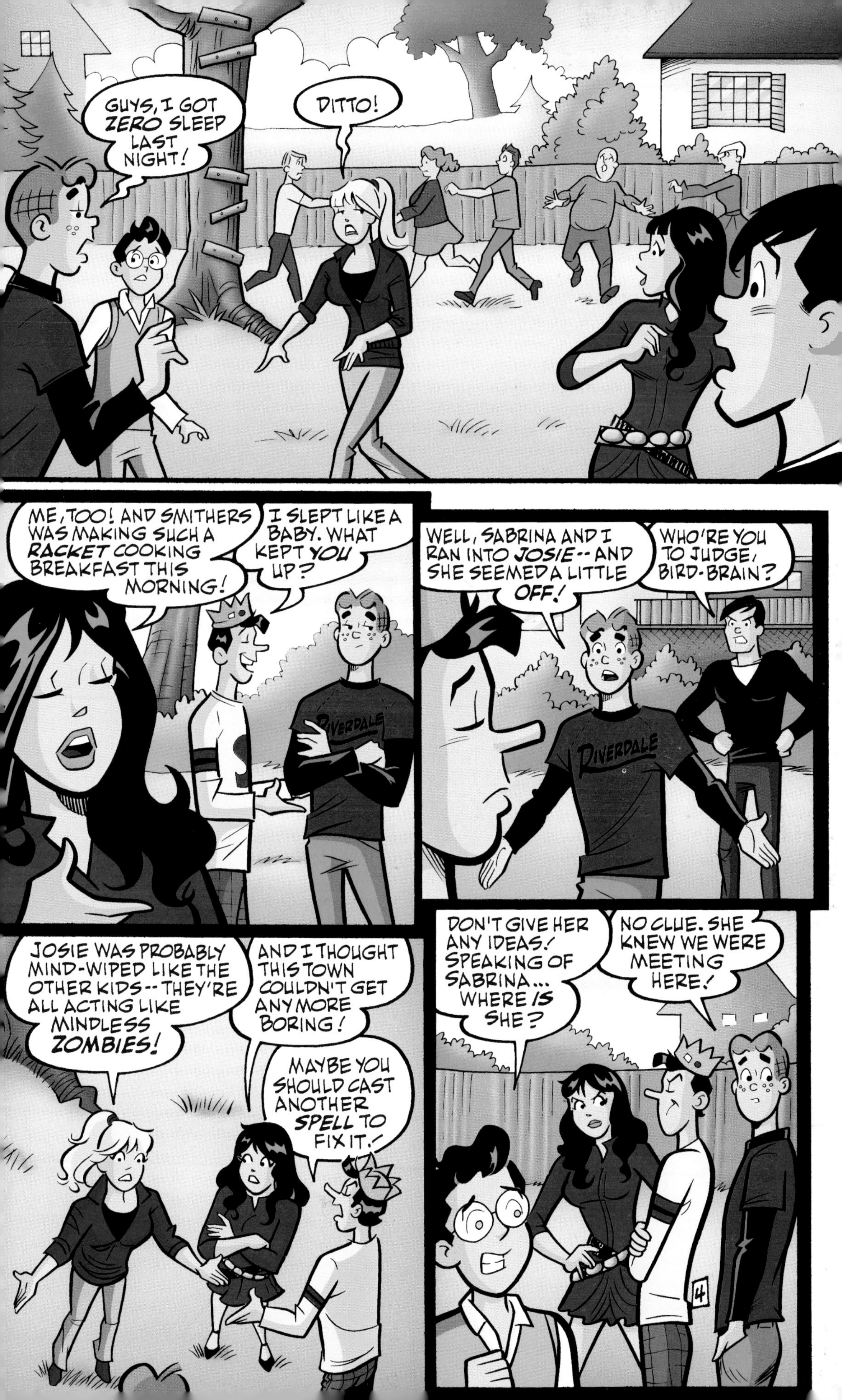
GUYS, I GOT ZERO SLEEP LAST NIGHT!
DITTO!
ME, TOO! AND SMITHERS WAS MAKING SUCH A RACKET COOKING BREAKFAST THIS MORNING!
I SLEPT LIKE A BABY. WHAT KEPT YOU UP?
RIVERDALE
WELL, SABRINA AND I RAN INTO JOSIE-- AND SHE SEEMED A LITTLE OFF!
WHO'RE YOU TO JUDGE, BIRD-BRAIN?
RIVERDALE
JOSIE WAS PROBABLY MIND-WIPED LIKE THE OTHER KIDS-- THEY'RE ALL ACTING LIKE MINDLESS ZOMBIES!
AND I THOUGHT THIS TOWN COULDN'T GET ANYMORE BORING!
MAYBE YOU SHOULD CAST ANOTHER SPELL TO FIX IT!
DON'T GIVE HER ANY IDEAS! SPEAKING OF SABRINA... WHERE IS SHE?
NO CLUE. SHE KNEW WE WERE MEETING HERE!
4

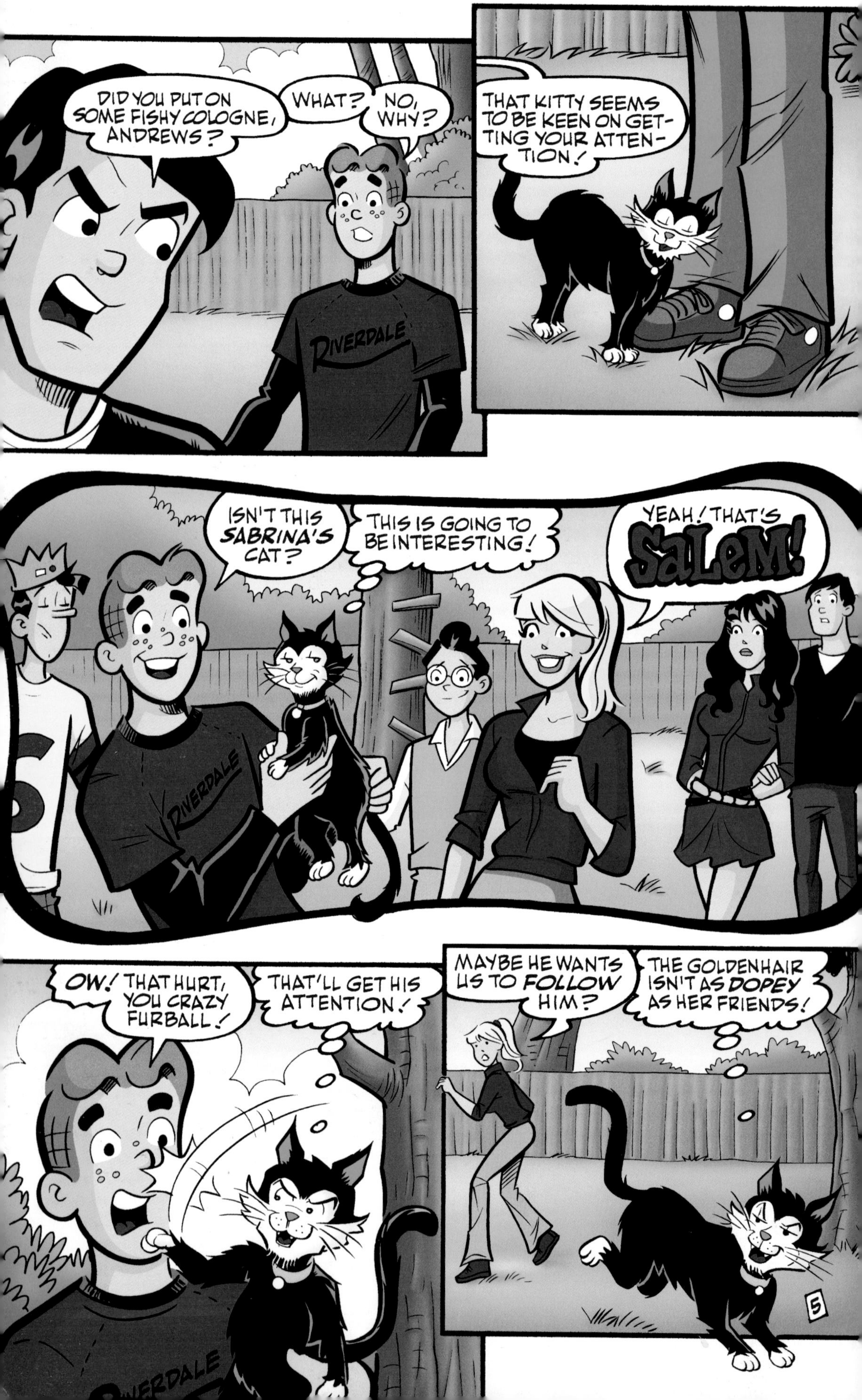
DID YOU PUT ON SOME FISHY COLOGNE, ANDREWS?
WHAT?
NO, WHY?
THAT KITTY SEEMS TO BE KEEN ON GETTING YOUR ATTENTION!
RIVERDALE
ISN'T THIS SABRINA'S CAT?
THIS IS GOING TO BE INTERESTING!
YEAH! THAT'S SALEM!
RIVERDALE
OW! THAT HURT, YOU CRAZY FURBALL!
THAT'LL GET HIS ATTENTION!
MAYBE HE WANTS US TO FOLLOW HIM?
THE GOLDENHAIR ISN'T AS DOPEY AS HER FRIENDS!
5

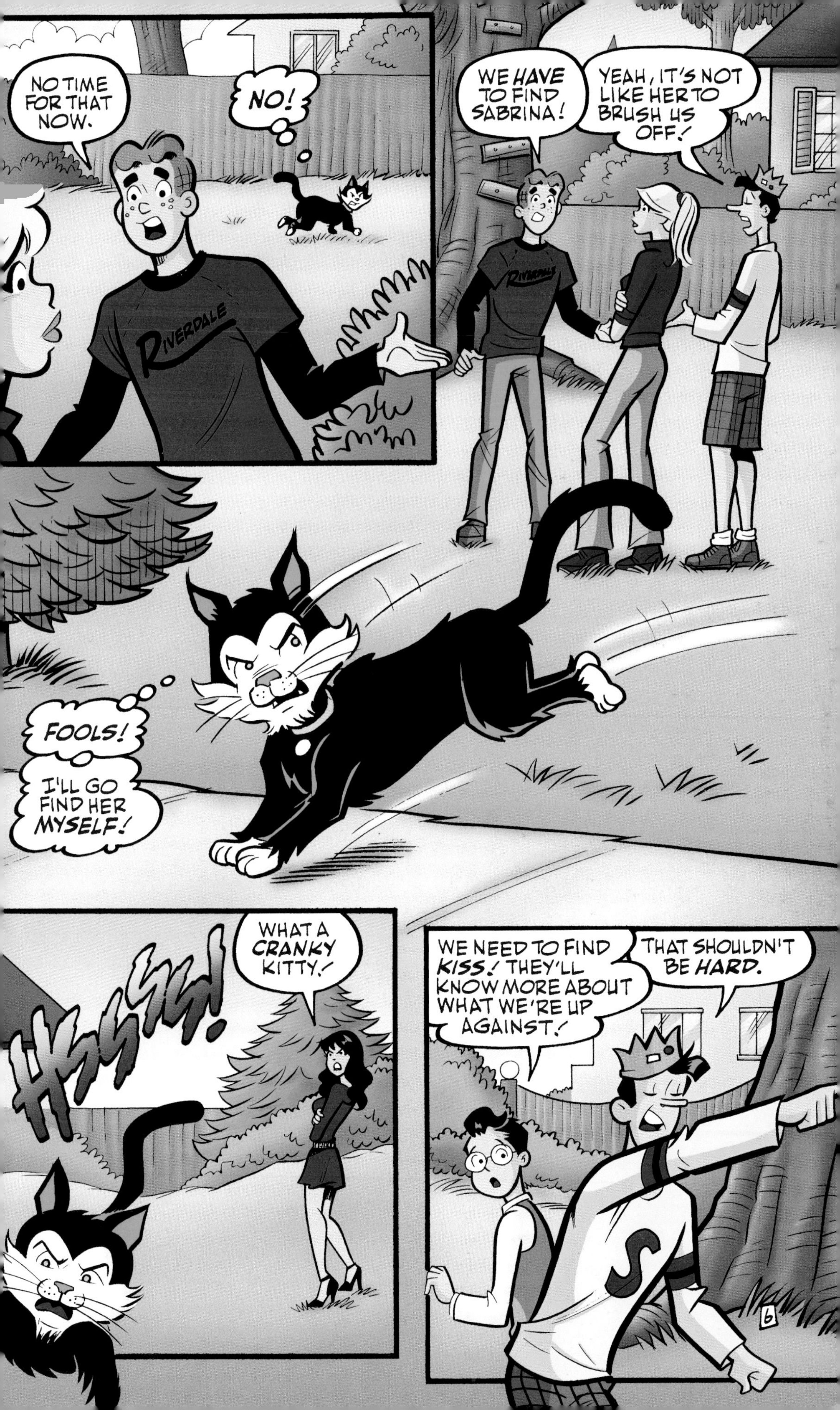
NO TIME FOR THAT NOW.
NO!
WE HAVE TO FIND SABRINA!
YEAH, IT'S NOT LIKE HER TO BRUSH US OFF!
FOOLS!
I'LL GO FIND HER MYSELF!
HSSSS!
WHAT A CRANKY KITTY!
WE NEED TO FIND KISS! THEY'LL KNOW MORE ABOUT WHAT WE'RE UP AGAINST!
THAT SHOULDN'T BE HARD.
6

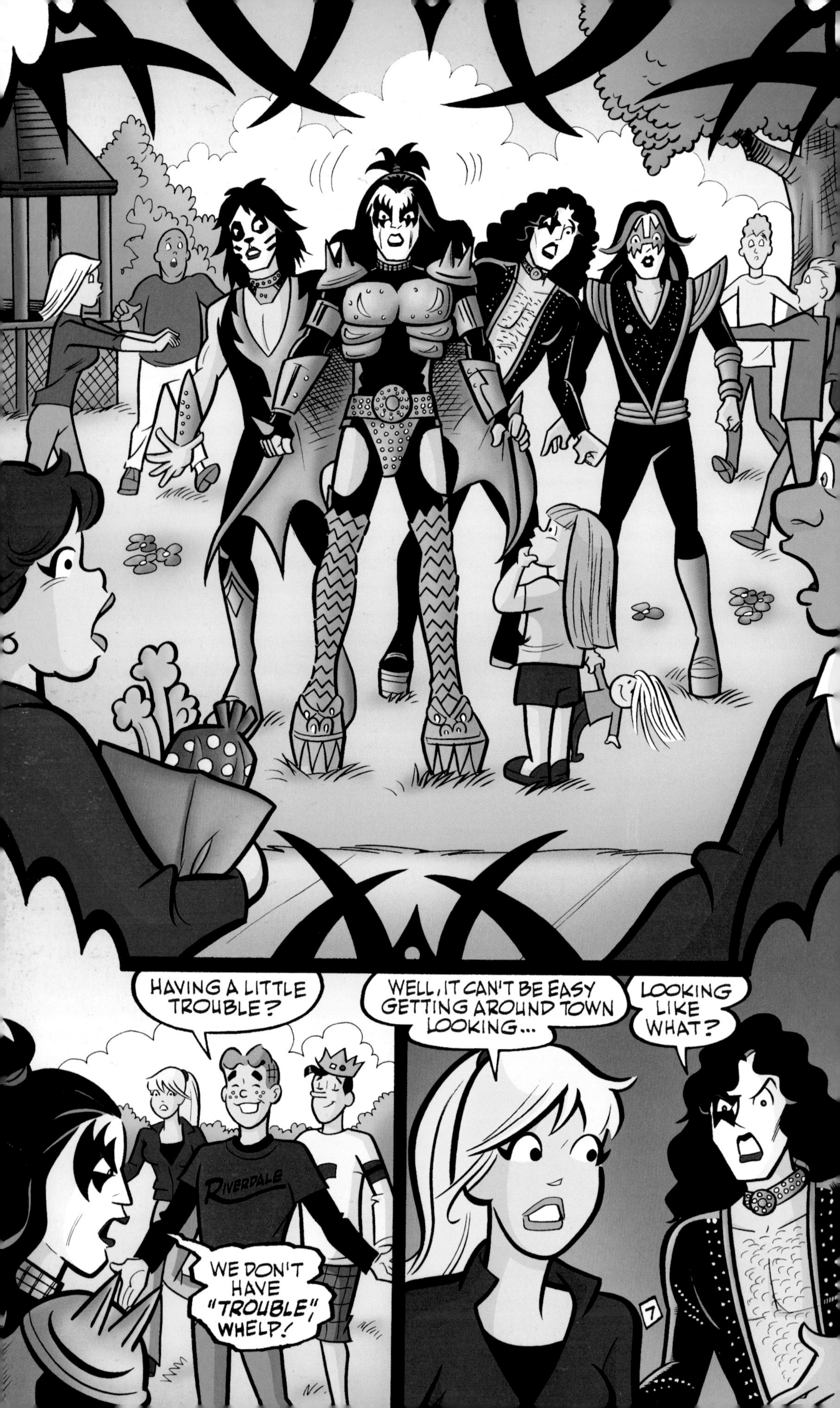

HAVING A LITTLE TROUBLE?
WE DON'T HAVE "TROUBLE," WHELP!
RIVERDALE
WELL, IT CAN'T BE EASY GETTING AROUND TOWN LOOKING...
LOOKING LIKE WHAT?
7

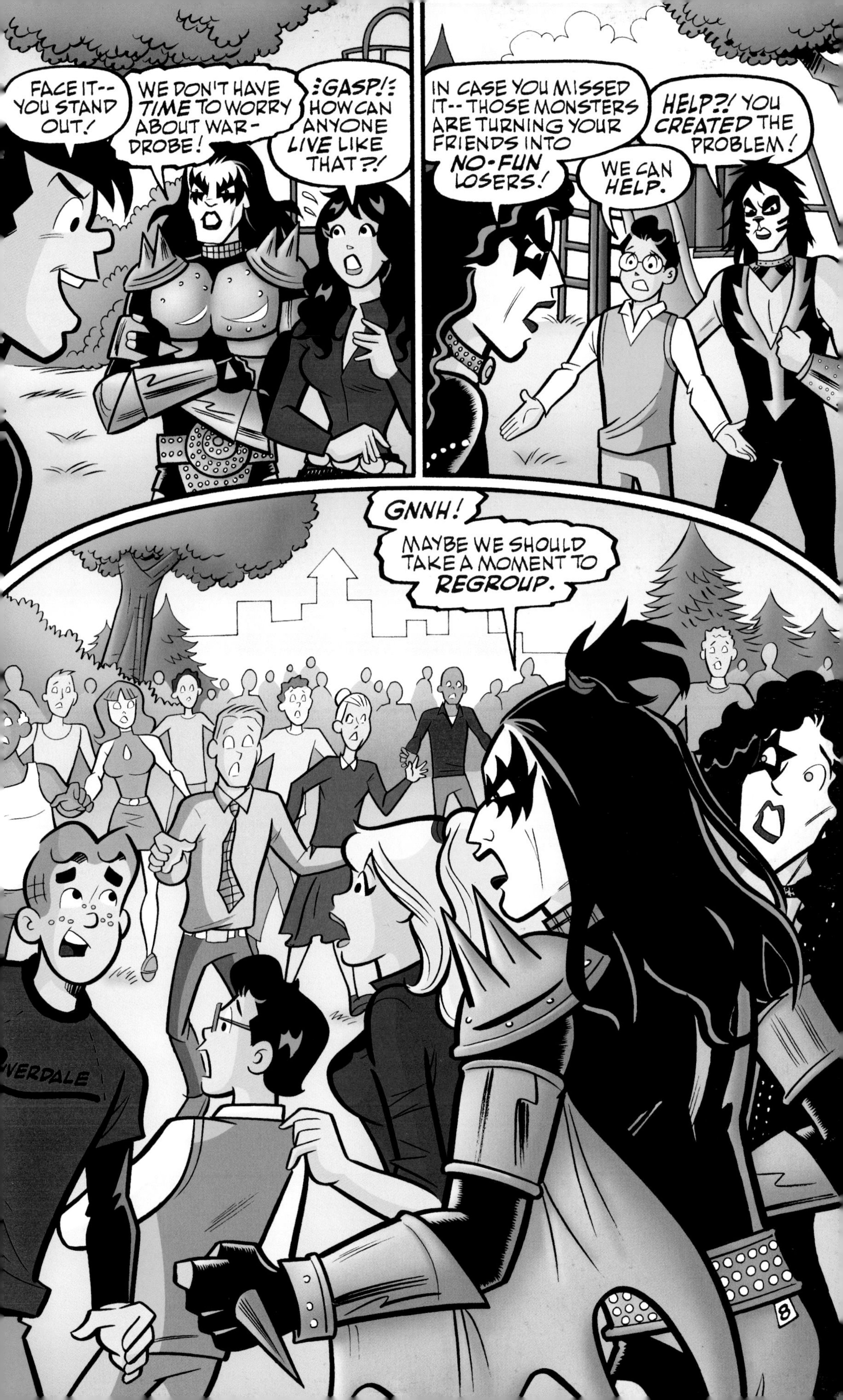
FACE IT-- YOU STAND OUT!
WE DON'T HAVE TIME TO WORRY ABOUT WAR-DROBE!
:GASP!: HOW CAN ANYONE LIVE LIKE THAT?!
IN CASE YOU MISSED IT-- THOSE MONSTERS ARE TURNING YOUR FRIENDS INTO NO-FUN LOSERS!
WE CAN HELP.
HELP?! YOU CREATED THE PROBLEM!
GNNH!
MAYBE WE SHOULD TAKE A MOMENT TO REGROUP.
RIVERDALE

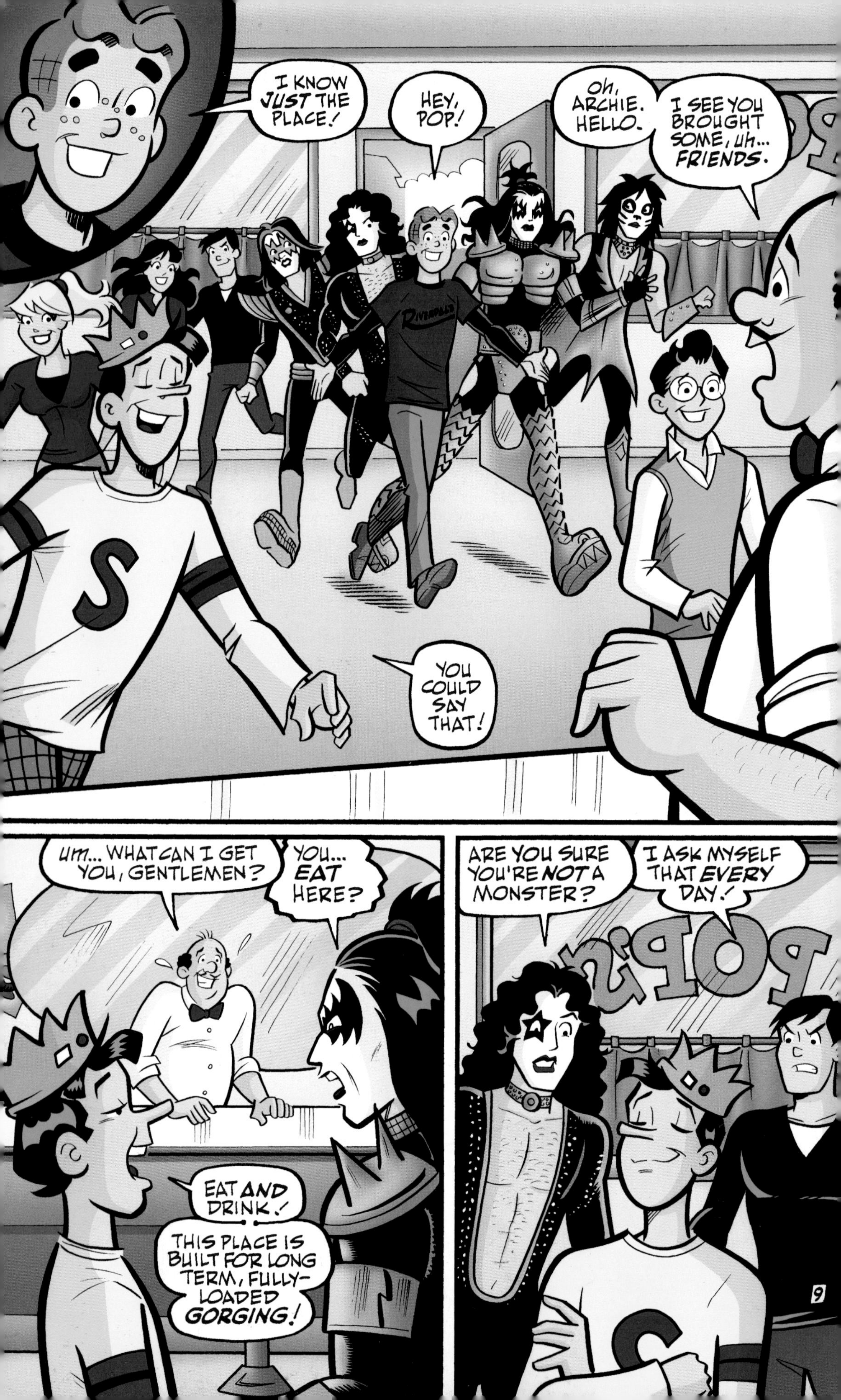

I KNOW JUST THE PLACE!
HEY, POP!
Oh, ARCHIE. HELLO.
I SEE YOU BROUGHT SOME, uh... FRIENDS.
YOU COULD SAY THAT!
Um... WHAT CAN I GET YOU, GENTLEMEN?
YOU... EAT HERE?
EAT AND DRINK!
THIS PLACE IS BUILT FOR LONG TERM, FULLY-LOADED GORGING!
ARE YOU SURE YOU'RE NOT A MONSTER?
I ASK MYSELF THAT EVERY DAY!
POP'S
9

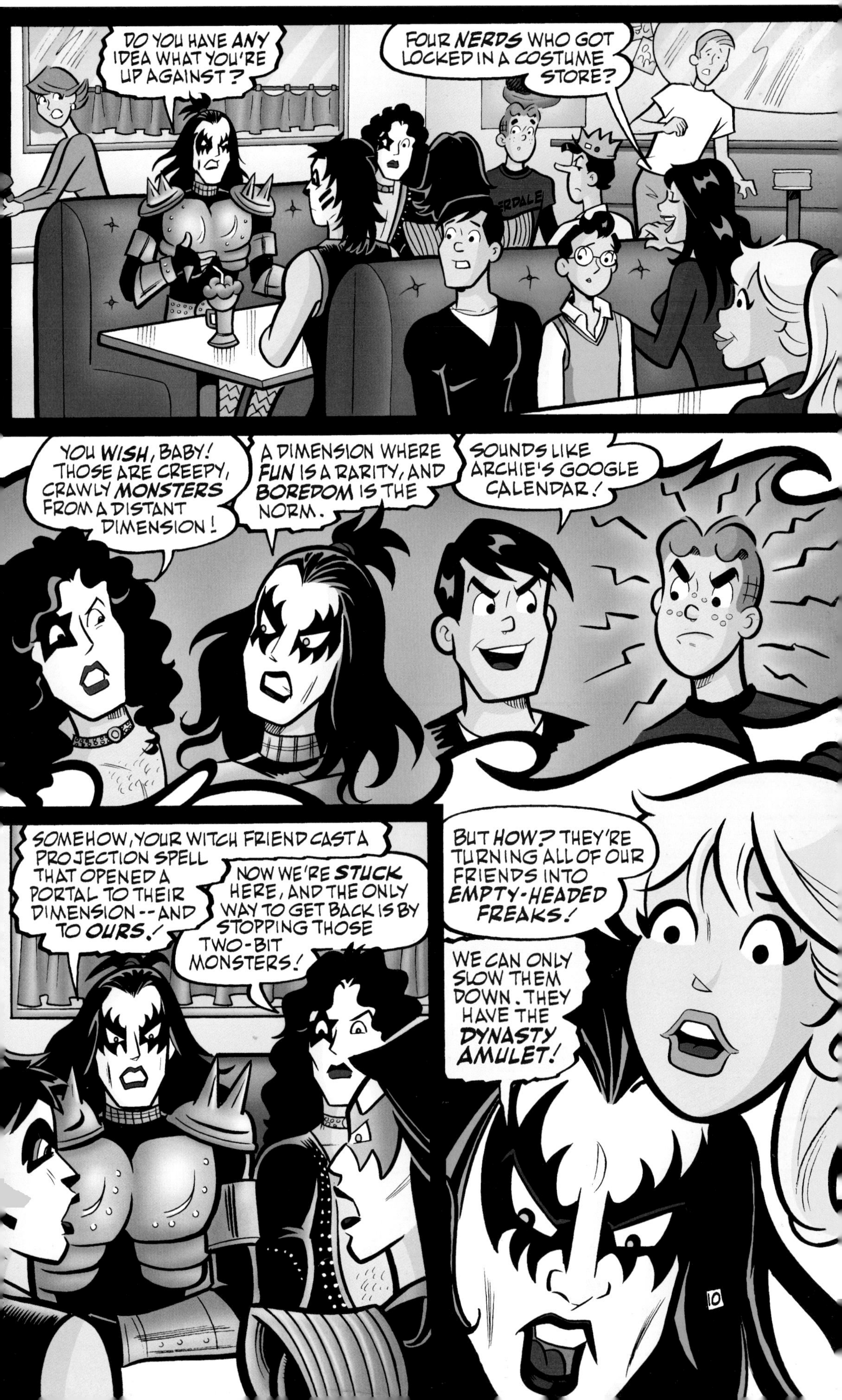
DO YOU HAVE ANY IDEA WHAT YOU'RE UP AGAINST?
FOUR NERDS WHO GOT LOCKED IN A COSTUME STORE?
RDALE
YOU WISH, BABY! THOSE ARE CREEPY, CRAWLY MONSTERS FROM A DISTANT DIMENSION!
A DIMENSION WHERE FUN IS A RARITY, AND BOREDOM IS THE NORM.
SOUNDS LIKE ARCHIE'S GOOGLE CALENDAR!
SOMEHOW, YOUR WITCH FRIEND CAST A PROJECTION SPELL THAT OPENED A PORTAL TO THEIR DIMENSION--AND TO OURS!
NOW WE'RE STUCK HERE, AND THE ONLY WAY TO GET BACK IS BY STOPPING THOSE TWO-BIT MONSTERS!
BUT HOW? THEY'RE TURNING ALL OF OUR FRIENDS INTO EMPTY-HEADED FREAKS!
WE CAN ONLY SLOW THEM DOWN. THEY HAVE THE DYNASTY AMULET!
10

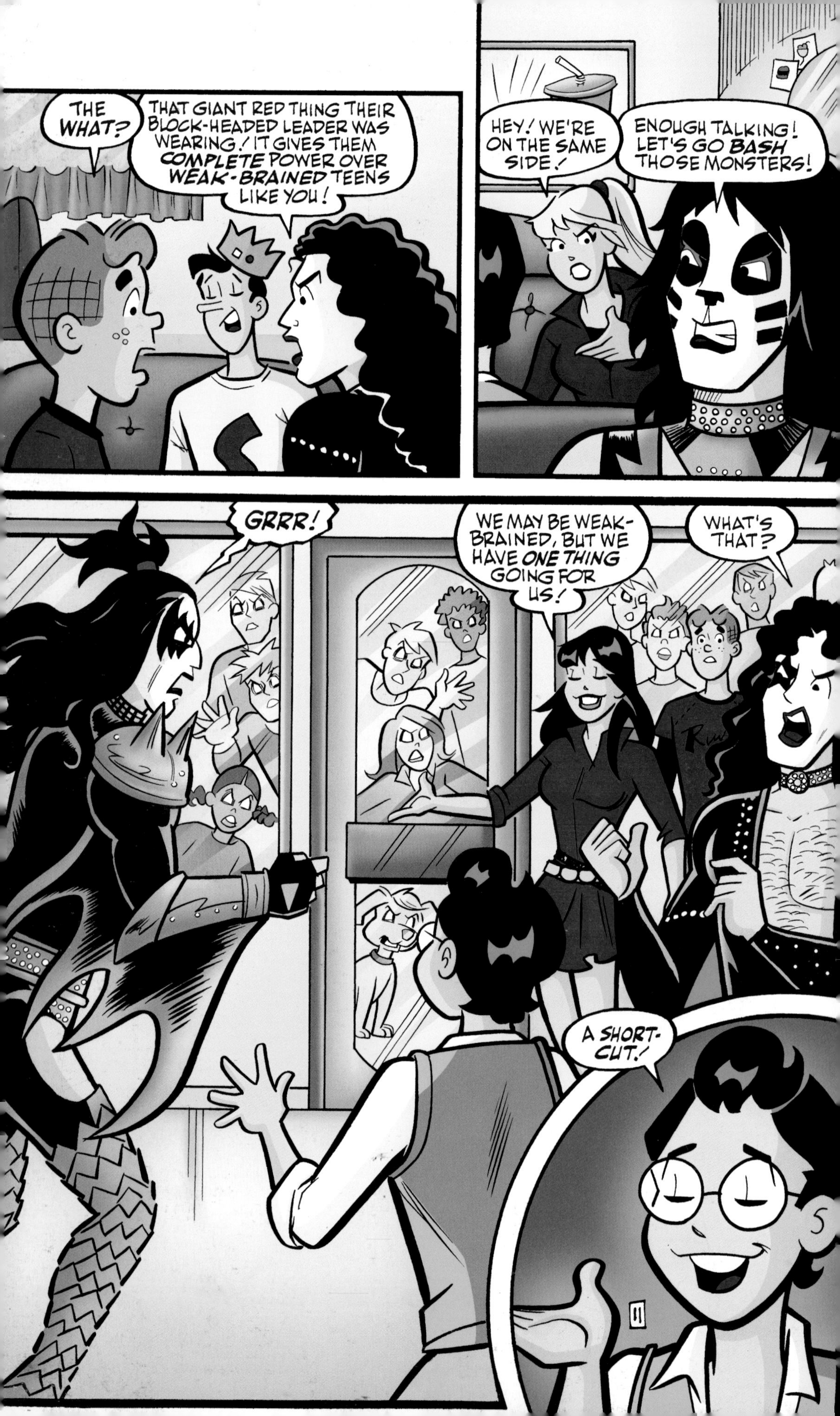
THE WHAT?
THAT GIANT RED THING THEIR BLOCK-HEADED LEADER WAS WEARING! IT GIVES THEM COMPLETE POWER OVER WEAK-BRAINED TEENS LIKE YOU!
HEY! WE'RE ON THE SAME SIDE!
ENOUGH TALKING! LET'S GO BASH THOSE MONSTERS!
GRRR!
WE MAY BE WEAK-BRAINED, BUT WE HAVE ONE THING GOING FOR US!
WHAT'S THAT?
A SHORT-CUT!
11

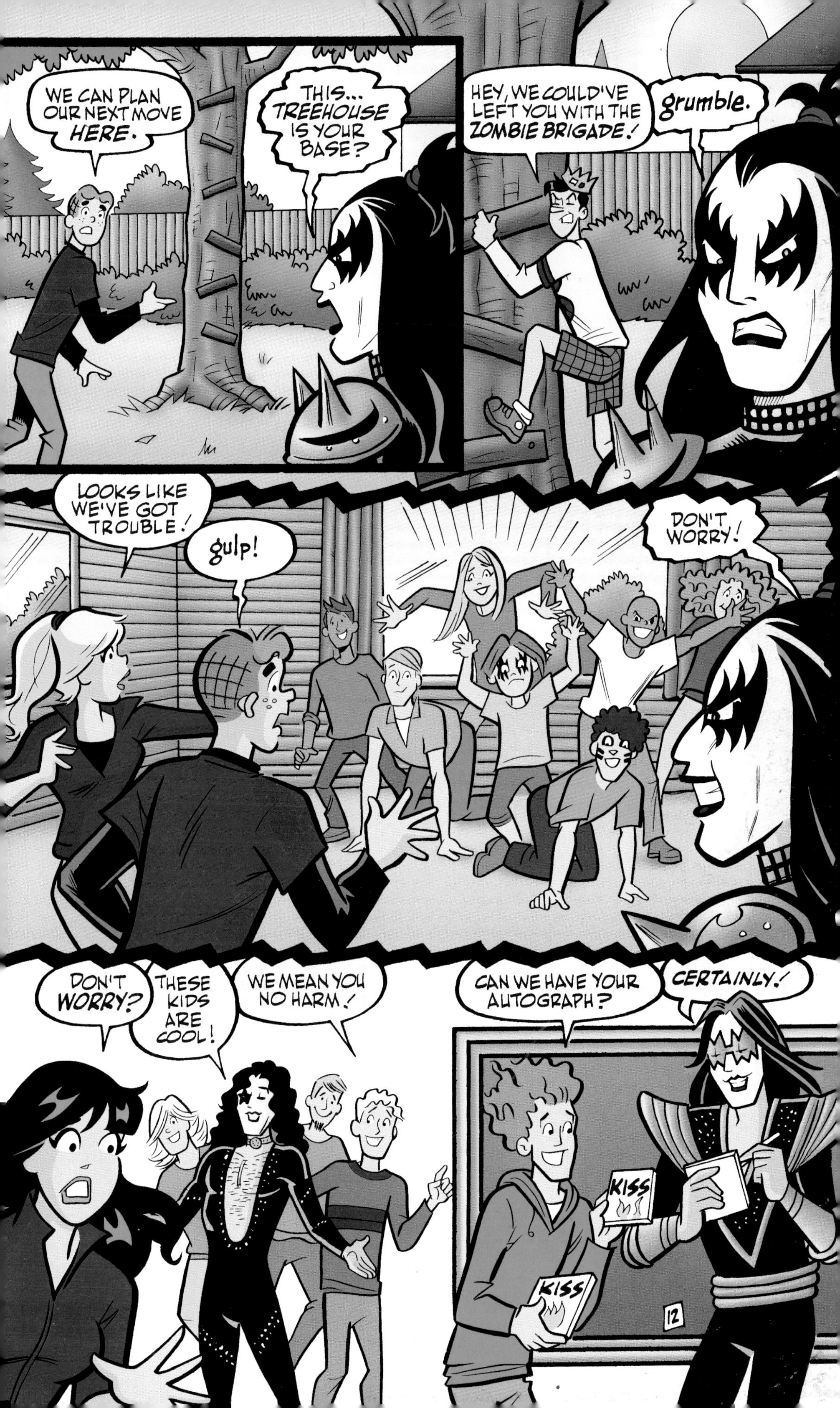
WE CAN PLAN OUR NEXT MOVE HERE.
THIS... TREEHOUSE IS YOUR BASE?
HEY, WE COULD'VE LEFT YOU WITH THE ZOMBIE BRIGADE!
grumble.
LOOKS LIKE WE'VE GOT TROUBLE!
gulp!
DON'T WORRY!
DON'T WORRY?
THESE KIDS ARE COOL!
WE MEAN YOU NO HARM!
CAN WE HAVE YOUR AUTOGRAPH?
CERTAINLY!
KISS
KISS
KISS
12

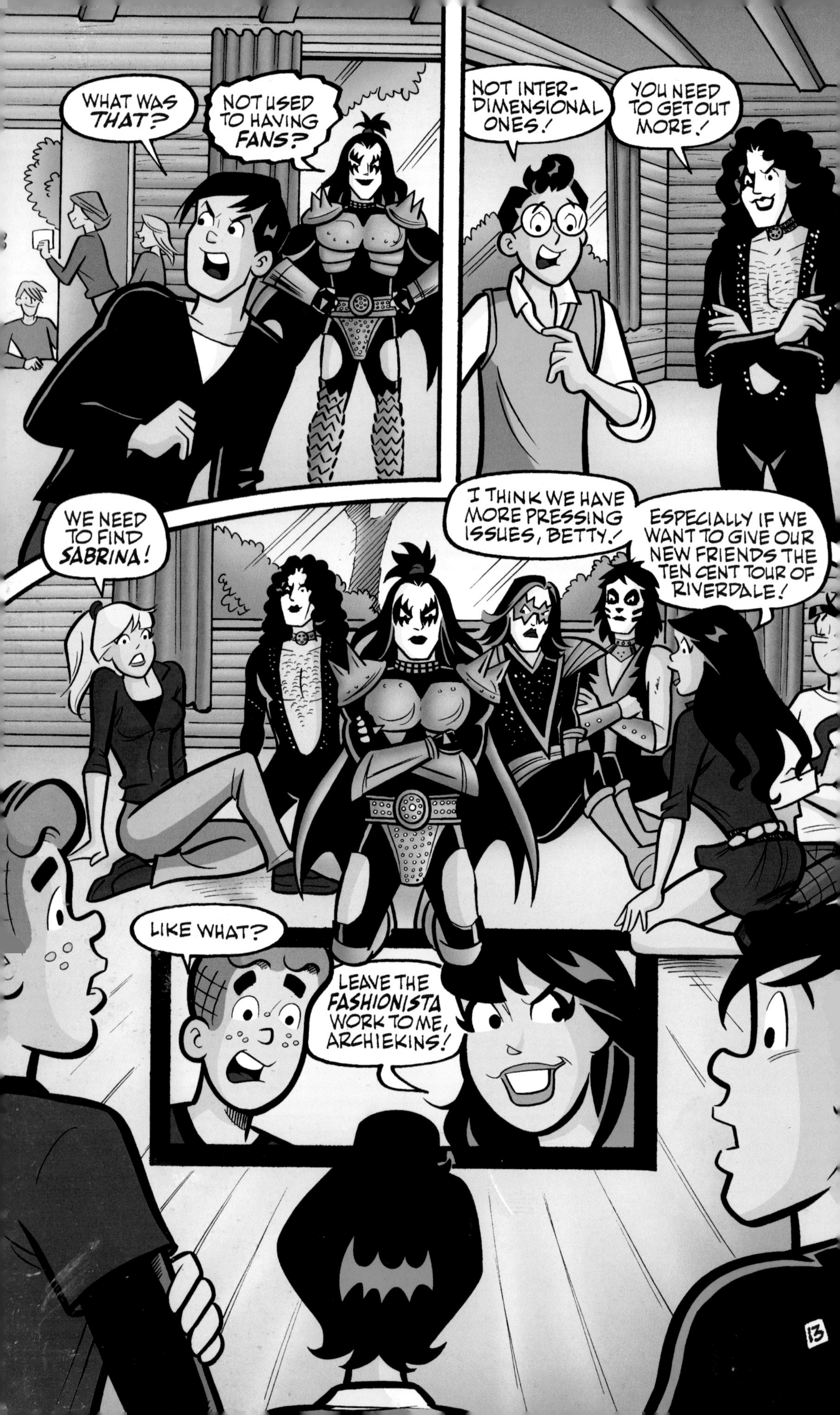
WHAT WAS THAT?
NOT USED TO HAVING FANS?
NOT INTER-DIMENSIONAL ONES!
YOU NEED TO GET OUT MORE!
WE NEED TO FIND SABRINA!
I THINK WE HAVE MORE PRESSING ISSUES, BETTY!
ESPECIALLY IF WE WANT TO GIVE OUR NEW FRIENDS THE TEN CENT TOUR OF RIVERDALE!
LIKE WHAT?
LEAVE THE FASHIONISTA WORK TO ME, ARCHIEKINS!

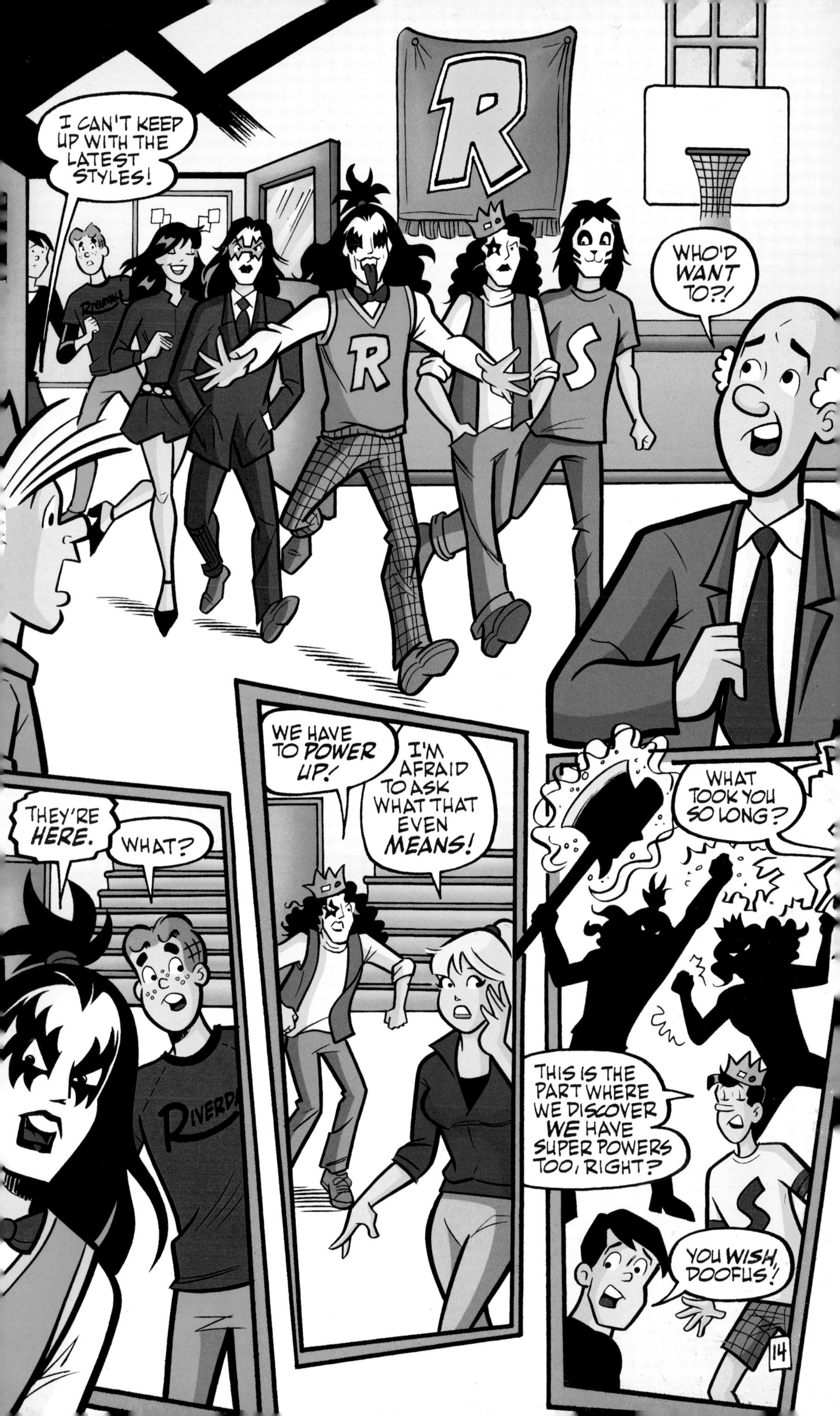
I CAN'T KEEP UP WITH THE LATEST STYLES!
WHO'D WANT TO?!
THEY'RE HERE.
WHAT?
WE HAVE TO POWER UP!
I'M AFRAID TO ASK WHAT THAT EVEN MEANS!
WHAT TOOK YOU SO LONG?
THIS IS THE PART WHERE WE DISCOVER WE HAVE SUPER POWERS TOO, RIGHT?
YOU WISH, DOOFUS!
14

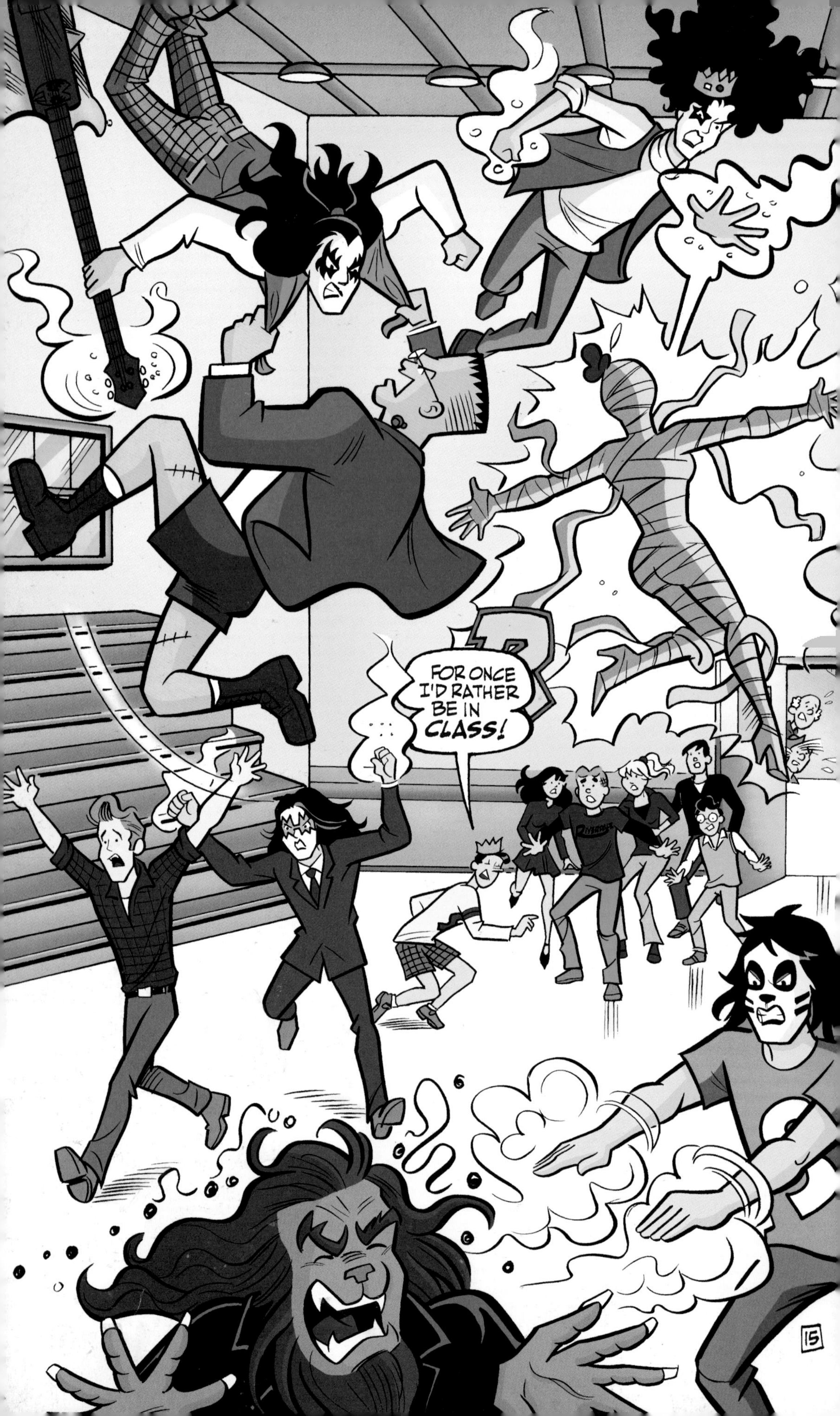
FOR ONCE I'D RATHER BE IN CLASS!

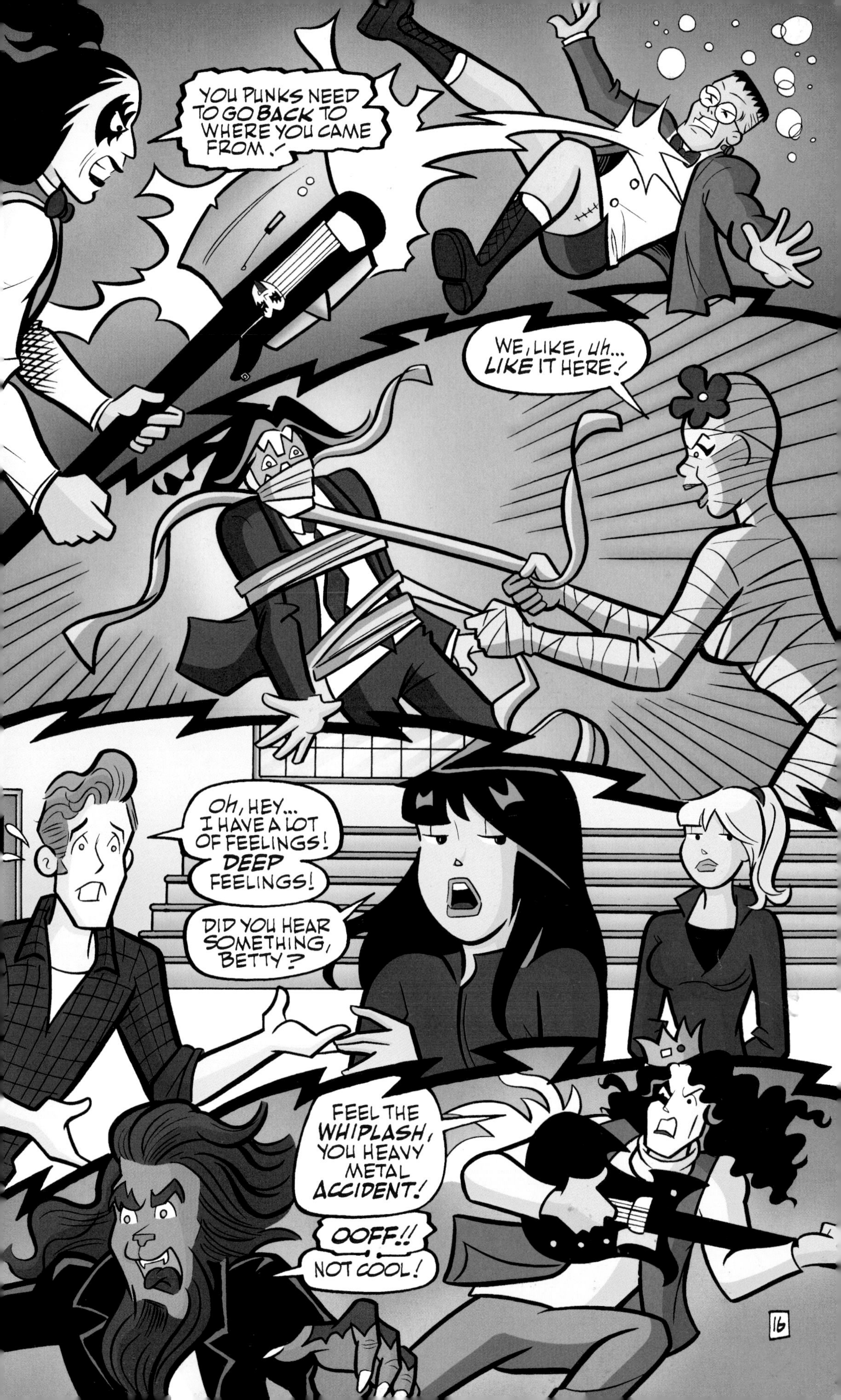
YOU PUNKS NEED TO GO BACK TO WHERE YOU CAME FROM!
WE, LIKE, UH... LIKE IT HERE!
OH, HEY... I HAVE A LOT OF FEELINGS! DEEP FEELINGS!
DID YOU HEAR SOMETHING, BETTY?
FEEL THE WHIPLASH, YOU HEAVY METAL ACCIDENT!
OOFF!!
NOT COOL!
16

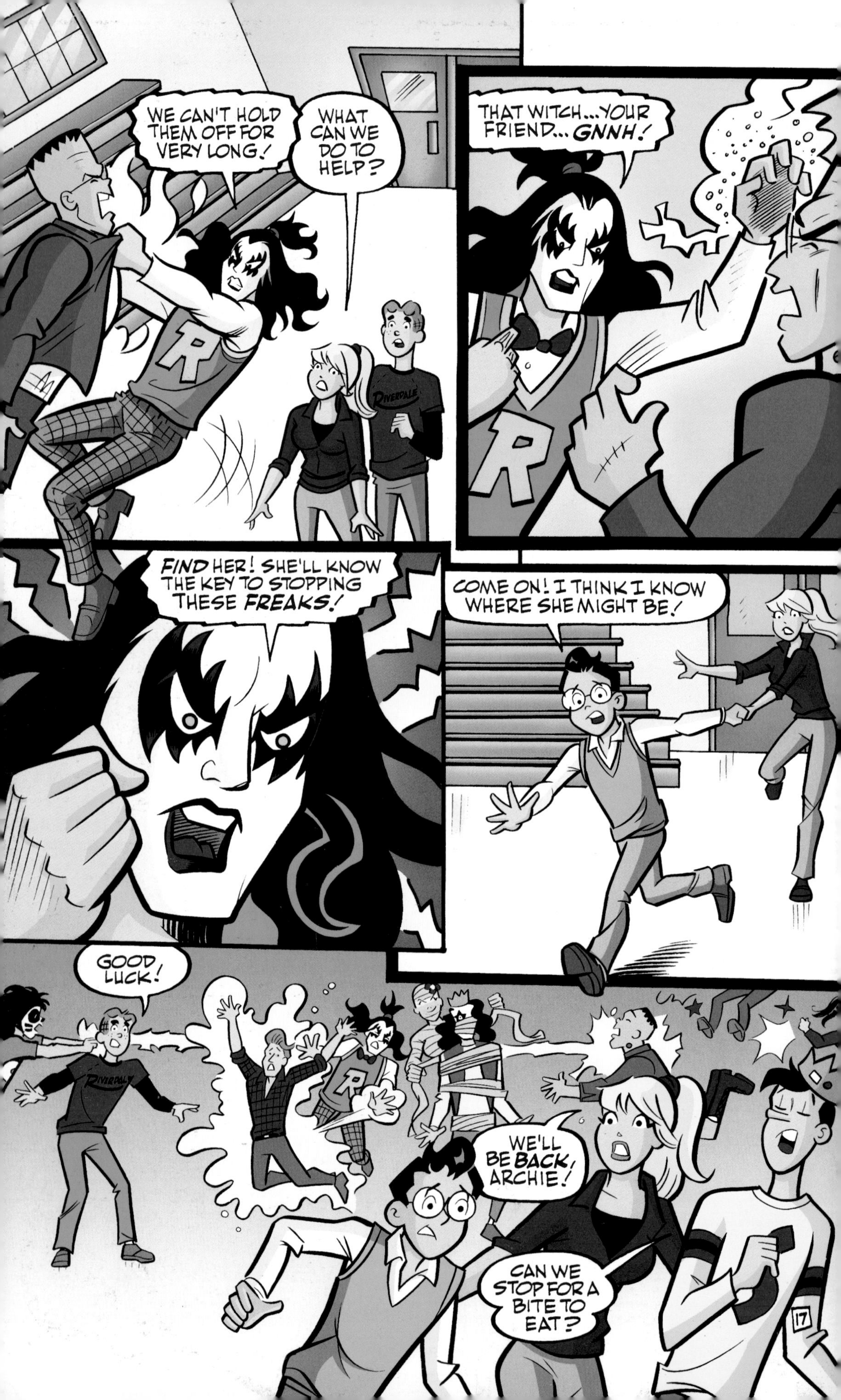
WE CAN'T HOLD THEM OFF FOR VERY LONG!
WHAT CAN WE DO TO HELP?
THAT WITCH... YOUR FRIEND... GNNH!
FIND HER! SHE'LL KNOW THE KEY TO STOPPING THESE FREAKS!
COME ON! I THINK I KNOW WHERE SHE MIGHT BE!
GOOD LUCK!
WE'LL BE BACK, ARCHIE!
CAN WE STOP FOR A BITE TO EAT?
17

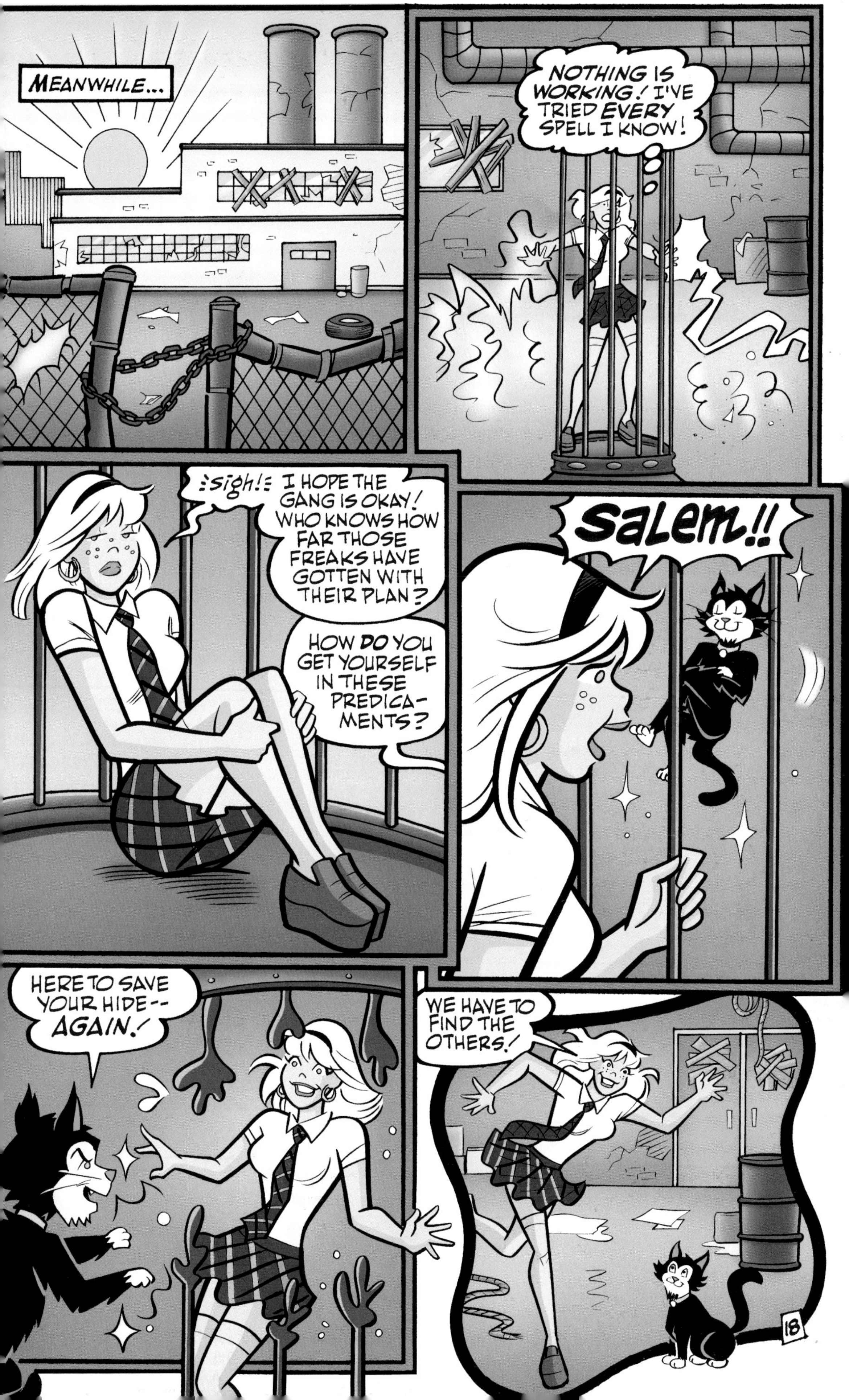
MEANWHILE...
NOTHING IS WORKING! I'VE TRIED EVERY SPELL I KNOW!
:sigh!: I HOPE THE GANG IS OKAY! WHO KNOWS HOW FAR THOSE FREAKS HAVE GOTTEN WITH THEIR PLAN?
HOW DO YOU GET YOURSELF IN THESE PREDICA-MENTS?
SALEM!!
HERE TO SAVE YOUR HIDE--AGAIN!
WE HAVE TO FIND THE OTHERS!
18

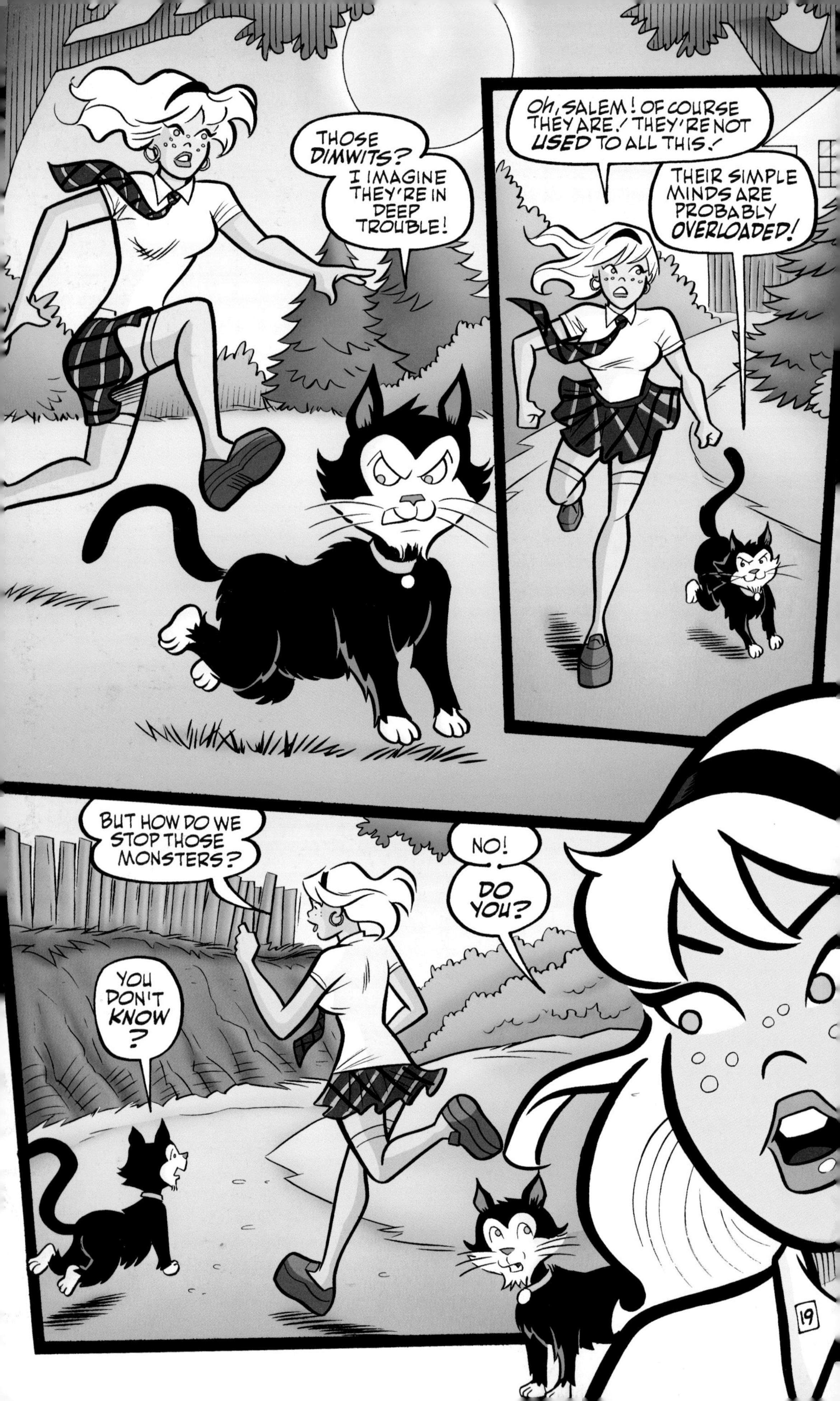
THOSE DIMWITS? I IMAGINE THEY'RE IN DEEP TROUBLE!
OH, SALEM! OF COURSE THEY ARE! THEY'RE NOT USED TO ALL THIS!
THEIR SIMPLE MINDS ARE PROBABLY OVERLOADED!
BUT HOW DO WE STOP THOSE MONSTERS?
YOU DON'T KNOW?
NO!
DO YOU?

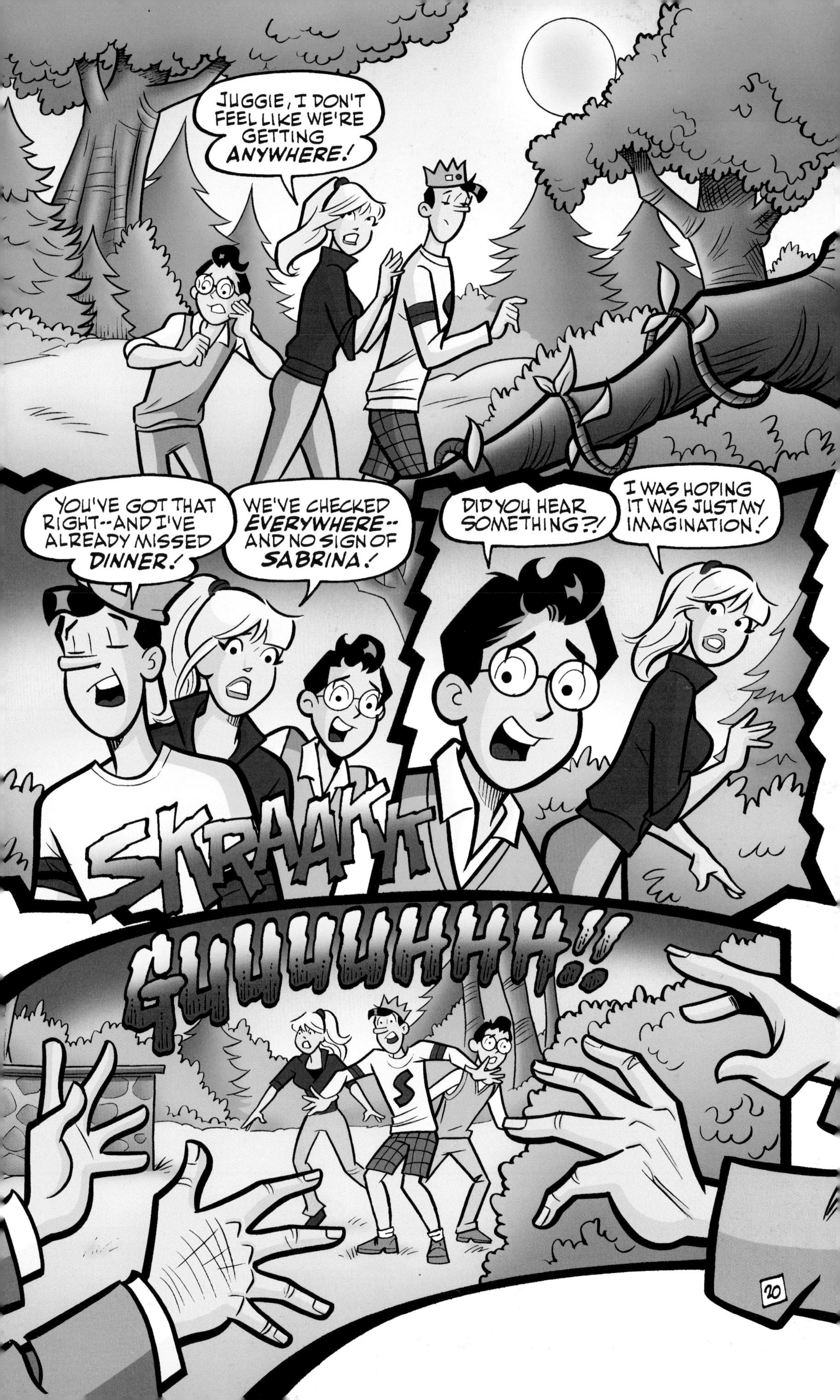
JUGGIE, I DON'T FEEL LIKE WE'RE GETTING ANYWHERE!
YOU'VE GOT THAT RIGHT--AND I'VE ALREADY MISSED DINNER!
WE'VE CHECKED EVERYWHERE--AND NO SIGN OF SABRINA!
DID YOU HEAR SOMETHING?!
I WAS HOPING IT WAS JUST MY IMAGINATION!
SKRAAKK
GUUUUHHH!!

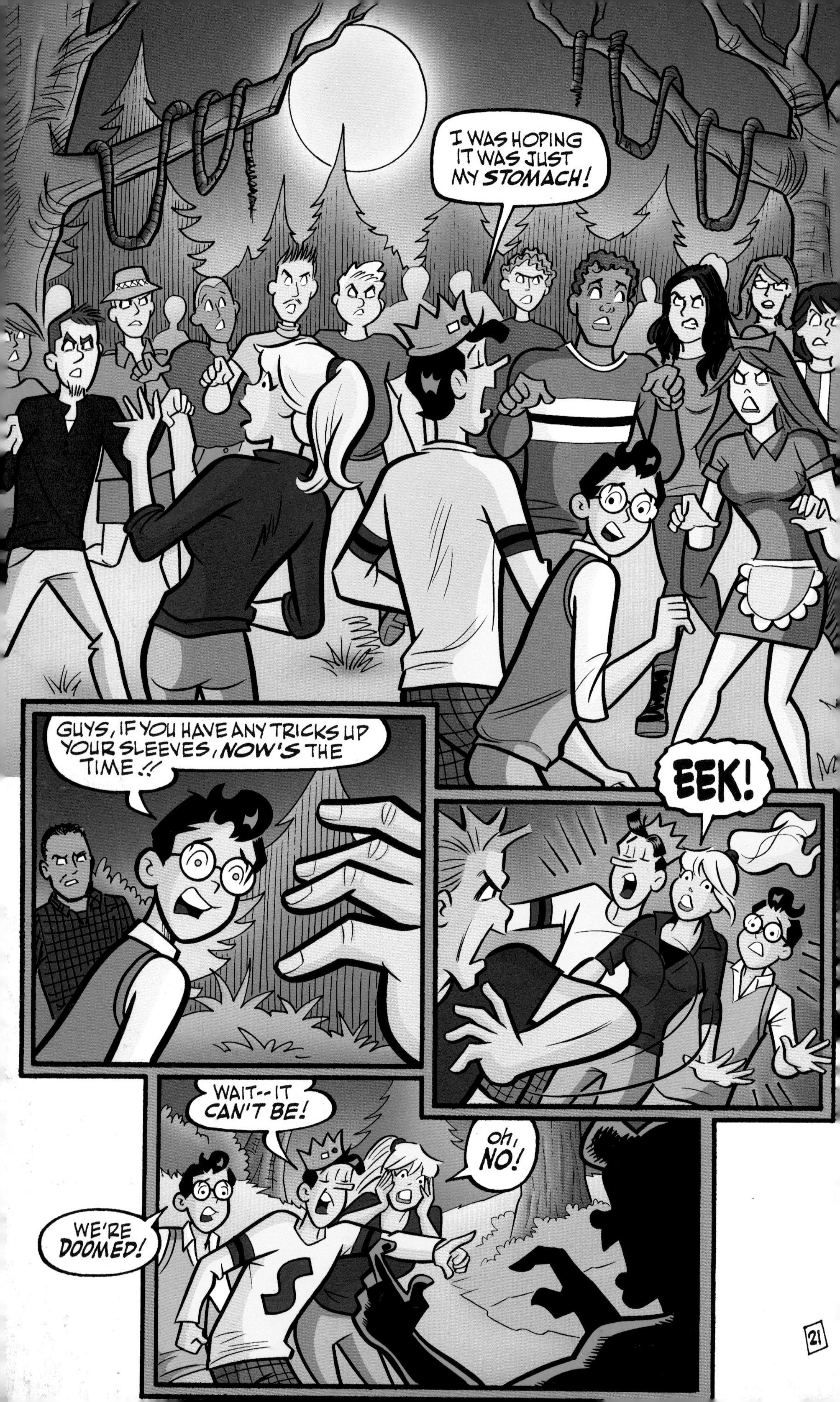

I WAS HOPING IT WAS JUST MY STOMACH!
GUYS, IF YOU HAVE ANY TRICKS UP YOUR SLEEVES, NOW'S THE TIME.!!
EEK!
WAIT-- IT CAN'T BE!
oh, NO!
WE'RE DOOMED!

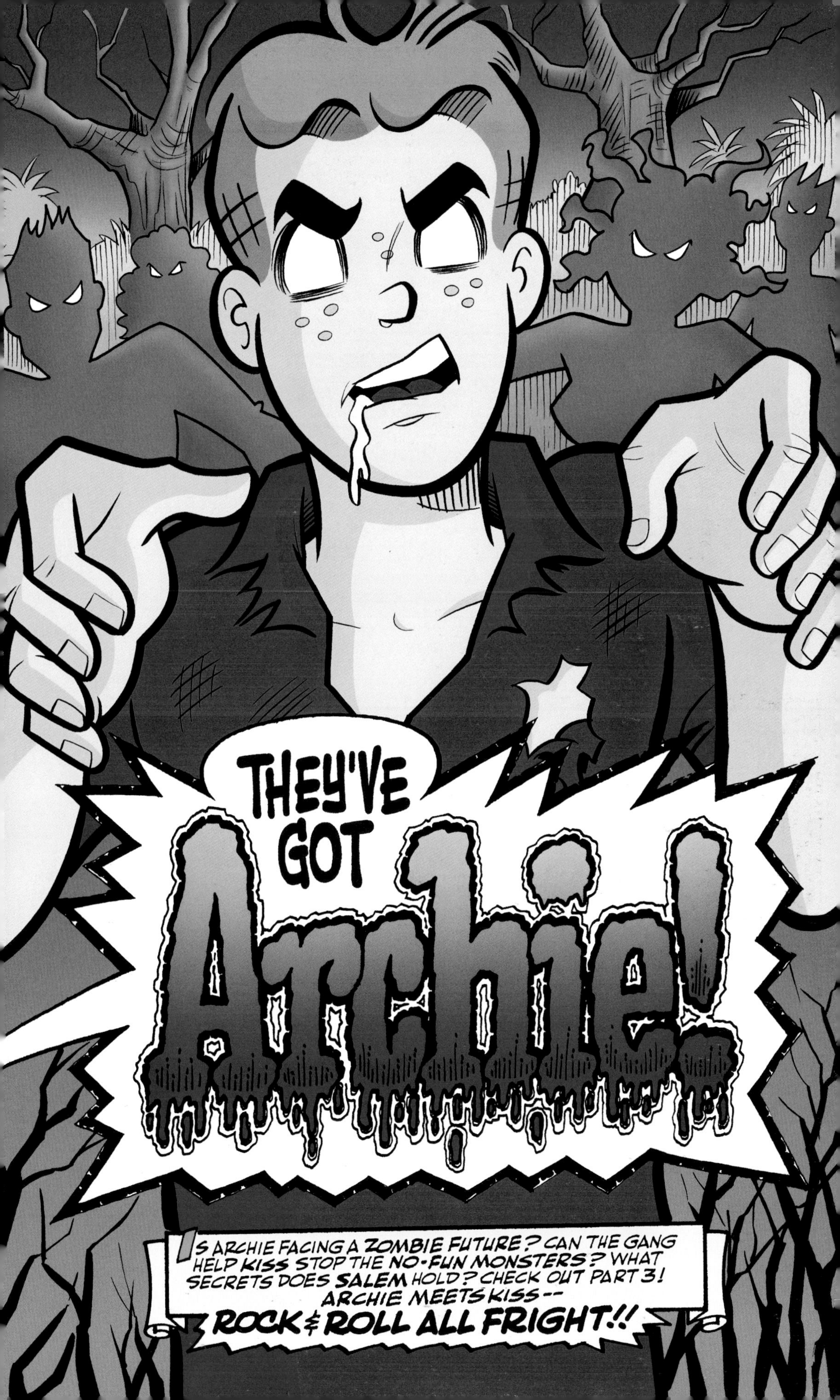

THEY'VE GOT Archie!
IS ARCHIE FACING A ZOMBIE FUTURE? CAN THE GANG HELP KISS STOP THE NO-FUN MONSTERS? WHAT SECRETS DOES SALEM HOLD? CHECK OUT PART 3!
ARCHIE MEETS KISS --
ROCK & ROLL ALL FRIGHT!!

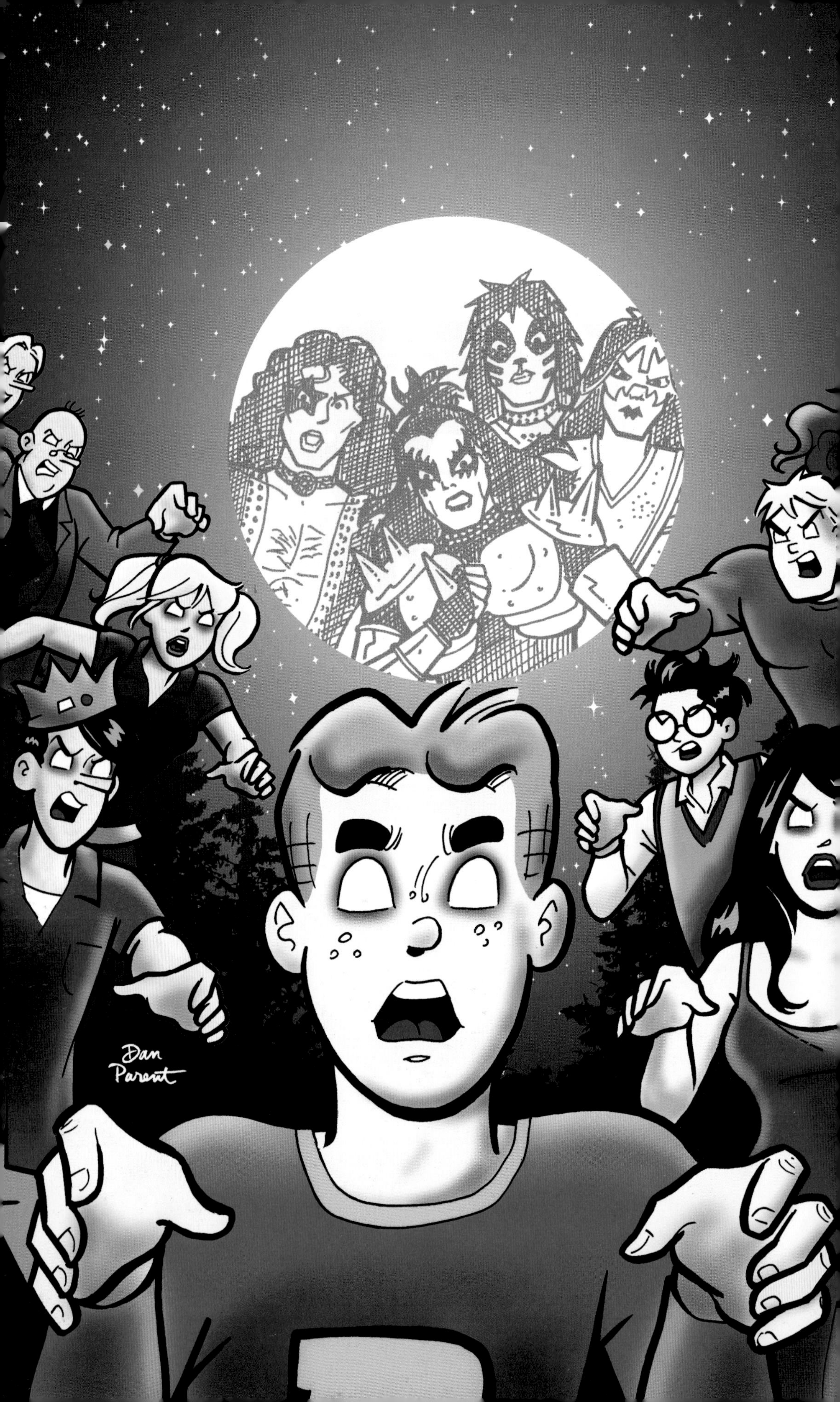
Dan
Parent

Chapter Three: Rock 'n' Roll All Fright

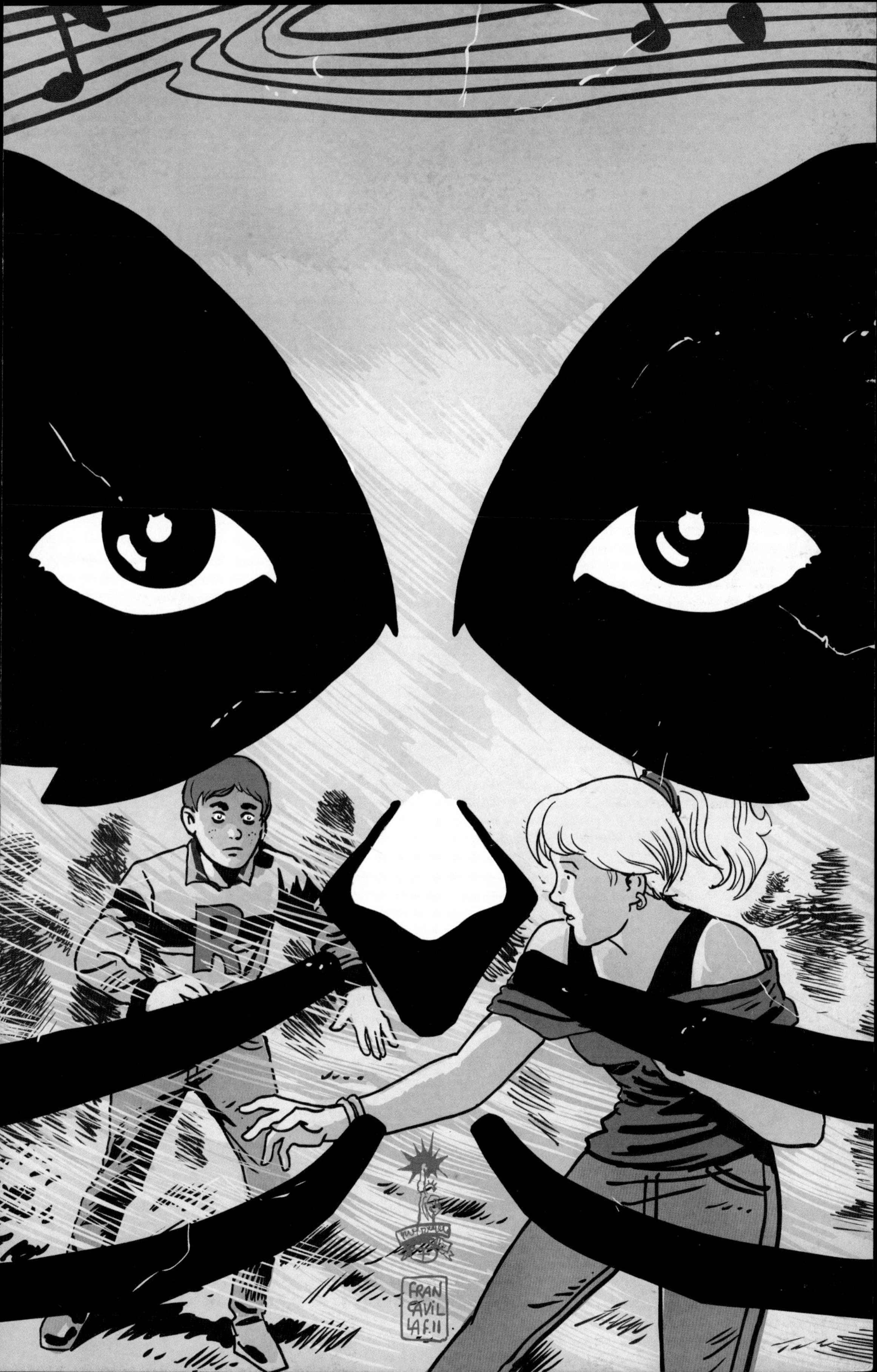

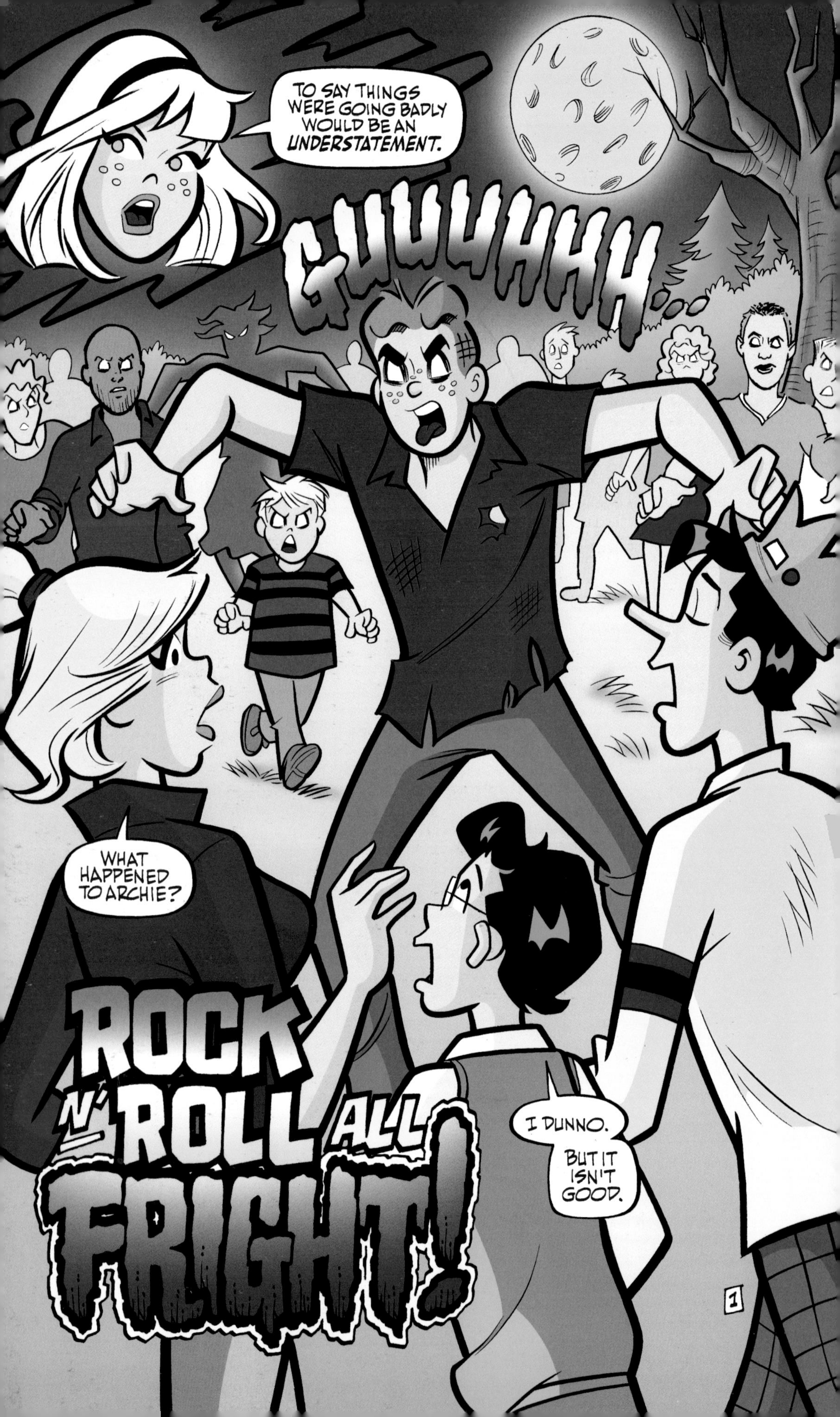
TO SAY THINGS WERE GOING BADLY WOULD BE AN *UNDERSTATEMENT.*
GUUUHHH...
WHAT HAPPENED TO ARCHIE?
I DUNNO.
BUT IT ISN'T GOOD.
ROCK N' ROLL ALL FRIGHT!
1

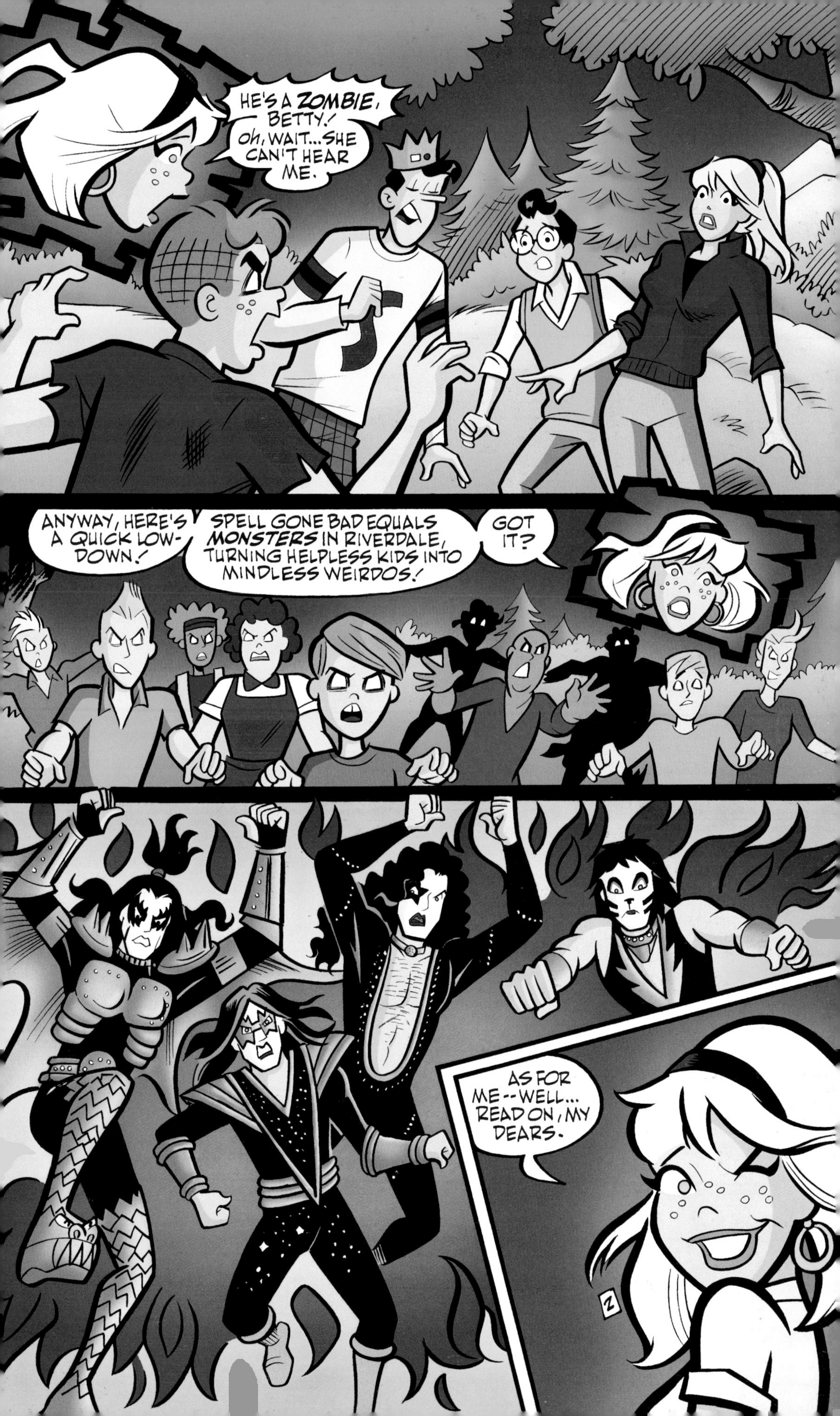
HE'S A ZOMBIE, BETTY! Oh, WAIT... SHE CAN'T HEAR ME.
ANYWAY, HERE'S A QUICK LOW-DOWN!
SPELL GONE BAD EQUALS MONSTERS IN RIVERDALE, TURNING HELPLESS KIDS INTO MINDLESS WEIRDOS!
GOT IT?
AS FOR ME--WELL... READ ON, MY DEARS.
2

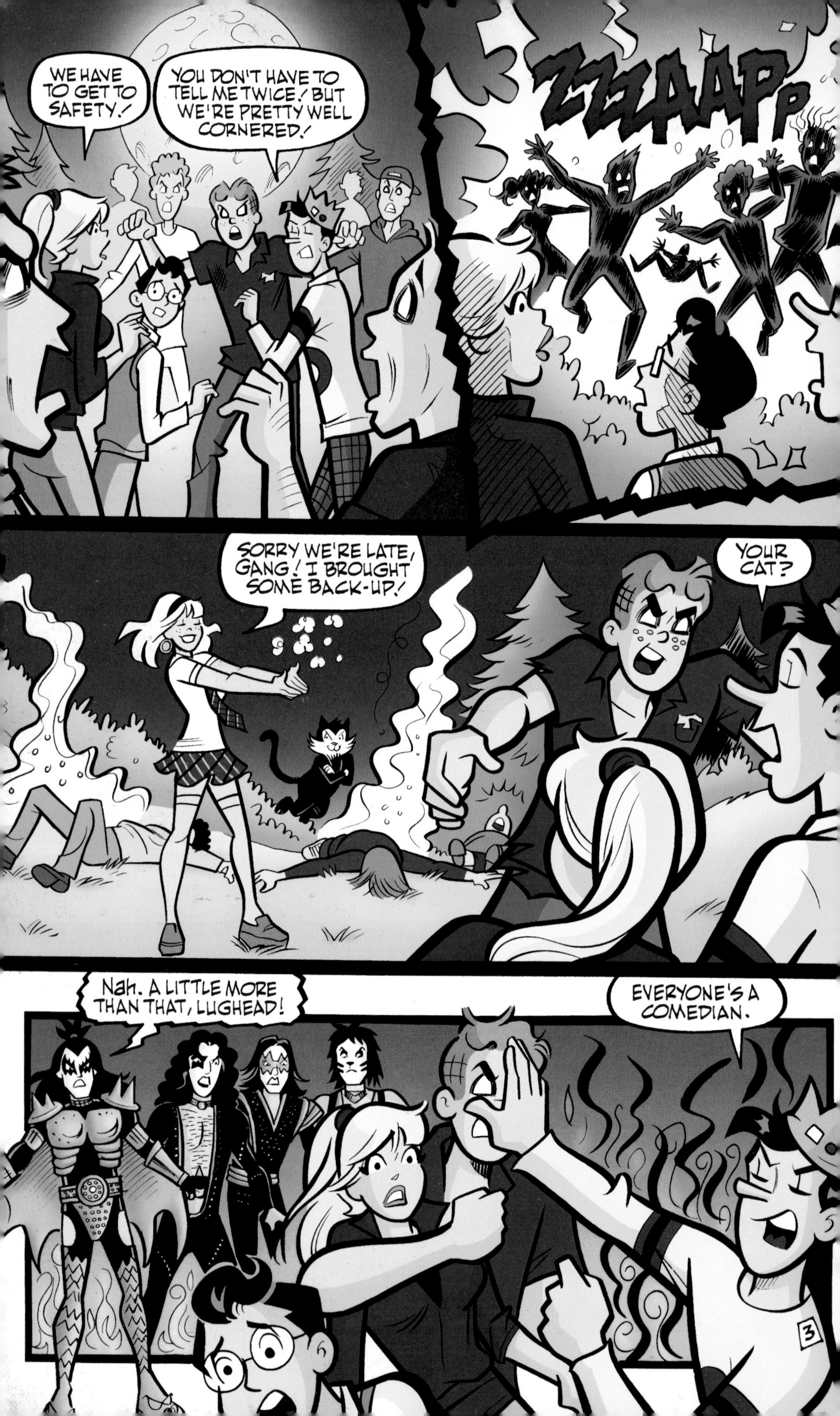
WE HAVE TO GET TO SAFETY!
YOU DON'T HAVE TO TELL ME TWICE! BUT WE'RE PRETTY WELL CORNERED!
ZZZAAPP
SORRY WE'RE LATE, GANG! I BROUGHT SOME BACK-UP!
YOUR CAT?
Nah. A LITTLE MORE THAN THAT, LUGHEAD!
EVERYONE'S A COMEDIAN.
3

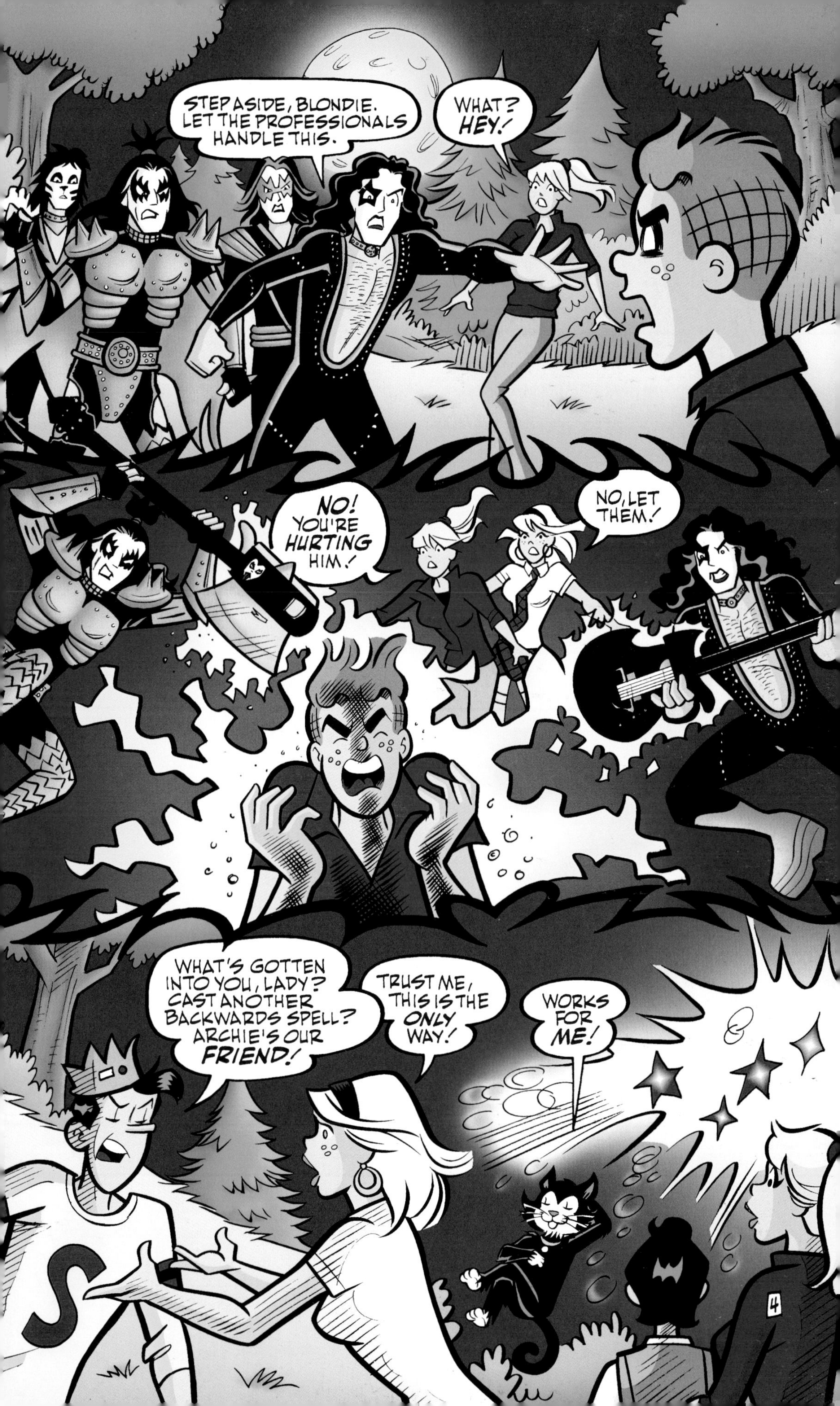
STEP ASIDE, BLONDIE. LET THE PROFESSIONALS HANDLE THIS.
WHAT? HEY!
NO! YOU'RE HURTING HIM!
NO, LET THEM!
WHAT'S GOTTEN INTO YOU, LADY? CAST ANOTHER BACKWARDS SPELL? ARCHIE'S OUR FRIEND!
TRUST ME, THIS IS THE ONLY WAY!
WORKS FOR ME!

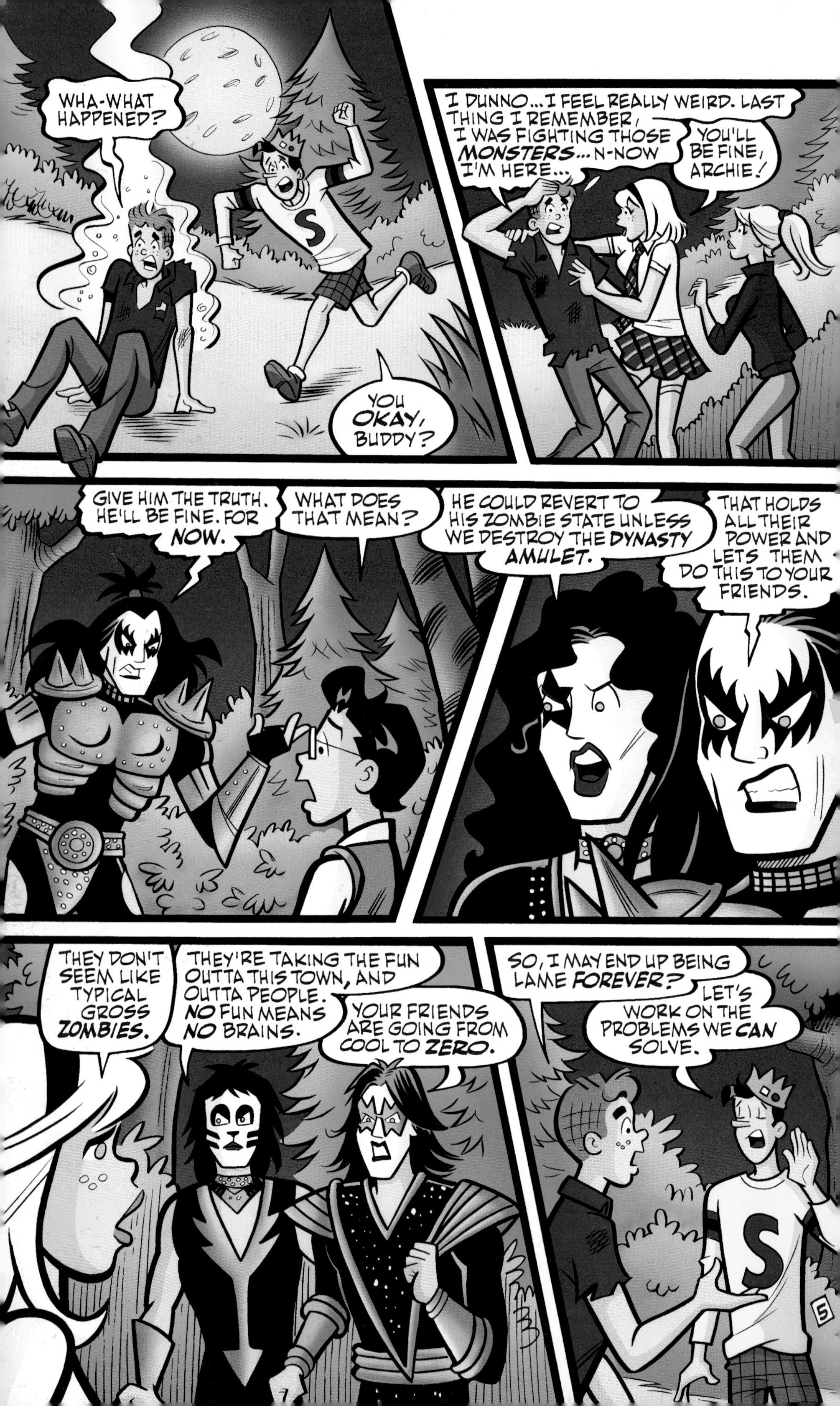

WHA-WHAT HAPPENED?
YOU OKAY, BUDDY?
I DUNNO...I FEEL REALLY WEIRD. LAST THING I REMEMBER, I WAS FIGHTING THOSE MONSTERS... N-NOW I'M HERE...
YOU'LL BE FINE, ARCHIE!
GIVE HIM THE TRUTH. HE'LL BE FINE. FOR NOW.
WHAT DOES THAT MEAN?
HE COULD REVERT TO HIS ZOMBIE STATE UNLESS WE DESTROY THE DYNASTY AMULET.
THAT HOLDS ALL THEIR POWER AND LETS THEM DO THIS TO YOUR FRIENDS.
THEY DON'T SEEM LIKE TYPICAL GROSS ZOMBIES.
THEY'RE TAKING THE FUN OUTTA THIS TOWN, AND OUTTA PEOPLE. NO FUN MEANS NO BRAINS.
YOUR FRIENDS ARE GOING FROM COOL TO ZERO.
SO, I MAY END UP BEING LAME FOREVER?
LET'S WORK ON THE PROBLEMS WE CAN SOLVE.
5

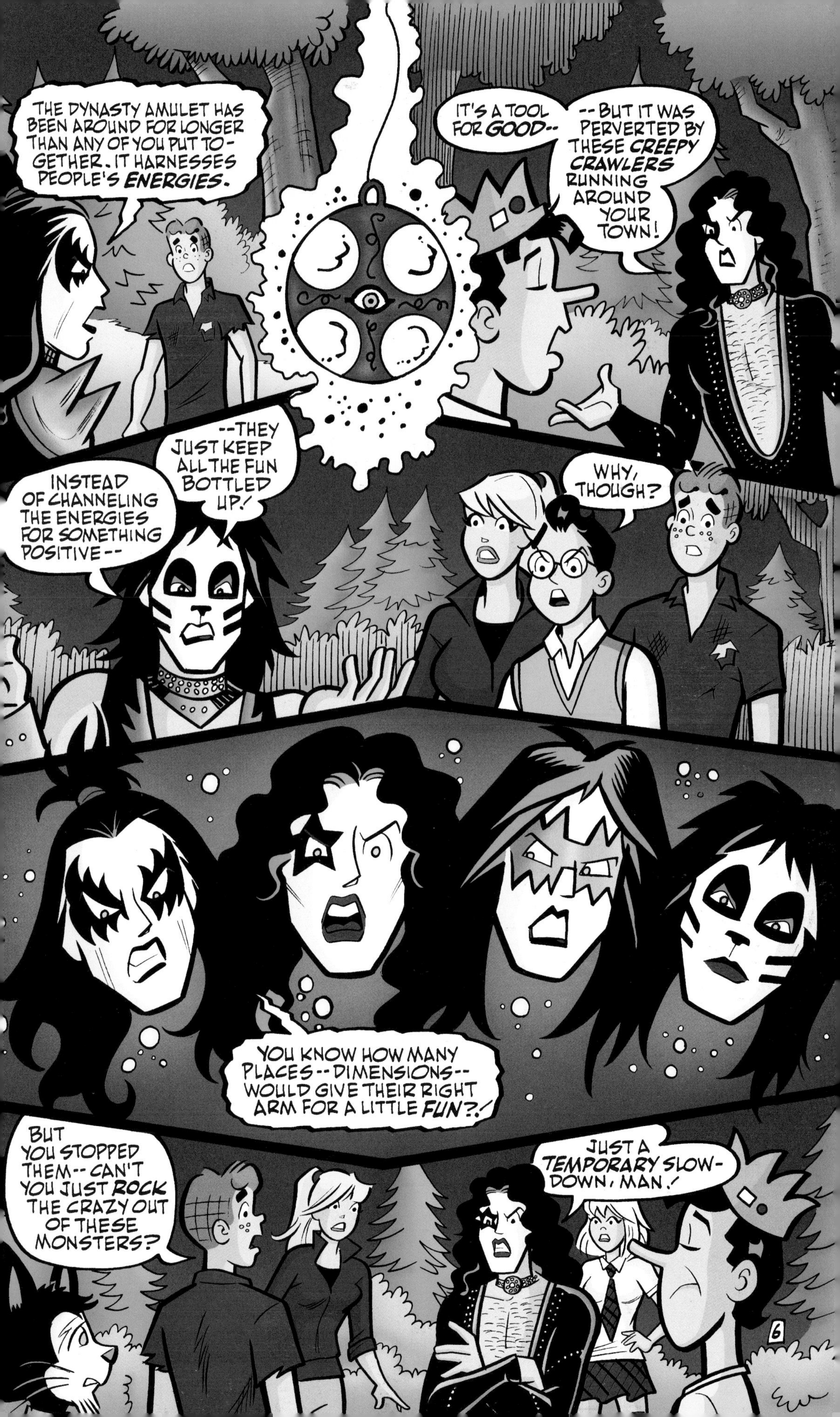

THE DYNASTY AMULET HAS BEEN AROUND FOR LONGER THAN ANY OF YOU PUT TOGETHER. IT HARNESSES PEOPLE'S **ENERGIES.**
IT'S A TOOL FOR **GOOD**--
--BUT IT WAS PERVERTED BY THESE **CREEPY CRAWLERS** RUNNING AROUND YOUR TOWN!
INSTEAD OF CHANNELING THE ENERGIES FOR SOMETHING POSITIVE--
--THEY JUST KEEP ALL THE FUN BOTTLED UP!
WHY, THOUGH?
YOU KNOW HOW MANY PLACES--DIMENSIONS--WOULD GIVE THEIR RIGHT ARM FOR A LITTLE **FUN**?!
BUT YOU STOPPED THEM--CAN'T YOU JUST **ROCK** THE CRAZY OUT OF THESE MONSTERS?
JUST A **TEMPORARY** SLOW-DOWN, MAN!

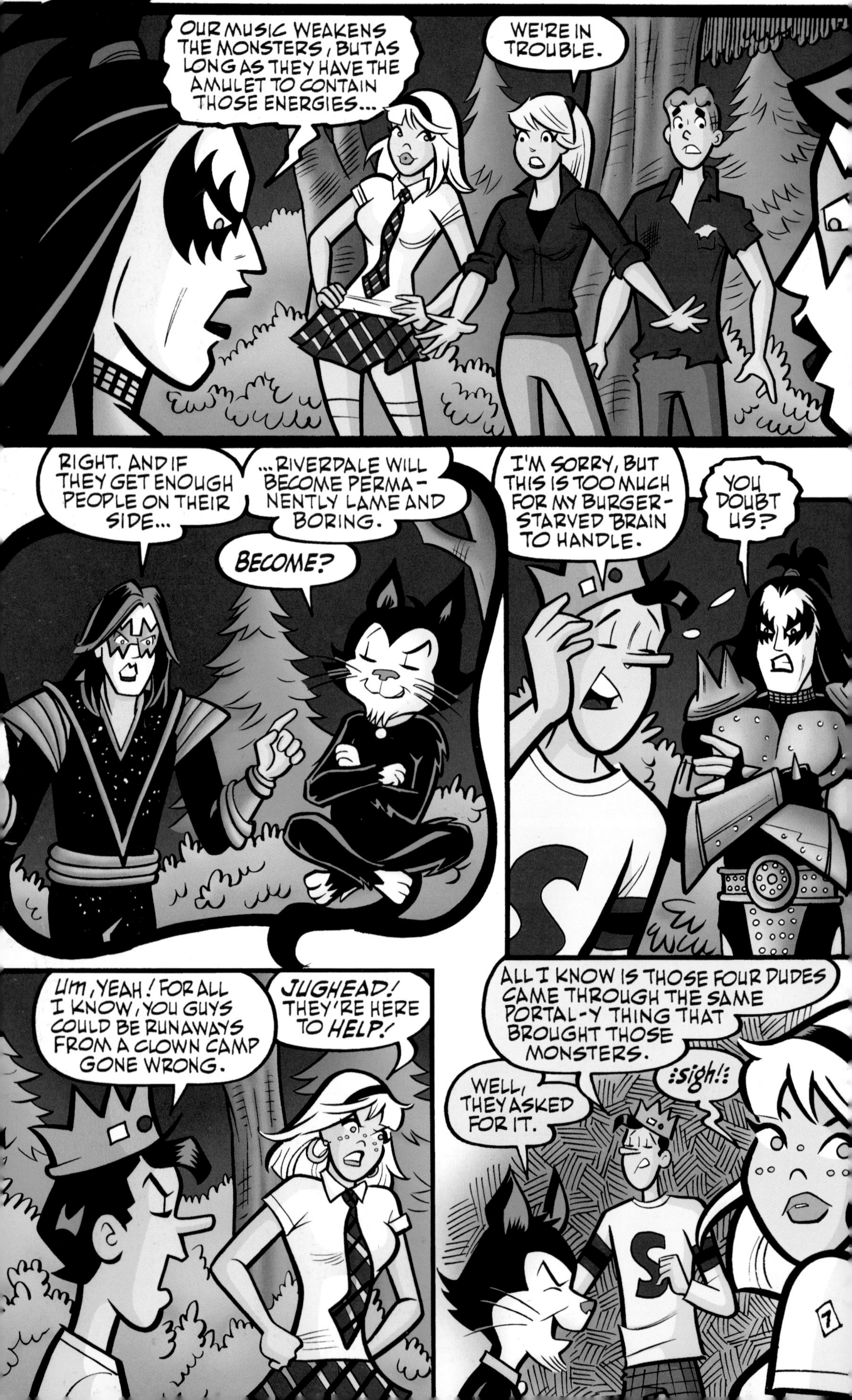

OUR MUSIC WEAKENS THE MONSTERS, BUT AS LONG AS THEY HAVE THE AMULET TO CONTAIN THOSE ENERGIES...
WE'RE IN TROUBLE.
RIGHT. AND IF THEY GET ENOUGH PEOPLE ON THEIR SIDE...
...RIVERDALE WILL BECOME PERMA-NENTLY LAME AND BORING.
BECOME?
I'M SORRY, BUT THIS IS TOO MUCH FOR MY BURGER-STARVED BRAIN TO HANDLE.
YOU DOUBT US?
UM, YEAH! FOR ALL I KNOW, YOU GUYS COULD BE RUNAWAYS FROM A CLOWN CAMP GONE WRONG.
JUGHEAD! THEY'RE HERE TO HELP!
ALL I KNOW IS THOSE FOUR DUDES CAME THROUGH THE SAME PORTAL-Y THING THAT BROUGHT THOSE MONSTERS.
WELL, THEY ASKED FOR IT.
:sigh!:

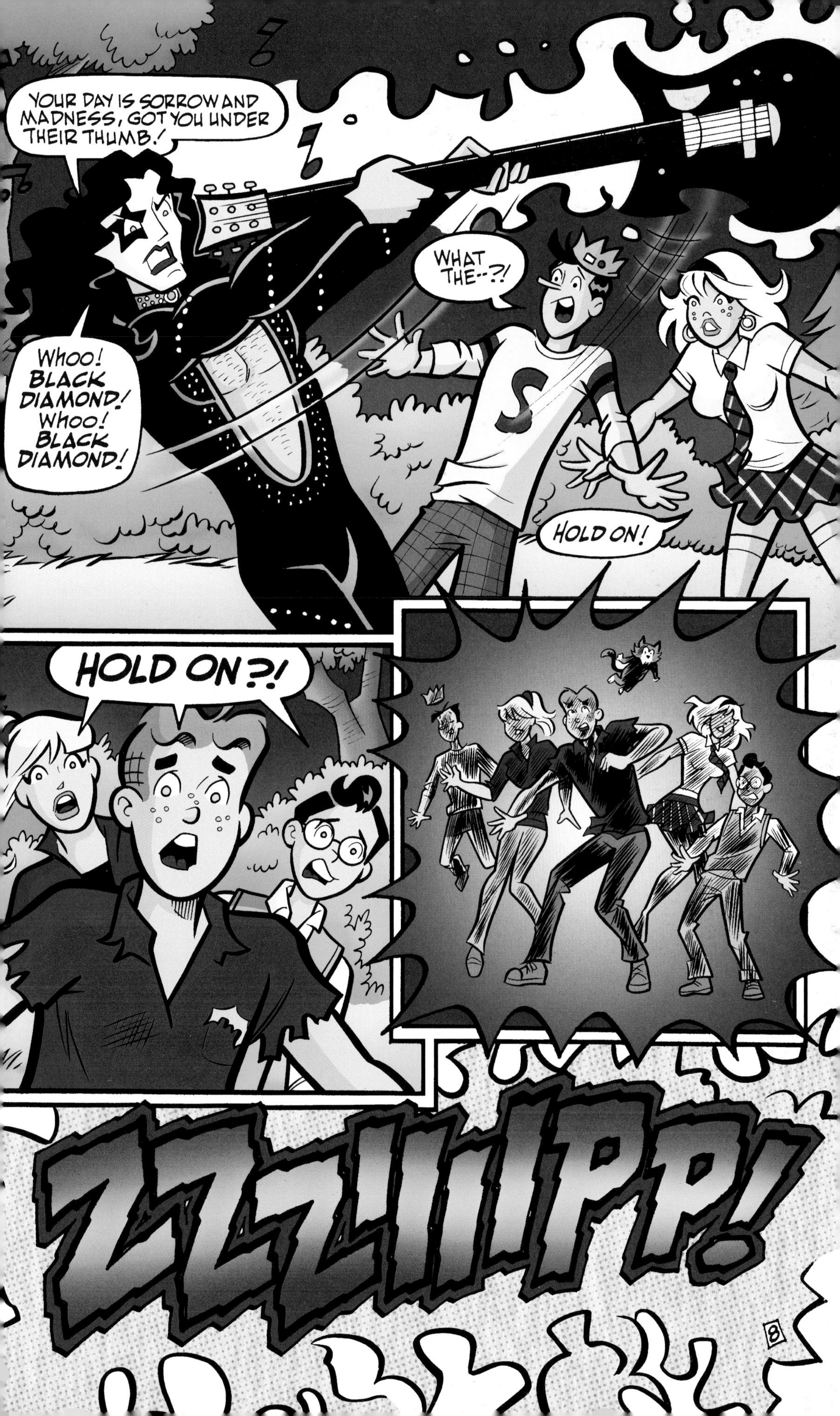
YOUR DAY IS SORROW AND MADNESS, GOT YOU UNDER THEIR THUMB.!
Whoo! BLACK DIAMOND! Whoo! BLACK DIAMOND!
WHAT THE--?!
HOLD ON!
HOLD ON?!
ZZZIIIIPP!
8

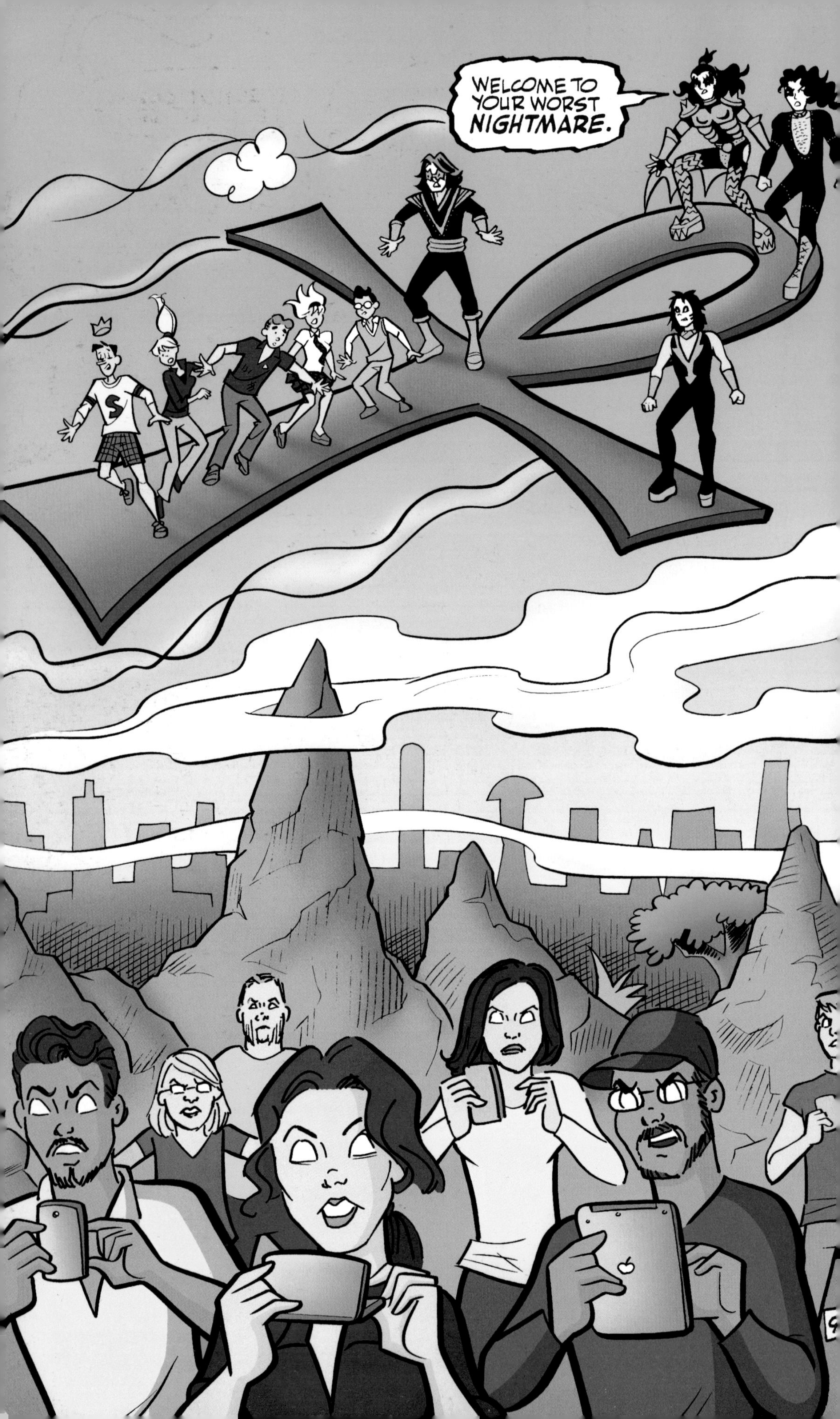
WELCOME TO YOUR WORST NIGHTMARE.

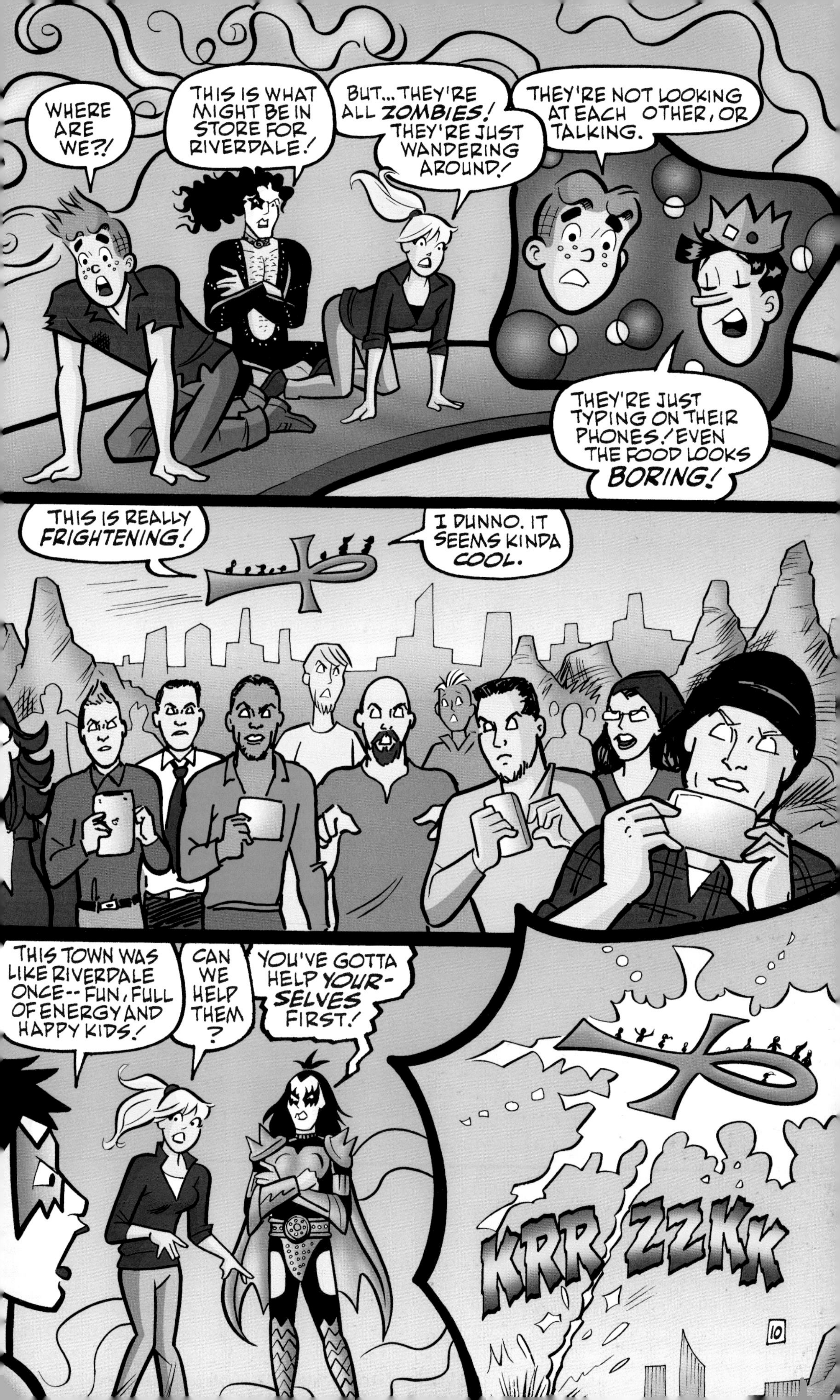

WHERE ARE WE?!
THIS IS WHAT MIGHT BE IN STORE FOR RIVERDALE!
BUT... THEY'RE ALL ZOMBIES! THEY'RE JUST WANDERING AROUND!
THEY'RE NOT LOOKING AT EACH OTHER, OR TALKING.
THEY'RE JUST TYPING ON THEIR PHONES! EVEN THE FOOD LOOKS BORING!
THIS IS REALLY FRIGHTENING!
I DUNNO. IT SEEMS KINDA COOL.
THIS TOWN WAS LIKE RIVERDALE ONCE-- FUN, FULL OF ENERGY AND HAPPY KIDS!
CAN WE HELP THEM?
YOU'VE GOTTA HELP YOURSELVES FIRST!
KRR ZZKK
10

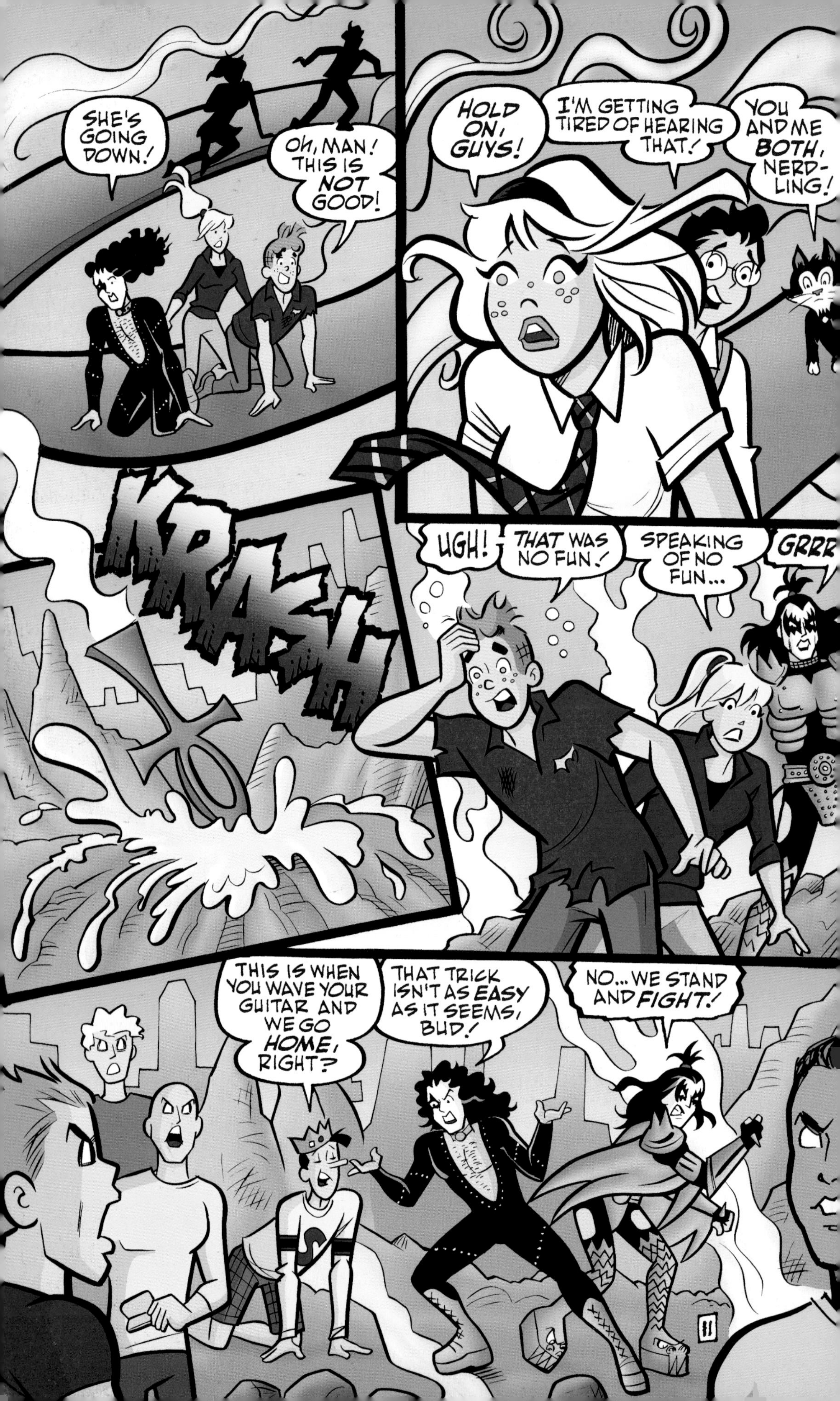

SHE'S GOING DOWN!
OH, MAN! THIS IS NOT GOOD!
HOLD ON, GUYS!
I'M GETTING TIRED OF HEARING THAT!
YOU AND ME BOTH, NERD-LING!
KRASH
UGH!
THAT WAS NO FUN!
SPEAKING OF NO FUN...
GRRR
THIS IS WHEN YOU WAVE YOUR GUITAR AND WE GO HOME, RIGHT?
THAT TRICK ISN'T AS EASY AS IT SEEMS, BUD!
NO... WE STAND AND FIGHT!
11

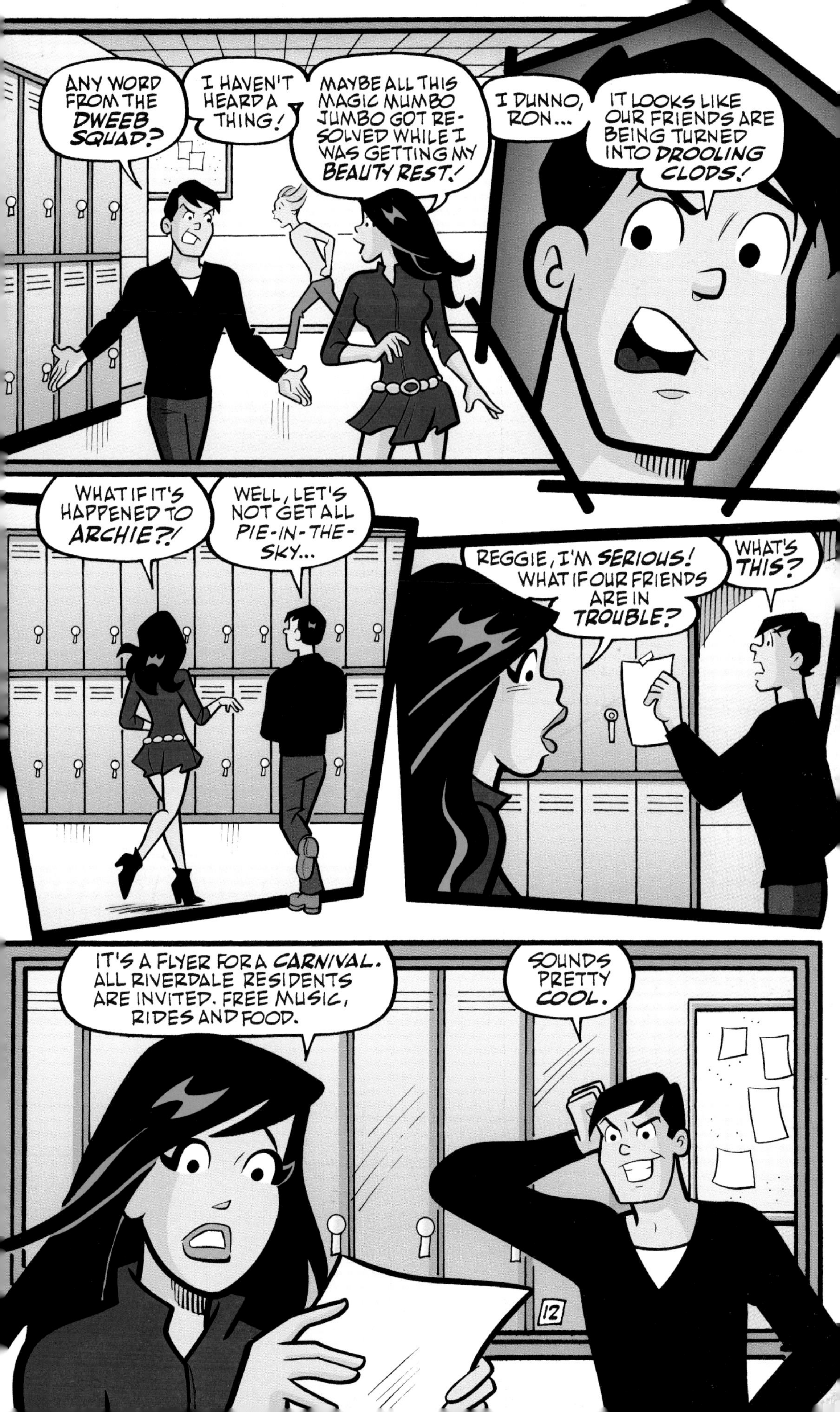
ANY WORD FROM THE DWEEB SQUAD?
I HAVEN'T HEARD A THING!
MAYBE ALL THIS MAGIC MUMBO JUMBO GOT RE-SOLVED WHILE I WAS GETTING MY BEAUTY REST!
I DUNNO, RON...
IT LOOKS LIKE OUR FRIENDS ARE BEING TURNED INTO DROOLING CLODS!
WHAT IF IT'S HAPPENED TO ARCHIE?!
WELL, LET'S NOT GET ALL PIE-IN-THE-SKY...
REGGIE, I'M SERIOUS! WHAT IF OUR FRIENDS ARE IN TROUBLE?
WHAT'S THIS?
IT'S A FLYER FOR A CARNIVAL. ALL RIVERDALE RESIDENTS ARE INVITED. FREE MUSIC, RIDES AND FOOD.
SOUNDS PRETTY COOL.
12

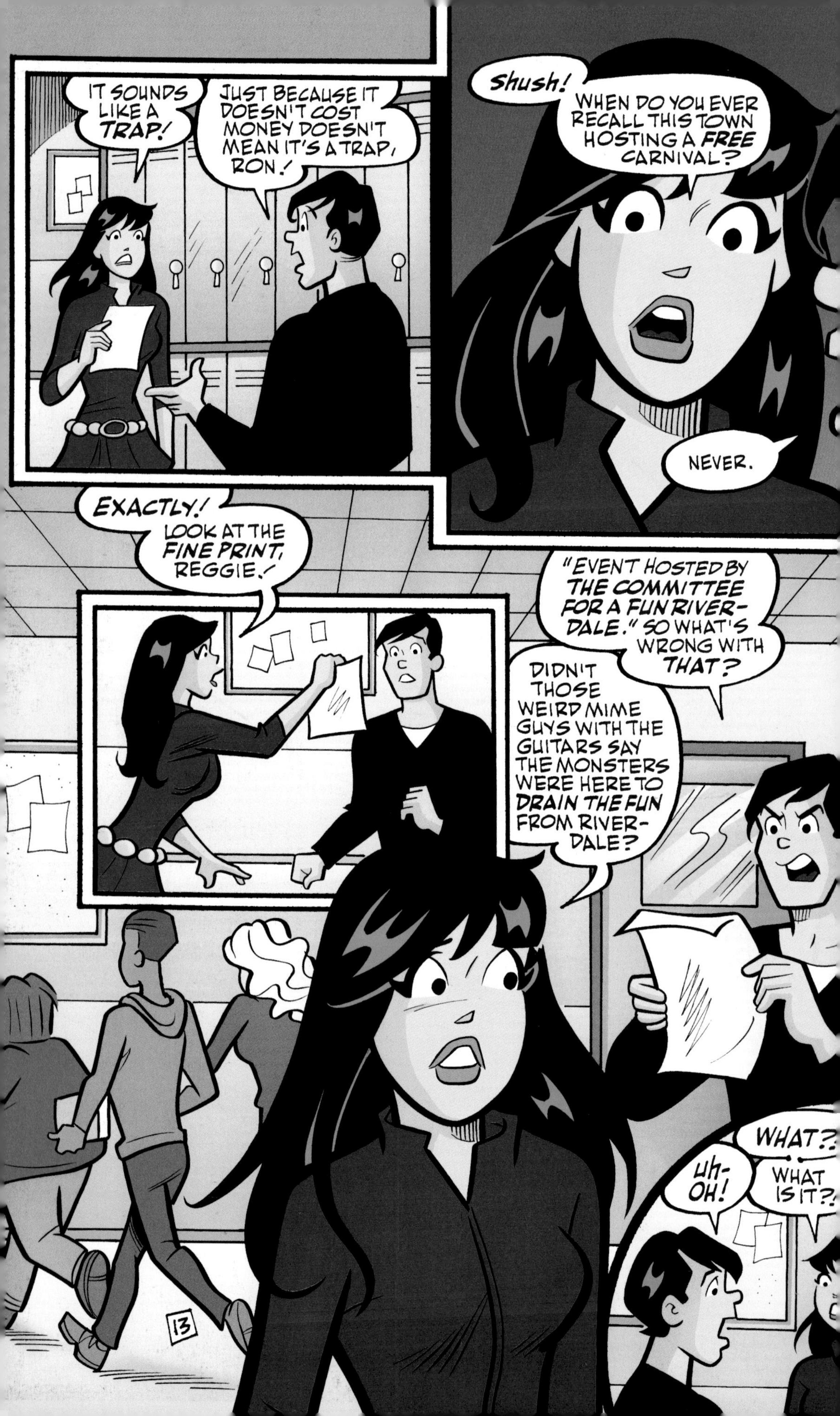

IT SOUNDS LIKE A TRAP!
JUST BECAUSE IT DOESN'T COST MONEY DOESN'T MEAN IT'S A TRAP, RON!
Shush!
WHEN DO YOU EVER RECALL THIS TOWN HOSTING A FREE CARNIVAL?
NEVER.
EXACTLY!
LOOK AT THE FINE PRINT, REGGIE!
"EVENT HOSTED BY THE COMMITTEE FOR A FUN RIVER-DALE." SO WHAT'S WRONG WITH THAT?
DIDN'T THOSE WEIRD MIME GUYS WITH THE GUITARS SAY THE MONSTERS WERE HERE TO DRAIN THE FUN FROM RIVER-DALE?
UH-OH!
WHAT?!
WHAT IS IT?!
13

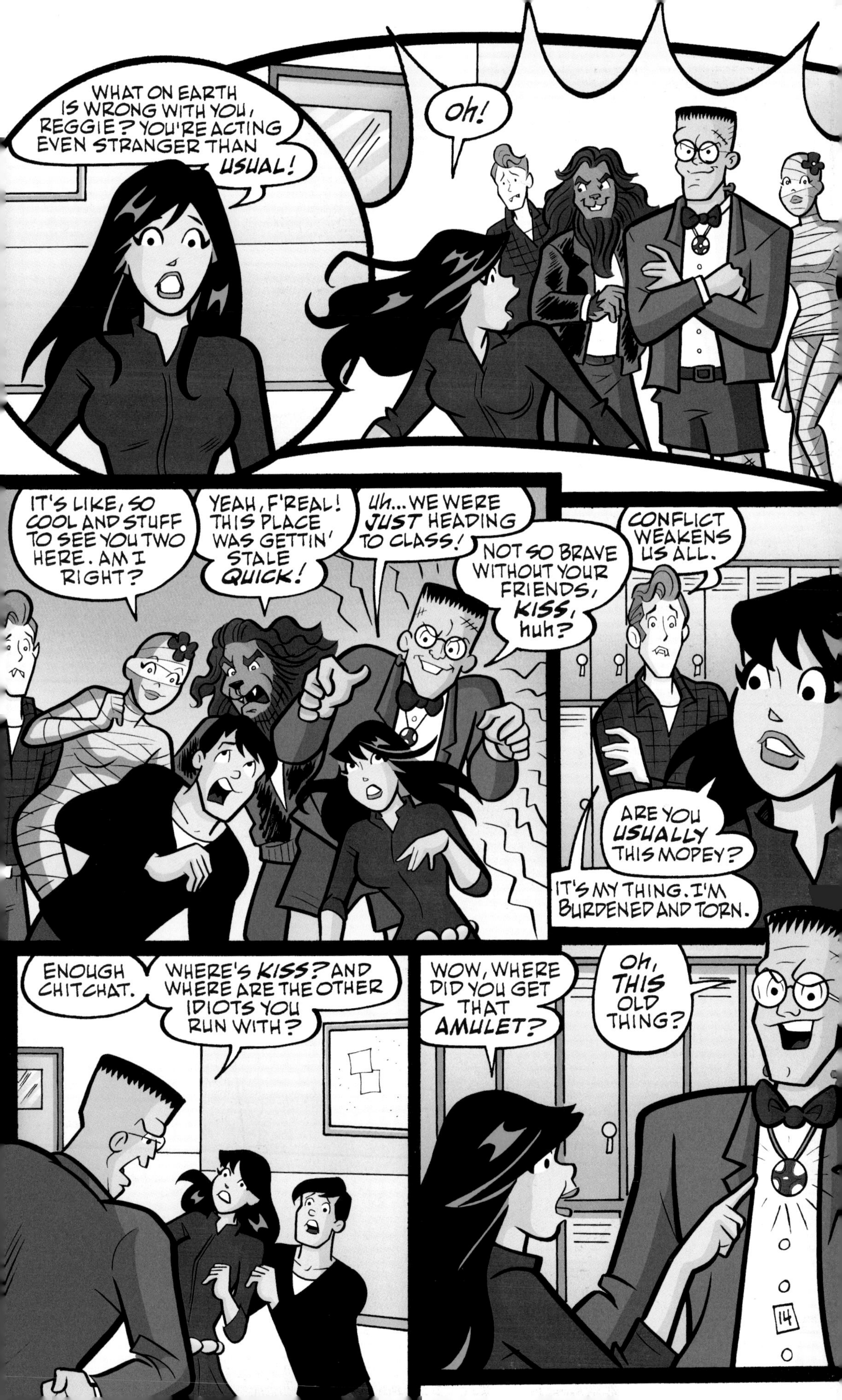
WHAT ON EARTH IS WRONG WITH YOU, REGGIE? YOU'RE ACTING EVEN STRANGER THAN USUAL!
Oh!
IT'S LIKE, SO COOL AND STUFF TO SEE YOU TWO HERE. AM I RIGHT?
YEAH, F'REAL! THIS PLACE WAS GETTIN' STALE QUICK!
Uh... WE WERE JUST HEADING TO CLASS!
NOT SO BRAVE WITHOUT YOUR FRIENDS, KISS, huh?
CONFLICT WEAKENS US ALL.
ARE YOU USUALLY THIS MOPEY?
IT'S MY THING. I'M BURDENED AND TORN.
ENOUGH CHITCHAT.
WHERE'S KISS? AND WHERE ARE THE OTHER IDIOTS YOU RUN WITH?
WOW, WHERE DID YOU GET THAT AMULET?
Oh, THIS OLD THING?
14

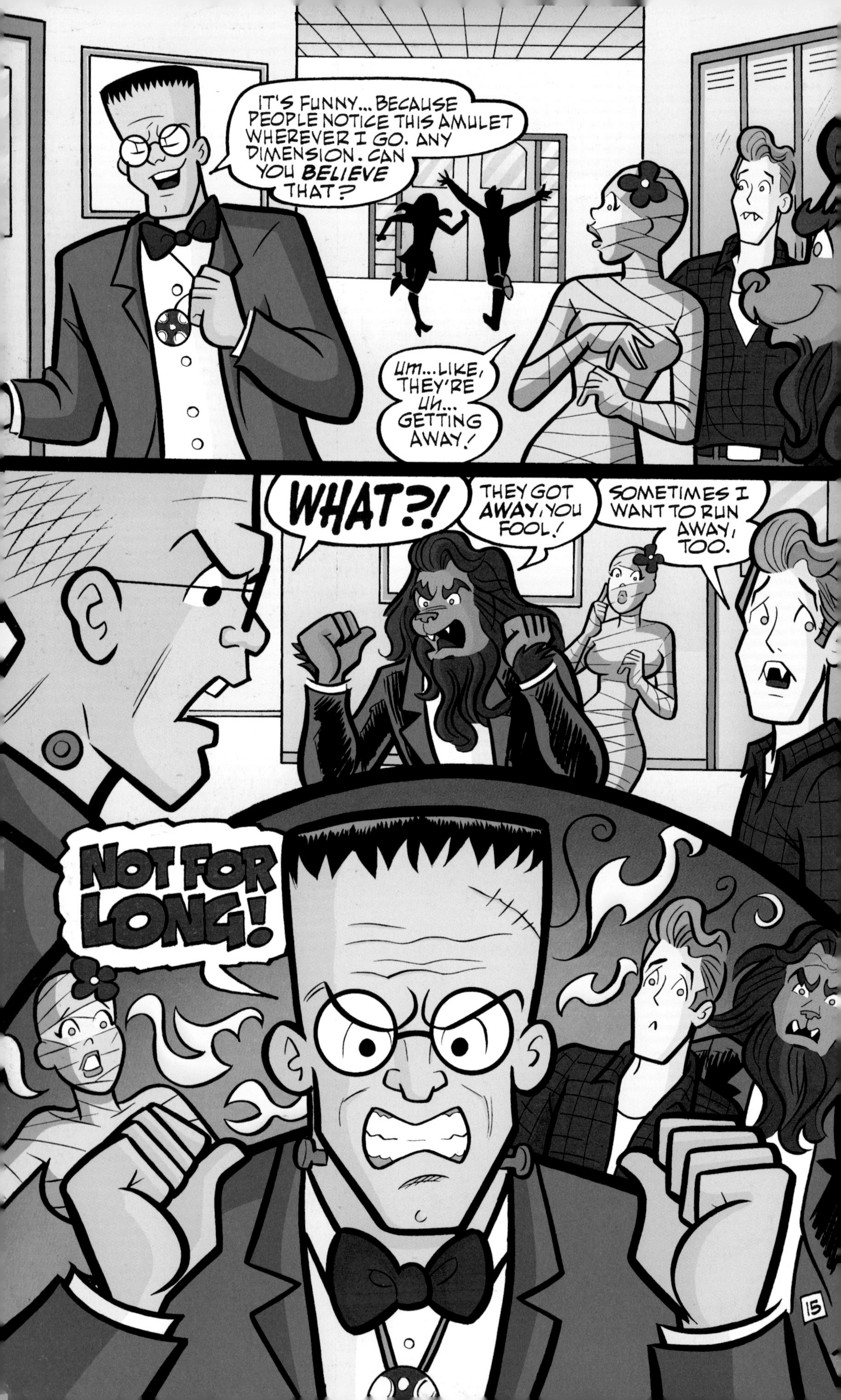
IT'S FUNNY... BECAUSE PEOPLE NOTICE THIS AMULET WHEREVER I GO. ANY DIMENSION. CAN YOU BELIEVE THAT?
UM... LIKE, THEY'RE UH... GETTING AWAY!
WHAT?!
THEY GOT AWAY, YOU FOOL!
SOMETIMES I WANT TO RUN AWAY, TOO.
NOT FOR LONG!
15

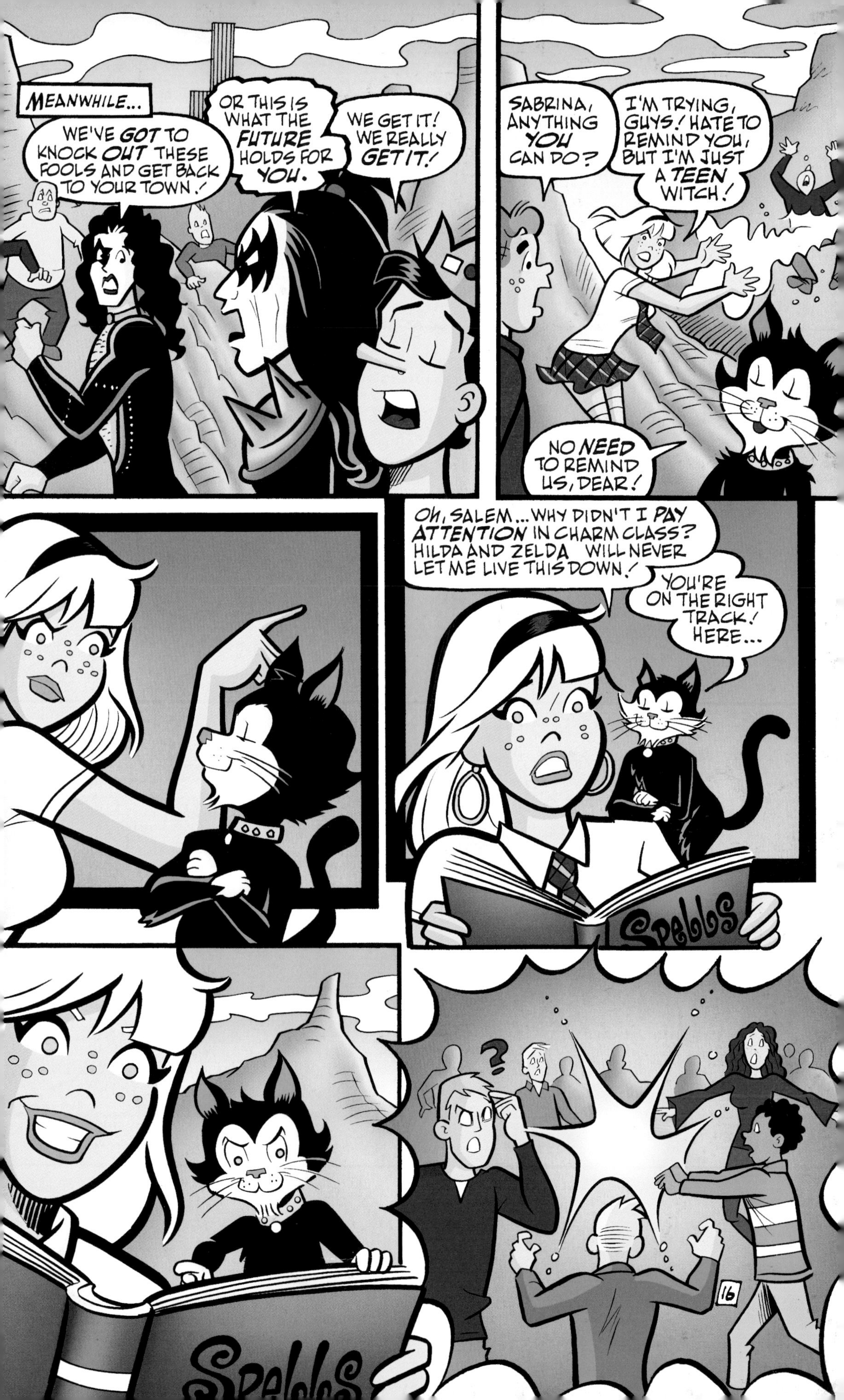
MEANWHILE...
WE'VE GOT TO KNOCK OUT THESE FOOLS AND GET BACK TO YOUR TOWN!
OR THIS IS WHAT THE FUTURE HOLDS FOR YOU.
WE GET IT! WE REALLY GET IT!
SABRINA, ANYTHING YOU CAN DO?
I'M TRYING, GUYS! HATE TO REMIND YOU, BUT I'M JUST A TEEN WITCH!
NO NEED TO REMIND US, DEAR!
Oh, SALEM... WHY DIDN'T I PAY ATTENTION IN CHARM CLASS? HILDA AND ZELDA WILL NEVER LET ME LIVE THIS DOWN!
YOU'RE ON THE RIGHT TRACK! HERE...
SPELLS
?
16
SPELLS

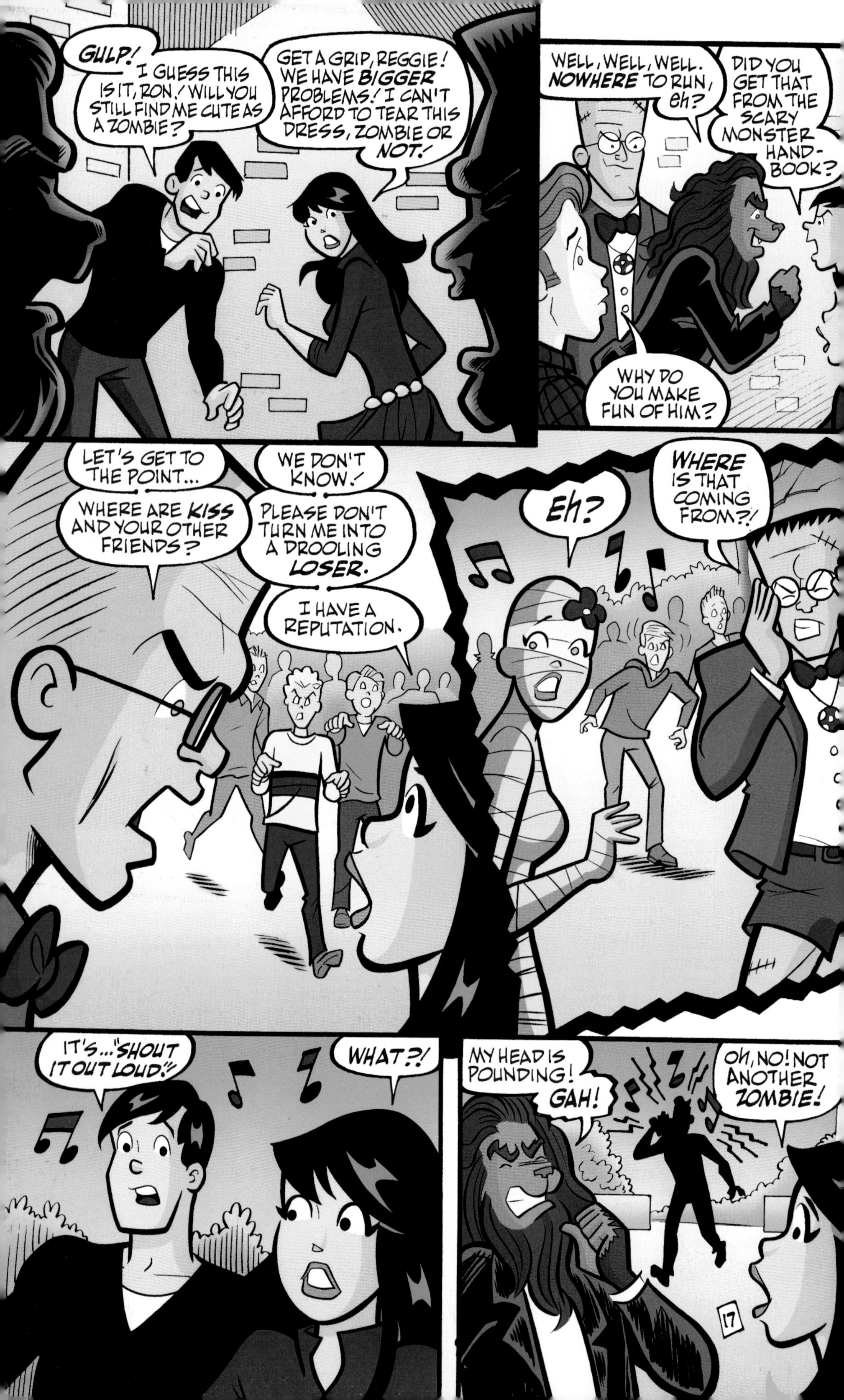
GULP! I GUESS THIS IS IT, RON! WILL YOU STILL FIND ME CUTE AS A ZOMBIE?
GET A GRIP, REGGIE! WE HAVE BIGGER PROBLEMS! I CAN'T AFFORD TO TEAR THIS DRESS, ZOMBIE OR NOT!
WELL, WELL, WELL. NOWHERE TO RUN, EH?
DID YOU GET THAT FROM THE SCARY MONSTER HAND-BOOK?
WHY DO YOU MAKE FUN OF HIM?
LET'S GET TO THE POINT...
WHERE ARE KISS AND YOUR OTHER FRIENDS?
WE DON'T KNOW!
PLEASE DON'T TURN ME INTO A DROOLING LOSER.
I HAVE A REPUTATION.
EH?
WHERE IS THAT COMING FROM?!
IT'S..."SHOUT IT OUT LOUD!"
WHAT?!
MY HEAD IS POUNDING!
GAH!
OH, NO! NOT ANOTHER ZOMBIE!
17

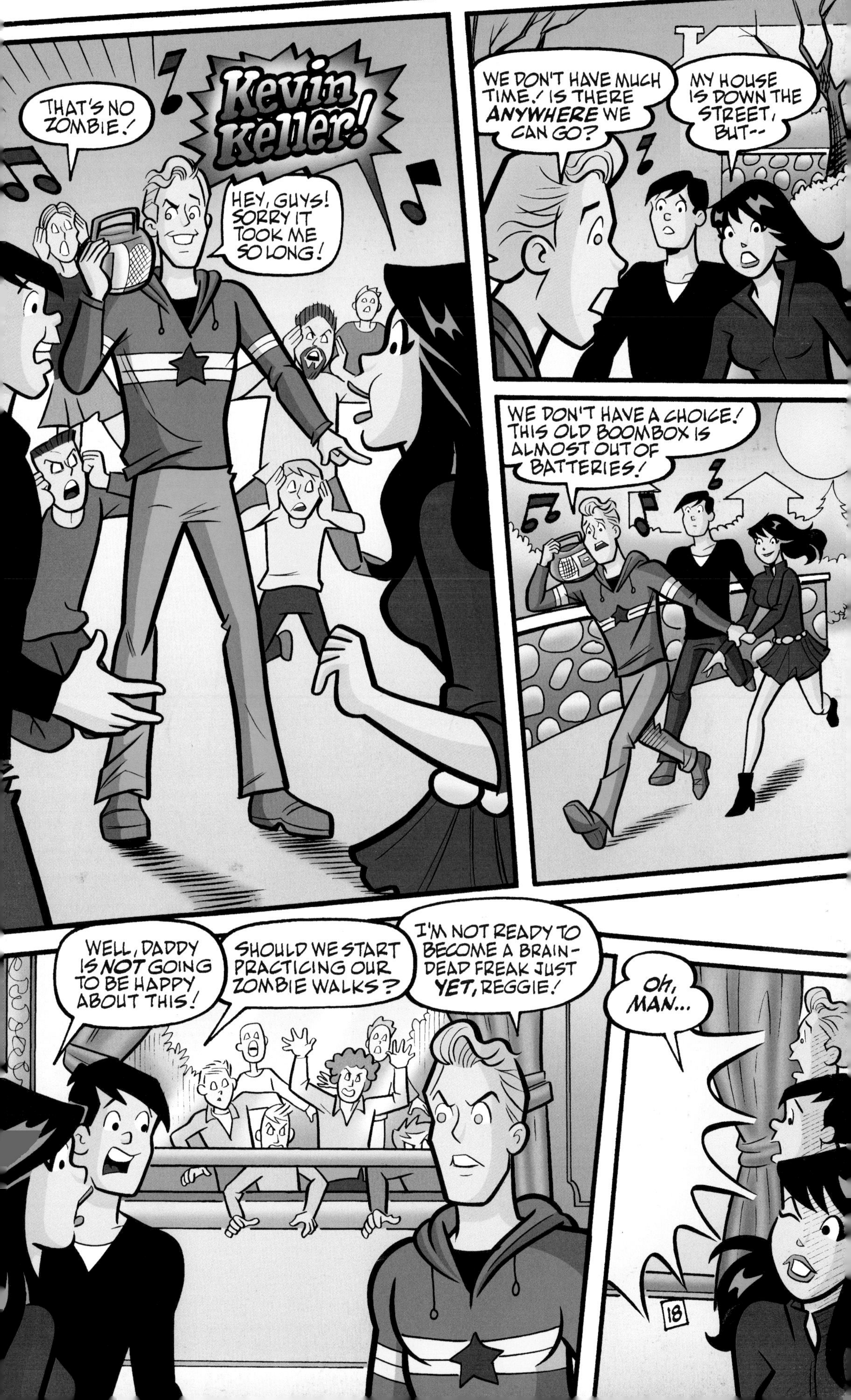

THAT'S NO ZOMBIE!
Kevin Keller!
HEY, GUYS! SORRY IT TOOK ME SO LONG!
WE DON'T HAVE MUCH TIME! IS THERE ANYWHERE WE CAN GO?
MY HOUSE IS DOWN THE STREET, BUT--
WE DON'T HAVE A CHOICE! THIS OLD BOOMBOX IS ALMOST OUT OF BATTERIES!
WELL, DADDY IS NOT GOING TO BE HAPPY ABOUT THIS!
SHOULD WE START PRACTICING OUR ZOMBIE WALKS?
I'M NOT READY TO BECOME A BRAIN-DEAD FREAK JUST YET, REGGIE!
Oh, MAN...
18

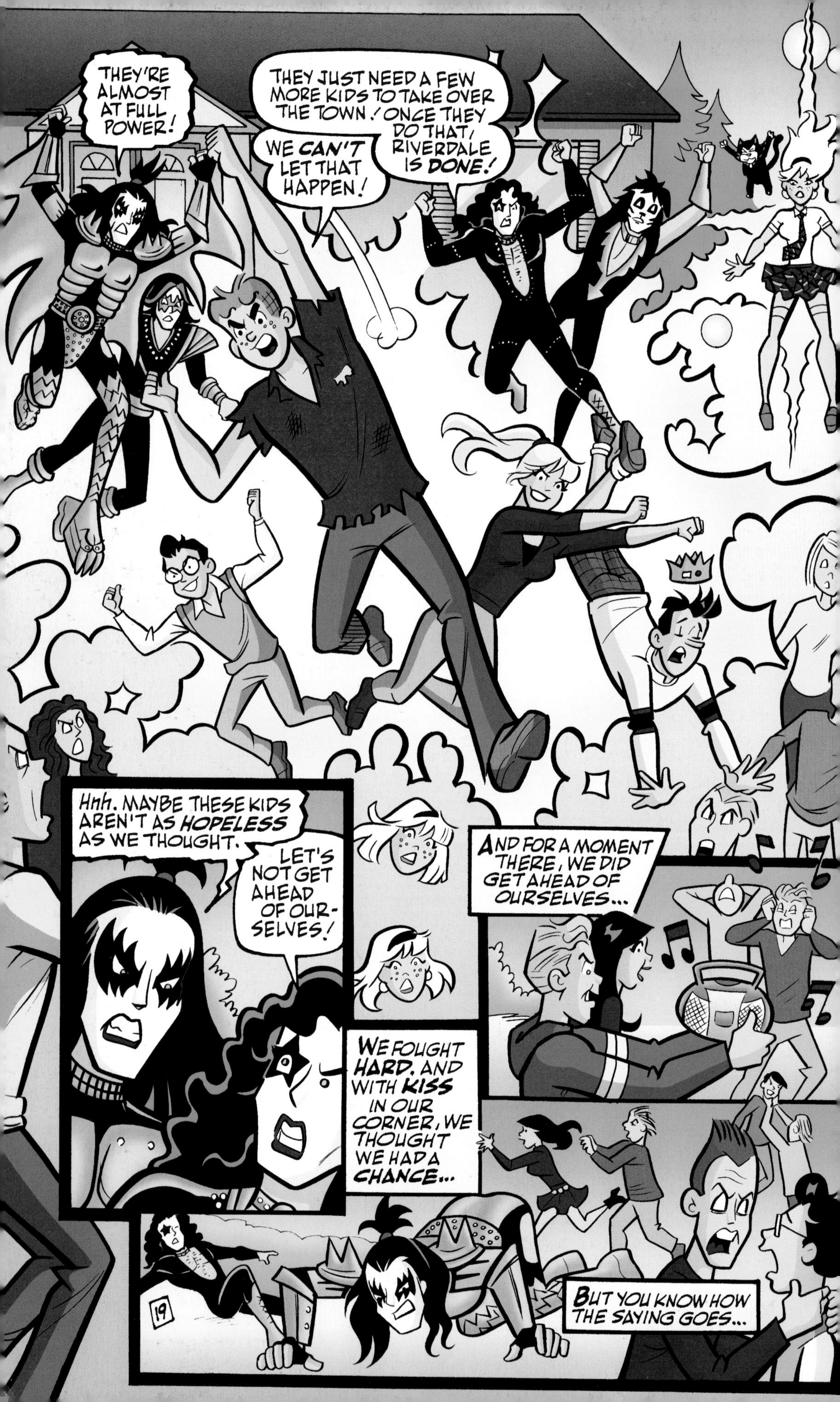

THEY'RE ALMOST AT FULL POWER!
THEY JUST NEED A FEW MORE KIDS TO TAKE OVER THE TOWN! ONCE THEY DO THAT, RIVERDALE IS DONE!
WE CAN'T LET THAT HAPPEN!
Hnh. MAYBE THESE KIDS AREN'T AS HOPELESS AS WE THOUGHT.
LET'S NOT GET AHEAD OF OUR-SELVES!
AND FOR A MOMENT THERE, WE DID GET AHEAD OF OURSELVES...
WE FOUGHT HARD, AND WITH KISS IN OUR CORNER, WE THOUGHT WE HAD A CHANCE...
BUT YOU KNOW HOW THE SAYING GOES...
19

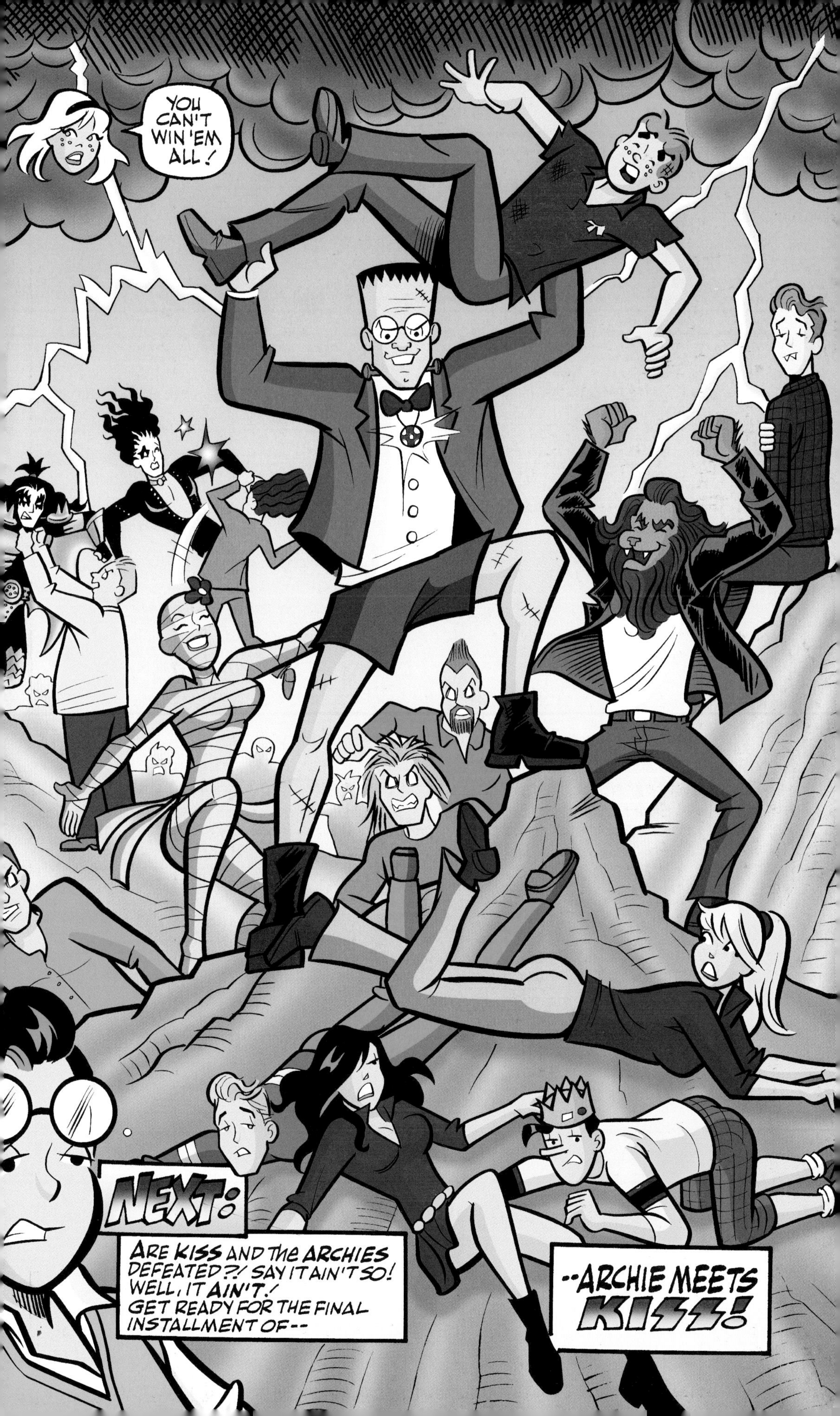
YOU CAN'T WIN 'EM ALL!
NEXT:
ARE KISS AND THE ARCHIES DEFEATED?! SAY IT AIN'T SO! WELL, IT AIN'T! GET READY FOR THE FINAL INSTALLMENT OF--
--ARCHIE MEETS KISS!

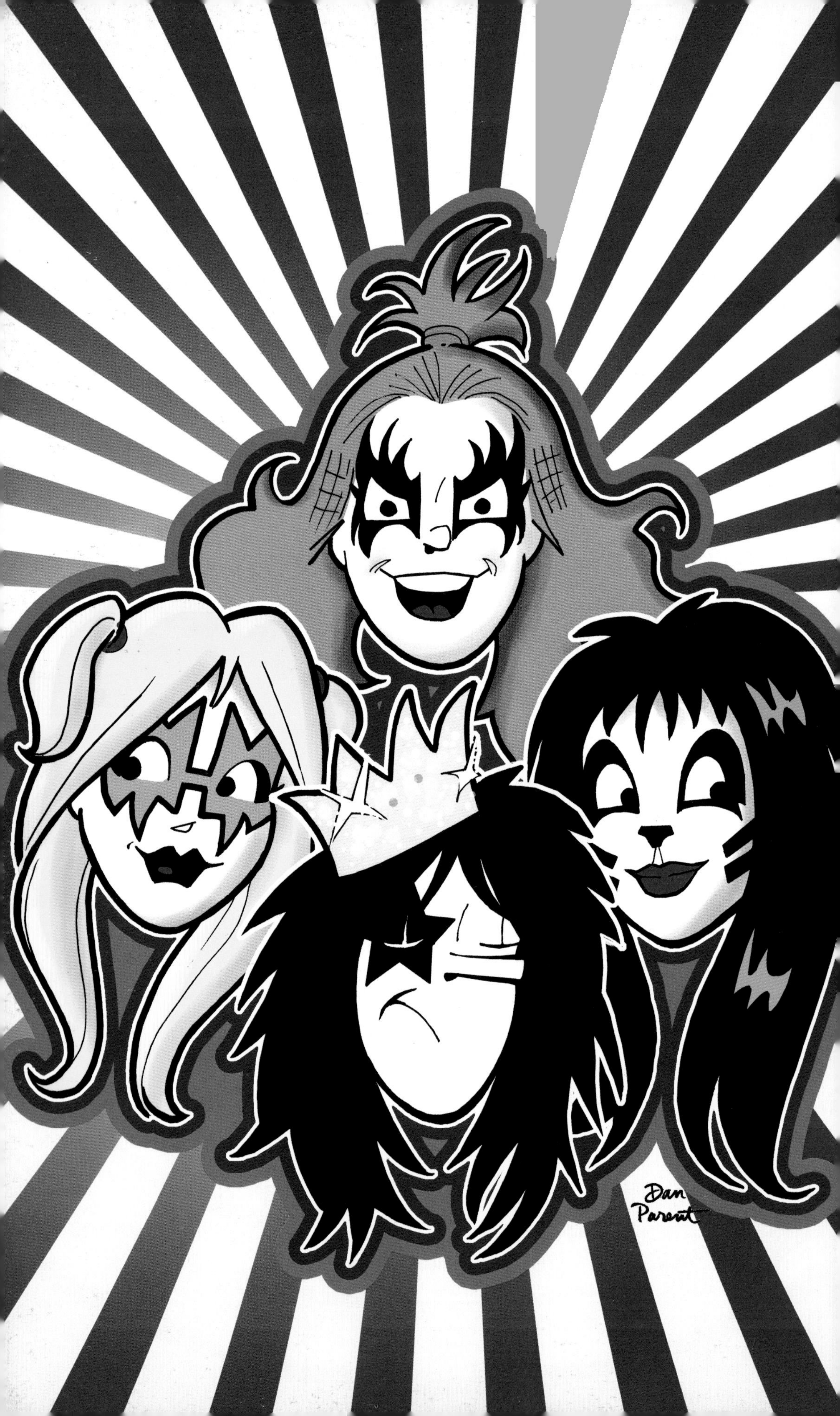
Dan
Parent

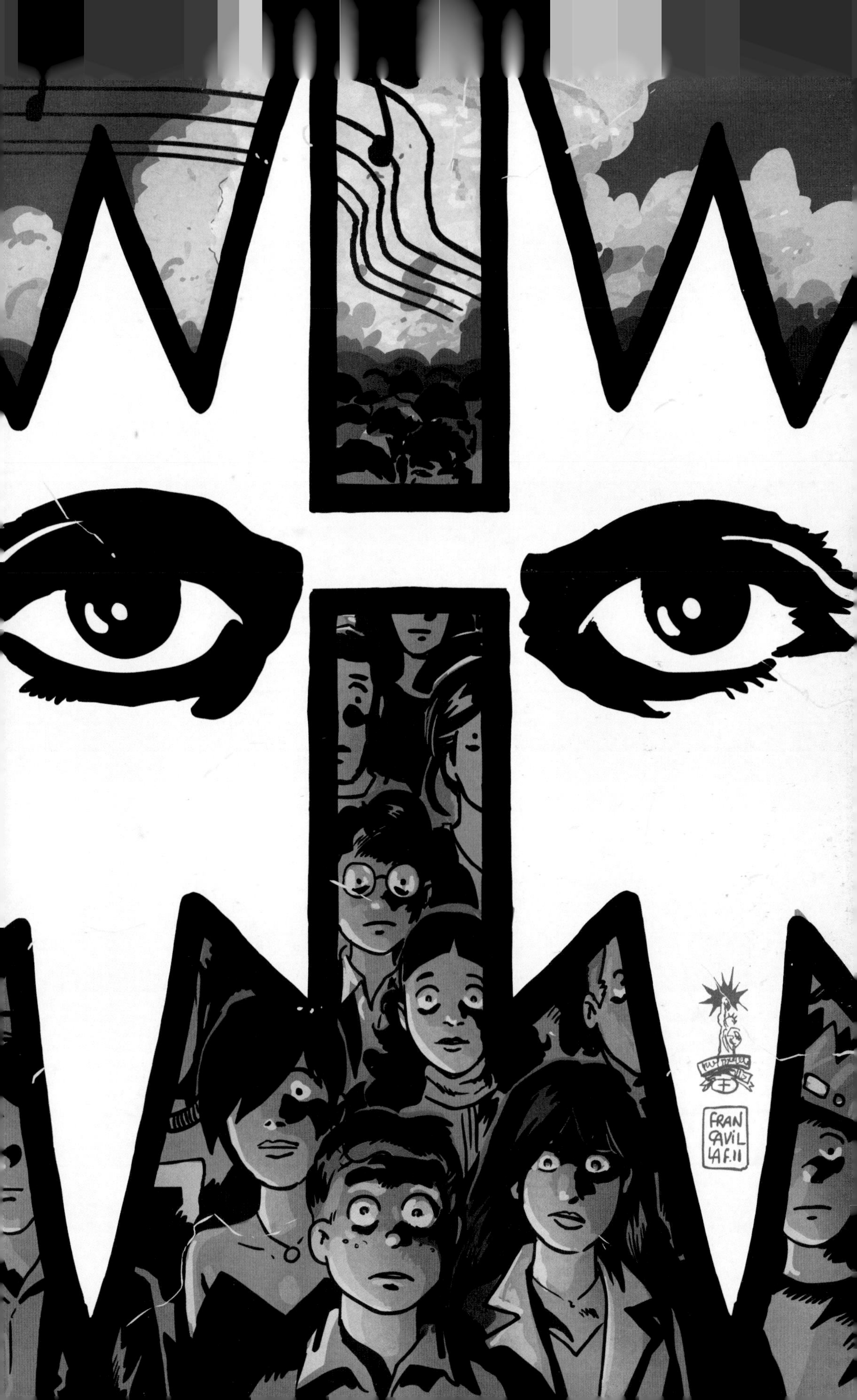
FRAN CAVIL LA F.11

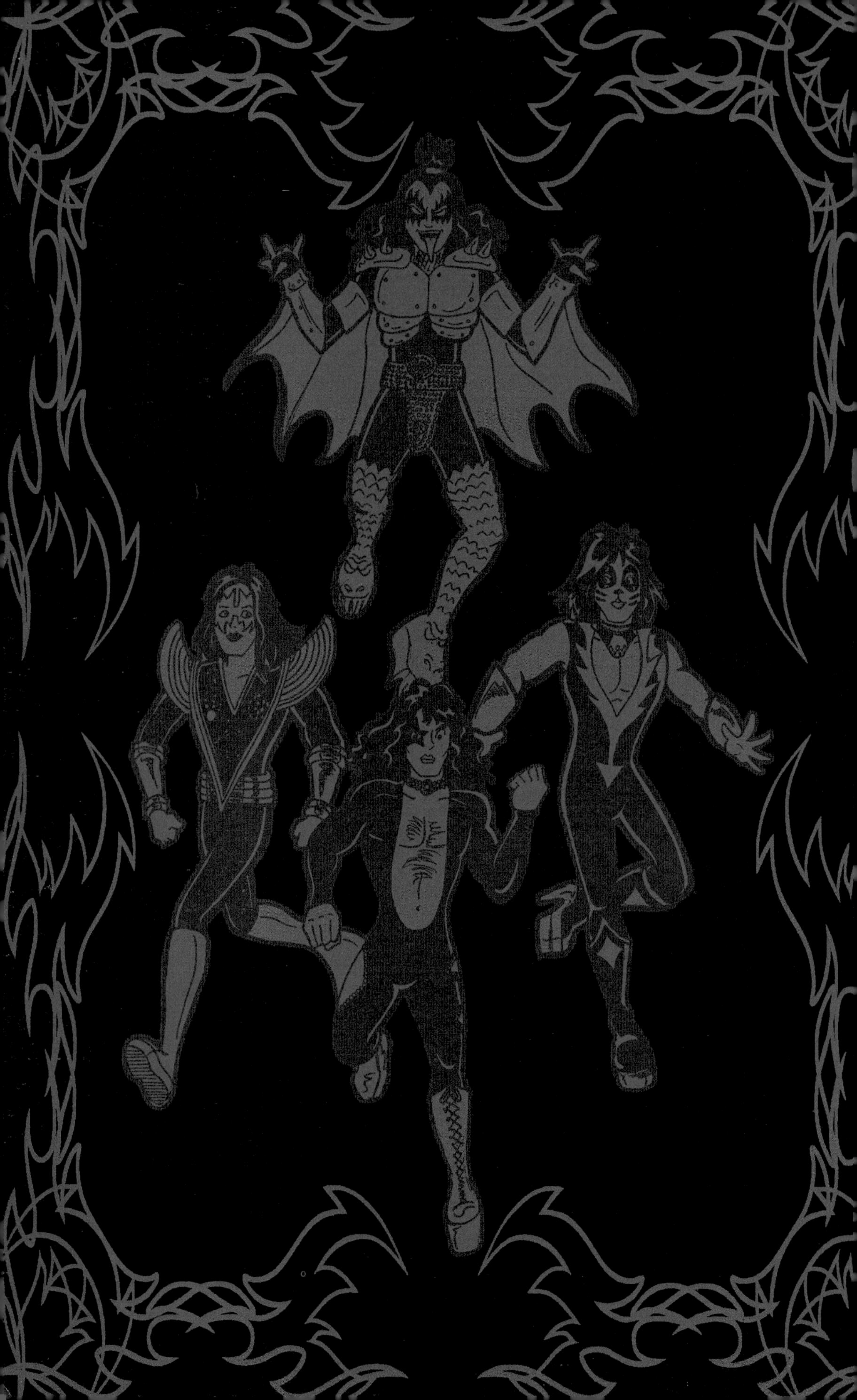

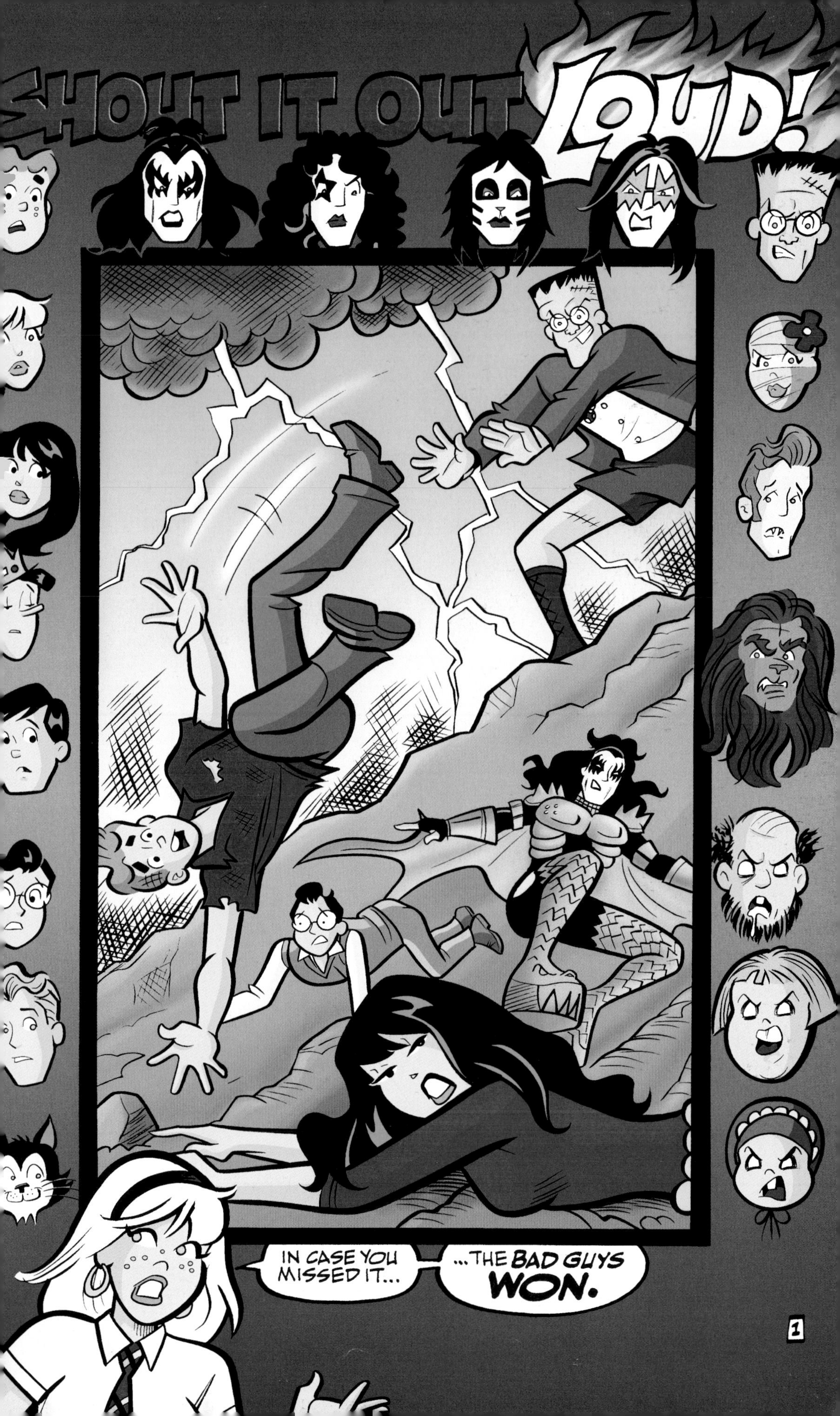

SHOUT IT OUT LOUD!
IN CASE YOU MISSED IT...
...THE BAD GUYS WON.

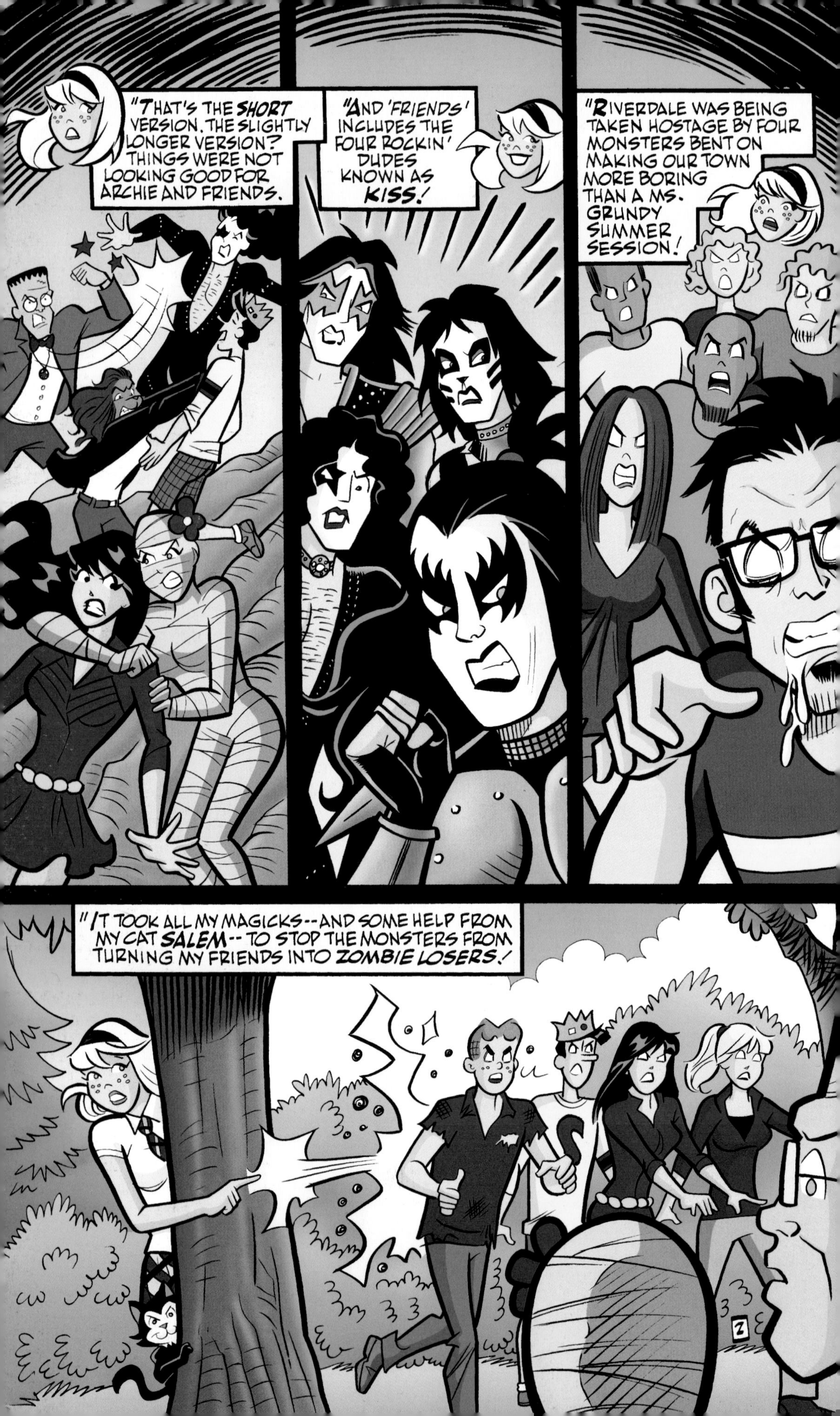
"THAT'S THE SHORT VERSION. THE SLIGHTLY LONGER VERSION? THINGS WERE NOT LOOKING GOOD FOR ARCHIE AND FRIENDS.
"AND 'FRIENDS' INCLUDES THE FOUR ROCKIN' DUDES KNOWN AS KISS!
"RIVERDALE WAS BEING TAKEN HOSTAGE BY FOUR MONSTERS BENT ON MAKING OUR TOWN MORE BORING THAN A MS. GRUNDY SUMMER SESSION!
"IT TOOK ALL MY MAGICKS--AND SOME HELP FROM MY CAT SALEM-- TO STOP THE MONSTERS FROM TURNING MY FRIENDS INTO ZOMBIE LOSERS!
2

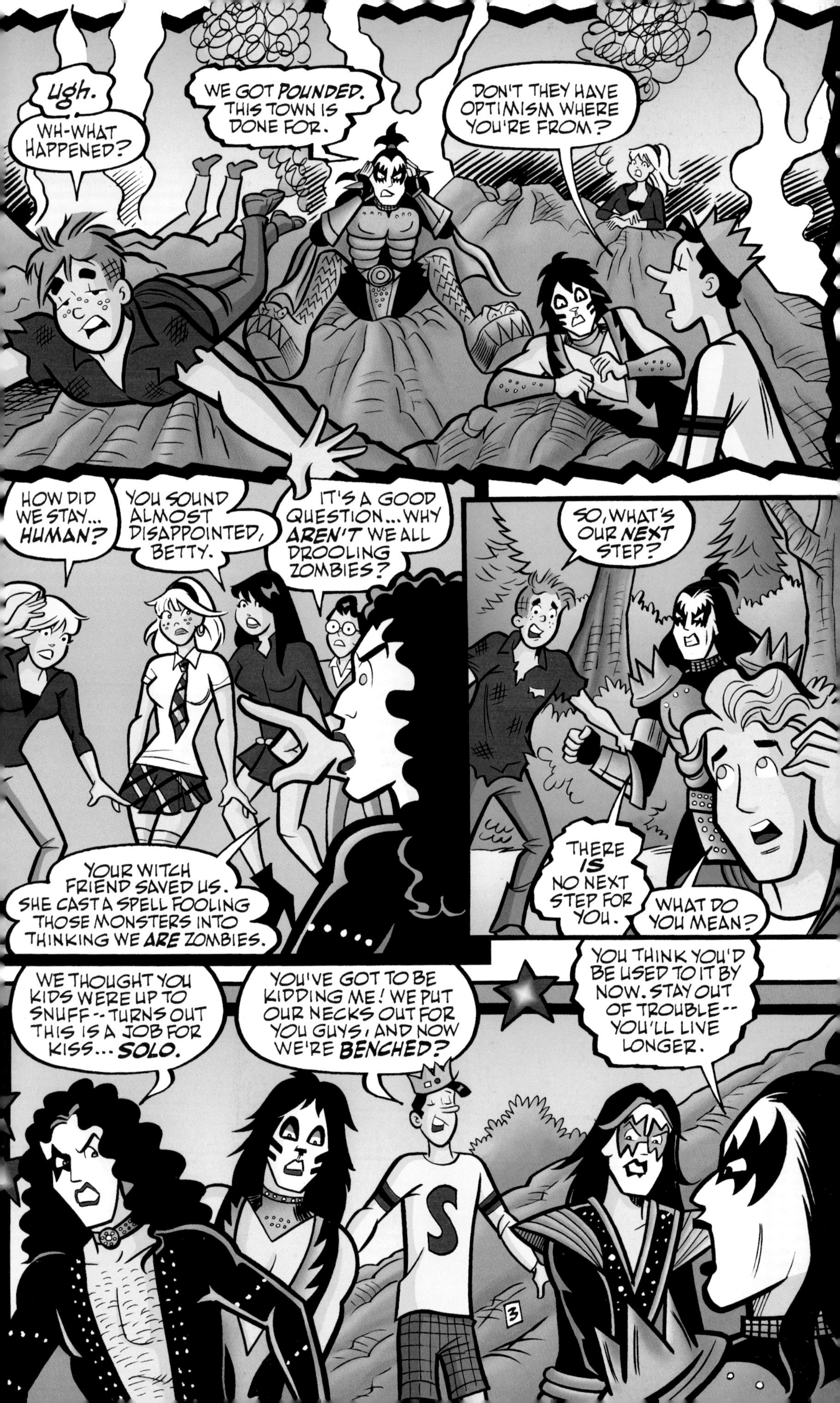
UGH.
WH-WHAT HAPPENED?
WE GOT POUNDED. THIS TOWN IS DONE FOR.
DON'T THEY HAVE OPTIMISM WHERE YOU'RE FROM?
HOW DID WE STAY... HUMAN?
YOU SOUND ALMOST DISAPPOINTED, BETTY.
IT'S A GOOD QUESTION... WHY AREN'T WE ALL DROOLING ZOMBIES?
YOUR WITCH FRIEND SAVED US. SHE CAST A SPELL FOOLING THOSE MONSTERS INTO THINKING WE ARE ZOMBIES.
SO, WHAT'S OUR NEXT STEP?
THERE IS NO NEXT STEP FOR YOU.
WHAT DO YOU MEAN?
WE THOUGHT YOU KIDS WERE UP TO SNUFF-- TURNS OUT THIS IS A JOB FOR KISS... SOLO.
YOU'VE GOT TO BE KIDDING ME! WE PUT OUR NECKS OUT FOR YOU GUYS, AND NOW WE'RE BENCHED?
YOU THINK YOU'D BE USED TO IT BY NOW. STAY OUT OF TROUBLE-- YOU'LL LIVE LONGER.
S
3

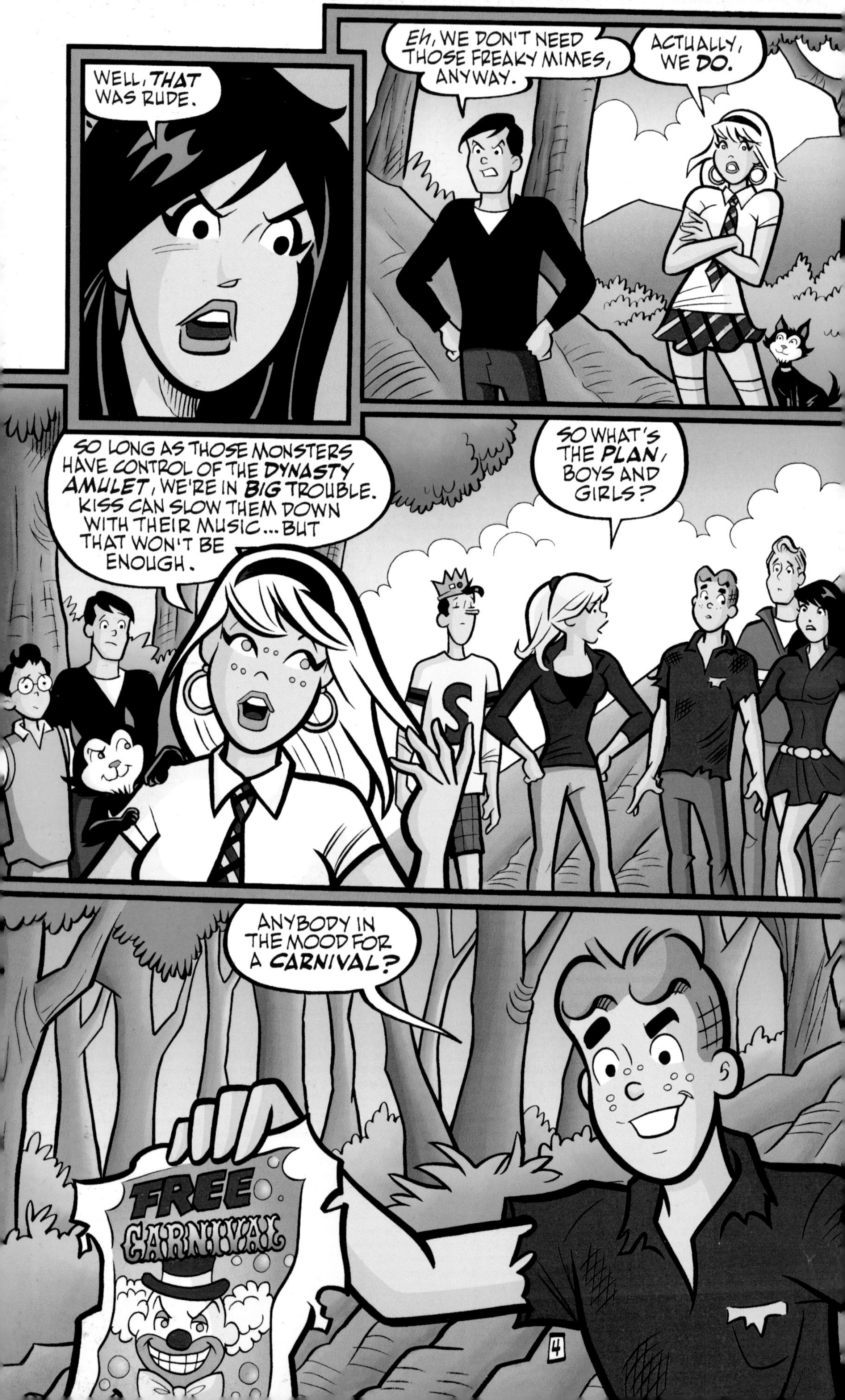
WELL, THAT WAS RUDE.
Eh, WE DON'T NEED THOSE FREAKY MIMES, ANYWAY.
ACTUALLY, WE DO.
SO LONG AS THOSE MONSTERS HAVE CONTROL OF THE DYNASTY AMULET, WE'RE IN BIG TROUBLE. KISS CAN SLOW THEM DOWN WITH THEIR MUSIC... BUT THAT WON'T BE ENOUGH.
SO WHAT'S THE PLAN, BOYS AND GIRLS?
ANYBODY IN THE MOOD FOR A CARNIVAL?
FREE CARNIVAL
4

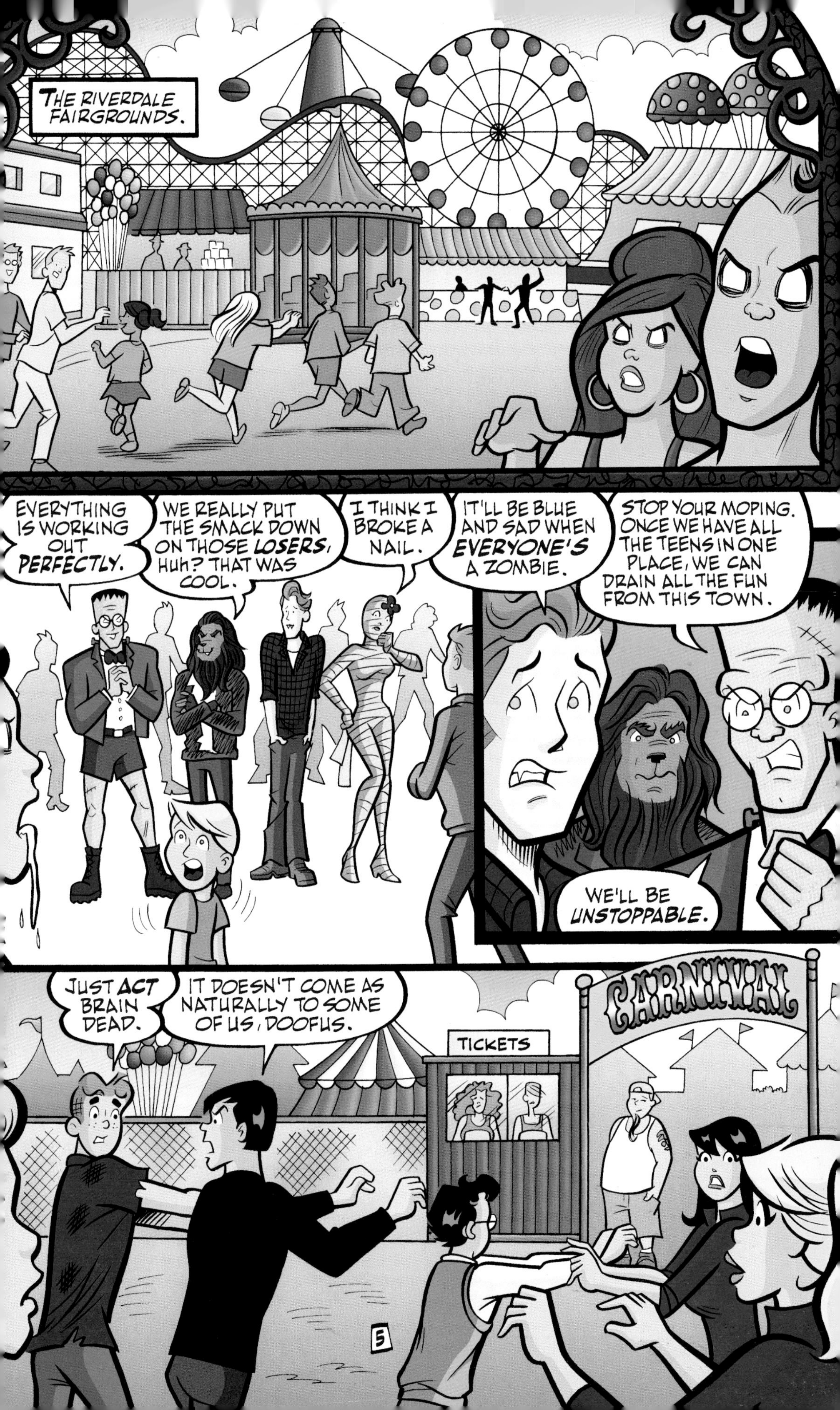

THE RIVERDALE FAIRGROUNDS.
EVERYTHING IS WORKING OUT PERFECTLY.
WE REALLY PUT THE SMACK DOWN ON THOSE LOSERS, HUH? THAT WAS COOL.
I THINK I BROKE A NAIL.
IT'LL BE BLUE AND SAD WHEN EVERYONE'S A ZOMBIE.
STOP YOUR MOPING. ONCE WE HAVE ALL THE TEENS IN ONE PLACE, WE CAN DRAIN ALL THE FUN FROM THIS TOWN.
WE'LL BE UNSTOPPABLE.
JUST ACT BRAIN DEAD.
IT DOESN'T COME AS NATURALLY TO SOME OF US, DOOFUS.
CARNIVAL
TICKETS

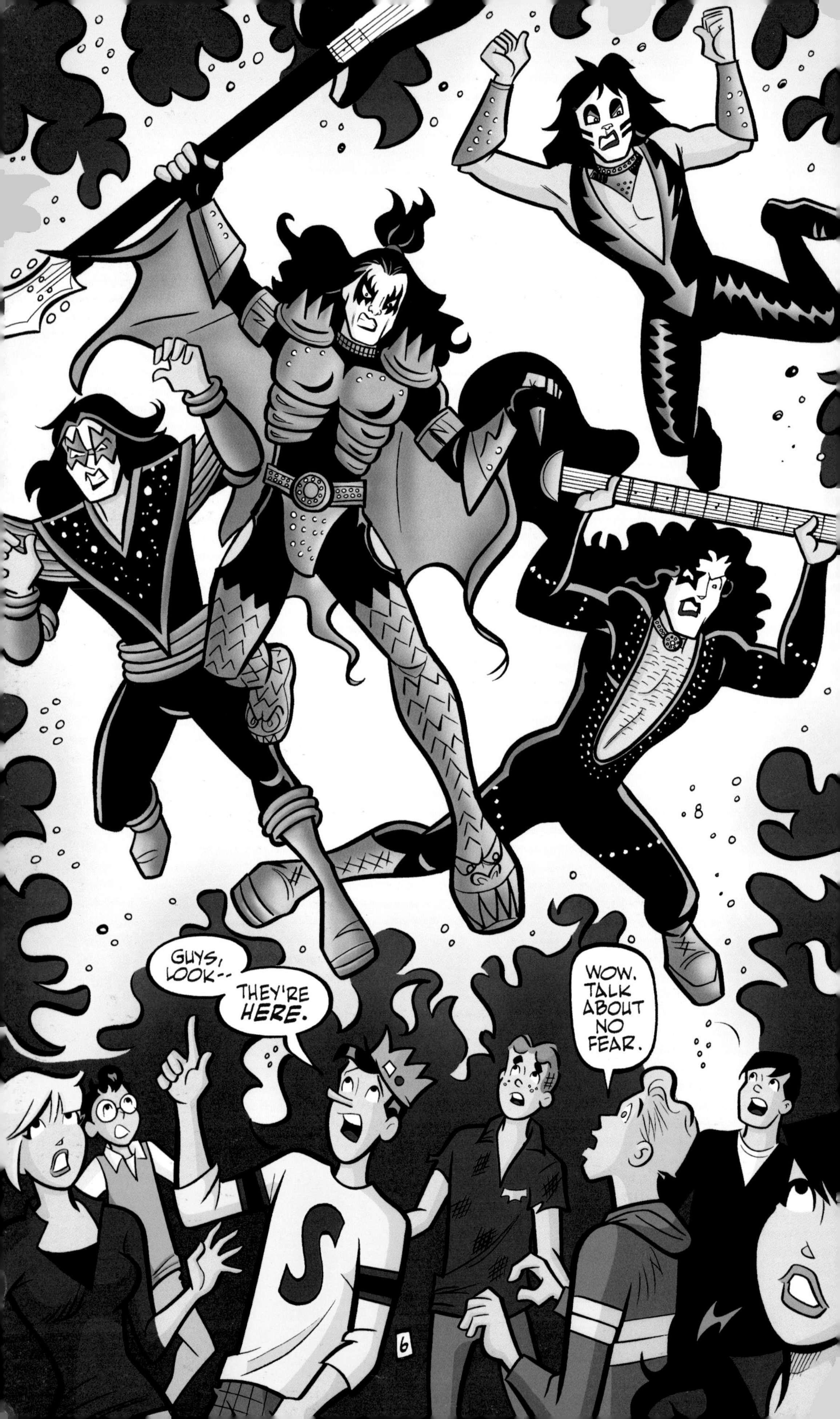
GUYS, LOOK--
THEY'RE HERE.
WOW. TALK ABOUT NO FEAR.
6

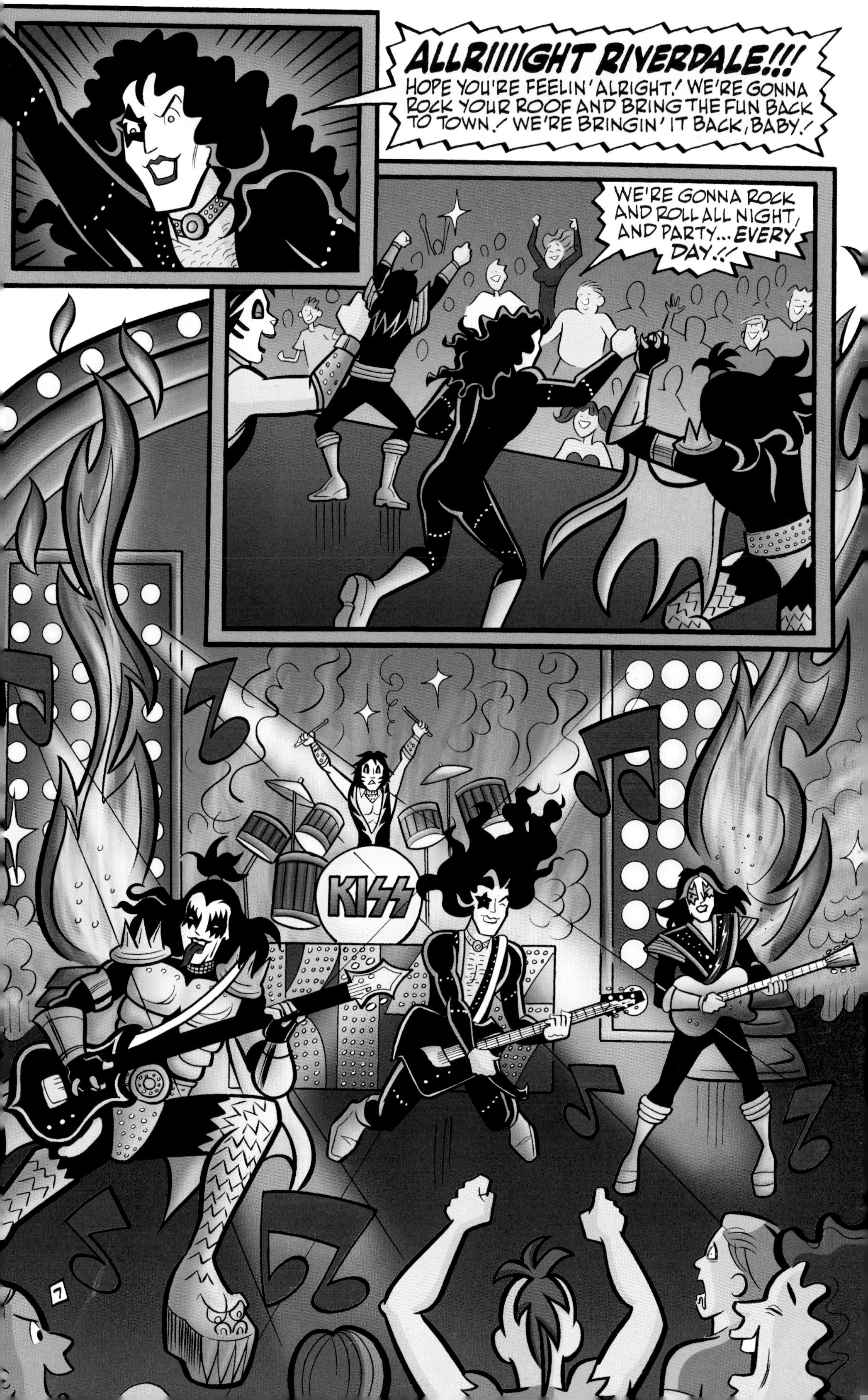
ALLRIIIIGHT RIVERDALE!!! HOPE YOU'RE FEELIN' ALRIGHT! WE'RE GONNA ROCK YOUR ROOF AND BRING THE FUN BACK TO TOWN! WE'RE BRINGIN' IT BACK, BABY!
WE'RE GONNA ROCK AND ROLL ALL NIGHT, AND PARTY... EVERY DAY!!
KISS
7

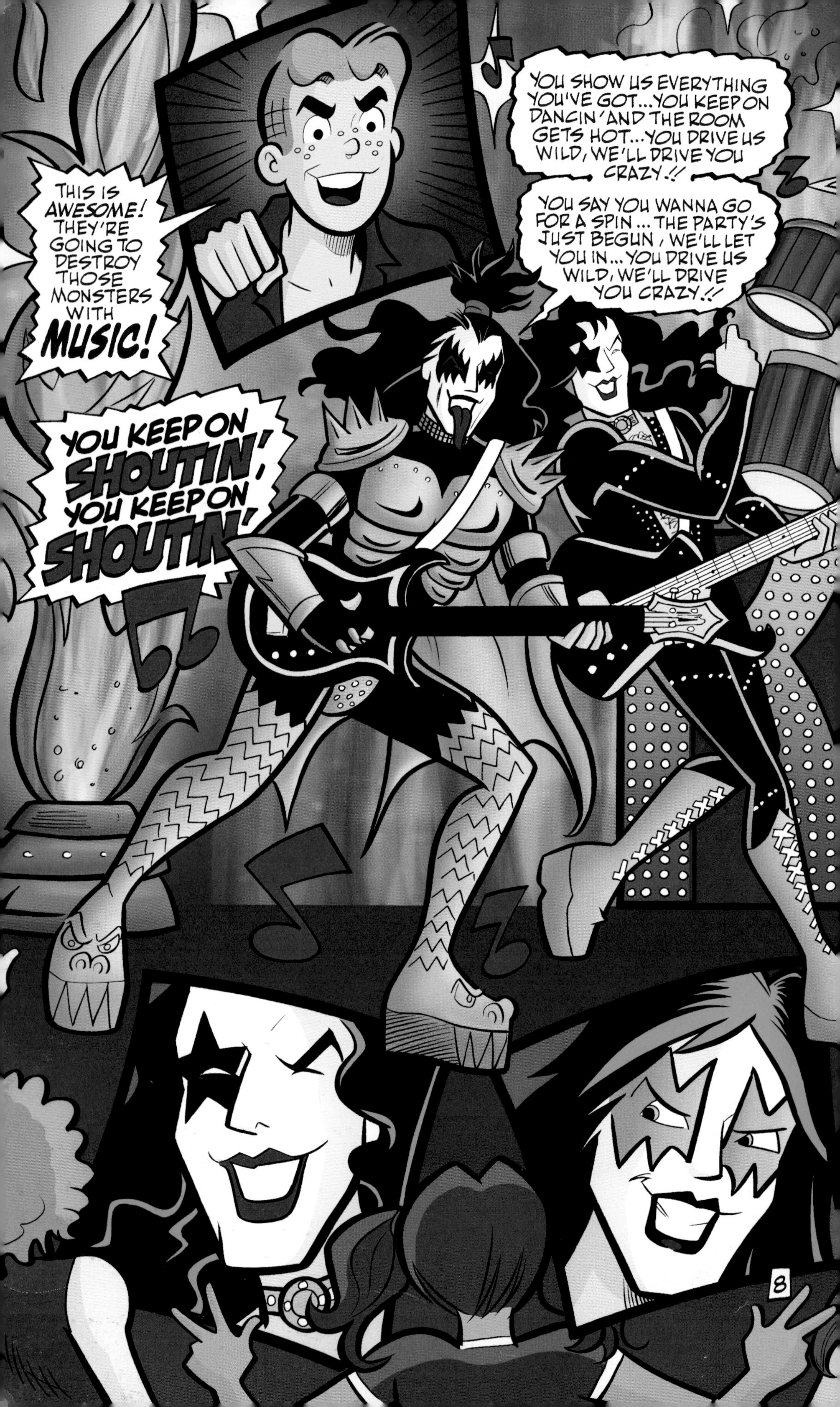
THIS IS AWESOME! THEY'RE GOING TO DESTROY THOSE MONSTERS WITH MUSIC!
YOU SHOW US EVERYTHING YOU'VE GOT... YOU KEEP ON DANCIN' AND THE ROOM GETS HOT... YOU DRIVE US WILD, WE'LL DRIVE YOU CRAZY!!
YOU SAY YOU WANNA GO FOR A SPIN... THE PARTY'S JUST BEGUN, WE'LL LET YOU IN... YOU DRIVE US WILD, WE'LL DRIVE YOU CRAZY!!
YOU KEEP ON SHOUTIN', YOU KEEP ON SHOUTIN'

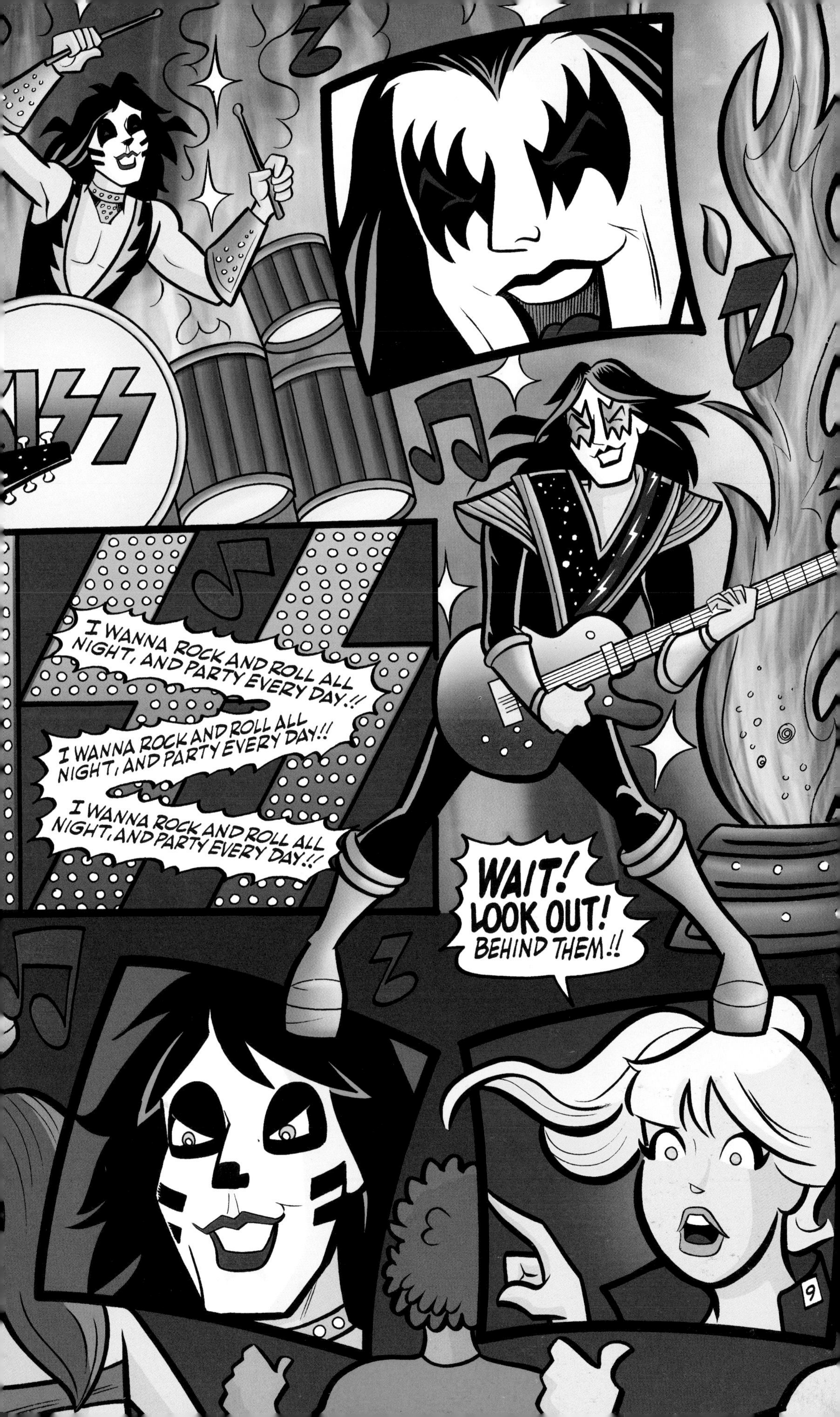
KISS
I WANNA ROCK AND ROLL ALL NIGHT, AND PARTY EVERY DAY!!
I WANNA ROCK AND ROLL ALL NIGHT, AND PARTY EVERY DAY!!
I WANNA ROCK AND ROLL ALL NIGHT, AND PARTY EVERY DAY!!
WAIT! LOOK OUT! BEHIND THEM!!

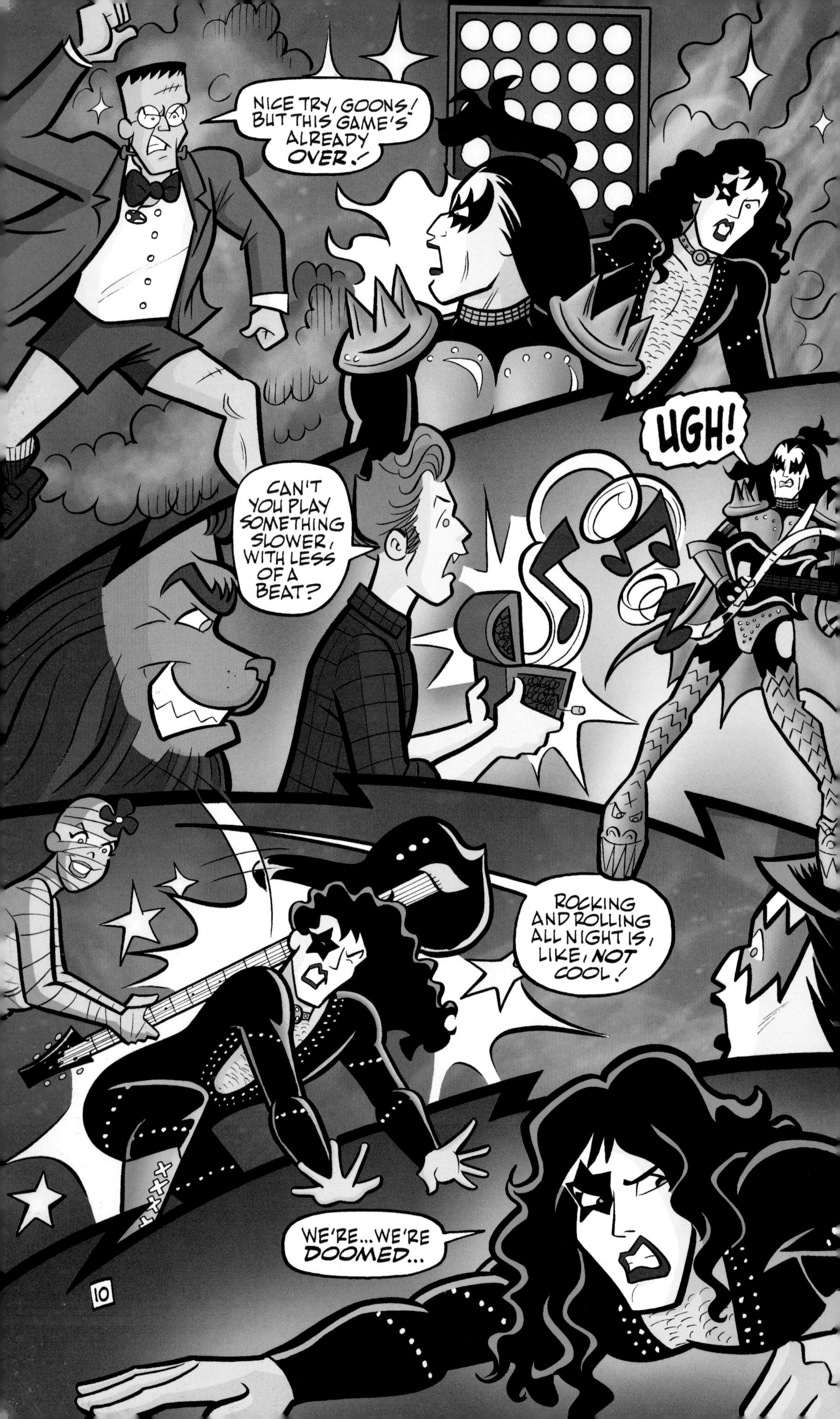
NICE TRY, GOONS! BUT THIS GAME'S ALREADY OVER.!
CAN'T YOU PLAY SOMETHING SLOWER, WITH LESS OF A BEAT?
UGH!
ROCKING AND ROLLING ALL NIGHT IS, LIKE, NOT COOL!
WE'RE... WE'RE DOOMED...
10

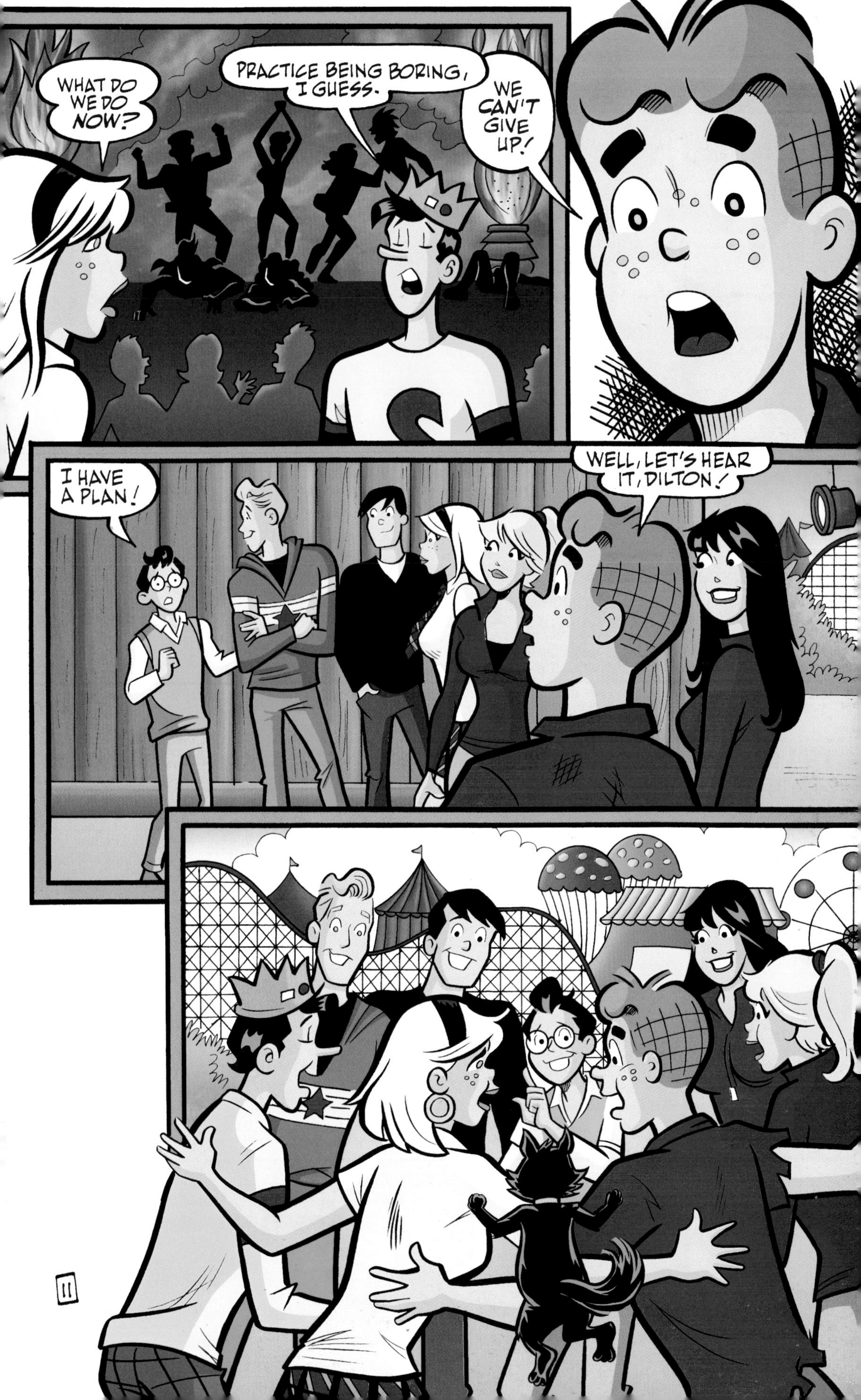
WHAT DO WE DO NOW?
PRACTICE BEING BORING, I GUESS.
WE CAN'T GIVE UP!
I HAVE A PLAN!
WELL, LET'S HEAR IT, DILTON!

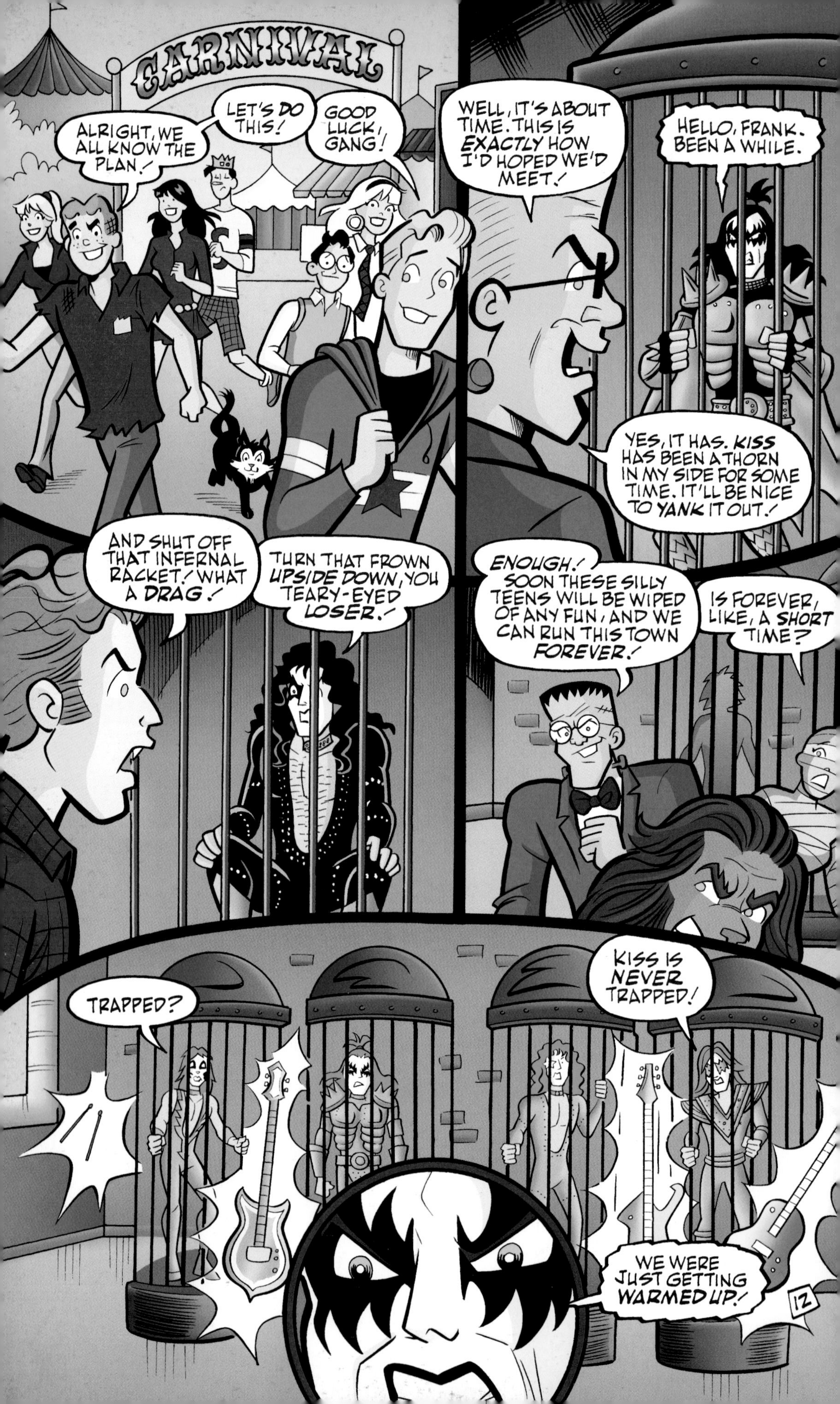
CARNIVAL
ALRIGHT, WE ALL KNOW THE PLAN!
LET'S DO THIS!
GOOD LUCK, GANG!
WELL, IT'S ABOUT TIME. THIS IS EXACTLY HOW I'D HOPED WE'D MEET!
HELLO, FRANK. BEEN A WHILE.
YES, IT HAS. KISS HAS BEEN A THORN IN MY SIDE FOR SOME TIME. IT'LL BE NICE TO YANK IT OUT!
AND SHUT OFF THAT INFERNAL RACKET! WHAT A DRAG!
TURN THAT FROWN UPSIDE DOWN, YOU TEARY-EYED LOSER!
ENOUGH! SOON THESE SILLY TEENS WILL BE WIPED OF ANY FUN, AND WE CAN RUN THIS TOWN FOREVER!
IS FOREVER, LIKE, A SHORT TIME?
TRAPPED?
KISS IS NEVER TRAPPED!
WE WERE JUST GETTING WARMED UP!
12

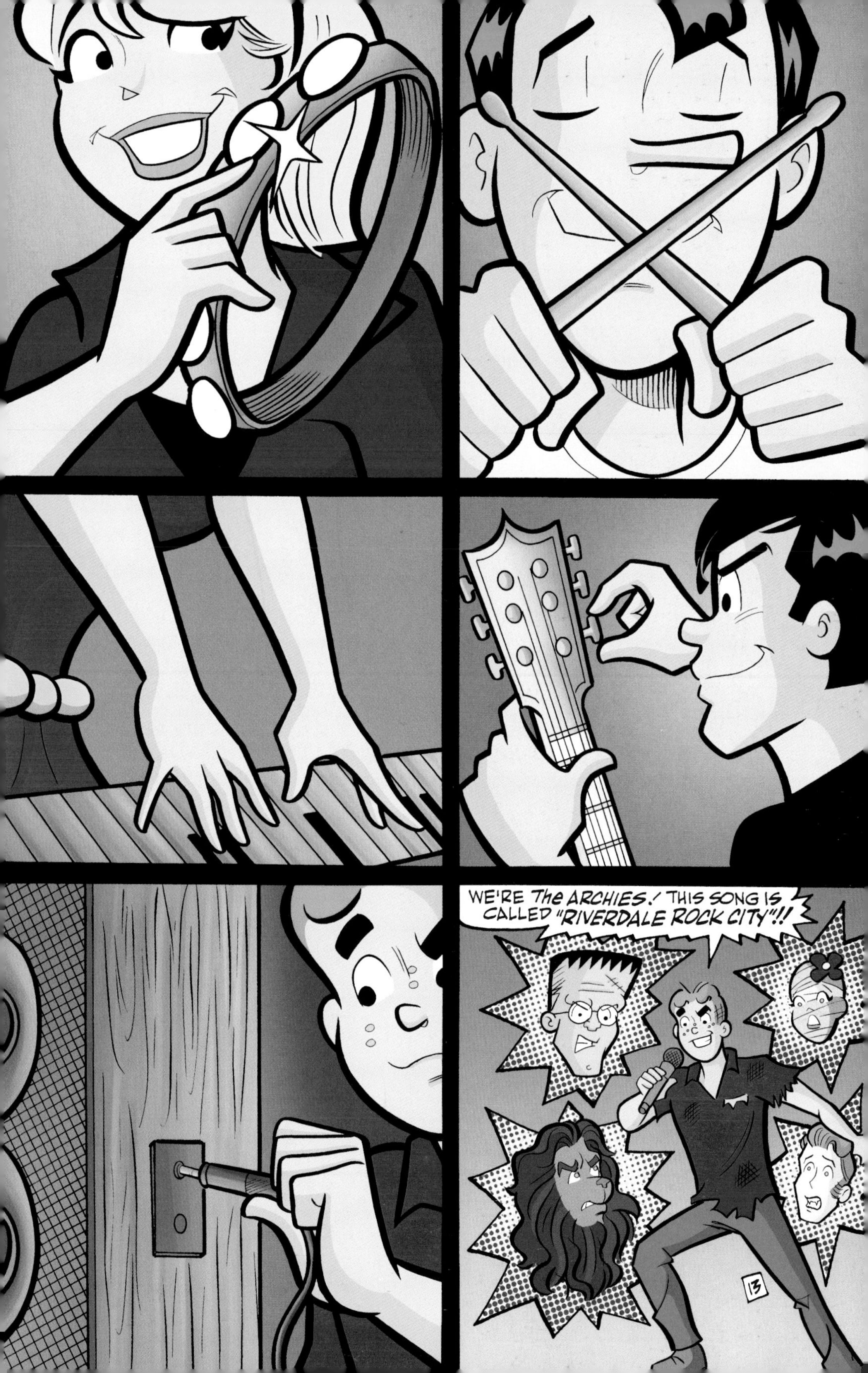
WE'RE The ARCHIES! THIS SONG IS CALLED "RIVERDALE ROCK CITY"!!
13

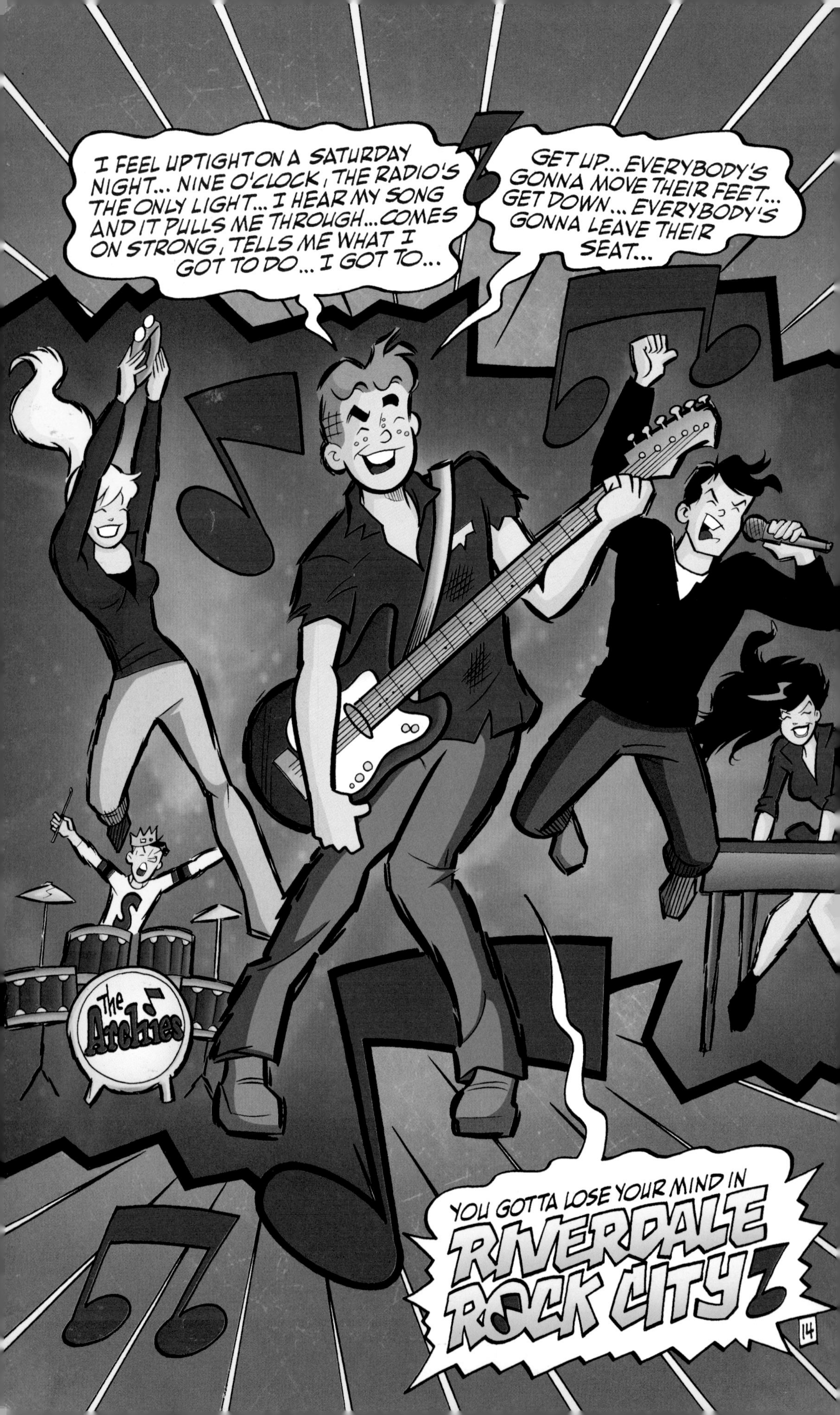

I FEEL UPTIGHT ON A SATURDAY NIGHT... NINE O'CLOCK, THE RADIO'S THE ONLY LIGHT... I HEAR MY SONG AND IT PULLS ME THROUGH... COMES ON STRONG, TELLS ME WHAT I GOT TO DO... I GOT TO...
GET UP... EVERYBODY'S GONNA MOVE THEIR FEET... GET DOWN... EVERYBODY'S GONNA LEAVE THEIR SEAT...
The Archies
YOU GOTTA LOSE YOUR MIND IN RIVERDALE ROCK CITY

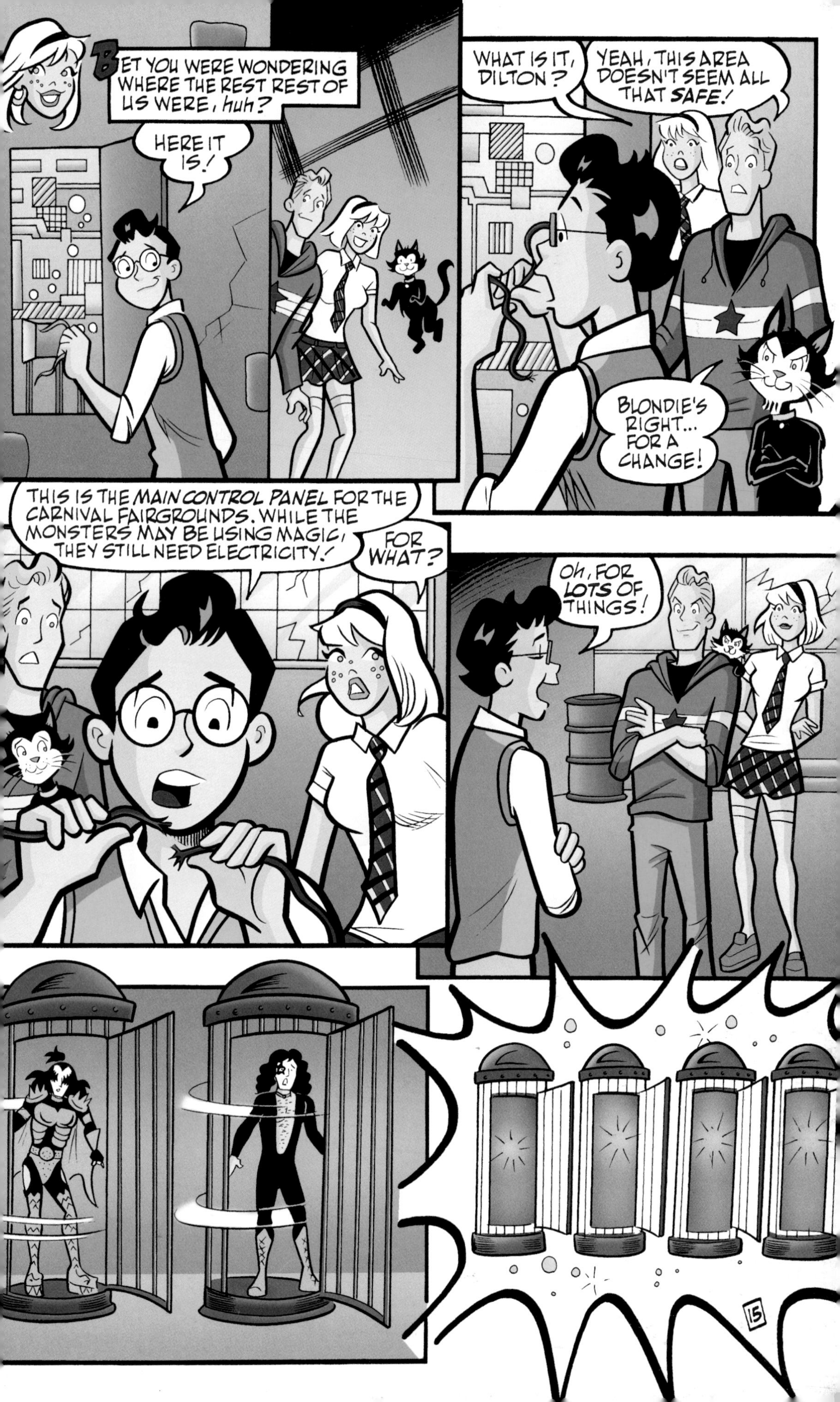
BET YOU WERE WONDERING WHERE THE REST REST OF US WERE, huh?
HERE IT IS!
WHAT IS IT, DILTON?
YEAH, THIS AREA DOESN'T SEEM ALL THAT SAFE!
BLONDIE'S RIGHT... FOR A CHANGE!
THIS IS THE MAIN CONTROL PANEL FOR THE CARNIVAL FAIRGROUNDS. WHILE THE MONSTERS MAY BE USING MAGIC, THEY STILL NEED ELECTRICITY!
FOR WHAT?
Oh, FOR LOTS OF THINGS!
15

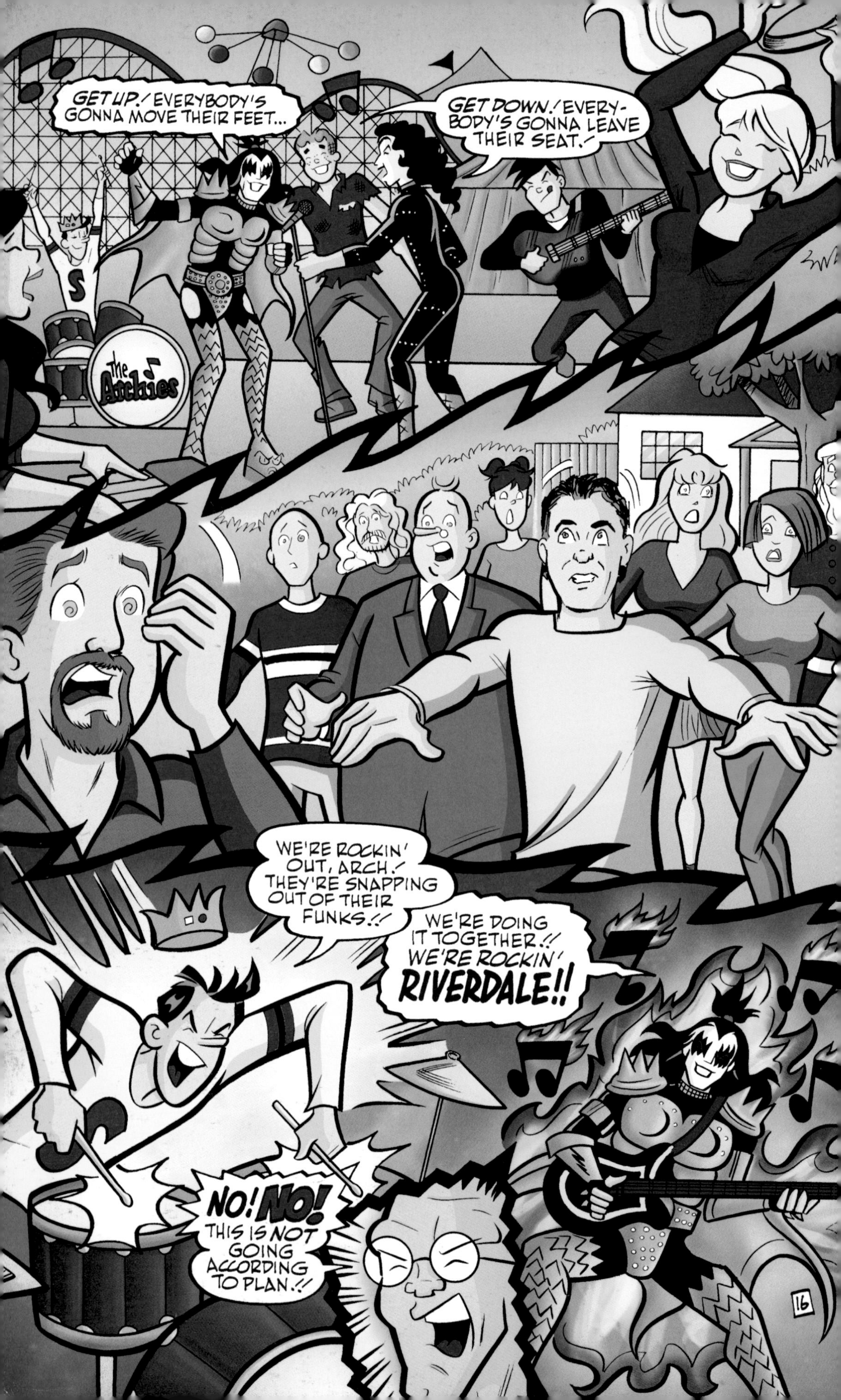

GET UP! EVERYBODY'S GONNA MOVE THEIR FEET...
GET DOWN! EVERYBODY'S GONNA LEAVE THEIR SEAT!
The Archies
WE'RE ROCKIN' OUT, ARCH! THEY'RE SNAPPING OUT OF THEIR FUNKS!!
WE'RE DOING IT TOGETHER!! WE'RE ROCKIN' RIVERDALE!!
NO! NO! THIS IS NOT GOING ACCORDING TO PLAN!!

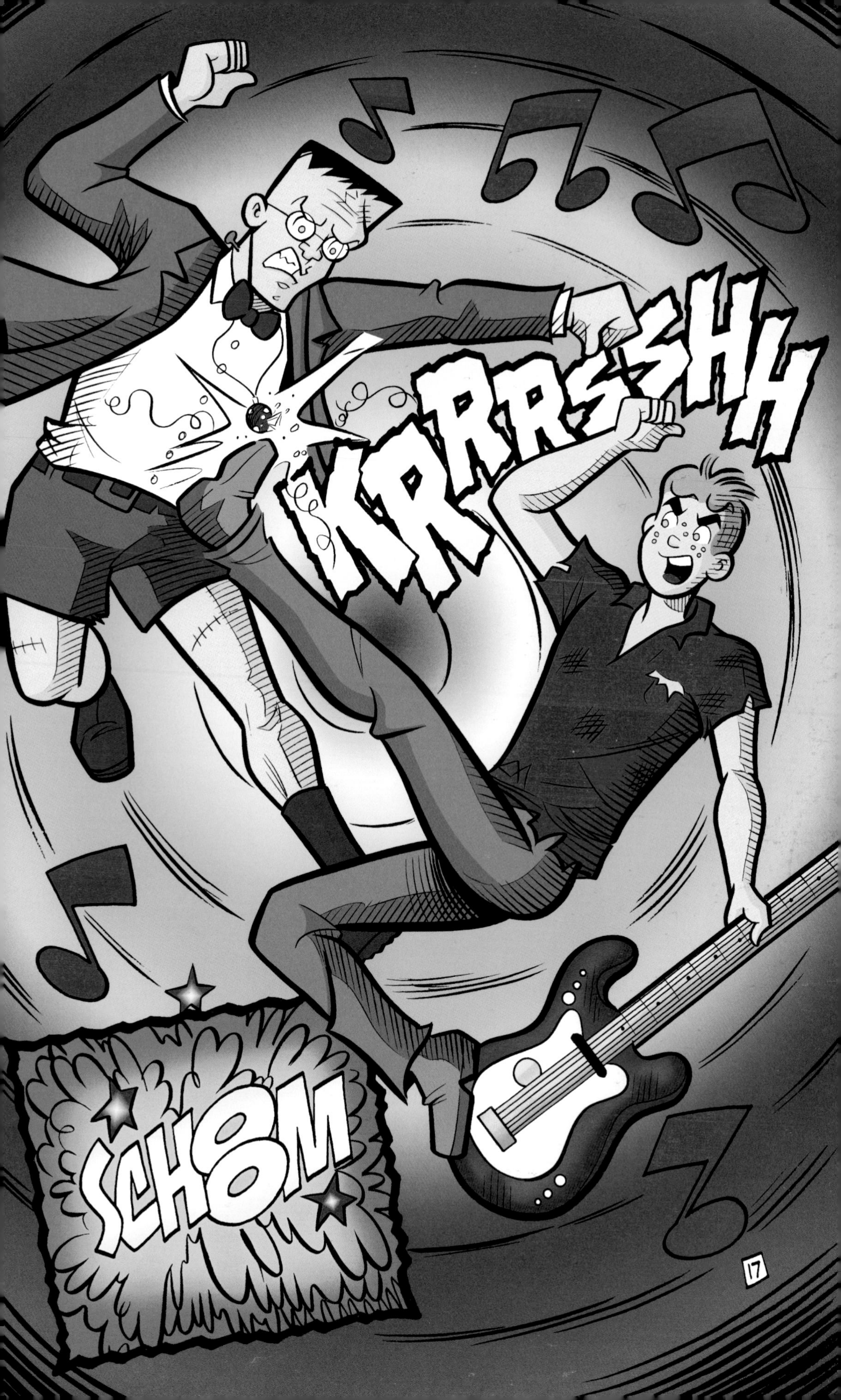
KRRRSSHH
SCHOOM

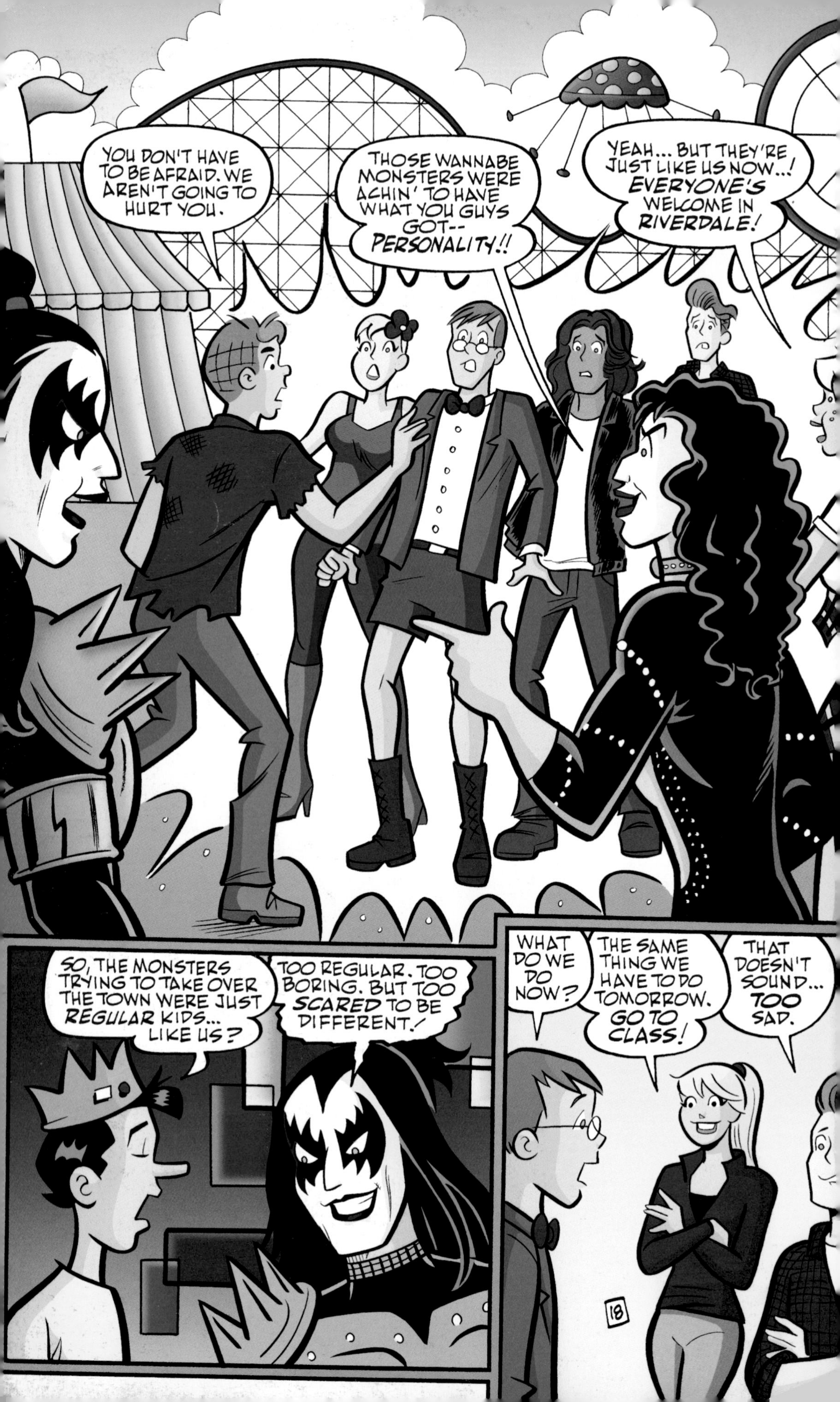
YOU DON'T HAVE TO BE AFRAID. WE AREN'T GOING TO HURT YOU.
THOSE WANNABE MONSTERS WERE ACHIN' TO HAVE WHAT YOU GUYS GOT-- PERSONALITY!!
YEAH... BUT THEY'RE JUST LIKE US NOW...! EVERYONE'S WELCOME IN RIVERDALE!
SO, THE MONSTERS TRYING TO TAKE OVER THE TOWN WERE JUST REGULAR KIDS... LIKE US?
TOO REGULAR. TOO BORING. BUT TOO SCARED TO BE DIFFERENT.!
WHAT DO WE DO NOW?
THE SAME THING WE HAVE TO DO TOMORROW. GO TO CLASS!
THAT DOESN'T SOUND... TOO SAD.
18

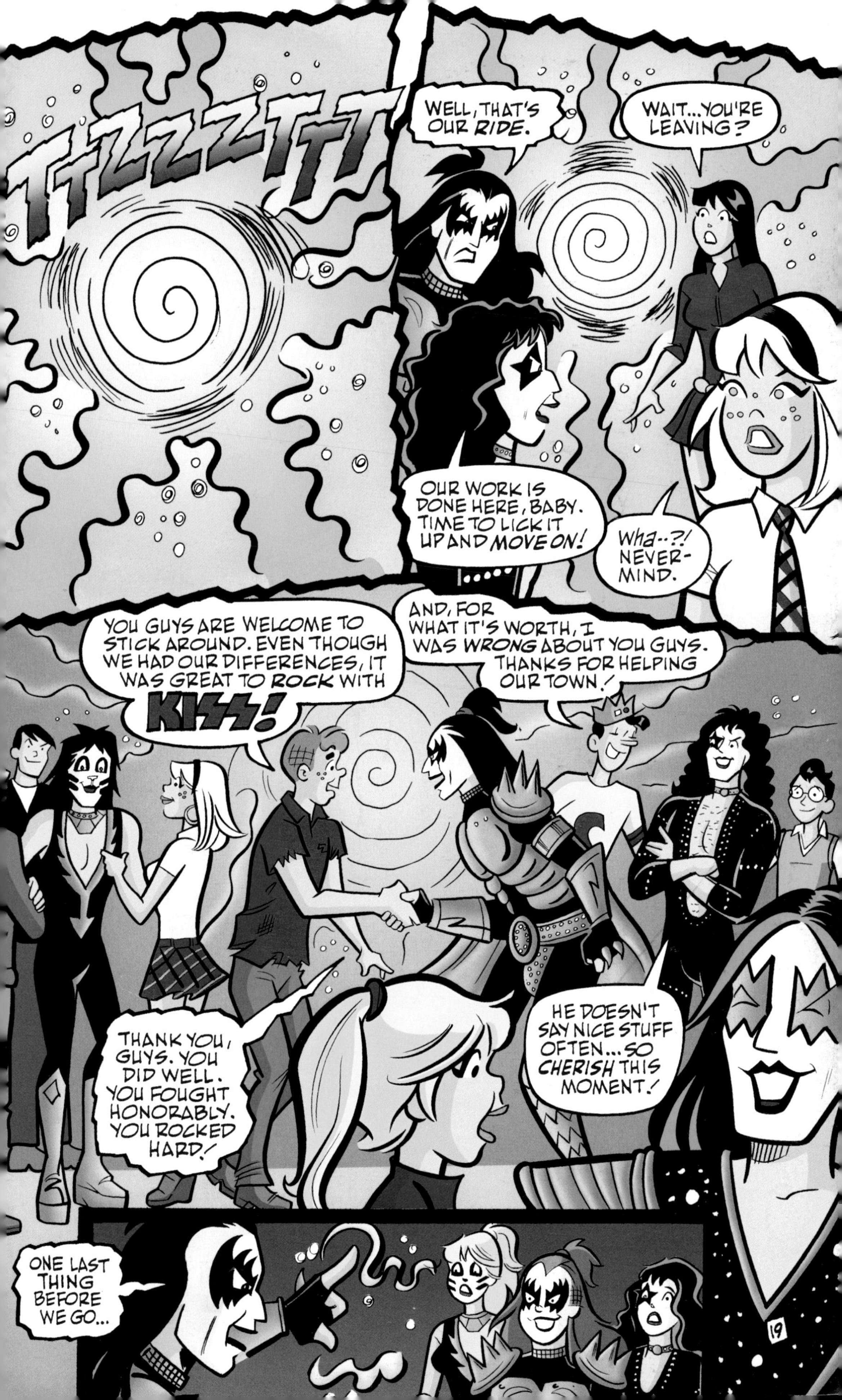
TTZZZTTT
WELL, THAT'S OUR RIDE.
WAIT...YOU'RE LEAVING?
OUR WORK IS DONE HERE, BABY. TIME TO LICK IT UP AND MOVE ON!
Wha--?! NEVER-MIND.
YOU GUYS ARE WELCOME TO STICK AROUND. EVEN THOUGH WE HAD OUR DIFFERENCES, IT WAS GREAT TO ROCK WITH KISS!
AND, FOR WHAT IT'S WORTH, I WAS WRONG ABOUT YOU GUYS. THANKS FOR HELPING OUR TOWN!
THANK YOU, GUYS. YOU DID WELL. YOU FOUGHT HONORABLY. YOU ROCKED HARD!
HE DOESN'T SAY NICE STUFF OFTEN... SO CHERISH THIS MOMENT!
ONE LAST THING BEFORE WE GO...

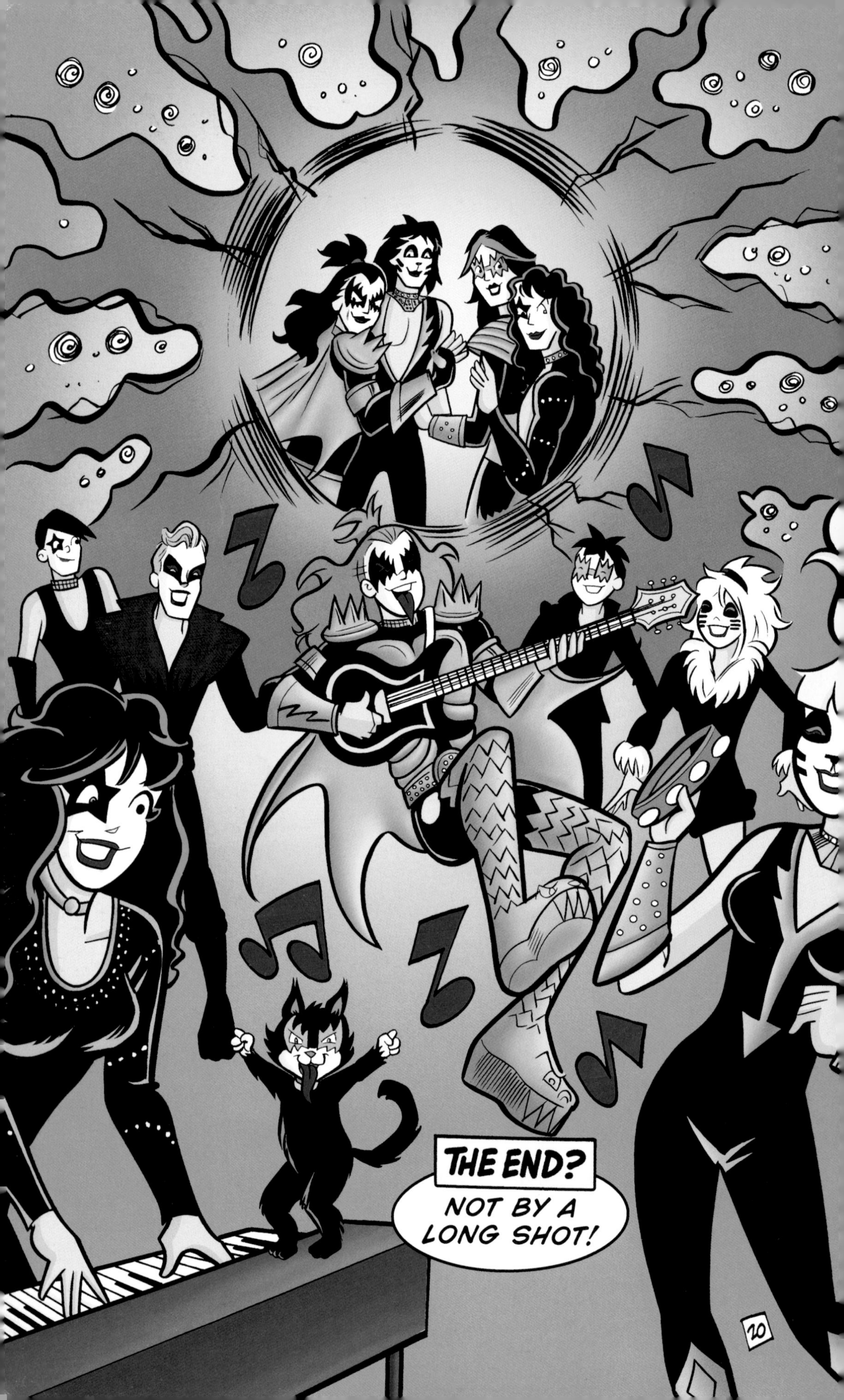
THE END?
NOT BY A LONG SHOT!

Archie® MEETS KISS®

SKETCHBOOK

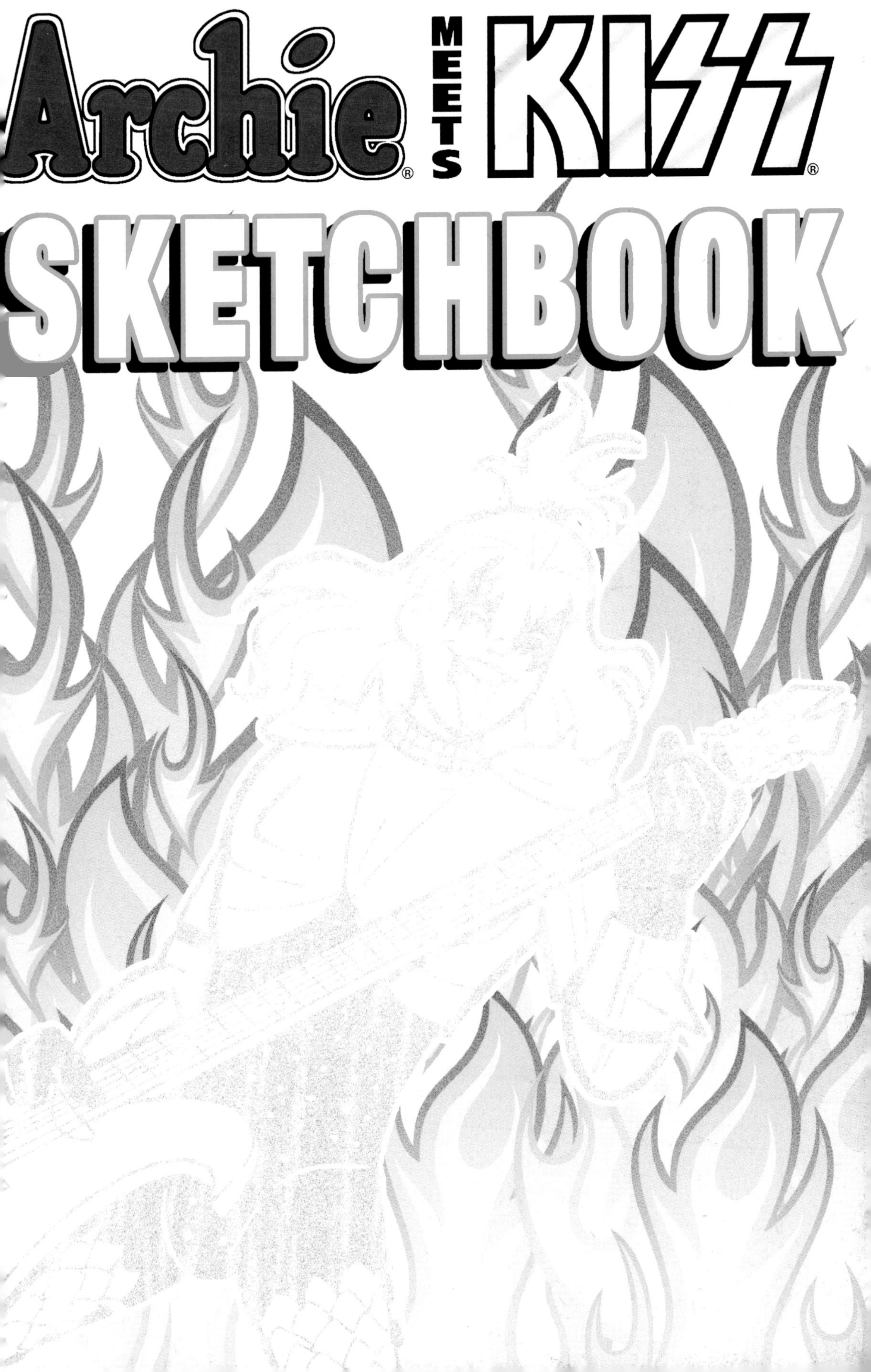

the very first sketch I did when I learned about the project.

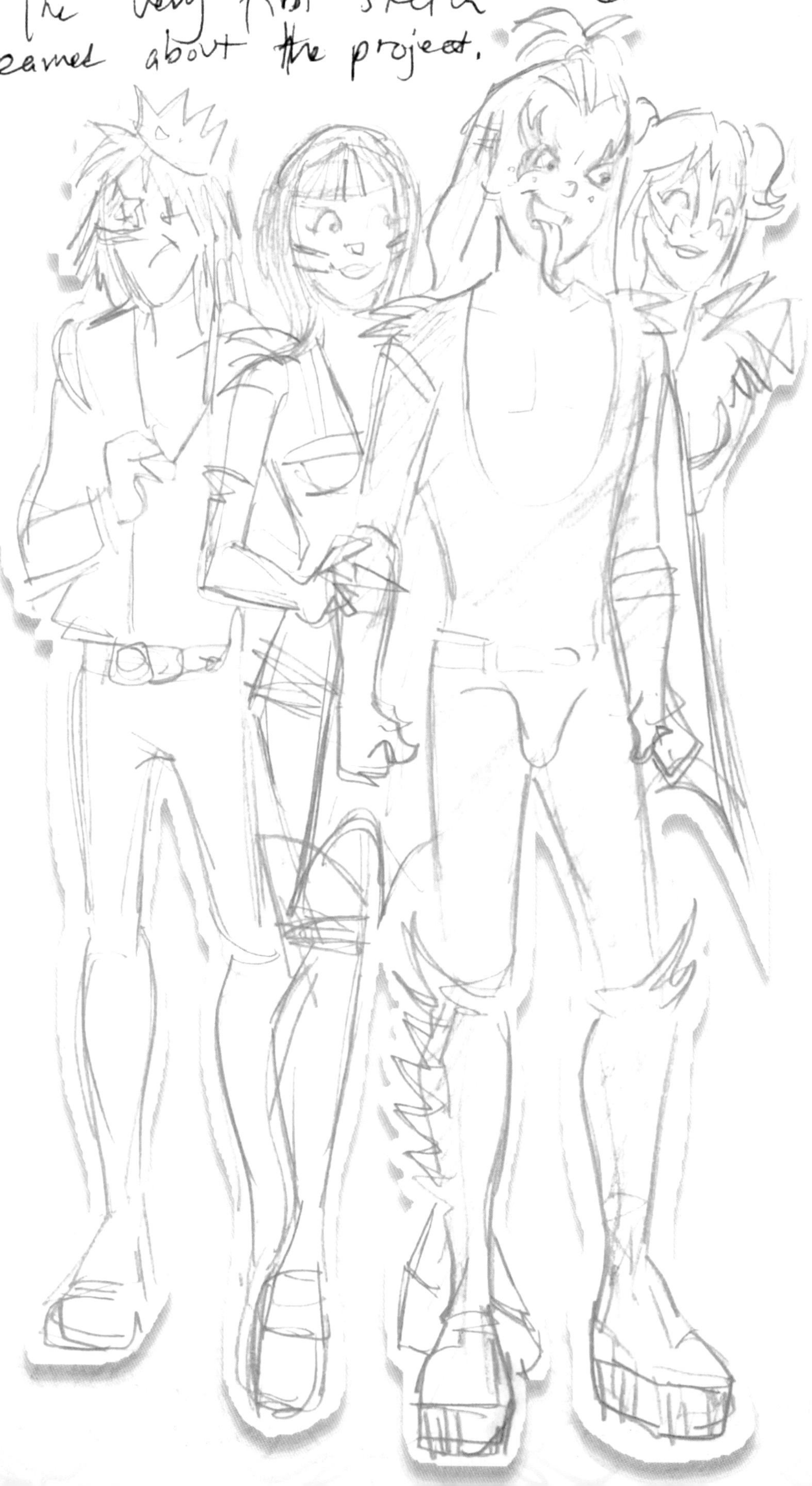

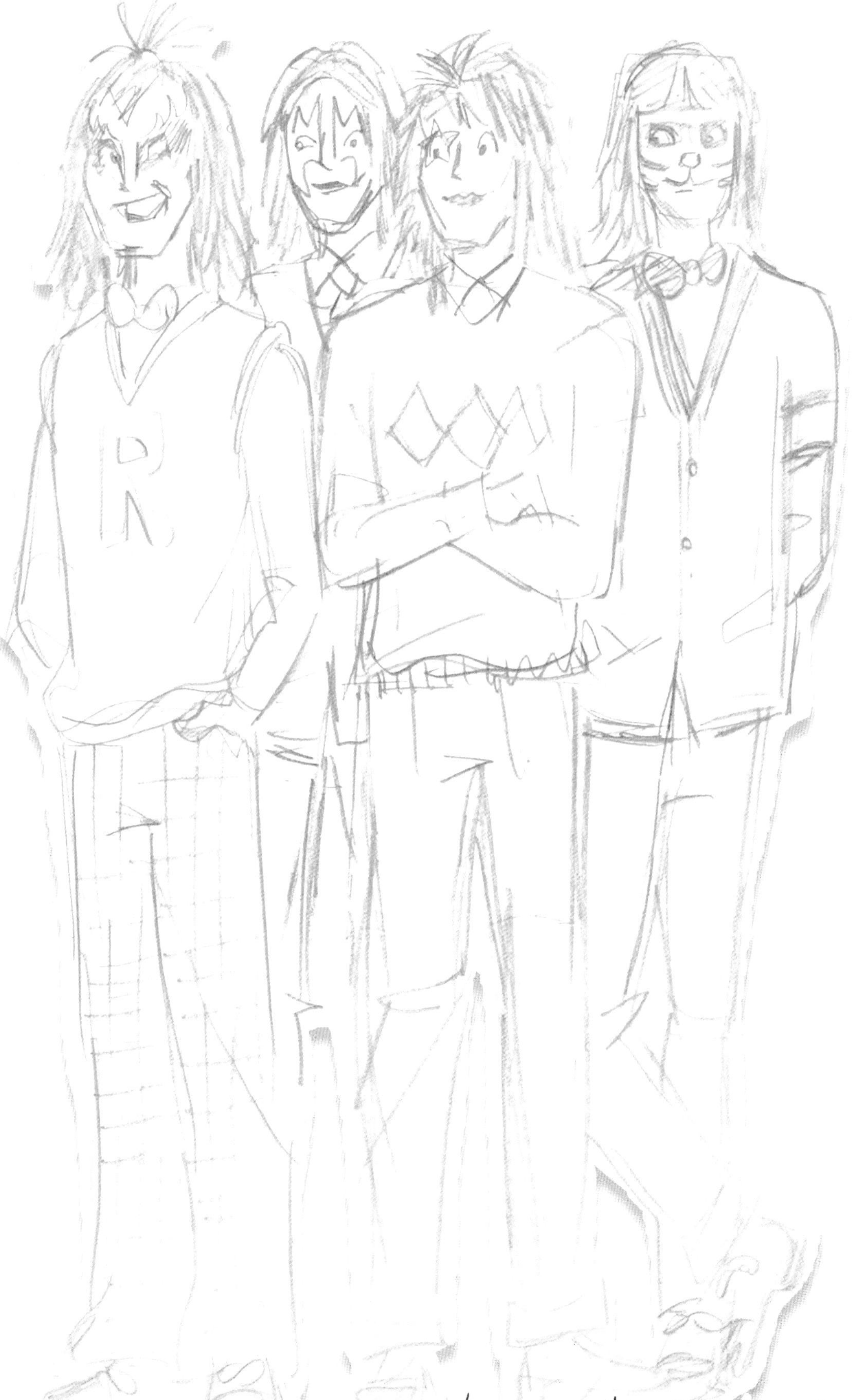
R

There was no story written yet, so I was "imagining" different scenarios!

an early sketch, when we didnt yet have a storyline

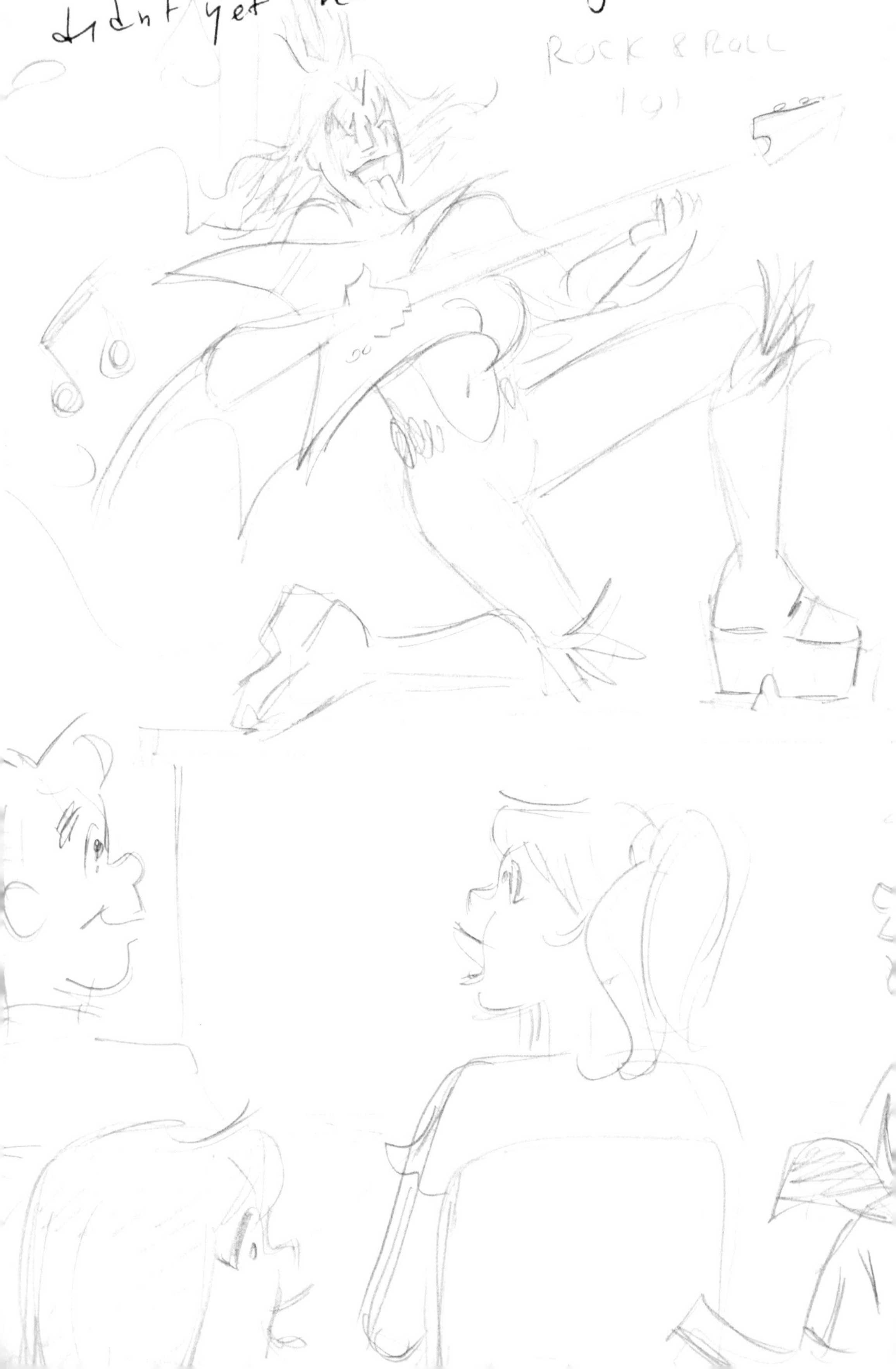
ROCK & ROLL 101

another goofy
idea very
early on --

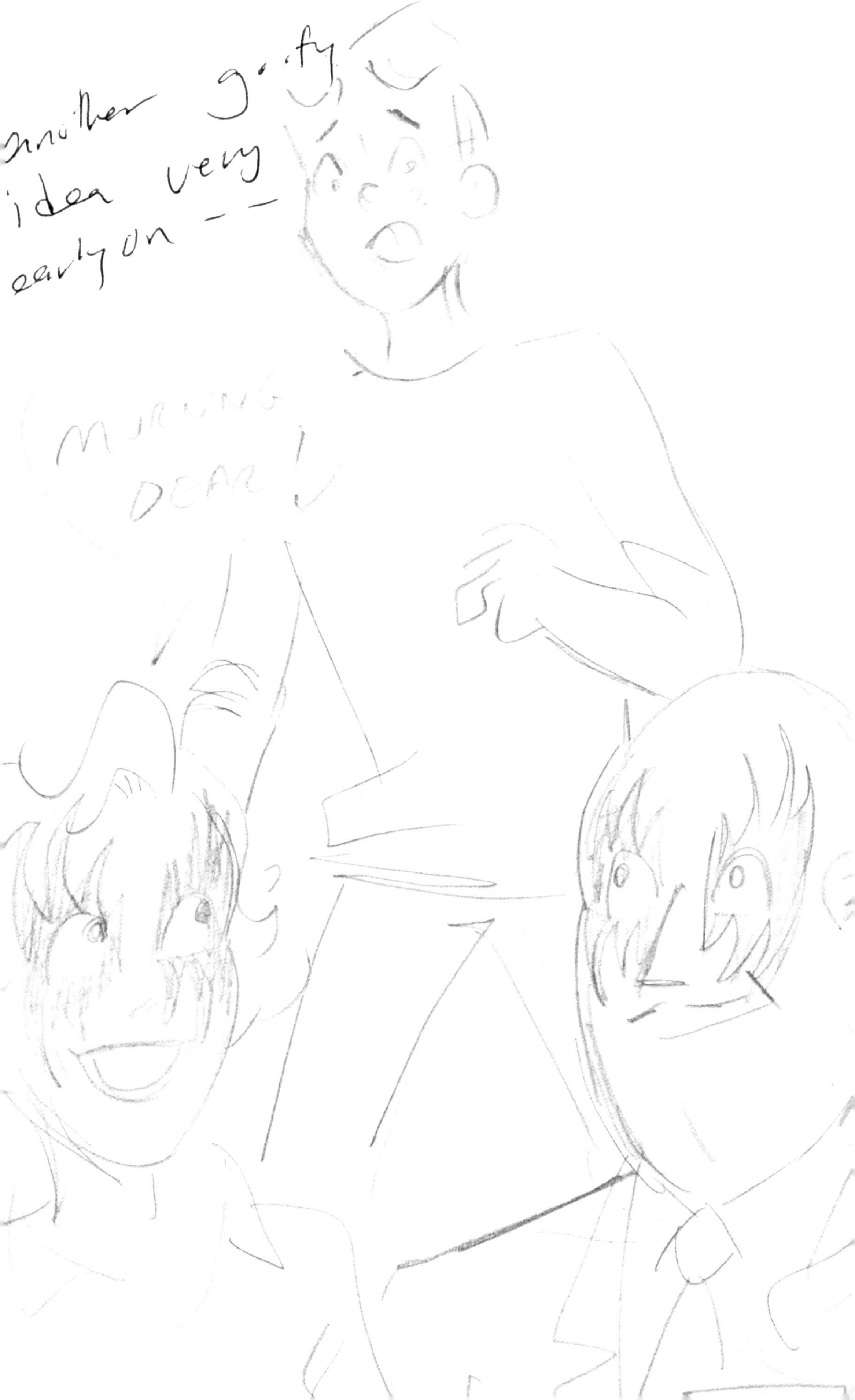
MORNING DEAR!

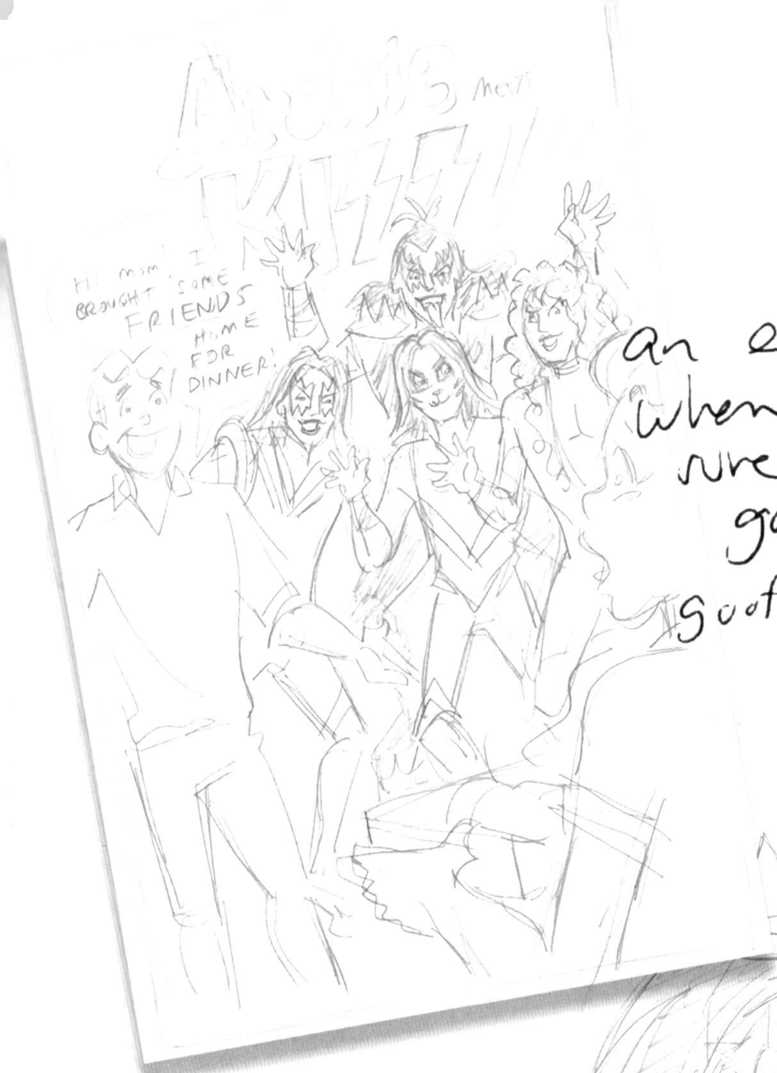
Meets
Hi mom, I brought some FRIENDS home for dinner!

an early approach when I wasn't sure if we were going for the goofy approach (we didn't)

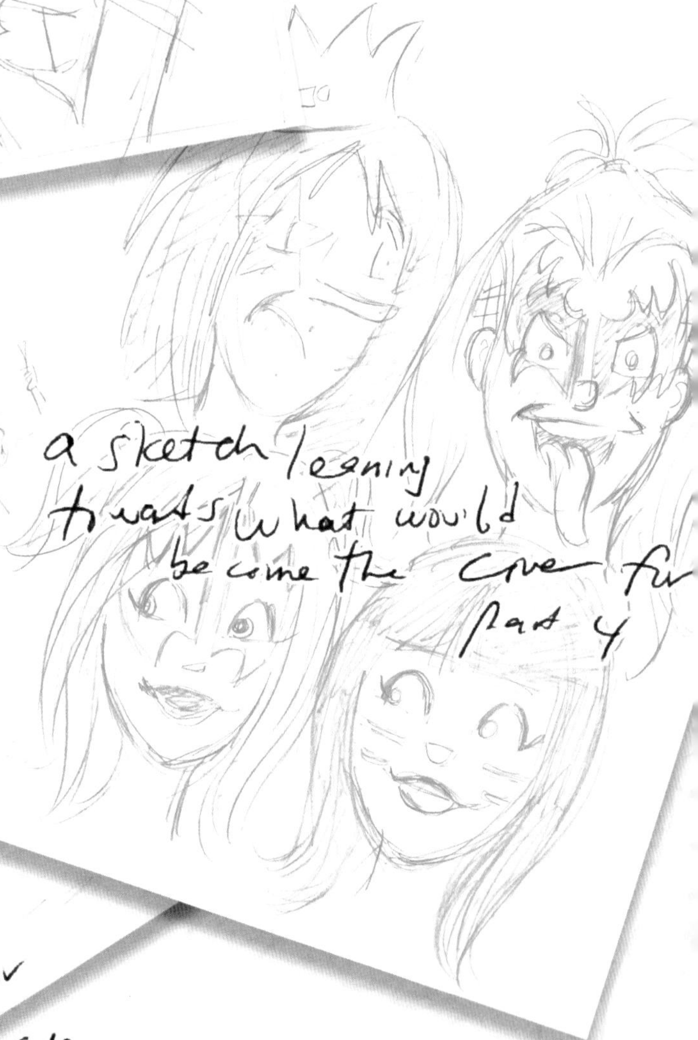

a sketch leaning towards what would become the cover for part 4

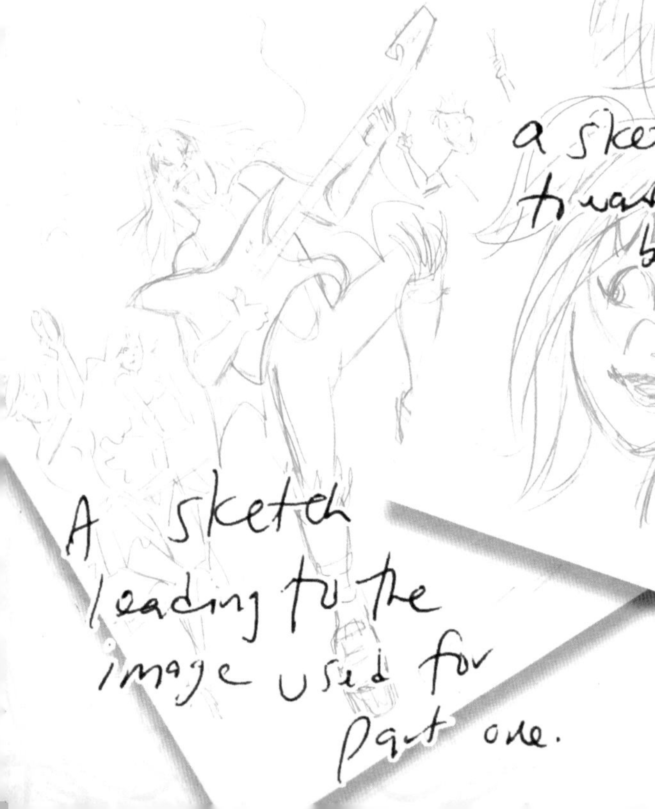

A sketch leading to the image used for part one.

Close version to what became cover for part 1

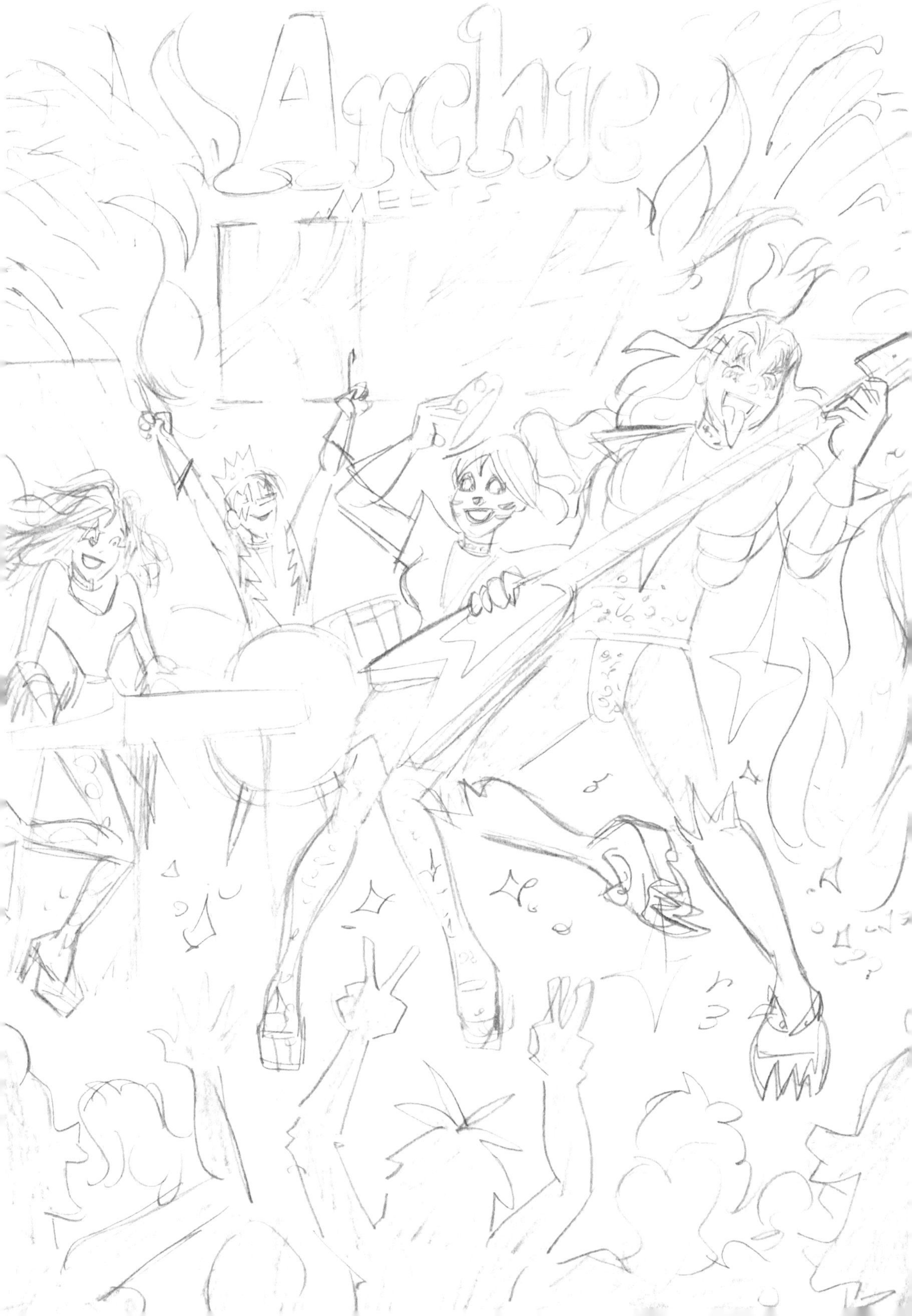
Archie
MEETS

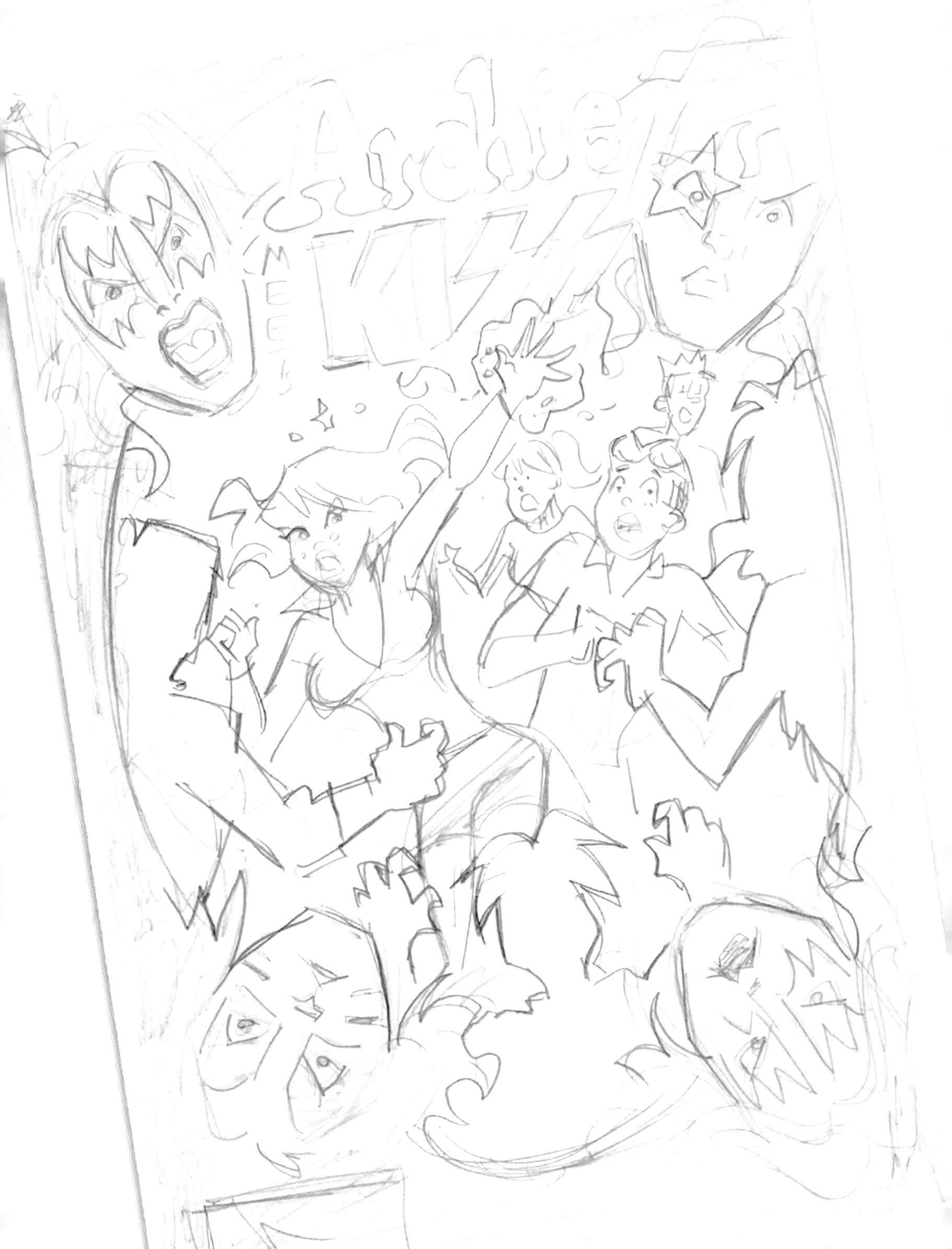
Archie
MEETS

sketch for part 2
– damn UPC box
ruined the design!

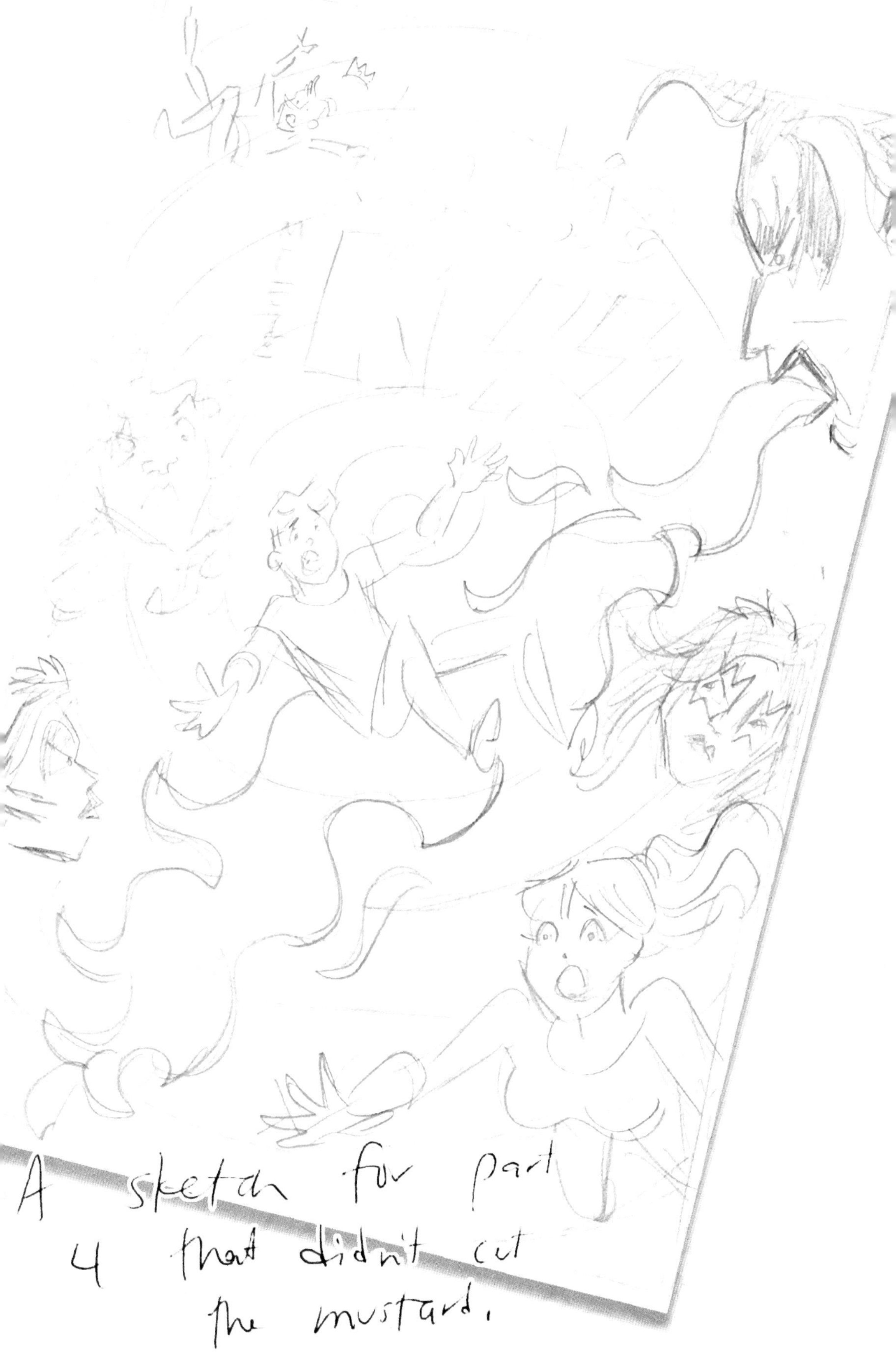

A sketch for part 4 that didn't cut the mustard.

Another idea I liked!

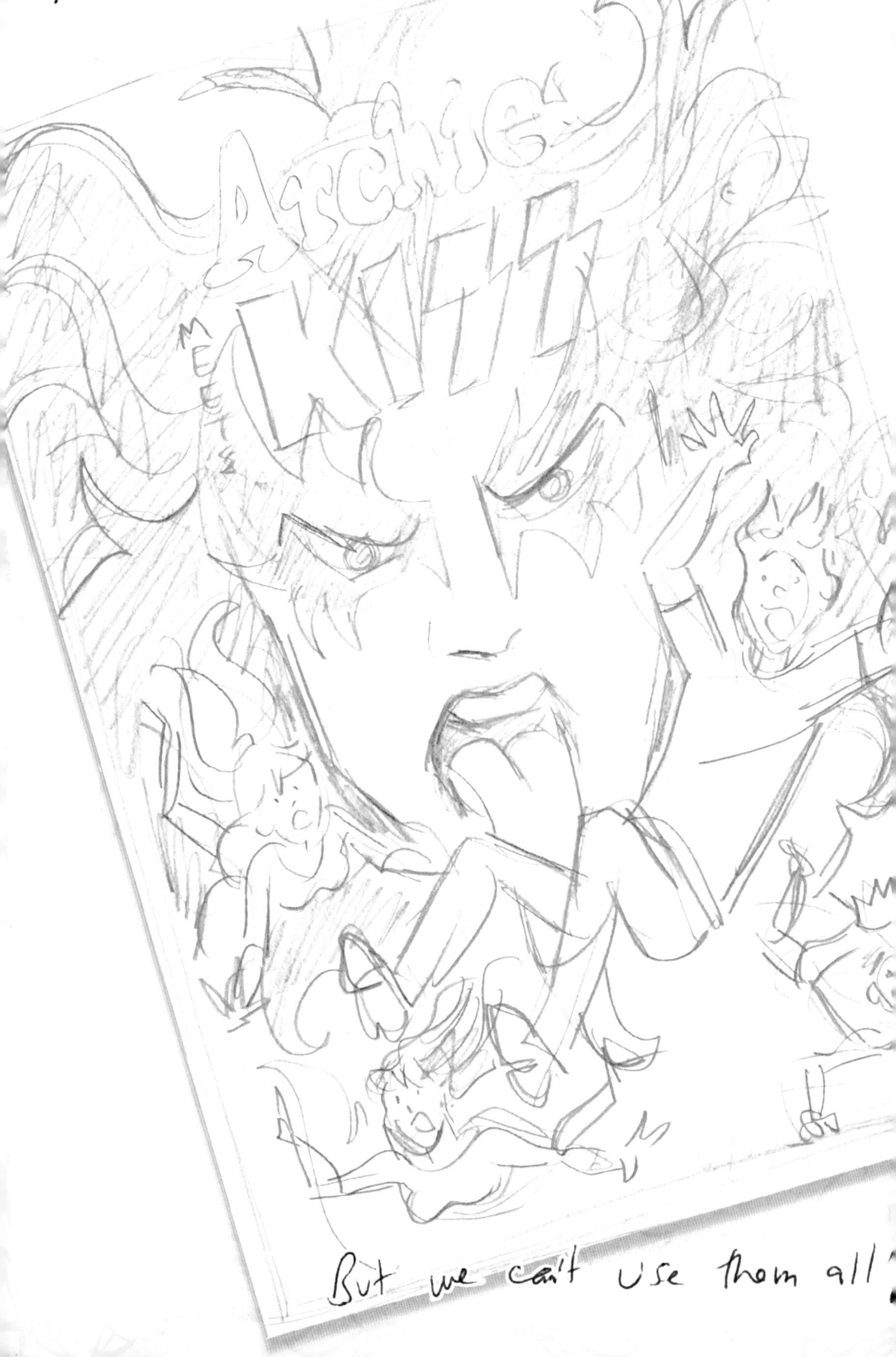
Archie
MEETS
KISS

But we can't use them all!

This is my favorite idea that didn't get used. It's a variation on the Destroyer album. I'd love to do it in the same style as the original cover. Maybe I'll still get the chance!

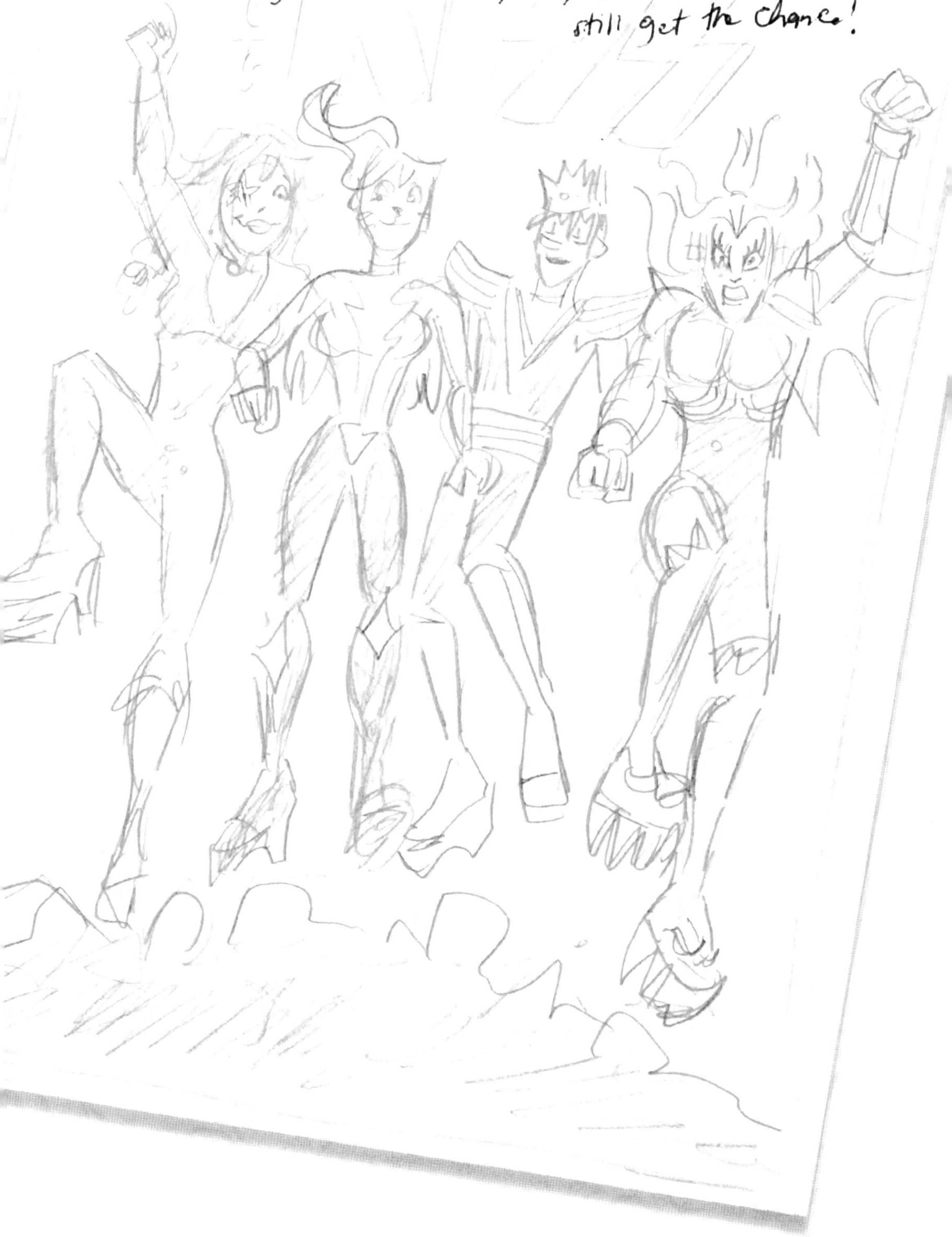

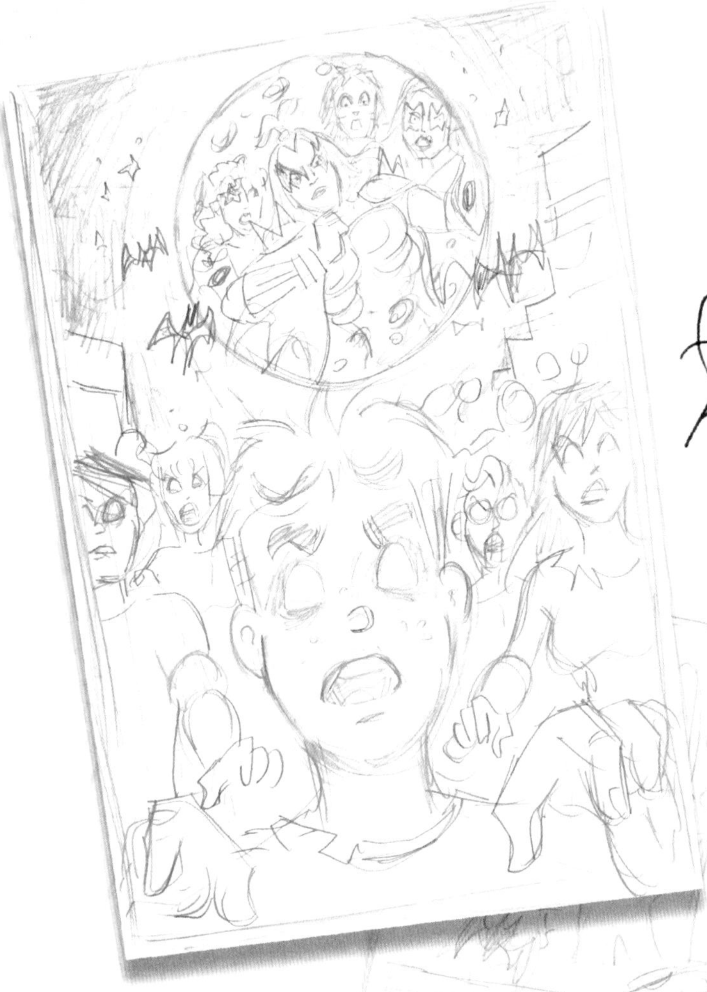

first sketch for Archie/Kiss part 3

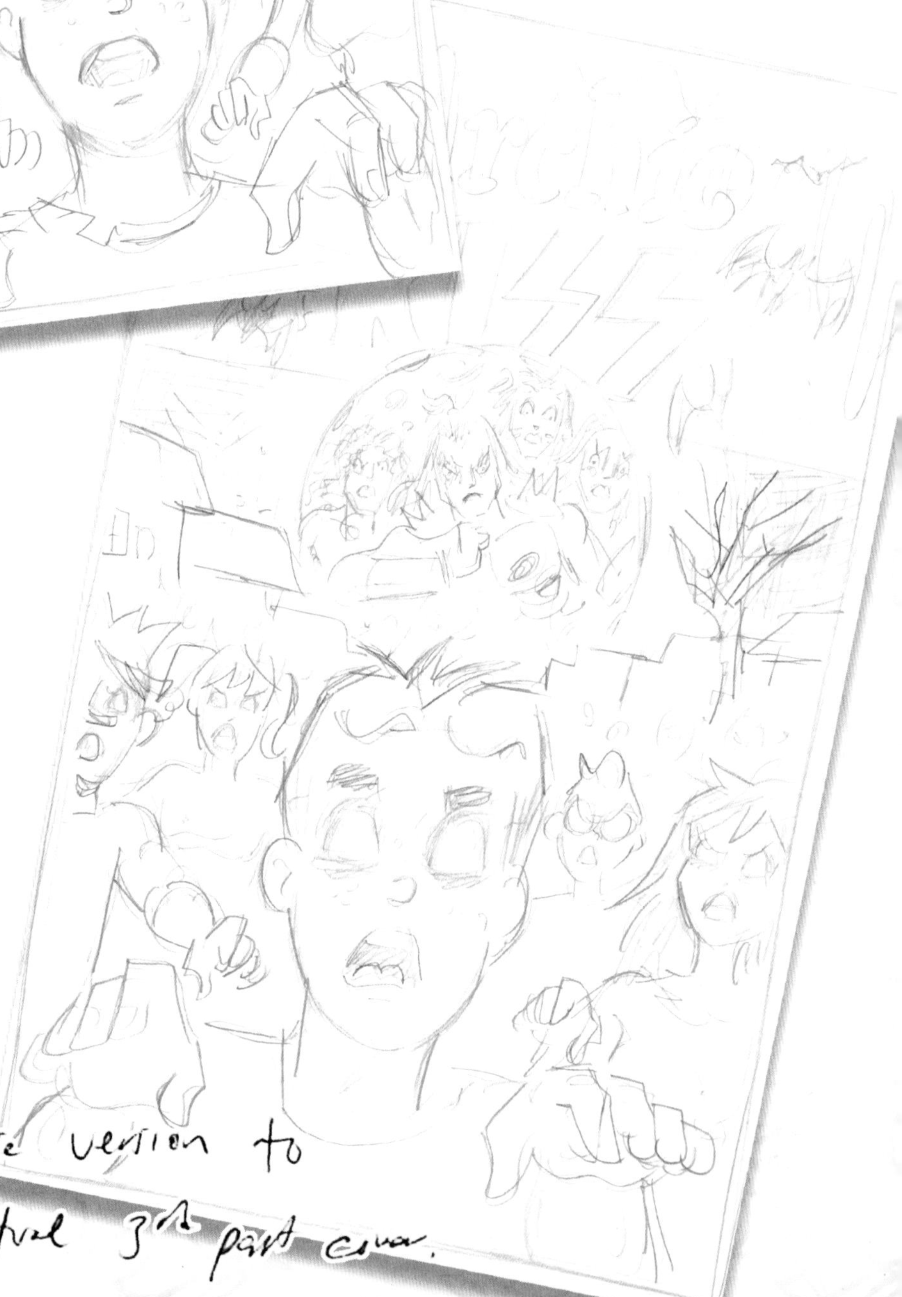

a close version to the actual 3rd part cover.

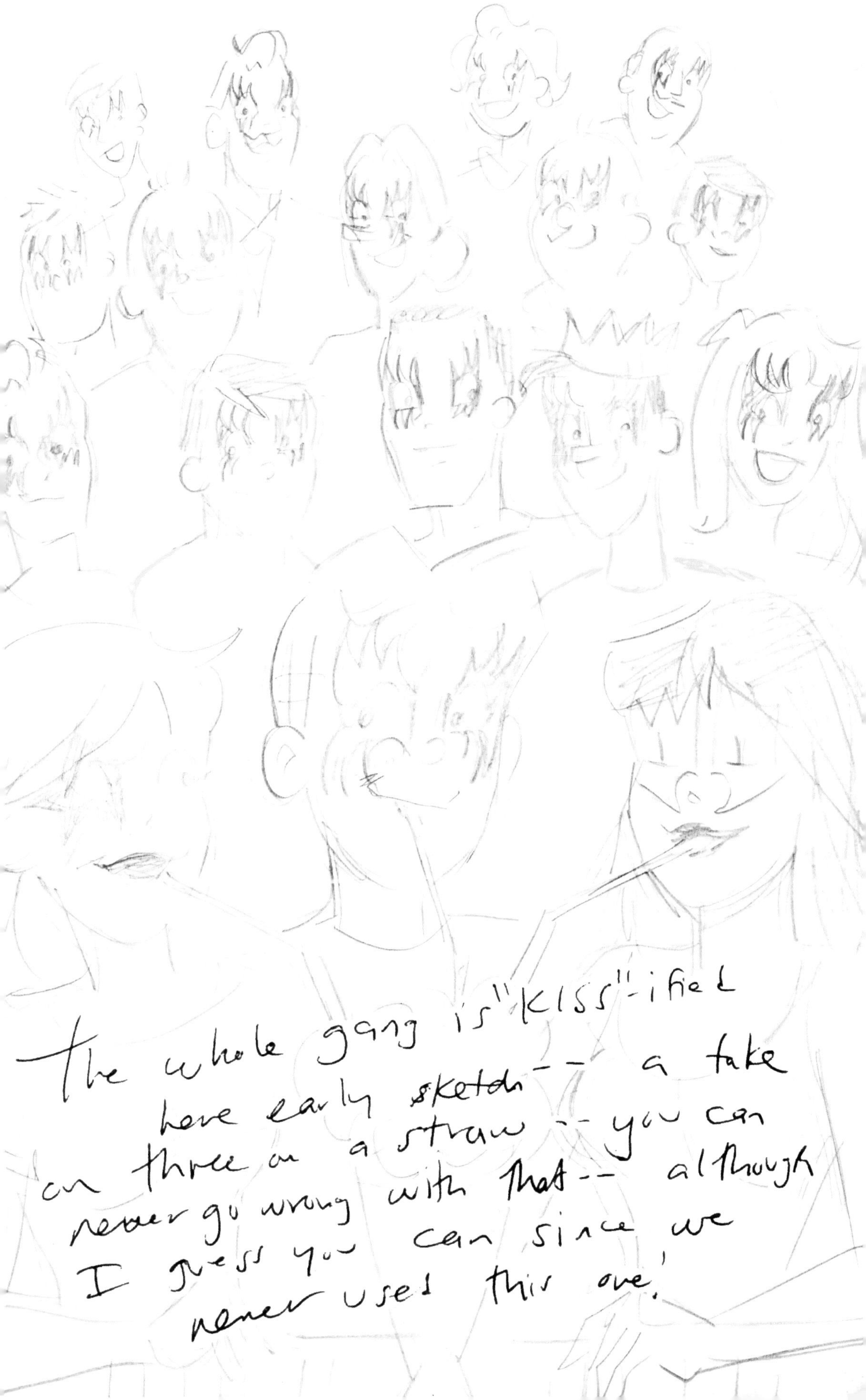

The whole gang is "KISS"-ified here early sketch -- a fake on three on a straw -- you can never go wrong with that -- although I guess you can since we never used this one!

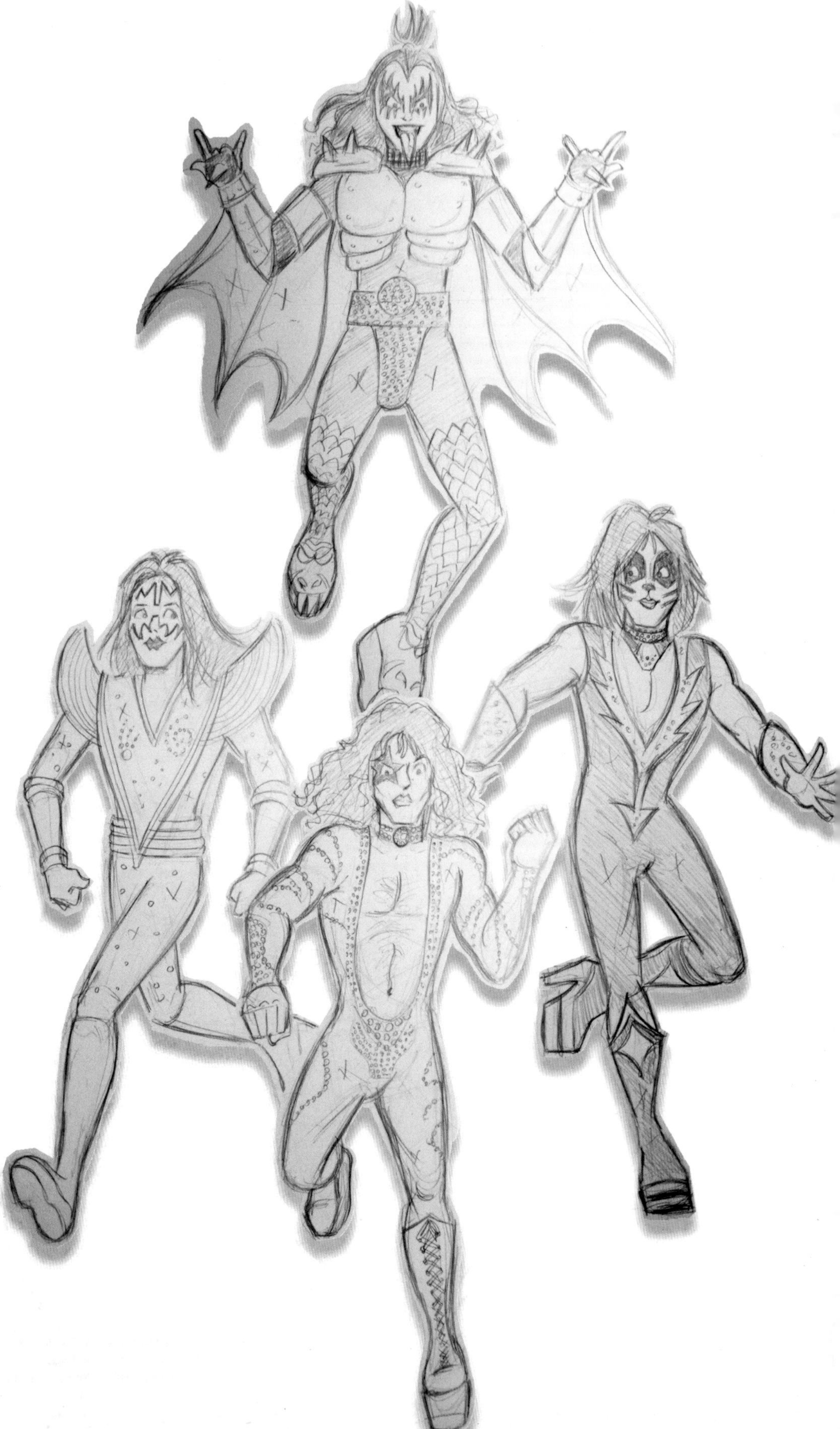